A Dragon & Her Girl

LTUE Benefit Anthologies

Trace the Stars
A Dragon and Her Girl
Twilight Tales (forthcoming)

Edited by Joe Monson

Join the Space Force Now! (forthcoming)
A Universe of Stories (forthcoming)

By Joe Monson

Hemelein Discovery (forthcoming)

Edited by Jaleta Clegg

Wandering Weeds: Tales of Rabid Vegetation (with Frances Pauli)
Soul Windows (with Frances Pauli)

By Jaleta Clegg

Dark Dancer
Autumn Visions (collection)
Brain Candy (collection)
Llama Tell You a Story . . . (collection)

Altairan Empire series
Nexus Point
Priestess of the Eggstone
Poisoned Pawn
Kumadai Run
Cold Revenge
Jericho Falling
Obsidian Tears
Chain of Secrets

AN LTUE BENEFIT ANTHOLOGY

A DRAGON & HER GIRL

Edited by
Joe Monson and Jaleta Clegg

HEMELEIN PUBLICATIONS

WITH

LTUE PRESS

A Hemelein Publications Original

Copyright © 2020 by Joe Monson and Jaleta Clegg. Except for brief excerpts in the case of reviews, this book may not be reproduced in any form without prior written permission of the publisher. All stories published by permission of the individual authors.

Story and content copyrights on page 290.

The stories in this book are works of fiction. Any names, characters, people, places, and events in these stories are products of the authors' imaginations, and any resemblance to actual people, places, or events is entirely coincidental.

Published jointly by Hemelein Publications and LTUE Press as a benefit anthology for *Life, the Universe, & Everything,* an annual science fiction and fantasy academic symposium held in Provo, Utah. Proceeds help students to attend for a greatly reduced price. We appreciate your support.

Cover artist: Kaitlund Zupanic, kaitlundzupanic.com

Cover art, *A Dragon and Her Girl,* copyright © 2019 Kaitlund Zupanic. Used by permission of the artist.

Editors: Joe Monson and Jaleta Clegg
Cover Design: Joe Monson
Associate Editor: Heather B. Monson
Interior Design and Layout: Marny K. Parkin

ISBN 978-1-64278-002-4 (trade paperback)
ISBN 978-1-64278-003-1 (ebook)
Library of Congress Control Number: 2019953737

First Edition
First Hemelein printing, February 2020
10 9 8 7 6 5 4 3 2 1

Hemelein Publications: http://hemelein.com/

LTUE Press: http://press.ltue.net/

To Linda Hunter Adams
For teaching so many of us the basics (and more) of
editing, writing, and publication.
Your influence reached farther than you knew.

Contents

Foreword:
The Dragonlady of Crandall House West   ix

A Game of Stakes   1
   Max Florschutz

Dragon Soap   37
   M. K. Hutchins

Li Na and the Dragon   51
   Scott R. Parkin

High Noon at the Oasis   61
   Jaleta Clegg

The Wild Ride   75
   Christopher Baxter

Rising Star   89
   Michaelene Pendleton

The Diamond-Spitting Knight   105
   S. E. Page

Amélie's Guardian   111
   Bryan Thomas Schmidt

Aer'Vicus   123
   Jodi L. Milner

Loyalties   137
    Josh Brown

Ash and Blood   153
    Hannah Marie

Therapy for a Dragon   183
    Sam Knight

Taking Wing   187
    Julia H. West

Lullaby   211
    John D. Payne

Rain Like Diamonds   221
    Wendy Nikel

Here by Choice   225
    Gerri Leen

Dragon's Hand   231
    David VonAllmen

Take out the Trash   247
    Melva L. Gifford

Burying Treasure   253
    Alex Shvartsman

Dragon in Distress   263
    Mercedes Lackey and Elisabeth Waters

Contributor Biographies   279

Acknowledgments   287

Foreword:
The Dragonlady of Crandall House West

THE SCIENCE FICTION SYMPOSIUM, *LIFE, THE UNIVERSE, & Everything*, wasn't the only amazing thing to come out of the "Class That Wouldn't Die" at Brigham Young University. The same group of organizers also created their very own semi-pro science fiction magazine, *The Leading Edge* (now simply *Leading Edge*).

From its first issue in 1981 to the latest (issue 75 in February 2020), it published—and continues to publish—some amazing fiction by pros and amateurs alike. It even won a Chesley Award for its April 2001 issue (edited by Brandon Sanderson, no less), featuring cover art by James C. Christensen.

For many years, *TLE* (as it was affectionately nicknamed) was housed in Crandall House West, a former residence-turned-Humanities-Publication-Center located to the west of the iconic Centennial Carillon on campus. One of the driving forces behind the "HumPub" was Linda Hunter Adams.

Linda always reminded me of weyrwomen such as Moreta and Lessa in Anne McCaffrey's *Pern* series, though I don't know that I ever discussed the series with Linda. The weyrwomen in those stories were strong leaders, compassionate (in many cases), and basically ran everything in the weyrs. They knew what they were doing and were happy to help others learn what needed doing. Everyone in the weyrs looked up to them and respected them. The HumPub was Linda's weyr.

Linda was fiercely protective of her weyr. She handled no end of political wrangling with the leaders of various other weyrs at the university. She stood up for what the students thought was best for the books and journals produced at the HumPub, gently guiding her students and interns through the ins and outs of the publishing business. With expert skill and grace, she walked the line between professional/academic advisor and the slightly-eccentric aunt everyone wishes they had. During the time I worked on *TLE* (off and on from 1993 to 1998), Linda was a constant fixture there. Her passing in 2016 had a huge impact on all *TLE* and *LTUE* alumni.

The stories selected for this volume of the *LTUE Benefit Anthologies* were selected with Linda in mind. We picked stories we think Linda would have loved. These stories feature strong women and girls doing hard things, going on difficult adventures, making tough decisions, and interacting with dragons in various ways. Basically, women like Linda, fighting the good fight—whatever the odds—in order to make sure their important people and places are protected and guided.

As with *Trace the Stars* (2019), all of the stories were donated by the authors (and the cover art by the artist) to help *LTUE* continue to let students attend for a greatly reduced price. If you see these creators anywhere, please thank them for their generosity. We couldn't do this without them. We hope you enjoy the stories in *A Dragon and Her Girl* as much as we did.

Before you go, I recently found this filk song in my archives (translation: I was cleaning a room). It has no attribution, but it appears to have been written on the occasion of Linda's retirement from BYU. Whoever the author is, thank you! This song is wonderful! If you see this, feel free to contact me on the Hemelein website and I'll update any future editions with proper attribution.

"Linda Hunter Adams"
(sung to the tune of "Maria" from *Sound of Music*)

She'll dot the i's and cross the t's
And give the words a stare.
Then briskly rolling up her sleeves,
She'll plant a comma there.
   In this whole world, there's never been
   An editor to compare
      With BYU's own Linda Hunter Adams!

She has a reputation for
Enhancing people's prose.
And with her own panache and flair,
She teaches what she knows.

And day and night, she never stops—
She goes and goes and goes.
    We're going to miss our Linda Hunter Adams!

    I'd like to say a word before we're through:
    She opened a *pub* at BYU!

Chorus:
    You are a legend, Linda Hunter Adams.
    No one would dare to try to take your place.
    One of a kind, that's Linda Hunter Adams.
    A style of your own, with a splash of flamboyance and grace.

    Think of the published authors you have nurtured.
    Think of the generations you have blessed.
    And think of the students who
    Admire and worship you.
    You're like a mother hen upon her nest.
    Oh, you are a legend Linda Hunter Adams.
    Now, cherished colleague, you deserve a rest.

In her office there's no space
For her guests to have a place.
She's been known at times to even lose her keys.
    And her phone just rings and rings.
    Sometimes she is late for things.
    And to send her emails, well, it ain't a breeze.
Student journals—see them grow,
For she never can say no.
And she always is surrounded by her "kids."
    She's a mentor. She's a guide—
    With disciples at her side.
    She's inspiring! She's untiring! She's a whiz!

Repeat Chorus

    Thank you for your support of the symposium.

Joe Monson
February 2020

A Game of Stakes
Max Florschutz

Departure

"Ah, Victoria," her father said as she lifted the last of her luggage into the coach. "It pains my heart to see you go."

"I know, Papa," she said as she turned to look at him. "But it will only be for a short time. A few months, half-a-year at most. The length of a short campaign, nothing more." She wrapped her arms around her father, hugging him through the stiff, black greatcoat he always wore.

"I know, Victoria. But this is different. With those, I left you. When you deigned to let me do so, that is." His arms wrapped around her, holding her close.

She wanted to bury her head in his chest. Not that it was easy to do so, not since she'd inherited her mother's height. She had to settle for resting her head on her father's shoulder instead and smiled.

"Do you remember the Sicarian campaign?" she asked.

"How could I forget?" Her father's chest shook with a short laugh. "Your mother was furious. I thought she'd never speak with me again. But this . . ." He finally unwrapped his comforting arms, stepping back and resting his hands on her shoulders. "This is still different. This time, my Victoria, you are leaving me." He smiled. "And on a campaign of your own."

"Papa, seeking a husband is hardly a campaign."

"No," he said, shaking his head with a laugh. "It isn't. It is far more difficult." For a moment a faint look of sadness slipped across his face, whether at her departure or at the mention of her late mother, she couldn't say. "But Victoria, are you . . . certain . . . that this is how you wish to go about it? Hiring a dragon?"

"It's a novel prospect, Papa," she said, taking one of his massive hands in hers and pulling it gently from her shoulder. "I'll be fine. Nothing is set in stone, you know that."

Her father nodded quietly. "Aye, I do." One of the first lessons he'd taught her. "But, are you sure you could not do the same here? My Victoria, you'll be putting your fate in the claws of a dragon."

"My fate will be in my own hands, Papa," she said. "The dragon is just a means to an end. A way to let the world know that the daughter of the famous Count Artares is seeking a companion."

"You could do that here, my daughter," he said, stepping back and giving her a better view of the honor guard around them. "You don't have to go to this dragon."

She smiled. "No, Papa, I must. It is because I am the daughter of Count Artares, the Wolf of Artares, that I must go." She stepped back, up onto the footstep of the coach that would take her away. "Don't you see, Papa?" She let out a little laugh. "Men are more ready to meet with a dragon than they are with the Wolf."

Her father smiled back at her, though she could see the tears in his eyes. "I know," he said. "But I want you to be safe, my Victoria. Give the word, and your guard will stay with you and this dragon."

"I know, Papa." She set a palm at the hilt of the sword that hung at her hip. "But I will be fine. I love you, Papa."

"I love you too, Victoria. Stay safe. And, good luck."

"I will, Papa. And thank you." She swung open the door of the carriage, but didn't climb in, instead hanging from the side of the coach, looking out over her father's estate and the guard arrayed there. They'd likely be on the move soon, hired for another campaign. There was only one thing left to do.

She threw up a fist. "For honor, and for victory!" she cried.

The guard, three dozen strong including the ones on horseback behind her, threw their own fists up. "For honor, and for victory!" The coach began moving forward, but she stayed hanging in the open door from the side, as was custom, until she had cleared her father's estate. At last, when the hills outside the coach gave way to farmland, she ducked inside and sat down, her mind and heart both racing.

"For honor, and for victory," she repeated quietly. "I will not let you down, father."

The dragon was waiting.

Arrival

The lair of Dostoy the Mighty was nothing like the name, or popular stories, suggested. The coach moved up a well-cared for gravel road, which in turn led to what could have been a simple estate home carved into the rocky face of the mountain itself. In fact, Victoria thought as the coach came to a stop, it likely hadn't, but the architects had taken great pains to ensure that it looked as though it had. But her eyes could see the faint jutting changes in the rock, the distant seams that could be used to perhaps find a weakness to exploit.

Draconic architecture, she thought, eyeing the high-vaulted windows and wide doorways. *Or human?* It certainly wasn't one of the other races, not that they had much to do with humans outside of border trade with the edges of the empire. The stone had been carved with simple reliefs, repeating patterns that added a pleasing aesthetic. She almost could have forgotten that it was home to a dragon, if not for the large size.

And, of course, the dragon himself standing by the front doors, waiting to receive her.

He was smaller than she'd expected. She gauged him to be somewhere between ten and eleven feet long—maybe a dozen at most—though it was only a rough estimate given the distance between them, and it was hard to tell with him sitting on his haunches, tail wrapped tightly around him. The tail would easily add another ten feet, maybe more. He held his wings tightly folded against his back, and while she knew dragons used magic to fly, she'd heard more than one old campaigner mention that their span was often larger than it appeared to be at first glance. She looked up at the dragon's raised muzzle—

And stopped in surprise. His eyes were looking right back at her and her coach, keen and inquisitive. More than one of her father's soldiers had spoken of dragons as "dumb brutes," but there was no mistaking the way those eyes were picking over her retinue, pausing here and there before moving on. This was a thinking, intelligent, aware being.

Her coach pulled to a halt, halfway across the wide open gravel clearing before the dragon's home. She took a deep breath. This was it. She stood, hunched in the interior of the coach, and then with great care opened the door. The dragon's eyes met her own as she stepped out, once again displaying a depth of intelligence and awareness that was surprisingly human, and then to her shock he bowed, spreading his wings as he bent low.

"Lady Victoria Artares." His voice was not quite as deep as she'd been expecting either, and bore an accent with traces of the northern nobility. "I welcome you to my lair and home. It is a pleasure to meet you."

She smiled. Most would have said "with the daughter of the Wolf" rather than "you." It was a small difference, but it helped ease her heart that she'd made the right choice.

"Dostoy the Mighty," she said, holding her voice steady at the title. "It is a pleasure to make your acquaintance at last." For some reason, when she'd exchanged letters with him, she'd been envisioning a mighty, commanding figure of red. But in truth, he was more a light tan, like faded tree-bark. "Was my payment received?"

"It was, Lady Victoria," Dostoy replied, coming out of his bow at last.

From the corner of her eyes Victoria saw several of her guard sitting in ready positions, their hands within easy reach of their muskets and crossbows.

"Will your guard be joining us?"

He had, she realized, noticed as well. *Of course he would have,* she thought. *It's been only thirty years since things were put to rest between our species. As well as they could.* There were soldiers in her father's army—likely in her own guard—that had gone against dragons during what the dragons called the Bad Days, when they were little more than pillagers and looters, blights across any kingdom that found itself beset by one. Before the dawn of the New Age when inventions had leveled the battleground between them, and forced a truce. The dragon himself would likely not remember those days, given that he was three years her junior and hatched after the truce, but the scars of those centuries ran deep.

"Guard," she called. "Ease. We aren't among foes here." Several of her followers nodded, lowering their hands. *Good.* They would follow her orders. "And no, Mr. Dostoy—"

"Just 'Dostoy,' if you please," he said quickly. "Just Dostoy."

"Very well." She nodded. "Dostoy, they will not be joining us. They will, however," she said, turning and gazing at them, "be camped some miles away, just to serve as a precaution against overenthusiastic suitors." There were towns with inns nearby, of course, but that would mean a higher public profile, and neither she, nor her father, wanted that.

"Very well," Dostoy said with a nod of his head. She wondered how many remnants of other similar camps her guard were likely to find out in the forest. "Do you have any attendants or ladies-in-waiting?"

She shook her head. "None. I can take care of myself."

"Very well. Do you require aid with your luggage? I am willing to lend a claw."

"That would be . . ." She glanced at the trunks atop her coach. "Very kind. Thank you."

Dostoy simply shook his head. "It is in my interests that you are as cared for as possible and have your needs met." He dropped to all fours and strode forward. Despite her height, she still had to look up at him. "Your guard, of course, may be of use as well. I can show you to your room, and once you are settled, give you a tour."

His words seemed to shock her guard, who began to dismount, no doubt with intentions to help with her luggage. She let them, stepping up on the sideboard of her coach and motioning toward one of the heavier trunks. "This one, if you please," she said, grabbing a trunk of her own. Dostoy complied, carefully and quite skillfully picking up the trunk and sliding it onto his back, where it lay held between wings. To her surprise, he then waited until she was ready before walking with her back toward the front doors.

"Your residence will be on the second floor," he said, his head angling in the direction of a set of windows. "From there, you will have a clear view of any suitors that come to complete your challenges."

She smiled. "I look forward to it."

Dostoy's home was, as expected, tailored to suit his needs rather than hers. The halls were large and wide, the ceilings lifted. Stairs elongated to suit a quadrupedal gait, like small terraces rather than steps. Her rooms were both wide and spacious, and far nicer than what she was accustomed to at home. Built for princesses, rather than a seasoned campaigner's daughter. She suspected that the wooden floor would be more comforting to her than the soft bed.

But there were other rooms available to her as well. A kitchen, for cooking needs. Human-styled facilities—magic, no less. Extra rooms for servants—not that she had brought any—and even a study with wide windows and a collection of books, everything from histories to children's stories. She'd raised her eyes at the selection, and Dostoy had admitted with a very human shrug that—after several complaints—he'd simply stocked a little bit of everything, but could acquire more if there was something specific she required.

Before long her trunks had been delivered, and she dismissed the guard, watching as they rode after the coach.

This is it, she thought, turning to look at Dostoy's home once more. The dragon himself was waiting by the entrance. *Now, we talk business.*

"So, Dostoy," she said. "Let us see how you are at a game of Stakes."

Stakes was an old game—centuries old, in fact—but it was why she was *here*. Stakes was a game of strategy, played on a board with near-infinite combinations and methods of play. It involved careful tactical consideration and warfare, and she'd been playing it since she was a child. As the daughter of the one of the most famous mercenary leaders who'd ever lived, how could she not? It was a primer across kingdoms everywhere for budding generals and captains.

And Dostoy was a dragon who played Stakes. Even more, from what he'd said, he was respectable at it. Which, for what she required, was key.

In the old days, a dragon's seizing the children—often daughters—of nobility had been a common enough tactic. They would take them someplace remote, demand a ransom, and wait. A prime method for a young dragon to acquire a horde.

In response, tradition had sprung up regarding the fate of those who were able to rescue one so kidnapped, not through monetary means but by besting a dragon in combat. Those who could do so, regardless of lineage or upbringing, were rewarded for their deeds. Knighthood, usually. A place in a noble's guard. Quite often the hand of the one rescued.

When the truce had been established, suddenly that avenue of success to some had been closed. At least, until one enterprising dragon had arrived at a king's court to announce a "matchmaking service" whereby he would serve as a challenge for potential suitors. For a small fee, of course.

Nevertheless, the new method let the old traditions live, while even allowing for the one-time "victim" to set their own terms of "combat," giving them the power to narrow their potential field of suitors from "good with a blade" to other areas of interest.

Such as Stakes and military strategy. As the sole heir to her father's company, control of his forces would be passed to her in due time. If she ever was to be married, she wanted someone who could live up to the legacy her father had built, someone who could command his armies alongside her with the skill and shrewd strategy the company was known for.

She needed an equal who could command. And Dostoy would help her draw one out.

The dragon led her to what she assumed was his own study, where an ornate wooden Stakes table sat near one long, broad window. A fire crackled nearby, though she could smell no smoke, and the other three walls were covered in shelves, each filled in turn with book after book.

"You enjoy reading?" she asked as she spotted a human-sized seat sitting next to the Stakes table.

"Studying," Dostoy replied, lying down on the floor across the table from her almost like a cat. His faintly inhuman—but bright and welcoming—eyes met hers. "Reading for pleasure as well, but when not otherwise occupied with my responsibilities around the mountain, I enjoy learning."

"An admirable trait." She looked down at the wooden tiles, marveling at their careful craftsmanship. Rivers, mountains, fords, roads, and cities were all carved into them in painstaking detail. Dostoy opened a compartment at the side of the table and began carefully picking out impressively detailed pieces. Pieces that were both expensive, she noted, *and* well-worn with use.

"I hope this isn't your only copy of Stakes?" she ventured, taking some of the pieces and setting them in place. "A table such as this shouldn't be left out in the rain."

Dostoy laughed. "Not a chance, Lady Victoria. This is my personal table. I have a travel set I will be testing your suitors with." The wooden pieces clacked against one another as he placed them with the ease of a seasoned player.

"Good. A work of art such as this deserves to be cared for—and played," she added, picking up more of her pieces. They were larger than she was used to, but then it made sense given who they had been made for. "When will the first suitors begin arriving?"

"Tomorrow," Dostoy answered. "At least, that is the first day announced that challengers may arrive. Between the appropriate times, of course. Ruleset?"

"Full," she answered without pause as the last pieces went into place. "Flip."

Dostoy nodded, a single claw tapping a spinner carved into the wood at the side of the table, a more luxurious option than the common coin flip. A dragon's head carved into one side of the coin represented, she guessed, his chosen token.

The other side of the piece came up, and she made her first move. A straightforward, if slightly complicated, opening gambit. To her satisfaction, Dostoy caught it immediately, reacting in kind. *Excellent. His claims were not in boast, then.*

Play proceeded for several turns in silence before Dostoy spoke. "You know, Lady Victoria, forgive my saying so if you find it indelicate, but you are already unlike most of the clients I've served before."

"Really?" She lifted one eyebrow at him while moving a formation of infantry in a very aggressive bait. "How so?"

Dostoy blinked, and she had the distinct impression that her reply had surprised him. "Well," he began, choosing instead to send scouts across her flanks. "You're tall for a human woman, for starters. No offense meant, but many of my other clients have been . . . thin. Waifish, really. You, on the other paw, carry a sword."

Her hand went to her hip, eyes going wide as she realized the truth of his statement. "My apologies," she said quickly. "I neglected to leave it in my room." To carry a blade in the home of one who had invited her—

But Dostoy was shaking his head. "I meant no slight. By all means, wear it wherever you wish. My home is open to you. I merely meant it as an observation. That is all."

"Very well," she replied, moving a few more of her forces in response to his latest push. Dice rolled in a wooden cup, assigning casualties as his tokens charged forward. "Thank you for taking no insult. I have worn a blade ever since I was a small child. In the future, I will leave it in my room until it is needed. No disrespect was meant." She pulled her forces back in the face of his attack, pressing them together.

"You also apologize with much more readiness and sincerity. Are you practiced with it? Your blade, I mean," he added quickly.

Her forces looked on the verge of loss. She pulled them further back. "Of course," she replied. "Hence the third challenge." The first was that a suitor had to be fleet of foot enough—or clever enough—to make it to the Stakes board with Dostoy defending it. The second was that they must beat him in a game. And the third was that she herself would duel them—openly as a test of their personal skill with combat, but privately as a test of their mettle, honor, and dignity. Only then would she *consider* giving them her hand. Victory in all three was not a promise.

"Your challenges are unique as well," Dostoy replied, leading his forces forward. Victory appeared imminent. Both went silent as he completed his movements. "I believe I will be quite interested to see what sort of suitors respond."

"Capable ones, one would hope," Victoria replied, checking the board carefully. *Perfect.* She flipped over one of the wooden cards, exposing her cannons, hidden in the forest from his view, as they unleashed a blistering salvo that cut deep into the side of Dostoy's army. Half his pieces were gone from the board in an instant.

"That was impressive," Dostoy replied, eyes wide with surprise as she moved the rest of her pieces forward, cutting into what was left of his pieces and wiping many more of them from the board. "I didn't even suspect there was something there."

"I've been playing Stakes since I was a child, too," she replied, ending her turn. Dostoy reached out with a single talon and knocked over the piece representing his commanding officer, a sign of surrender. "A grasp of strategy and tactics is vital, considering what I stand to inherit. Hence the challenge. If I could find someone who could be a match for me at Stakes, or even defeat me, then the company's future will be in good hands." She glanced at his remaining pieces, noting the count. "What was your hidden piece?" He smiled and flicked the barrier down.

"A dragon?"

"A personal favorite of mine," he replied. "I almost never play without it. Powerful in the right claws—or hands—but prone to weakness in the wrong place."

"Well," she said, dismantling her pieces. "Perhaps a second chance to prove yourself?"

"It would be my pleasure."

"In fact," she added as they began to set the board up once more, flipping and moving tiles to new locations. This time the battlefield became a long, narrow valley. "If you don't mind, I suggest we play nightly, to hone one another's skills."

"And further test those suitors who come calling?"

"Precisely." She spun the spinner, the dragon's head coming up. "Your move." Dostoy's claws came down, and the second game began.

Day Two

By midday of the second day after her arrival, she was already bored.

Not a single suitor had shown up, potential or otherwise. She had gotten her hopes up when she'd seen a young man approaching up the road, but he'd turned out to have been one of the local farmers Dostoy watched over, there to discuss something to do with crops on the eastern side of the mountain. Tedium had returned with his departure, and she'd retreated to one of the books she'd pulled from the shelves.

But by midday, she was through with it. Her muscles were already sore from an extended sword practice the night before and that morning, and she was growing tired of reading about ancient kings. *Surely there must be more to occupy myself with.* She left her rooms behind her, wandering about the "lair"—she was starting to think of it more as an estate—and looking for something or someone to pass the time with.

She found Dostoy lying in his study, bent over a large book and reading intently. To her surprise, a pair of glasses were perched across his muzzle, and she tried to keep her expression neutral as he turned to look over them at her. "Yes, Lady Victoria? Did you need something?"

"Nothing more than a change of pace," she said. "I needed to get out and do something other than read."

"I understand," Dostoy said, plucking the glasses from his face with surprising care and placing them atop the book. "I believe that is usually why so many of my clients decline to come alone. Then again, sharp minds require constant stimulation. Would you care for another game of Stakes?" He'd yet to beat her, and she suspected he was building a grudging admiration of her talent at the game.

"No no," she said quickly, shaking her head. "I wouldn't want to take time away from your studies. They are yours after all. What . . . are you studying, actually? I don't believe I've asked."

"Magic," Dostoy replied. "Primarily."

"Magic?" She stepped forward, taking a quick look at the pages of the book he'd left open. "Are you a wizard?"

Dostoy let out a laugh, the tone surprisingly bright for one so large. "No," he said. "As far as I know, there never has been a dragon wizard. But that doesn't mean there couldn't be." He held up two of his talons, and a soft glow began to pulse from between them. "That also doesn't mean that there have not been dragons who have used magic. We are, after all, creatures of innate magic. But become a wizard? Apply at a formal academy?" He shook his head. "Perhaps if fate led me that way. I merely find the study of magic interesting. And it gives me something to do and learn when not attending to my other duties."

His words made sense. Magic was a discipline of great effort, like any other, but to a being that was already infused with it . . . "Are you proficient at it?"

"A bit. Nothing like your skill with strategy. Or with the sword. But I know more than a few spells. Many of them are simple, practical things, such as light, heat, or even taking away pain so that a healer can do their work. But I have tried my hand at more complicated spells. Or ones that are mostly useless. For example . . ." He held up his talons, and a moment later, without warning, his tan scales became a bright, vivid purple.

"Hah!" The laugh was free of her before she had a chance to catch it, but there was no calling it back. "That's incredible!" It was, but she also had to admit the shade of purple he'd chosen looked ridiculous. Thankfully, Dostoy was smiling as well.

"Of limited use save amusement," he said, his scales returning to their usual shade. "Or perhaps distraction. I've made some progress with illusion as well." She blinked, and there were two Dostoys lying before her. Then the one to her left stood and began to grow, filling his half of the room. "But I can't mix them with sound yet, nor maintain them very far," the first Dostoy said as the second vanished.

"Even so, I am impressed," she said. "I've never had a chance to learn magic myself. What few wizards we've employed have been quite expensive and very secretive. Overly so, if you ask me."

"I agree," Dostoy said, turning and motioning to the book lying at his desk. "Which was one reason why I purchased these books. It was far cheaper to learn on my own and make my own discoveries than to pay a wizard to teach me a few tricks. Thus, I gain understanding."

"Is there anything you'd like to do with it?" she asked.

He shrugged. "As of yet, I am unsure. There are a myriad of uses detailed across the various tomes I have collected, and I must admit some curiosity to various schools on my own part. Much of it is powerful magic, some of it is not, but . . ."

"You are Dostoy the Mighty, after all."

"I prefer Dostoy, myself," he said. "But true nonetheless, if only by my innate magical ability. Would you like to study here for a change of pace? I was in the middle of something, but—"

"Yes." If nothing else, reading magical theory would be interesting. "I'll leave you to it. Where would you recommend I start if I wished to learn a little about magic?"

"'Adricarle's Treatise Magicka,' on the second shelf," Dostoy said, his tail pointing at the row in question. "It provides a thorough and mostly concise overview."

"Thank you."

"You're welcome." The dragon returned to his study of his tome, and she in turn picked out the book he'd pointed her toward, heavy in her hands. A light spell *would* be useful. As would an illusion, or a spell that reduced pain. Her curiosity aroused, she sat down, her back against the wall, and began to read.

Day Five

It had taken until the third day for a potential suitor to show up. He'd been turned away by Dostoy without even reaching the Stakes table. To no one's surprise, even the suitor, who admitted upon surrendering that he'd not expected much, but felt obligated to try. Not a strong start, not a strong suitor.

The fourth saw the appearance of two more suitors, both of which had made it to the Stakes table before being soundly outmaneuvered by Dostoy. She had to admit, he was a very capable player with a clear talent for thinking ahead and trapping his opponents. Their nightly games had grown longer, though he'd yet to beat her. But it put a high requirement on those who came pursuing her.

Thus far the fifth day had been silent. She set down the treatise she'd been reading, taking a brief break and glancing at the clock. Dostoy wasn't there at the moment, having been called away to deal with something on one of the local farms, leaving her alone in the study. After the second day, she'd moved some of the spare chairs from her rooms down to the study to give her some additional seating options for when she wanted to read about magic.

The book was a tome, there was no doubt. Wordy and detailed, she had to admit it gave her a far better grasp on how magic worked than any of her tutors had ever taught her. The myriad of notes scrawled in the margins had helped. It wasn't until she'd spotted Dostoy dipping a claw in ink and making notes in the margins of the tome he was currently reading that she realized who had penned them. Or in this case, clawed them.

I should go prepare something to eat. Dostoy's larder was well stocked, her kitchen well equipped, and she'd been making her own meals since she arrived. She rose and moved across the room. *Something simple but—* "Oh, Dostoy," she said as she spotted the dragon coming down the hall. "I was not aware you'd returned. What was going on?"

"Animal attack," Dostoy replied, coming to a stop. His paws were damp—recently washed. "Something, likely a bear, attacked and ate several sheep. If it happens again, I'll need to go looking for it."

"Is that common around here?"

"Common enough," he said with a nod. "It's why this land wasn't settled and my ancestors were able to possess it. Local legends say the place is cursed. Personally, if it was, magic fades, but every now and again something strange occurs, so there may have been some truth to it. In any case, I must eat. By your leave, Lady Victoria."

"Actually," she said, her voice halting his turn as an idea occurred to her. "I've been eating alone for days now. Would you care to share lunch?"

Dostoy thought for a moment and then nodded. "Your company would not be unwelcome. I would honored if you would join me. You may want to bring your own food, however."

"I will." Several minutes later, she joined him in his dining room, setting her sandwiches down across from a large, cold roast of mutton, if her guess was right.

"I must admit this is a first," Dostoy said, tearing a bite out of his meat with his teeth and swallowing. "But your company thus far has been nothing if not pleasant. Which does make my mind wander a bit. If my inquiry is not too forward, tell me: Why did you feel you needed my services in acquiring a companion? I have been under the impression that most human societies value the traits you've demonstrated thus far."

"Truthfully? Because of my father." It was no secret, so there was no shame in telling him. "Don't misunderstand: I love my Papa dearly, and he's never been anything but the best father he can be, which given his responsibilities is no small feat, but . . . He is the Wolf of Artares. Men that have expressed interest in me have found themselves at the end of his glare, and by extension that of his entire company."

"Such as your guard."

She nodded. "Exactly. I love my Papa, but he is . . . overwhelming. And while yes, I suppose many would say my 'traits,'" she smiled, "are of value, it becomes something else when choosing a partner. Sometimes our values, despite our claims, are not as highly prized as some would say. Though it doesn't help that my upbringing in some ways goes against the standards and expectations of polite society."

"Such as carrying a sword through someone's home?" Dostoy suggested with a toothy smile, and she nodded.

"Like that. In many places a woman carrying a sword is a rare sight of its own, in others, a shame. And there are the requirements of the company."

"Could you not marry someone from the company? Surely there are plenty of skilled tacticians to choose from."

She let out a little laugh. "No, because that's missing the point entirely."

"Enlighten me?"

"If I were to marry," she said, setting her sandwich down. "I would want to marry someone who was capable at strategy and command, but not defined by it. My father, for example, paints and runs the estate, as well as a school of learning. To many, he is the Wolf, but to me, the Wolf is only part of who he is."

"I see. You desire someone more than just a military figurehead."

She nodded. "Yes. Which is why I came up with the tests I did. Besting you at Stakes speaks to one aspect of their character, but how they behave afterward and for the third test, another."

"Very wise. What does your mother make of all this? I noticed you haven't spoken of her, only your father."

"I hope she approves," Victoria said, taking another bite. "She passed some ten winters ago. In childbirth. My younger brother didn't survive either."

"I'm sorry." His words sounded both heartfelt and genuine. "That is a great loss."

"It was," she said, pausing for a moment, her meal forgotten. "I still miss her. She used to take me stargazing on clear nights, point out all the constellations. She's gone, but she's not gone. Not entirely. I do regret that she did not get to see me find someone who cared and loved me as much as Papa loved her, but, all things in their proper time."

"Was she a soldier?"

"Of a sort. She could be, when the time called for it, but preferred to be a mother. And she was wonderful at it." Memories spilled through her mind like warm embers. "She was a very capable woman."

"And it would seem you've followed in her footsteps." Dostoy swallowed the last of his roast, then licked the platter clean.

"Maybe," she offered, and changed the subject. "Your notes have been most helpful, by the way. In learning about magic."

"Thank you for your gratitude," Dostoy said, seeming somewhat surprised. "I hadn't considered their effect when giving you access to my books. They were written from my own mind and with my observations. I am glad to hear that they were helpful."

"They are, especially along some of the drier passages."

Dostoy smiled. "Adricarle is indeed quite dry. Sometimes I wonder if his intent was to make the study of magic rarer still by putting those who would wish to follow in his footsteps to sleep. Nevertheless, his observations are most detailed and useful . . . if one can stay awake."

"Your notes help with that."

"Have you attempted any magic of your own yet?"

She shook her head. "No. I'm still immersed in theory."

"Well, if you do, please let me know. It would be a delight to see someone other than myself master a basic spell." She nodded, and he rose, picking up his platter in one paw. "Thank you, Lady Victoria, for the pleasure of your company during this meal. It was enjoyable. And now, if you'll excuse me, I'm fairly certain I saw another suitor coming up the road on my way back."

There was, and Dostoy beat him at Stakes just as soundly as he'd beaten the others.

Day Eight

One week, Victoria thought, looking out the window of what she'd come to think of as "her" drawing room. *One week, and not a single successful suitor yet.*

There had been several more that had tried since the day she'd shared lunch with Dostoy. One had even beaten the dragon, employing a very aggressive charge that had routed the his pieces and forced him back, capturing his command post, only to lose when she herself had come out to meet the final challenge. His skill with a blade had been respectful, but not enough.

Especially not after she'd seen him backhand one of his servants for offering the wrong blade. Prince or not, she had no desire to wed or even court someone so dishonorable. She'd met his smirking stance with a devastating rush that she'd only restrained out of the expectation that it would have been too much a blow to his ego to find himself thrown to the ground. As it was, she had disarmed him in moments, and he'd slunk away in disgrace.

Since then there had been fewer suitors, but Dostoy assured her that this was normal. "The challenge thins those out who doubt themselves as time goes on," he had said. "In the beginning, when the challenge is fresh, many can convince themselves that they can overcome it because few understand it. With each fallen suitor, however, the difficulty of a challenge is better understood, and fewer that are honest with themselves attempt it, as they know they have no chance."

Not that she would have minded those who had no chance trying. There was something to be said for perseverance after all. If they displayed an aptitude for humility and a willingness to learn . . .

She frowned. *Unfortunately, humility seems to be trait few of my potential suitors possess.* Her mind slid to the night before, when a prince from a fairly wealthy province had shown up in a grand announcement, and had actually declared to Dostoy that he should be able to skip portions of the challenge because he was 'no peasant.' Dostoy had thankfully seen no reason to do so, and the prince had been beaten by him in a quick, ruthless game of Stakes. He'd demanded the "right" to the third challenge. It had been denied. His comments as he had slunk away had given her cause to suspect that to him, she'd been nothing more than access to her father's company and his own military designs anyway.

I could never love a fool such as that, she thought, staring down at the empty gravel clearing. Dostoy was nowhere to be seen, likely in his study once more, leaving her with a clear view of the mountainside stretched before the manor and the tall pines flanking it. The sky was a crisp, clear blue, devoid of any clouds. As she watched, the tops of the pines waved slowly from side to side in some faint breeze. Would there be another suitor today? There was no way to tell, but there hadn't been one so far.

What to do with my time . . . ? She hadn't fully considered just how much *waiting* there could be in such a situation. Even with Dostoy's kindness in allowing her to study his precious tomes of magic, there was only so long she could read through Adricarle's lengthy, flowered prose before she felt like her brain was overburdened. *I should have asked my guard to leave a horse. At least then I could go for a ride, or—*

Movement at the front door caught her eye, and she leaned forward to see Dostoy walking out, a small pack of some kind strapped across his back. *What is he up to?*

There was one way to find out. She opened the window, ignoring the harsh bite of the mountain's spring air across her cheeks, and leaned out. "Dostoy!"

"Lady Victoria," he said, his head turning on his flexible neck to look up at her. "Is all well?"

"Fine, thank you. What are you doing?"

"Going hunting," he replied as if it were the most ordinary thing in the world. "One of the farmers informed me of a small herd of elk nearing my lair, and I spotted them during my early morning flight. A few of them will restock my larder nicely, and it will only take a short time. I will return –"

"Wait!" she called as he began to spread his wings. She chose to ignore the suddenness of her outburst. "Would it be all right with you if I were to accompany you? I have hunted many times before, and it would be nice to see more of the mountain."

For a moment Dostoy simply stared at her, his expression unreadable, caught in surprise or consideration, she couldn't tell. But after a few moments, he spoke again. "It would be some distance," he replied. "You would need to walk, as you do not have a horse."

"I'm no stranger to long hikes," she replied. The thought that she could ride atop his back occurred to her, but she dismissed it almost immediately. He had not offered, and he was a sapient being. It would be rude of her to ask as if he were some beast of burden. "That is, if you're open to the company."

This time his reaction came with more swiftness. "Of course, Lady Victoria. As I stated the other day, I have found your company quite pleasant so far. You are more than welcome to join me in my hunt."

"Then if you please, could you wait several moments while I prepare? I won't be long." She ducked back from the window at his nod, almost forgetting to close it in her hurry. *A hunt!* That was something she enjoyed, and was no stranger to. Often her father's forces hunted while on the campaign, seeking out extra supplies of food for the camp followers. She herself had learned at a young age, and her father had coached her personally, along with several of his best trackers. She was no master, but it was something she could enjoy with any of them, and did from time to time.

And it was the *perfect* way to stave off a little boredom. Several minutes later, she met Dostoy at the front door, a little harried from her quick change into attire more suited for hunting.

"There," she said, giving the dragon a grin. "I hope you weren't kept waiting long."

"Not at all," Dostoy said, looking at her with evident surprise. "You brought a bow?"

"Of course," she said, holding the recurved item in question in her hand. Her quiver was already across her back. "I wouldn't travel without one."

"Lady Victoria, you continue to prove to be a pleasant surprise among all my clients," he said, letting out a soft chuckle. "Now then, we'd best get walking if we're going to catch up to the herd. This way," he said, turning and pointing with his head toward a break in the trees. "I'll keep my pace slow as to not—"

"Don't," she replied briskly, already striding at his side. There was a reason she'd chosen to change into thick trousers and a good pair of boots. Years moving with her father's forces had left her more than capable of handling a stiff hike. And if the winter had seen her lose some of her capacity, then that was simply something she'd need to deal with. "Not unless I need it," she added quickly. "But I should be able to keep up, provided you don't intend to run to the hunt."

"Very well," Dostoy replied. "And no, I did not." They entered the forest, trees looming even over Dostoy's large form, rich scents flooding her senses, from the smell of fresh pine stinging at her nose, to the earthy moss underfoot. She took a deep breath, a smile on her face as she let Dostoy lead the way, and followed.

Several hours later they returned to the clear space in front of his manor, leaving the comfort of the woods behind but returning with several dead carcasses, already cleaned. Between her bow and Dostoy's incredible speed and bulk they'd been able to down five elk from the herd, gutting them in place before loading them aboard a small, collapsible sledge Dostoy had brought in his pack. It hit the gravel with a raspy *thud*, and Dostoy dropped to his belly, letting out a faint *whoosh* of breath.

"That was quite a haul," he said, looking at her as she stood panting, her legs burning. True to her request, he'd kept his speed up on the way back, though it appeared he'd perhaps overestimated his own pace slightly. "My thanks for your assistance, Lady Victoria." He set his head down atop his forepaws for a moment, a satisfied rumble emanating from his chest. "My larder will be well-stocked with elk for the next few weeks."

"It was my pleasure," she replied, shrugging and dropping to the gravel with her legs crossed. "I enjoyed it. Though if you feel inclined to share, I do know of a few ways to prepare elk. Including flame-roasted."

"I may be able to help there, Lady Victoria," Dostoy said, lifting his head with a smile. A small lick of flame left his lips.

"Call me Victoria, please," she said, leaning back on her hands, base of her quiver prodding the ground. "A good hunt shared between friends is reason enough for you—for us—to forgo formalities in one another's company, wouldn't you think?"

"Very well, Victoria," Dostoy said, nodding. Then he paused, staring at something down the road. "Oh. It would appear that we have company."

"What?" It took a moment for his words to register, her mind caught on the sight of five gutted elk atop Dostoy's sledge. They would need to be fully butchered— "Company?"

"Yes," Dostoy said, rising and untangling himself from the sledge. "A coach." She could see it too, now that he'd drawn her attention to the road. "A suitor, I would guess."

"Oh dear." And here she was with her hair tightly bound back, dirt and sweat covering her body, and bloodstains on her hands. There was definitely no time to change or freshen up, but maybe she could rush inside and stay out of sight—no, the coach was moving swiftly, hoofbeats thundering up before it. She glanced at Dostoy, staying silent as the ornate carriage drew closer and closer.

And it *was* ornate, festooned with gold filigree and carved, painted wood. The crest upon the door identified it as that of the Rietillian Royal Family, and its occupant thereby one of the inheritors of one of the wealthiest of the kingdoms of man. At least two dozen knights, each clad in armor that gleamed under the sun, followed in the coach's wake, arraying themselves out to the sides with banners and lances held high. The coach came to a swift stop, kicking up gravel and rock as its driver pulled the reins back, stopping it perfectly in the center of the yard. A herald rose from the seat next to the driver, his voice booming across the clearing.

"Announcing his royal highness, Prince Teravin Rietillian of the Royal Kingdom of Rietillian, long may it stand!" The door of the coach swung open, the prince stepping out with a dramatic flourish of his cape.

Victoria felt her breath catch in her throat. If nothing else, the prince was *handsome*, his chin sculpted like it was the work of a master artist. His eyes were bright and welcoming, and his smile was stunning. Then he spoke, and his voice was surprisingly light, with only a bare hint of resonate deepness.

"Dragon," he said, smiling at Dostoy. "If you would be so kind to inform the Lady Victoria Artares that I, Prince Teravin Rietillian, have come to fight for her hand, that she may see our contest!"

"Prince Rietillian," Dostoy said, bowing. "There is no need. She is already present."

"Your highness," Victoria said, opting for a bow. She caught a gasp of surprise from someone atop the coach, driver or herald she couldn't say, then rose to see a curious sort of shock on the prince's face.

"I . . . see," he stammered at last, perfect jaw closing. "On second thought . . . Dragon? Lady Victoria? I . . . um . . ." He gave them both a quick nod, then turned and ducked back into his coach, almost shutting the door on his cape.

With a cry of "Hyah!" the coach leapt forward, completing its tight turn and heading back down the road from whence it had come, the knights falling in behind it without so much as a backward glance.

She and Dostoy simply stood in silence for a minute watching the coach depart. Then, just as it began to move out of sight, they turned and looked at one another. A smile teased at her lips, and she could see Dostoy's shoulders shaking.

Laughter exploded out of them like a storm, echoing across the clearing in the wake of the prince. She couldn't say how long they laughed, only that she was clutching at her sides, tears leaking from her eyes and chest aching for breath by the time both of them settled down to small titters. "I suppose," she said, her voice breaking for another giggle. "I suppose that he wasn't the right one either."

"No," Dostoy said, his voice echoing between larger laughs. "Not at all."

She took a deep breath as they finally quieted, glancing down at the disheveled state of her clothing. "So," she said at last. "Shall we butcher the elk?"

"Butcher the elk," Dostoy agreed, hitching up the sledge once more. "Let's see to it."

The rest of the day passed with light spirits.

Day Twelve

"Hah!" The loud shout echoed across the clearing. "I have you now, dragon!"

His opponent did, too, even she could see that. The knight had taken Dostoy by surprise, his cavalry charge a feint for his real strike. Unless Dostoy had a counter of some kind in store, the game would be over in several turns.

She could see his side of the board. He did not have any such plan at the ready. With a sigh, she turned away from Adricarle's tome and moved to the bed, where her sword hung in its scabbard from the footboard. She changed quickly, and from down below she heard the knight's triumphant cries as the game came to its forgone conclusion. She'd need to teach Dostoy how to read such a feint and react to it, assuming she still was a guest in his home after the next part of the challenge. But for some reason, she felt she would be.

"Victory is mine, dragon, though you fought well. And now for the third challenge!"

"The Lady Victoria will be here momentarily," she heard Dostoy say. She left the window open as she strode out of the room. The day was warm enough that it wouldn't matter.

"Ah," the knight said as she strode out the front door. "The Lady Victoria." He knelt, extending a hand toward her. "I long for the—"

"This is not a poetry competition, Sir Pendel," she said, cutting him off. "There's no sense in wasting time. Take up your blade." Dostoy had already moved to one side, taking his board with him, so she raised her blade in challenge, waiting on the knight.

"You wish to proceed with haste?" The knight nodded, raising his own blade. "Very well. You've been here some time already. I can see why you would be impatient, lady." He was wearing light armor for mobility, and she could see that he was exaggerating his own movements, playing at being slower than he was.

Two can play at that game, she thought. *And I wager I can do it better than you, Sir Pendel.* "Then let us begin," she said, and moved forward.

Pendel charged, as she had expected he would, bringing his blade around in a flash. Like hers, the edge was covered in padded leather, to keep a blow from being truly dangerous, but the impact could still hurt. She blocked his probing slash, countering and sending out a probing poke of her own, which he pretended to appear almost too slow to block.

Almost, but she could see the way he held himself. The block was too neat, his footwork too precise. He was trying to goad her into being too aggressive.

She could work with that. She took the offensive, striking out and—like lightning, the knight retaliated, springing forward with sudden speed to batter her blade aside and make a killing blow.

Save that their blades never connected. At least, not as he had intended. Her sword was already out of reach, darting back and then forward to mirror his own strike, slapping it aside right when his balance was at its weakest point. He all but fell forward, the padded tip of her sword striking him right in the chest.

He froze there for a moment, on one knee, eyes locked in surprise first on her blade, then moving up to her. Then he smiled. He *was* handsome, in a rugged sort of way, but . . .

"My admiration for your skill, Lady Victoria," he said, recovering his balance and rising. He gave her a sheepish grin. "I don't suppose two out of three would be appropriate?"

She considered it for a moment before shaking her head. "No," she said. "My apologies, Knight Pendel, but you have failed this test." The knight's face fell, as did that of his squire's, watching from the clearing. "You fought with honor, but you did not pass the third challenge."

"Very well." Pendel sheathed his sword at his hip and bowed. "You are an impressive sort, Lady Victoria. May your quest bring you what you seek. I shall return to the road."

She watched him go, her sword sheathed at her side. After a few minutes, Dostoy spoke up. "I thought he might be the one, if I am honest, Victoria. I'm surprised you let it end so quickly."

"I thought so too, at first," she said, finally turning from the road. "But his character did not impress me."

"Really?" The ridge of scales between Dostoy's horns furrowed. "What was it that he did, if I may ask?"

"He wouldn't call you by name," she said, moving for the front doors. "That was all."

Day Eighteen

She awoke to hear loud shouts, hand already grasping for her sword. The ground beneath her was hard but warm, where was she—?

Her mind caught up with her. Dostoy's manor. The challenges. Her sleeping atop the rug due to the softness of her bed. And she had been dreaming something, though she couldn't quite remember what. Only that she had felt safe and warm. And there had been the scent of cinnamon.

Shouts. Calls of alarm. They were not normal. She threw her bedding back, ignoring the chill of the room as she grasped her sword and ran to the window in her undergarments.

The front door had been thrown wide open, light spilling across the yard. Dostoy was silhouetted by it, hastily trying to calm whomever he was speaking to. She cracked the window.

"—wolves. Fell wolves, led by that bear. They're slaughtering the flocks. They've killed four men already. They're going to go for the homes!" The speaker was obviously out of breath, as was the wheezing horse standing behind him, both heaving for air.

The bear. She remembered Dostoy's comments about the mountain. *And now wolves.* And it was Dostoy's duty to protect his people. Already she could see him spreading his wings, preparing to take to the air.

"Dostoy!" she called. "Wait!"

"Victoria?" he cried, looking up at her. "Wolves and that bear have attacked!"

"I heard!" she called, her eyes catching a glimmer up the road. "My guard and I will help! Just wait!"

"The watchman will guide you!" he shouted, pointing at the man who'd brought the message and then launching himself into the sky with a mighty beat of his wings. He vanished into the dark in seconds.

She dressed in moments, her leather cuirass falling over her form with practiced ease. By the time she reached the door, hair waving behind her but sword and bow in hand, her guard were already almost at the clearing, thundering up the road in response to the commotion. She took one look at the farmer's horse and discounted it immediately. It was a draft animal, heavily winded. Not a warhorse like she was familiar with.

"Lady Victoria," the captain of her guard called as they neared. "What—!"

"Fell creatures!" she cried, running for them. "Attacking Dostoy's people! We ride to their aide!" Just as she had expected, her guard had come with a spare horse and ready for combat. She swung herself into the saddle with practiced ease.

"You!" she shouted at the farmer as she urged her horse toward him. She held out a hand as she came close, pulling the man up behind her. "Guide us to your home!"

Then she turned, guard following with a cry. The wind whipped at her hair, and she took advantage of the ride to bind it down, out of the way.

Her guide seemed hesitant to wrap his arms around her until she took one arm in hers and pulled it around her gut, urging her mount on faster. The road they were on wound through the forest, at times so narrow she doubted two wagons could pass one another, and at other times so twisting she thought the very act of turning would pull her from the saddle.

Soon she could hear roars ahead, and her blood began to pound even harder. *Dostoy!*

They burst free from the trees into what looked to be small pastures and farmland, though it was hard to tell in the dark. Ahead of them, she saw a small cluster of homes bunched together behind a low wall, lit only by scattered torches and lamps. And past that, Dostoy, breathing fire that burned against the night. Something howled in pain as his flames licked across the ground.

She could make out several groups of locals bunched together as well, trying to hold the wall against dark, twisted forms that darted in and out of the night, snarling. As she watched, one of them locked its jaws around someone and pulled them away, out into the darkness. Screams rent the air.

"Guard!" she called, eyes flicking over the village. "Five squads! Assist those defenders, get them to their homes, then hold those streets!" She brought her sword up, the hands around her waist vanishing as the watchman jumped from her charger. "For honor, and for victory!"

The company's oath rang through the air after her as her horse leapt into motion, thundering down the road toward the village center. She sheathed her sword, switching to her bow and firing as soon as a target presented itself. A fell wolf that had been leaping for one of the villagers crashed to a stop, an arrow jutting from its throat.

Her guard roared as they swept down on the wolves, their horses crushing skulls beneath their hooves and the soldiers hacking with blades. A sharp explosion filled the air as one fired a pistol, the musket ball tearing through a wolf in a spray of hot gore.

She left them to their work, galloping for Dostoy's position. He was surrounded by wolves on all sides, lashing out with claws, teeth and flame. Her charge caught them by surprise, and she let out a roar as her blade bit through a wolf's flesh, cleaving its head from its body. Hot ichor, foul and *wrong* leaked out of its corpse, hissing smoke as it struck the air. *Fell creatures indeed.* It was magic. Evil magic.

"Haaah!" she cried, skewering another wolf on her blade. Claws tore at her mount's sides, cutting deep wounds into its flank. She dove free before it could go down, landing atop one of the wolves and driving her blade through its skull with a sharp *crack*. Blackness stained the blade.

Then she was beside Dostoy, guarding his side as more wolves rushed forth out of the darkness. She'd never seen so many.

All of them would die. Her blade was a shimmer in the light of Dostoy's flames. He fought with a ferocity she'd never seen him exhibit, claws tearing wolves asunder and flames burning them to ash. With each breath, she could feel the flash of heat even on his other side, and she gave the world a grim smile.

Ichor and blood in equal parts splattered her armor and her face, but she fought on, cutting and stabbing until the tide of wolves slowed. It had felt like hours, but her own experience told her that it had been a minute or two at most, the world slowing during the haze of battle.

Then something roared and crashed into Dostoy from the side, throwing him to the ground. His wing came out reflexively and slammed into her back, throwing her through the air to land in the baked soil. A bear of titanic size stood over Dostoy, roaring as it brought its front paws down on his head.

Dostoy slumped, dazed, and the bear opened its jaws, bending down toward Dostoy's neck.

"*Light!*" The word tore free of her throat as she leapt to Dostoy's defense, her open hand coming up with a white blaze so bright it made her eyes water. The bear recoiled, blinking and howling in agony as she blinded it. She stabbed with her sword, driving the blade deep into the bear's gut, black ichor oozing around the hilt.

Something slammed into her shoulder with the force of a war-maul, throwing her into the air even as she cried out in pain. She hit the ground and rolled, her shoulder throbbing, sword torn from her hand by the force of the impact. The bear had hit her. She pushed herself up with her good arm as the beast fell to all fours, rushing toward her. *First rule: Get your feet under you!* But the bear was too close.

Dostoy's entire weight slammed into it from behind, shoving it into the ground with an impact that made the world shake. He roared, driving his claws deep into the bear's back and rending flesh. It tore at the earth, trying to push itself up and fight back, but Dostoy's size held it down.

Victoria pulled her bow from her back, threaded an arrow in one smooth, practiced motion, and fired. It struck the thrashing beast in the cheek, drawing out another roar. She fired again, this time striking it in the neck. Still it fought, pushing up and rocking Dostoy back and forth.

Her next arrow found its mark, catching the bear in the eye with a spray of black goo. For a moment the bear slowed, in shock, surprise, or pain, she didn't know, but it was all Dostoy needed. Flame spewed forth from his maw, bathing the bear's head in flames and scorching it until nothing was left but a charred, brittle skull, shrouded in ash.

Silence fell across the battlefield for a brief moment, almost as if the fallen beast had been the standard-bearer of its army, and then with howls the remaining wolves began to flee. A series of shots from her guard said that none of them would make it very far, and as she watched one of the fleeing wolves was cut down, its leg shattered.

"You . . ." Dostoy moved off of the body of the bear, speaking as she turned toward him. "You did magic."

"I . . . I did," she said, looking down at her hand in shock. "It was all I could think of. That dumb light spell."

"It might have just saved my life, Victoria," Dostoy said as the last of the wolves was cut down. The farmers began to cheer, doors opening and light spilling over the ground as they hurried out with lamps and aid. "Thank you."

"You're welcome," she said, before stepping over and pulling her blade free of the bear's corpse. "Now let's burn these bodies before they cause any more trouble."

Day Twenty-three

Things had settled again, since she and her guard had rushed to the defense of Dostoy's people. A few of her soldiers had been wounded, but not seriously, and the mount she'd ridden would need care for some time, as would her right arm where the bear had struck her. It was swollen, but a healer had pronounced nothing broken, and she'd returned to Dostoy's manor to clean up and return to her wait.

Still, she thought as she sat in her room, eyes fixed on the darkness outside the window. *We did a good thing.* Her arm would be stiff and sore for another week or so, limiting her swordplay, but the collection of prospective suitors had slowed as well, only one beating Dostoy in the last week, and mostly by luck, before being easily bested by her, so it didn't seem as though it would be a problem.

At least if the hunt for a suitor wasn't going well, nothing else seemed to be going wrong. The locals had thrown her and her guard a celebration in thanks for their help in thwarting the fell attack. Her skill with her magic was growing, as if her sudden success had opened the dam in her mind to—not a flood, or even a river, but at least a creek. And Dostoy himself had been most appreciative of their aid, paying her guard handsomely for the help. She'd turned down her own part of the payment. Taking it had felt . . . wrong, and not just because she'd saved his life. He didn't owe her. And besides . . . *He saved my life as well,* she thought.

The hour was late, and she turned from the window, about to draw her shirt over her head when a knock at the door brought her to a stop.

"Victoria?" It was Dostoy. She snapped her shirt back down. He had been quieter than normal during their game of Stakes that night, though his performance had improved. Perhaps he felt guilty for something? *Maybe I should have taken that payment,* she thought. *Or maybe he feels guilty over nearly losing a charge.* Or he was starting to suspect as she was: that her search for a suitor wasn't working.

Or maybe he was just quiet because I beat him so soundly when he thought he was winning, she thought as she moved to the door. "Yes?" she called, opening it.

Dostoy stood in the hall, looking down at her with an unreadable expression on his face. "Are you busy? If you're not, I would like to show you something. Dress warm."

"That's . . . cryptic," she said. She gestured at her clothes. "But very well." His face was neutral now, but she could see from the faint twitches of his wings and the way his tail was sweeping back and forth that he was hiding something. She had quickly learned that he often made the same motions when was setting up an ambush in Stakes. She still hadn't told him.

She threw on another layer of clothing, and then at Dostoy's urging, added a coat. "This is . . . quite warm," she said as she followed him through the manor.

"Don't worry," came his reply. "It will be quite cool in a moment." He led her out of the front door, out into the night. It was almost black outside, the sky overcast with low, heavy clouds, and the only light coming from the windows of the manor.

"All right," he said kneeling. "Now, I'm going to have to ask you to climb onto my back."

"What? Onto your back?"

"It's a great honor I wouldn't give to just anyone," he said, still kneeling. "But you . . . You have earned it, Victoria."

"I . . . Flying?"

"No," he said, and smiled. "That's not it. But we'll need to in order to . . . Well, to get there, so . . ." Slowly, hardly believing what was about to happen, she climbed onto his shoulders, just forward of his wings. His scales were smooth and warm to the touch.

"Wrap your arms around my neck if you need to," he said, rising. "I won't let you fall." His wings unfurled, gave a mighty downward *push*—and suddenly the earth was falling away beneath them, her stomach falling into her gut as they rose into the dark night. She let out a faint gasp of surprise, her arms and legs tightening by reflex.

"Ouch," Dostoy said with a faint chuckle. "Not so tight." The night air whipped against her clothes, and suddenly she was grateful for his warning to dress warm. She loosened her grip as the air became damp, and she realized they were in the clouds.

"It won't take long," he said as they climbed through the darkness. Her ears popped. "Not long at all."

Then with a rush they broke through the clouds, and she let out a gasp as she saw the night sky sprawled out before them, hundreds of thousands of pinpricks of light shining in all directions, backed by a misty stellar cloud that filled the horizon and ran from east to west.

"There," Dostoy said, his massive wing-beats slowing, and she tore her eyes away from the sky around her to see the peak of the mountain ahead of them. He set himself down atop it so lightly she didn't even realize they had landed until he folded his wings and knelt, and she slid off, eyes already drawn back to the stars around her.

"Levindias' Daughters," she said, her eyes alighting on a distant constellation. Then another. "The Sword of the Creator."

"I remember that you said you enjoyed stargazing when you were younger," Dostoy said from behind her. "And I've been up here myself on a few cloudy nights when the conditions are right. I wanted to do something to repay you for saving my life and helping my people, so—"

She spun around and wrapped her arms around his neck, her face pressed against his warm chest even as she blinked away tears. "It's perfect," she said. "Thank you."

They sat in silence for some time, watching the stars shine.

Day Thirty

He's good, Victoria thought as she watched her latest—and likely last, the way she was feeling lately—suitor maneuver against Dostoy. *Very, very good.* She'd already seen Dostoy try several of the tricks she'd taught him, only for his opponent to read and counter every one. She'd even glanced at the knight's team of squires and apprentices, watching them to make sure they weren't aiding him in any way. But they weren't. He was simply that good.

And yet . . . while she could feel a glimmer of excitement, the way she had been the first few times a suitor had come, something just felt . . . off. She watched as the knight, Sir Artur Kines, made another brilliant move at the game, cutting off two of Dostoy's attempt to counter it simultaneously. The move was brilliant. It should have had her gasping. Instead she just felt . . . intrigued, certainly. Impressed. But all the same . . .

What's wrong with me? she wondered as she watched Dostoy play a furious defense that nevertheless fell steadily to his opponent's careful strikes. *He's not bad looking. Sure, there's that scar, but it makes him look dignified. And he's only six years my senior. Educated, and he treats his squires well.* His was even a name she'd heard of before. *His reputation is of a man who values honor and right,* she thought as she watched Dostoy's last pieces fall. *Why am I so . . . unaffected?*

Down below, the defense she'd taught Dostoy failed at last, and he surrendered, tipping over his command post before Kines could do it for him. "You have won," he said, his voice echoing across the clearing. "And I don't think I've seen a more splendid game."

"You deserve commendations yourself, Dostoy," Kines said, rising from his seat and offering his hand with a smile. "That was an impressive defense. I've not had to play that carefully in years! You're truly remarkable!" They shook, and Dostoy began to gather up the board, the knight helping him, and even discussing their game.

I should be ecstatic right now, Victoria thought as she turned and walked to her sword, making sure that the leather guard was in place. *Papa would love him. His reputation is astounding. He's kind, certainly good–looking, and brilliant at strategy.*

Why do I feel like he's just an ordinary suitor?

No answer came to her as she walked through the manor, down the long steps and wide halls she'd spent the last month in. All she felt was apprehension. She put on a smile as she walked out the front door, accepting Kines bow of respect and responding in kind. She settled into a combat stance, ready to duel, when Kines held up a gauntleted hand.

"Wait," he said. "What's wrong with your arm?"

"I injured it a week ago," she said. "It's still a little stiff."

"Well that's not fair." Kines shook his head, gesturing to one of his squires. "Penua, grab some of the stiff training leathers. I'll bind my arm so that we're not unfairly matched. Please, a moment," he said in her direction.

Honorable, she thought as he began binding his arm with the stiff leathers, limiting his movement. *Certainly a trait worthy of admiration.* And yet she felt nothing but respect. Respect . . . and that was it.

"There!" Kines said, his arm bound tightly. "Now that we're evenly matched, Lady Victoria, we can have a proper, fair duel."

I . . .

"Are you ready?"

I . . .

Kines held his blade up.

She couldn't do it. She had her honor. To duel him now, when she felt so . . . strangely . . . about it, would be a slight against him, as well as a mark against her. "I yield," she said, lowering her blade. "I cannot."

"Pardon?" Kines seemed mystified—as did Dostoy—by the sudden drop of her blade.

"I'm sorry, Sir Knight Kines. You are a brilliant tactician, and I have no doubt you would best me with a blade, but even if you were, I could not—"

Kines held up a hand, forestalling what she was about to say, though she didn't even know what it was to be. "I understand," he said quietly. "I see the look in your eyes. You and I . . ." He shook his head, a soft smile on his face. "We are not meant for one another. You know this already."

"I'm sorry," she said quickly, but he shook his head again.

"Say no more," he said, lowering his blade and bowing. "I am not so without honor I would be unable to admit that I have lost this challenge, but the truth of it is in your eyes. May the Creator be with and bless you, Lady Victoria, and may our paths cross again." He saluted, albeit with a stiff arm, smiled, then turned on his heel and strode back to his squires. Many of them were giving him looks of confusion, but he held out a hand, and they were silent.

"Victoria?" Dostoy was looking at her in confusion. "What . . . ?"

"I'm sorry," she said. "I . . . he . . ." Then, unable to think of what to say, she turned and walked back into the manor, leaving his confused expression behind her.

It was almost evening when she ventured down to his study, still feeling as confused as she had been earlier. *Kines was everything I should have wanted. Everything Papa would have wanted.*

And she'd turned him away. For some reason, some cause, she'd said no. Her insides felt twisted.

"Dostoy," she said as she entered the study. He was lying at his desk, several books in front of him, though his eyes were fixed on none of them. "I . . . apologize for my behavior earlier. It was rude. After all you've gone through, and that amazing game of Stakes, to simply turn Knight Kines down so abruptly, and without explanation . . ."

"It was a good game," Dostoy said quietly. He reached out and closed his books. "Never fear, Victoria. As I believe I have said before, you are far from being my worst client. In fact, I would readily say that you have been the best, and I find your company truly delightful. If it takes another month, two, or even three, I'll gladly continue to test suitors for you. At a discount, even."

"Thank you, but . . . I'm not sure I should."

"Really?" he asked, moving to the Stakes table. She'd miss it when she was gone. It was such a beautiful board.

"Really," she answered, taking a seat opposite him and helping set up the pieces. It was an old, familiar practice now. "When I came to the idea, I thought for certain it would be a way to help me find a partner, not just in the company, but in love. But after this afternoon . . ." She let out a sigh. "I worry I may have been looking for the wrong thing." Pieces set, they flipped, and she made her move.

"You could change the test," Dostoy said as the pieces began to move back and forth between them. He'd gotten better under her tutelage. He was good. *Very* good. "Try something else. It's been done before."

She shook her head as she exposed an ambush and reacted. "Maybe, but I think . . . I think that while it was a worthy test, and I will treasure my time here, I don't know if changing the test will be enough. Somehow . . . Sometimes . . ." Her words trailed off. *Why is this so hard to explain?*

"Sometimes we know what we think we want, but not what we need?" Dostoy offered. She nodded. "My mother used to tell me that," he said, letting out a light chuckle even as his forces moved forward. He was trying to bait her with a surprise assault again, cut through her forces with cavalry or cannon fire. "So you would . . . leave, then?"

"I would," she said, her chest letting out an aching pang. She would miss the manor, with its sweeping halls and tall windows. And the mountain scenery. And the warm, cinnamon scent that seemed to pervade it. "Back to Papa and the campaigns." She moved her forces forward building a defense around the lee of a cliff.

"I will miss you, you know," Dostoy said. "As I said, I have enjoyed your company immensely. You've brightened my home with your curiosity and . . ." He moved a few pieces, engaging her forces. "You've taught me much about Stakes, among other things."

His words brought a smile to her face. "I've enjoyed your company a great deal," she said, gathering her forces to punch through his. It would be a slugging match, but she held the upper hand. Her chest let out another pang. "I'll miss you as—"

Her words stopped as Dostoy reached out and picked up one of his few remaining hidden pieces, revealing it to be the dragon. It moved across the board, soaring over the battle . . . and came down to rest on her command tent. She froze, her jaw hanging open as he looked at her with a sad smile—happy because he'd won at last, but sad to see her go—and suddenly everything in her mind, everything her heart, *clicked*.

"Victoria," Dostoy said, looking down at her with that same expression, with his wide, bright eyes she'd battled against every night, fought beside, and spoken with. "I think I just—"

She almost burst from her seat, clasping his cheeks with her hands as she pulled his lips into hers. For a moment, Dostoy seemed frozen, stiff with surprise. A flash of panic darted through her like a bolt of lightning. And then his lips melted into hers with a fiery passion.

The world seemed to *sing* around her, an electric thrill cascading all the way down to her toes, everything alight in a single, perfect moment that stretched on like it would never end.

At last she pulled away, short of breath, looking him right in the eyes, and found her voice. "I was wrong," she said. She *knew* now why she had been so hesitant, so listless, during Kines' challenge. "Someone did pass: You." She bent down, his stunned eyes following her every move, and tipped her command post over. "*You*. Will you accept?"

"I . . ." Dostoy seemed at a loss for words, his wings almost fully extended. "But I . . . Dragon . . . human . . . I mean, yes—"

The world *rippled*, something in her chest burning and leaping with joy.

"—but how—?"

She kissed him again, this time more slowly, then pulled back and smiled. She already had an answer. "The people can say what they want," she said. "I know what *I* want. I've heard wizards speak of the magic of shifting shape before. Father even once hired one who could make himself a crow and scout a battle. Think you can make a dragon a man . . . or a woman a dragoness?"

It seemed to take Dostoy a moment to find his voice. That wonderful, lightly deep voice. "For you?" he asked. "I'd give you the stars."

"You already did. But I'll settle for a second viewing. You?"

"Whenever you want."

She wrapped her arms around his neck, holding him close against her, even as his wings wrapped around her. She felt warm and safe, and his scales smelled of cinnamon.

The listless feeling in her chest had been burned away by something grand.

One Week Later

"Papa!"

Victoria leaped from her coach into his arms, an exuberant smile on her face as she rocked Federico Artares, the Black Wolf, back on his feet.

"Victoria!" It was all he could get out before her arms clasped against him so tightly he could hardly breathe. But finally she let go, stepping back with a bright, beaming smile that said as much as he had suspected when he'd received her short letter. Her search had been successful, and she had found a prospective husband.

He felt his suspicions rise slightly at the thought. Whoever his daughter wed had better be a great man indeed, to stand beside such a daughter. Not in front, or behind, but beside. He knew his Victoria.

"You return bearing good news," he said, smiling. *She looks so happy*, he thought. *Ah, my angel. If only you could be here to see this.*

Victoria's smile only grew, and she nodded.

"Well," he said, extending a hand to the coach. "Let him come out!"

"Oh, he didn't ride in the coach, father," she said, and he frowned in confusion. "Nor did I, save the last mile or so."

"What? But—?"

"Father," she said, turning as a large *whooshing* sound began to fill the air. "I'd like you to meet my fiancé, Dostoy the Mighty."

Federico's jaw dropped as the tan dragon landed beside his daughter, tucking his wings in and bowing. "Count Artares," he said, his words holding a trace of a northern accent. "My name is Dostoy, and I love your daughter Victoria. It would be my greatest pleasure to stand beside her as a husband, and as your son-in-law."

Federico continued to stare, words failing him as Victoria leaned over and kissed the dragon on the lips, right in full view of everyone around. A hundred different thoughts boiled to his head, teasing at the edge of his tongue . . . and then he laughed.

His daughter had returned with *a dragon*. One she intended to wed, no less. And as far as grandchildren were concerned, well . . . he could see the look in their eyes. Wizards were expensive . . . but he had money. *And of course, that would be why Victoria mentioned learning magic in her final letter.* It came together in his mind like a battle plan, every piece revealed, and he spread his arms.

"Welcome, Dostoy, soon-to-be-husband of my Victoria, and my future son-in-law!"

"Huzzah!" the cry went up from all his guard, filling the air.

"You two!" he cried, stepping forward and wrapping his arms around both of them. Or as close to it as he could with his left trying to wrap around the large body of a dragon. "You must be tired from your journey. Go inside. Freshen up. We have *much* to talk about! I'll see to the guards.

Go! Go!" He stepped back and shooed the pair away, watching as they walked up the steps to his home, Victoria's arm wrapped around one of the dragon's—Dostoy's—forelegs.

He smiled and clapped his hands together. He could *see* the joy radiating between the couple. Dostoy would make a fine son-in-law, species notwithstanding. He was already sure of that. Victoria was wise beyond her years.

And when the time comes, he thought as he began ordering the guard back to their posts. *The Black Wolf of Artares will step down.*

And the Dragoness of Artares will take my place.

He had to admit, it was not at all what he had expected. But Victoria was happy.

And that was all he could ask.

Dragon Soap
M. K. Hutchins

Gran never did like it when I used the Winchester to deal with dragons—so I went and did a damn fool thing and set out to hunt them in the dead of night. It wasn't hard to sneak by Gran. She snored twice as loud as she barked, which was saying something.

I clambered down the hill from our farm and into the swamp. A half-moon glowed above the trees, casting strange shadows over the curtains of moss and standing pools of water. It almost made the mud look like opals, but that didn't change the smell.

I kept the rifle at a ready carry. The smooth, well-worn wood felt solid in my grip, despite the apothecary's anti-mange lotion I'd slathered on my hands—and every other inch of exposed skin on my body. I wasn't keen on coming home riddled with bug bites.

Something splashed behind me. I whirled. But it wasn't no dragon—just my ten-year-old little brother Ted, tripping into a pool and soaked half-way up his britches.

"Tarnation, Ted! You shouldn't be here!" I slung the gun over my back. Not my favorite way to carry it, or the quickest draw, but at least with it pointed straight up I could guarantee Ted wouldn't run in front of my muzzle. Probably.

"You shouldn't be here, either."

Ten-year-olds are all smart-mouths. "Get on home."

"Send me home, and I'll wake up Gran. I'm the man of the house, Maisy. I belong out here," he said.

He tried so hard to be grown-up, but if he were a man, he'd know how to swallow his pride and do what was important. If Gran woke, she'd froth herself into a right fit with us both gone. If Ted had stayed, she'd at least have a body to complain to. "Your pants are wet."

He did his best to walk forward in a dignified-like manner. "You're not sending me away. We've got to cull the dragons back. I know one of them tore up a row of radishes and made off with a chicken last night. You and Gran ain't good at hiding nothing from me."

Maybe even more pressing, we needed the money. The apothecary in town didn't pay much for a swamp-dragon—but she paid something. I'd been planning on selling that chicken to get Gran more of her tonic. Now we only had one, and we needed her bad for eggs and eating up grubs in the garden.

"Fine. Be quiet. And stay behind me. I'll be shooting things in front."

Ted pulled a face. "I'm not an idiot."

He was almost adorable when he pouted like that. Would have been, if he'd been five years younger.

I couldn't see much in the way of tracks, but I could smell the blood-rust tang of mange eggs. I followed it. The little mange-bugs would bite anything that moved, but they needed fresh dragon blood to hatch their eggs.

Ted seemed to trip over every branch and stick behind me. Man of the house, indeed.

We walked and walked, the mange-stench getting stronger with every step. With this kind of reek, we had to be coming to a dragon's nest or something. Couldn't be less than twenty of them ahead. I pulled my shirt over my nose, but I still didn't see nothing.

"M-Maisy?" Ted asked nervously, like he'd just realized he was afraid of the dark.

I brushed more moss aside, mud sucking at my boots. Water stretched ahead of me—we'd have to go around. It was at least thirty feet wide, practically a pond.

"Maisy?" he tried again.

I squinted. Three, maybe four, lithe adult dragons, each a bit bigger than a raccoon, wriggled in the shallows on the far side of the pond. Strange. Four dragons couldn't make a mange-stink this bad. Maybe I just couldn't see the others in the moonlight.

"I'm going to get a closer look." If I sold a whole mess of dragons into the apothecary, I could buy Gran's tonic and a new flock of chickens. Maybe we could finally really get on our feet and I wouldn't have to sneak out to shoot dragons. "You stay here."

I wasn't particularly worried about getting bit or clawed by the critters. I knew what I was doing—but Ted didn't and thought he did.

"I'm all itchy."

"Yeah. Wet pants'll do that to a man." I started off.

A slap. Another slap. He was hitting himself, swatting at bugs. "I keep getting bites. It hurts, Maisy."

I turned round. Even in the bad light, I could tell this wasn't good. Wasn't no mere mosquitoes. The blisters on his face and hands were turning black.

"Ted. Did you follow me without rubbing down with anti-mange?"

"I . . . I didn't want to lose you. You move fast through the swamp."

Idiot. "We've got to get you back."

"Back where?" he asked, but he was already wobbling on his feet.

I put my arm around his shoulder—the arm without the Winchester slung around it—and dragged him along. "The longer we wait, the worse it'll be. Trust me."

We didn't have none of the apothecary's anti-mange soap, so I sent Ted out with the lye stuff to wash by the rain barrel. I left him the lotion—it worked best as a repellent, but it might help some. He stumbled back inside soon enough, curled up, and went to sleep.

I woke to Gran screeching, "What the devil, Ted!"

The mange got him bad. The bites were still black, and the skin round them had turned purple. I felt like I was looking at a boy who'd suddenly grown a hundred tiny black eyes.

After that, it didn't take long for the story to come out.

"Neither of you got more sense than a newborn chick!" Gran ranted. "What were you thinking, trying to shoot up dragons? And at night?"

I'd been thinking that she wouldn't have to know a lick about it. Her gnarled old hands were already trembling, and it wasn't noon. She must've started rationing her tonic down.

Gran knelt next to Ted and rubbed a cut-open radish over his bites, to help with the pain and the itch. Poor kid. Laying groaning on his pallet with his sweaty hair plastered to his head, he looked a lot younger. Like he did before Ma and Pa went up to heaven.

"They're tearing up the radishes, they've eaten most of the chickens, and we needed a couple corpses to sell in town," I said. "Looks like we'll need more than a few now. He has to have the anti-mange soap, Gran. Lotion ain't strong enough."

"Ask Beth to sell us her soap on credit," Gran said.

I choked on air, laughing. Credit?

"I won't have you shooting no more dragons. It's killing dragons what brought this horrible mange plague. Spilling their blood everywhere."

"Gran." I didn't outright say she was plain dead wrong. I didn't know how the mange had gotten so bad so quickly, but it'd surely be worse if folks weren't shooting their breeding ground.

"Don't you Gran me, young lady. You really think it's coincidence that as soon as Beth offers to buy up corpses, the mange gets ten times worse than it's ever been? Used to be you'd get a dragon maybe once every other year sneaking out of the swamp and tearing up radishes to rub on himself for a bad case of mange. But now!"

I shook my head. "That doesn't account for the chickens."

"So long as you're going to hike for a radish, why not snatch a snack?"

She had a point there.

"Beth's so proud of her apothecary skills, so proud she found some way to make use of lesser dragon bones. But if folks round here had a lick of sense, they'd stop selling carcasses to her. Including you, Maisy!"

She'd worked herself up and was scrubbing Ted like he was a pile of Saturday laundry.

"Can you stop trying to skin me?" he groaned. "I'm not a rabbit. I'm your grandson. Promise."

Gran took herself a deep breath and calmed down, but I still spoke slow and careful. For Ted's sake. I had no love for that stuck-up Beth, but Gran could blame bad weather on the woman. "Honestly, I can't feel bad about selling dragons to her. Even if I wish someone else were profiting by it, the medicine she makes out of the bones seems to do a world of good for all those folks up north with coal miner's lung."

"Folks up north," Gran muttered it like she was cussing. "What about folks here? Beth's medicine probably doesn't even work."

Based on how many fancy new clothes she'd been able to buy lately, I doubted that. "Do you have some other idea of how to make quick money?"

Gran pursed her lips. Of course she didn't. "Beth ought to be right ashamed of herself and all this mange she's caused. All this damage to people's farms. You tell her she owes us, then come back with that soap."

"I can say that, but it won't do a lick of good. Beth ain't just giving us soap." Gran thought about it for a second. Then she snatched a wooden carving of a bird off the mantle—Pa had made it. "Take this."

It felt heavier than lead in my hands. "It's not worth nothing." Not except to us. I remembered watching Pa make it—his long, calloused fingers gently turning the wood in his hands. Ted moaned again. I don't know if he was just in pain, or if he was protesting, too.

"It's not to pay her. It's collateral for our loan."

That might actually work. Beth would get a kick out of taking something we cherished. She'd probably burn it as soon as I left.

"Maisy," Gran prompted sharply.

I'd just been standing there, looking at it and dawdling. If my folks were still around, we wouldn't be like this—me and Gran and Ted scratching just to get by. "Yes, Gran. I'm going."

Beth had a nice spot in town, between the tinsmith and the leatherworker. The wooden sign was painted in garish red, with letters so flourished they were hard to read: Madame Jade's Apothecary. Best Tonics, Medicines, and Restoratives.

I pushed inside, setting off a small bell hanging from the door. The inside was worse than the out—every inch covered either in bottles or in red-and-gold tassels and posters. Usually it reeked like pickled cabbage in here, but today the air was thick with the smell of rendering tallow.

Beth strode out of the back, dressed-up in a silk robe with her hair stuck on top of her head with sticks and a lot of make-up all over her face—like she was really from the East, where they had the world's most brilliant apothecaries. They'd figured out how to use dragon bones in the first place, and out there, they had proper dragons bigger than houses.

"Greetings and welcome to my humble store," she said, giving a bow that reeked of arrogance.

I casually stuck my hands in my pockets. "Heya Beth. How you been?"

Beth bristled. She hated it when people didn't play along with her, when they didn't bow and scrape and call her Madame Jade. But she wasn't from the East any more than I was, and I wasn't going to pretend otherwise. She pursed her red-painted lips. "I don't see any carcasses, Maisy. Do you actually have business here?"

"Need some anti-mange soap. Ted's covered in bites."

Beth gave me a flat glare and held out her hand for coin. I'd already outstayed my welcome.

"Gran wants you to take it on credit. We'll pay you back."

"I don't take credit from customers."

"We're not customers. We're family."

She let out a bark of a laugh. "I think that makes it worse. I know exactly what your Gran thinks of me."

Well. It's not like Gran ever claimed to be discreet or mild-tongued. I liked that about her. You never could say she didn't speak her mind. "It's for Ted, not her. And I brought some collateral."

I pulled out that fine little bird.

Beth smirked. "I'm not in the business of storing other folks' trash. It looks like something an owl vomited up. Your Pa make that?"

She was trying to rile me up, but I hadn't expected Beth to stoop so low as to insult the dead. I wanted to give her an earful until her skull burst, but the weight of the bird helped me remember why I was there. I could waste my breath insulting Beth when Ted was better.

"I'm one of your best dragon-suppliers. Cut me a half bar of soap and I'll get you a carcass within the week."

"I only sell whole bars and I'm not about to make exceptions. Go shoot me a pair of dragons and bring them back here. Then we can trade like civilized people," Beth sniffed.

Surely even Beth could have compassion for a kid. "Ted's already bruising. He needs it bad."

"So go hunting, Maisy. Stop wasting time here."

A new scent prickled my nose. "Something burning back there?"

Beth gasped and ran. I followed her a few paces. She did in fact have a pot full of white tallow, trimmed and cubed, rendering down on her fancy pot-bellied stove. She snatched a pair of towels and pulled it off the heat.

"You gotta do some kind of magic apothecary thing during the rendering to make the lotion or soap work? Cause if not, you really should've let the butcher do that." Old Carson charged a fair price, and he had a pot big enough to do half a cow at a time.

Beth ignored me, red lips pursed as she poked at her tallow with a spoon.

"Is that whole batch ruined?" I asked hopefully—it'd serve her right.

"It's fine," she snapped. "I only render it myself to ensure my ingredients are quality. Unfortunately, I have much less control over the caliber of my customers. Get out, swamp rat. Now. Or do I need to chase you with a broom?"

I walked back home parallel along the canal, but a good ways from it. Townfolk had cut it a decade ago so they could let the swamp compost their trash instead of doing it themselves. Corn husks and chicken bones bobbed downstream with considerably less-attractive human waste. Right then, I hated folks who were too good for a normal latrine like everyone else. People like Beth. She was worse than most, pretending to come from a noble place she'd never even seen.

Still, I should've begged better. Bowed and scraped and put on a show, calling her Madame Jade and everything, but I've got too much Gran in me for my own good.

I veered from the canal and up the hill to our little farm. The succulent smell of boiling chicken filled the air. I frowned, then jogged the rest of the way.

"Gran?" I pushed the door open. "What are you doing?"

"Cooking."

I groaned. "Tell me we've still got a chicken."

"Liars go to hell, Maisy, and while my old bones wouldn't mind some warmth, I'm fixing on spending my afterlife with your folks." Gran nodded toward Ted. "Look at him. He needs all the help he can get, and chicken broth is good for any ailment. We don't have the luxury to think about tomorrow—we have to survive today first. You got the soap?"

I stepped all the way inside and knelt by Ted's mattress. His skin shone feverish, and his bites glittered. They were already transforming into tiny scales.

Tarnation. I should have begged Beth nice. I set the bird carving next to him, hoping it might bring him some comfort or luck.

Ted blinked at me, like he couldn't quite focus. "Maisy?"

I took his hand and squeezed it, his scales scratching my skin. He must be allergic. Most cases never got this bad. The anti-mange lotion might slow it, but without soap, the scales would just keep spreading, until his whole body was locked down stiff in them. And when a body can't move, it eventually wastes away into a skeleton.

"You'll be right as rain soon, Ted." I brushed his hair out of his eyes, then grabbed the Winchester off the wall.

Gran glared at me. "I won't have you shooting no dragons! That's what caused this in the first place."

I pointed at Ted and spat her own words back at her. "We don't have the luxury to think about tomorrow—we have to survive today first."

Gran's face wrinkled up tight like she was sucking down a sour pickle. Her right hand started to tremble. She had to be rationing her tonic. "I don't like it."

"Got any other ideas? You want me to take this gun into town, shoot Beth, and steal the soap instead?"

Gran paused.

"I wasn't serious, Gran."

"I know, I know. I just need time to think. I left the chicken head and guts out by the stump. Go take care of them. I'll come up with something before you finish."

I slung the gun over my back, headed outside, and grabbed a shovel. I dug a two-foot hole and dumped the feather, skin, guts, and head into it. Then I turned our compost pile overtop—that would ensure critters wouldn't smell the carcass and go digging for it. The compost itself smelled good—warm and earthy. Real. I wasn't no town-dweller, sneering at others because I was too self-important to work up a sweat.

By the time I finished, Gran hadn't come outside with any brilliant ideas. So I rubbed on some anti-mange lotion and headed down the hill to the swamp. I'd need two dead dragons to buy the soap, and more than that for Gran's tonic.

I prayed that I really had found a nest last night. I'd worry about spilled blood spreading the mange and itchy dragons tearing up the farm in search of produce latter.

Soon as I reached the swamp, I switched to a two-hand carry, ready to shoot quickly. I ducked around moss and watched my step. Long before I reached the pond, though, I caught a wiff of rust. Had a mangy dragon been this way recently?

I slowed down. I watched the sunlight and shadows over the stagnant pools of water. Not a ripple.

Carefully, I stepped over a rotten log. Right onto a dragon's tail.

I stumbled back, too slow. The dragon burst from the log, hissing. Claws raked into my calf. That burned something fierce.

I cracked the butt of the Winchester against its scaly face. It screeched in anger, flopping backwards. Giving me just enough time to get my feet under me proper.

I shot. The Winchester cracked the air, making my ears ring. I pumped another cartridge into the chamber, but I didn't fire. Dragon wasn't moving. I'd gotten him clean between the eyes.

Well, that was one carcass I could haul in. One more and I could buy the soap. I hobbled over to a nearby rock to get a proper look at my injured calf. Little beast had torn through my boots and shredded the bottom of my pants. I ripped the bottom of the latter clean off and tied it tight around the gashes. They weren't deep enough to threaten bleeding out, but they hurt like the devil. And with part of my leg exposed, I was sure to get some mange on it.

"Thanks, big fellow. Just what I needed today."

He didn't respond of course, what with blood running down his snout from that third eye I'd given him. The little flurries of mange all around him clouded to his head, licked it up, and began laying eggs. The white froth looked just like soap scum—it matched the patches already on his back and forelegs. The little bugs must not have realized he was dead, yet. Mange liked fresh blood—they always left soon as a carcass bloated open or other critters tore into it.

Gran was wrong. This fatal wound wasn't any different than one he could take from a fall or fighting another dragon. No reason why it ought to make the mange spread.

I didn't want to haul him to the pond with me, so I slung his carcass up into the branch of a tree. Not real professional, but I hoped it would prevent scavengers from dragging him off.

Something itched my calf. I slapped at it, then swore as pain flared across my wound. Sooner I got this done, the better.

I hurried as fast as it was wise across the swamp. My whole leg throbbed by the time I reached the pond. With an open wound, I was probably going to need anti-mange soap as bad as Ted.

Once we healed up, we'd figure out how to get Gran's tonic. And replace the chickens. And eat when winter came, given the dragons had torn up so much of the garden looking for radishes.

My leg better heal up right quick. I was going to spend the rest of my life in this swamp, hunting dragons so we could survive.

I edged along the pool, trying to find a better vantage. Once again, I pulled my shirt over my nose, trying not to gag on the sharp, metallic reek of mange. There was swamp-reek, too, and something sickly sweet and potent in the hot afternoon.

But I only found six dragons, nosing around several largish shapes bobbing in the water, not the huge nest my nose had led me to believe there would be. I found a tree not too far away that looked solid and clambered up. Then I crawled out along one long branch and aimed the Winchester.

But there were those uncanny shapes in the water. The dragons were whimpering and pushing them around. And was that—half a pumpkin? Then I spotted a brown rum bottle. Other bits of floatsam bobbed in that curve of the pond.

The trash from the canal must gather here. Were the dragons eating it up, like pigs taking to slop?

I held still, ignoring my hurt leg and the uncomfortable angle of the branch digging into my stomach. A pair of dragons managed to flip one of the large, bobbing things up onto the bank.

It was another dragon. The corpse of one. All flayed open. Had to be one Beth had butchered—no animal teeth made those kind of nice cuts. And it was covered—tail to snout—in the pale froth of mange-eggs. I thought it might be a trick of the light, but then I spotted another dozen carcasses on the shore. No wonder this place stank so bad.

The live dragons sent up a mournful, haunting wail and rubbed up against their dead fellows. That only got them covered in its blood and guts and eggs. The mange swarmed thick around them and the open carcasses.

What had Beth done to those bodies, to make the mange take to dead dragons like that? Had she done it on purpose, so more people would need to buy her soap and lotion? She should have just hired someone to compost them for her. I'd have done it, if she threw in some of her soap.

But as the dragons nestled their fellow and grieved, I saw the reason for her secrecy. They rubbed away the guts and slime, showing bones sticking out. All the bones.

Beth wasn't buying those carcasses because she'd figured out how to use the skeletons of lesser dragons. She wasn't making medicine for no miners up north. I'd been a damned fool. I should have realized something was wrong when I caught high-and-mighty Beth rendering her own tallow.

I hauled the fellow I'd shot earlier back home, then asked Gran to help me butcher him up.

"Weren't you going to sell this?" she asked, sitting next to me outside.

"I think I can do better for Ted than that."

Gran didn't ask more questions. She was old, but when her hands weren't shaking, she was one deft butcher. Soon we had nice, white-yellow chunks of dragon fat. I asked her to start rendering them into tallow inside, while I buried the messy leftovers with the chicken carcass.

I scooped up some water from our leeching barrel and boiled it down into right strong lye. By then it was long past dark, but neither me nor Gran had any thoughts of going to sleep. Gran cooked the lye and the tallow together until we had something that looked like mashed potatoes. Gran crammed most of it into our soap mold. Some she just plopped onto a plate so it'd cool faster.

"Anti-mange soap," I said. "The bugs might like dragon blood, but they apparently can't abide dragon fat. That's why they stick with live dragons—all their fat is still safely inside."

Butcher out all the fat and dump the rest of the carcass in the swamp, and you'd create the perfect mange breeding ground.

Gran poked at the lump on the plate. "Looks like fine soap. You sure?"

"Do you think Beth's a no-good lazy charlatan?"

"Right. Let's try it on your leg first, then."

The soap would have been harder and better with more time to cure. It stung like the devil, but the itch disappeared as soon as we rinsed my calf off.

We sponge-bathed Ted's limbs. Half the little scales flaked off him, and the swelling went down. He groaned softly at first, but then started protesting out loud.

"Ain't natural to wash a body so often," he mumbled, slurring the words, eyes still closed.

I tried to reassure him. "We're helping you get better."

"Get offa me, or I'll kick you in the shins, Maisy."

"You'd have to stand up first. Besides, we're done now," I said. Gran was already taking away the rags.

"You're done 'cause you're scared of me."

I gently brushed the hair from his eyes. "That's right. You're terrifying. Now shut up and go back to sleep, sweat pea."

For once, Ted listened. The feverish sheen to his skin had gone away, and he was breathing slow and regular. Looked like he'd be fine.

"Come eat," Gran said, filling two bowls with chicken soup. "Shouldn't go to bed on an empty stomach."

I joined her by the fire. My eyes felt dry as cotton and my bones ached with tired, but my soul finally felt light.

Gran was smiling, too. "Beth caused this mange outbreak, throwing dragon carcasses in the swamp like that. Whether she's daft or whether she did it on purpose to prey on innocent folks so they'd buy more soap, I figure we can get her run out of town by tomorrow night."

For an old woman who couldn't abide a soul shooting dragons, she sure had a mean streak. "Gran. Then everyone'll be shooting up dragons for tallow. You think all of them are going to handle their carcasses any better than Beth?"

Gran's face puckered again. Nope. "Beth deserves it. She's family and she left Ted to rot."

"We can do better than a mob, Gran. Once that soap is hard enough to cut, I'll start selling it in town at half Beth's price. I'll buy carcasses for double."

I'd make lotion, too. That was easy—just add a little oil to the tallow so it spread easy.

"But the mange—"

"We'll compost the dead dragons proper ourselves. That'll get the mange under control, eventually. Dragons will stop bothering folks' farms for radishes all the time, we'll cut Beth out of what I suspect is her best business, and we'll make a tidy profit on the side. Once the mange is back to normal, I'll stop paying for carcasses and just go hunting myself—just enough to keep folks supplied with what little lotion and soap they'll need."

By then, we'll have more than enough money to replace our chickens and buy Gran a mess of tonic. We wouldn't be scraping by anymore—we could plan for tomorrow. Though I might have to hike to the city for tonic, if Beth was feeling disagreeable with us.

Gran took a few more spoonfuls of soup, thinking it over. "Beth will watch her business wither away?"

"Yup. Much worse than being driven clean out of town."

Gran nodded. "I like your plan, Maisy. Just promise me you'll sell the soap right in front of her store, where she can watch."

"Yes, Gran."

Li Na and the Dragon
Scott R. Parkin

L I NA FELT HER BODY BREAK IN THE FOURTH HOUR OF HER labor as she squatted down and curled tightly around her swollen belly, screaming for her reluctant seventh child to come quickly.

Not the sharp pang and long sting of skin tearing to make way for the baby, but a sudden snap and release deep within her body, as if jabbed in the spine between her hips with a blunt pole. Almost before the dull thud registered came a sudden heat spreading outward and taking her strength as it moved into her chest and face, arms and legs, ears and fingers and toes.

She fell backward against her rest chair but was too weak to catch hold of its shallow arms. She slid sideways and flopped to the floor as the midwife reached out with fingers that flailed at empty air. Hands tugged her away from the plain wooden chair and laid her flat on the lacquered floor, pressed down on her belly, and tugged at the baby as it emerged.

Li Na heard voices, but words fled behind an insistent ringing, like the thin metallic voice of Huanglong, the yellow dragon whose shrine she served.

"Let the child be a boy," she whispered, her leaden lips fighting to form each word. "Great Huanglong, guardian of rivers and master of words, give my husband a son to carry on his name. Bless my long service to your shrine with this one comfort. Please."

But as she felt her life spill onto the pale yellow floorboards, she knew it would not be. This was the curse of her family—that the women of her house would bear only daughters. Penance for the sin of a long-forgotten ancestor who had angered Huanglong's master and doomed the family name to extinction.

She should have told her husband, Li Zhou, of the curse in the very beginning so he could release her and find a wife able to fulfill that most basic duty. But they had been so much in love, and the idea of parting seemed so much deeper a pain . . .

The midwife brought the baby to her, and Li Na saw that she was right; her seventh and last child was indeed a girl. She tried to lift her hand to caress her beloved daughter, but her arm would not obey. Li Na tried to whisper a blessing of comfort to this child who would suffer both the burden of her own curse and the blame for her mother's death, but her lips would no longer move.

So Li Na gazed at her daughter as she stole rapid, shallow breaths until first whiteness, then darkness took even this simple joy from her.

She wept silently that the only gift she could bestow on this, her last child, was a memory of sorrow.

Li Na awoke to the soft tickle of her daughter's breath on her neck, the baby's reassuring weight pressing against her breast. She lay quietly, eyes closed, and enjoyed the moment.

She had not died, after all. Still, she would bear no more children. It was for the best.

Though her face still felt flushed, her hands were icy, even beneath the thick blanket that covered her. A dull ache pulsed deep inside, an insistent throb that flared with each breath. Her mouth was sticky-dry and tasted of the bitter herbs Li Na recognized as lei gong teng laced with a powerful narcotic meant to keep her still and asleep so she could heal.

She heard the rustling of slippered feet and felt hands tug at her blankets and adjust her headrest. She caught the sharp scent of cinnamon and ginger and cloves—her husband. He had left the care of his warehouse to others so he could watch over her. Of course.

Li Na felt light pressure on her chest and probing fingers checking her daughter's wrap. When he began to lift the infant away, Li Na reached up to stop him and gasped as sharp pain sliced through her core. Her eyes snapped open, and Li Zhou knelt over her, his own eyes wide in surprise.

"Let me hold her," Li Na croaked from a dry throat.

"You should be asleep," Li Zhou said and gently touched her cheek. He reached above her head and brought back a dark green wu lou gourd.

He tipped its long neck toward her mouth so that thick, bitter potion spilled onto her lips. She swallowed three sips before she let the potion pool and run off her lips, and he took the medicine away.

"Water," she said.

He lifted a yellow, dust-colored gourd, and Li Na let cool water soothe her dry mouth and parched throat. She emptied two gourds and still wanted more. It was no surprise, considering how much she had bled.

"Hui-Ying, bring more water!" Li Zhou hissed over his shoulder.

A moment later, light, hurried footsteps announced her oldest child's arrival, and cool water again touched her lips. The narcotic potion had begun to take effect and dulled her pain enough so she could turn her head and see her tall, slightly built, eleven-year-old daughter kneeling at her father's elbow, the young girl's eyes wide and her lips tightly pressed.

Li Na finished the third gourd and smiled at Hui-Ying as Li Zhou pressed the dark green bottle on her and bitter potion again washed her lips. She dutifully swallowed three more times and saw her daughter's expression soften. Hui-Ying studied the healing arts and was quite adept even at such a young age. She had most certainly created this unfamiliar potion as the fruits of her own study and talents and was clearly relieved to see it work.

Li Zhou reached out again and snatched the baby from her chest, handing her off to Hui-Ying. "Take that away and change the wrapping; it's soaking wet."

Li Na wanted to protest, but the potion had taken what feeble strength remained and she could only watch as Hui-Ying hurried away.

"Sleep, dearest," Li Zhou whispered, and she struggled to focus on his face. Though his eyes were now tender and his manner gentle, she had seen the hard look on his face and felt the harsh tug when he snatched the baby away.

As forced sleep took her, Li Na wondered how it was possible that her husband could love her in the same moment that he clearly despised her precious daughter. Were they not the same flesh, each created in her own time from love and hope?

The baby's cries from the next room woke Li Na. Not the simple fuss of wetness or the long wails of hunger, but the sharp, strangled shrieks of pain or abandonment. Why was her daughter in the dragon temple? That was Li Na's personal stewardship; no one entered except in her company.

She struggled to sit, then stand as she heard the angry rumble of Li Zhou's voice beneath the cries of her daughter. Pain pulsed in her center, but it was still dulled by the bitter potion, and she was able to tolerate it, though it stole her breath away.

Li Na staggered to the small room's single door. It was deep night and only the light of a single, small lamp wavered on the low teak table at the end of the short hallway to her left. She stumbled forward, gripping the door frame, then lurching to the side and leaning heavily on the small table. There was wetness on her thigh; she had begun to bleed again.

". . . ignored her pleas and let this mistake happen." Li Zhou's voice was hard, his words clipped and spat out as though hurling stones at an enemy. "You have stolen her time and devotion from me, yet given nothing in return."

She leaned against the wall beside the narrow doorway and gasped against the lightness in her head, the weakness in her legs, and the rising pain deep in both body and soul. She gazed through the curtain of amber beads that separated the bright light of the great yellow dragon's temple from the darkness of her husband's house.

Li Zhou knelt before the simple cedar and river stone shrine, his hands raised as if in prayer, but his fingers were clenched into tight fists. Her newborn daughter lay naked on the shrine's offering board, tiny arms and legs shivering in the chill of the late-night breeze from off the great Huang He River. Her skin was mottled purple and white from cold and distress as she shrieked without cease.

Her husband stood suddenly, and she saw the long, white linen wrap that should be protecting her daughter wadded in a heap on the floor.

"If you will not grant her wish, then hear my demand." He snatched up the linen and shook it at the brass statue of Huanglong that stood atop the small shrine. "I have no use for a living daughter, a dying wife, or a dragon shrine that wastes my resources to no benefit."

She heard a high, rich metallic sound like the pure ring of a bell and recognized it as the voice of Huanglong. The great yellow dragon was growling, a sound she had heard only once in her life—years ago, when Huanglong had used the word of its power to vanish a mischievous tortoise after it had damaged the dragon shrine.

Her husband seemed unaware of the sound.

"This is my bargain and my oath," Li Zhou spat through clenched teeth. "Change that mewling thing into a son or else take it away and use it to restore my wife's health. If you fail to do one of these things by sundown tomorrow, I will tear this temple from off my house and cast its parts into the great river."

He flung the wad of linen at the small brass dragon statue and stalked through the temple's open front gate and out into the cold night.

Li Na gathered the remains of her paltry strength and stepped forward, despite the growing pain. Huanglong's ringing metal growl never abated, and she stumbled through the curtain of amber beads. Her heavy feet knocked into each other, and she sprawled forward toward the dragon shrine where she lay still, her face flat to the worn wooden floor. Though her daughter shivered and shrieked only two arm's-length away, Li Na knew Li Zhou was in greater danger.

"Great Huanglong," she whispered, "guardian of rivers and master of words, please forget the foolish words of my husband."

"It is unforgivable!" the tiny metallic voice cried. The ringing growl grew louder and more resonant. "To deny the worth of creation in which he had part—"

"He is afraid," Li Na said, her voice thin. "His one great hope lies unfulfilled on your offering board; his one great comfort lies broken before you. It has made him desperate."

"It has made him stupid!" Huanglong shouted and sailed down off the top of the cedar shrine, its small brass body moving with fluid grace. It plucked the linen wrap from its tiny horns and draped it over the shrieking baby, then gazed down on Li Na.

"If he is stupid, great Huanglong, it is because I have lied to him these fifteen years. He knows nothing of the curse that your master rightly breathed out against my ancestor, and so does not understand that what he asks is impossible."

The ringing growl suddenly stopped and heavy silence filled the small temple, broken only by the distant rush of the mighty Yellow River—the Huang He—and the soft susurrus of night wind. Even her daughter's shrieks ceased for a moment.

"He wishes your daughter dead and has named her a mistake," the yellow dragon said as the infant's cries rang out again. "To imagine that a dragon would seek the life of an infant in exchange for *anything*... How can I forgive such disrespect?"

Li Na gathered her arms under her and pushed up. Sharp pain arced through her hips and gut and brought bile to her throat, but she faced Huanglong.

"I don't... I can't..." Tears streamed from her eyes. "His dying hopes have driven him mad in this moment of frustration. I know Li Zhou to be loving and kind and generous."

"And yet."

"No," she said, her voice stronger. "No. He wishes for my health, not her death. If he has spoken vainly, it only proves the depth of his fear."

Huanglong gazed down at Li Na, and she gazed back, unfazed. "He feels nothing at all for her," the dragon said, though its mouth did not move. "That much is true."

"Can you protect her?" she asked, then quirked the barest hint of a smile that faded instantly. Words had power and meaning, especially to the great Huanglong who had taught the secret of writing to Humanity. "*Will* you protect her?"

"If your daughter asks, I will answer. Whether she hears is hers to choose."

No promise of protection, then. No detail as to *how* the great dragon would answer—whether by direct word or by indirect symbol. Li Na bowed her head. It was the best she could hope for. It was not in the nature of a dragon to give a specific answer when an indistinct one was possible.

"And Li Zhou?" she asked.

"I will grant neither of his demands."

Will not rather than *cannot*. It was still possible, then.

Li Na took a deep breath and gathered her feet under her. Pain screamed throughout her body and made spots dance before her eyes. Blood flowed freely; it streaked her simple gray shift and slicked both her thighs and ankles. Her life would end here this night—that much was clear—but there were still tasks to perform.

She clasped her hands above her and bowed low until her head touched the floor. "Great Huanglong, guardian of rivers and master of words, please forgive the vain words spoken by my husband, Li Zhou, who is in anguish."

The baby shrieked louder and kicked at the thin linen covering her.

"Your daughter needs you," the dragon said.

"Great Huanglong, guardian of rivers and master of wor—" She gasped again, and her arms began to shake. The potion had failed, and she felt the slow tear of her own flesh deep inside her body. "Master of words, please forgive . . . both me and my husband." Her voice was the barest whisper.

Li Na waited for the dragon to speak, but the only sound she heard was her daughter's abandonment crying into the chill night. She made to repeat her prayer a third time, but her strength had fled and all she could do was wait. As she listened for the sound of the dragon's high, tinny voice, her daughter's cries began to fade.

Yet even as her sorrow welled up at the dragon's silence, she could not blame Huanglong either for her lies or for the terrible oath Li Zhou had made. Her husband's misunderstanding was her own fault; in her reverence of the dragon, she had kept too many things to herself.

Her breath came slower now, and the pain began to ebb, first to a dull ache and then vanishing altogether. So this was the sensation of dying; not unpleasant. Li Na felt a touch on her head and was surprised that she had the strength to sit back.

Huanglong stood before her, its golden body no longer a tiny brass statue, but fully twice the length of a man and made of iridescent flesh that pulsed with life. Where the statue was smooth and vague, the true shape of Huanglong clearly revealed each tawny hair on its long, camel's face with its scant beard and branching, golden stag's horns. Each of the glistening amber carp's scales on its wingless, serpentine body spoke of perfect balance between necessary opposites—yin and yang, discipline and compassion, thought and deed. Even down to the five hand-length eagle's talons that protruded from each of its soft lion's paws.

It was the first time Li Na had seen the dragon's true form, and it quietly spoke of so much more power than even she had ever imagined.

Though its body curled back and around the small cedar shrine, its head was level with her own, and it looked her straight in the eye with its piercing amber gaze. In its upturned right paw rested her daughter, quiet now and snugly wrapped in linen. Li Na took the child from the dragon and hugged her tightly to her breast.

"I cannot undo your injury, but I can ease your pain," the dragon said in the same high, tinny voice she had always known. "I have heard your words and they are true. So by the word of *my* power, I declare the oath of Li Na's husband forgotten."

She bowed low. "Thank you, great Huanglong."

When she raised her head, the dragon spoke again. "While I can forgive your husband his words, I cannot change his heart. He has called this child a 'mewling thing' and a mistake; he sees her only as a failed promise."

If only she had more time. But the dragon could not undo her injuries, so she could not explain to Li Zhou that no promise had ever been made to her.

She nodded her understanding. "Is it possible at least to remove my family's curse from this child? She will bear enough burdens without this additional weight."

The yellow dragon closed its eyes. "I did not speak those words; I cannot rescind them."

Li Na wept, and a wave of fatigue washed over her. Her time had come. She reached down and gently kissed her last child on the forehead. "I'm sorry, little one. Find peace as you can."

She lay down carefully on her side and pressed the child to her face. As her eyes fluttered closed, she heard a voice. Not the high, tinny voice of Huanglong, but a deep, rich voice that echoed in every part of her being. Not loud, but penetrating.

"The curse declared against the line of Pang Ji is ended," the voice said.

Li Na opened her eyes, but saw only Huanglong, who now bowed its head and crouched low to the ground. She tried to sit up so she, too, could give honor to this unseen dragon to whom even the mighty Huanglong bowed, but her body refused to obey.

"Can you give my daughter peace, great dragon?" she asked, her voice barely a whisper.

"I can watch over her," the encompassing voice said. "If that is your wish."

"What must I do to earn this great blessing?" she asked. "I have little left to offer."

"Any bargain is between you and me alone; not even your husband may know of it."

"But he is my love and my strength, and he has already suffered so much for my secrets. Is there no other way?" Silence. No, then. "Then I will hear the costs, great dragon."

"This child will live in loneliness until the last days of her life. She will be buffeted by forces and powers she can neither see nor imagine. Her destiny is to be utterly forgotten in this world."

"Must you heap such misery upon her?" Li Na asked.

"I do nothing; such are the natural consequences of choices already made," the penetrating voice said, and she knew it to be true. The nature of dragons was to aid, not interfere; to give counsel, not direct; to buoy up, not crush down.

Though she felt no pain, her strength had gone. There was no more time.

"But you will watch over her," Li Na said, "if I consent?"

"Yes."

Footsteps sounded on the sandy ground outside the front gate, and Li Na struggled to keep her eyes open. Li Zhou stepped into the temple holding a bowl of rice and a cinnamon stick—the same offering she made every day in this temple. He stopped when he saw her lying on the ground before the shrine, clutching their daughter, her dress streaked with her own blood. He dropped the bowl and rushed to her.

Li Na saw that Huanglong had returned to its perch as a brass dragon atop the simple shrine and smiled. She wondered if her husband could even have seen a dragon in its natural form. He clearly could not hear their voices. Of course, he did not serve them, and so did not earn their blessing; she was their messenger at this time and in this place.

"Choose her name," the penetrating voice said.

Li Zhou knelt by her side, oblivious to the great dragon's powerful voice. "Forgive me," he said. "I've made a terrible mistake."

She wanted to pull him close, to whisper comforts into his ear. She wanted to ease his pain and soften his heart. But it was too late. All she could do now was answer the dragon and believe in both the dragon's power and her husband's good heart.

"My child shall be called Kai," Li Na said and let her eyes droop closed.

"Don't leave me," her husband cried and bent over her, clutching her close. "I need you."

The great dragon's voice echoed throughout her being.

"You act with compassion and wisdom. Serve me here, and I will not only watch over Li Kai, the last child of Li Na, but I will ensure that she chooses her own fate—though destiny must still have its due. Yours is the power of creation; ours is the magic of inspiration. By this pact, Li Kai shall know and wield both."

And while she knew her husband would misunderstand her words as speaking to his bargain and not her own—that he would be injured by them every day until his heart grew cold and hard—it was a necessary thing. She had chosen her daughter's name carefully, knowing the words of Li Zhou's vain oath.

"The bargain is accepted," Li Na said with her last breath as her husband wailed out his grief.

He had demanded that either Li Na live or the child be made into a boy. Though such was impossible in this life, she nonetheless chose a man's name for her daughter—at first to give her husband peace, but later to give her daughter hope.

This last creation of her flesh would be called Kai, which meant *victory*. She would choose her own fate by the power of her own soul and with the aid of dragons who alone among creation were honorable in all things.

There could be no other choice.

High Noon at the Oasis
Jaleta Clegg

THE FIRST RAY OF SUN KISSED THE TOP OF THE DUNES. PHAEDRA shook her mane, lifted one black hoof. She paused. Hoof? Mane? Sand cascaded from her black hide as she scrambled to her feet. She stood, legs splayed, sides heaving. Her head hung low, horn brushing the sand. Her shadow stretched down the dune.

She took a tentative step. Her front hoof sank into the loose sand. She shifted a back hoof forward, sliding a step down the side of the dune. She planted her feet to stop the slide. Her body felt awkward, her center of mass shifted oddly.

A breath of air stirred her mane. She raised her head, nostrils flaring at an unfamiliar scent. Images of cool water and green grasses nudged her toward it. The errant breeze died, but not before she fixed the direction in her mind. Down the dune, over the next, angled away from the blazing sun climbing over the horizon.

Phaedra attempted another step. Coordinating four slender legs took all her concentration.

She tossed her head. Where had that thought come from? Four legs? She swished her tail in frustration. If she focused, the thoughts scattered. She couldn't remember anything before waking up in the sand. But those little tastes of memories floated loose as she concentrated on other things.

She moved without thinking, her legs managing quite well on their own. Until she realized she was walking down the slippery dune slope. A back leg kicked into a front hoof, shattering her rhythm. She flailed with all four legs, her tail rising in her panic. She tumbled down the dune in a tangle of long legs, ending in an undignified heap at the bottom.

A high whinny escaped. She huffed a couple of breaths, then scrambled back to her feet. The packed sand at the base of the dune made balancing easier. She tapped her front hoof, testing the hard crust. Her foot clacked on a rock. She took a step, feeling for the rhythm of four legs. If she let go and just let her body move, her gait was smooth and even. When she tried to consciously think about it, she faltered.

Like breathing.

No voice, then, nothing but a neigh. She'd turned into a horse, somehow, although she couldn't remember what she had been before.

She trotted toward the scent of water, moving easily while her mind chewed over other things. Her hip muscles twitched at a sudden itch on her flank. She whipped her head around to bite whatever had caused the itch and almost impaled herself with her horn.

Horn? On her head. She crossed her eyes trying to see it. Glimpses showed a gleaming obsidian spike.

I'm a unicorn.

She wanted to laugh, but all that came out was a bray of horse noises.

Someone turned me into a freaking unicorn. Once I remember who that is, I'm going to skewer them on my horn, then use all four feet to stomp them into the dust.

Her hooves clattered over stones as she rounded the dune. This time, she heard a distinct metallic clatter. She stopped, then backed slowly until she heard it again. She kicked experimentally with her back hoof. Yep, definitely metal somewhere down there.

"Do you mind? I just got things settled and now you're knocking everything sideways!"

Phaedra reared, twisting to face the source of the feminine voice. Her front hooves came down on either side of a plume of fuchsia smoke.

"Never fails. I get all relaxed, ready for a break for a few decades, then wham! Someone knocks on the lamp again."

The smoke resolved itself into a very curvaceous dark-haired beauty in a skimpy harem outfit. She blinked at the black unicorn, her full lips compressed in consternation. "Who are you?"

Phaedra. And someone turned me into a unicorn.

She tried to speak, but her mouth only nickered.

The woman grinned, then leaned on a puff of smoke that settled into a divan underneath her. "You're not from my usual clientele, obviously.

The horn and the whole 'I'm a unicorn' thing kind of give that away. Well, you summoned me so the rules say I have to give you three wishes." She spread her hand, examining her flawless manicure. "You got a limit, though. New rule. You can only summon me three times. Some lawyer got hold of a djinn and abused the system until headquarters got involved and changed up the rules." She flicked a glance at Phaedra. "Not much for words, are you? Well, we've got time. I'm here until you make your wishes. Landscape hasn't changed much," she said as she glanced at the towering dunes.

Phaedra made frustrated noises and stamped one hoof. *You talk too much. Listen, please!*

"Are we going to lounge here all day? It's going to get extremely hot soon and I'd rather not be out in the sun. I believe there is an oasis that way." She pointed with one lacquered nail. "Just pick up my lamp and carry it. I'm rather attached to it. Literally." She laughed at her own bad joke.

Phaedra rolled her eyes. It wasn't very effective as a horse. Too much like panic and not enough like contempt. Not horse, unicorn. Whatever. She wrapped her lips around the handle of the lamp to work it out of the sand before she clamped down with her square teeth.

"Nicely done. I always thought unicorns were smarter than horses. You just proved it, sweetie. Name's Jadwiga, by the way. It would be nice if you could tell me yours. Maybe I should try guessing. I can't grant any wishes until you speak, though, rules are rules."

You talk enough for both of us.

Phaedra hated the taste of metal in her mouth but didn't dare drop the lamp. Jadwiga might be the only chance she had of being something other than a black unicorn in an increasing hot desert. The promised oasis had better appear soon.

Or what? I'll die of thirst. If her chattering doesn't make me kill myself first.

Jadwiga kept up her rambling monologue as she drifted on her vaporous cushions. "I've only been a djinn for maybe three centuries now. Long enough to get bored, let me tell you. Lying around, buried in sand, with nothing but that lamp, that gets old in a hurry. It's roomy enough inside, pocket dimension you know, but you can only do so many things by yourself for days on end. A little company is nice, but rules are rules.

We get one week every ten years when we can go visit the other djinn in the grand stone city hidden in the heart of the desert."

Phaedra's ears pricked. She remembered stone streets, clusters of strange people made of smoke and moonlight, staring at her, shouting at her. Cursing her.

She almost dropped the lamp. The djinnis had done this to her, made her into a unicorn. And they could just undo it. Somehow. She could wish herself back to her natural form, if she could speak.

Her hoof clacked on red stone as she stamped.

"There's shade at the oasis. But," Jadwiga fanned herself, "we're never going to get there if you keep stopping. Come on, pick up the pace."

Phaedra let a string of drool drip down the lamp. She had been holding her horse instincts back, but now, she let her tongue explore the odd metal.

"Ew! Stop that. You're getting spit in my kitchen. It's messing up all my linens."

Serve you right, you magical cow. See how you like the tables turned.

Jadwiga shouted muffled curses as she smoked back into her lamp. Her chatter faded until the only sounds left were the susurration of sand grains rolling as the wind pushed them and the occasional clack of hoof against stone.

Phaedra flapped her tail and trotted between the dunes, wending her way toward the scent of fresh water and palm trees.

The terrain grew more rocky, less sandy. At least a unicorn's body was built for running. Similar to a horse's build, but with longer, more slender legs, sleeker body, and of course, the horn. She tried to hug what little shade the stone banks offered as she wound between dunes that were halfway to being hills. Clumps of thorny bushes began to dot the ground. Sand drifted in long tongues out from their bases, pointing where the restless wind blew.

And there, between two hills, a glint of deeper green caught her eye. Like an emerald set in a brooch, the tops of palm trees shivered in the heat, brilliant green against the red of the cliffs that had grown to replace the dunes. Her hooves fairly danced through the heat waves. It wasn't just a mirage. She drew in the scent of wet stone, flowing water, and green grass.

I can see color.

Random thought, but a strange one. Did horses see in color? She didn't know. And didn't really care. She was a freaking unicorn, at least until she could figure out how to turn back into whatever she'd been before.

Her sides glistened with sweat long before she reached the first hint of shade. The sun was brutal and that hint of green farther than she thought. She twisted through another narrow wash. Tough grass grew in cracks in the red stone. Her horse instincts urged her to snatch a bite, but she'd have to drop the lamp to do that. No, not yet. She wanted, *needed*, those three wishes. Unicorns could survive in the desert, but she'd never thrive here.

The sun was sliding toward the west before she finally reached the bushes marking the outskirts of the oasis. It was a small one, a tiny trickle of water over stone that flowed into a larger pool. A dozen palm trees marked the spot. Their fronds drooped in the still air. An insect buzzed past Phaedra's nose. She blew it away absently, focused on the water.

She trotted into the tiny stream, her hooves barely splashing in the shallow flow. She deliberately kicked up what spray she could as she approached the pond. Her mouth was dry and tasted of brass from the lamp. She waded into the pool until water touched her knees.

She would have smiled, if her unicorn lips could bend that way. In order to drink, she had to drop the lamp. Where better than into the pool? The water was clear enough she could see the sand on the bottom, see the tiny fish darting away from her shadow. Jadwiga's lamp could use a good wash. She opened her mouth, let it tumble into the pool, then carefully planted one hoof on top. It wouldn't do to lose her best hope of becoming herself again.

But what am I? All I can think of is four hooves, a horn, long tail. The longer I'm a unicorn, the more it feels natural. What was I before this morning?

She watched her reflection for a minute, then dipped her head toward the water. Sand fountained up in a bubbling froth. She jerked her head back. The lamp slipped away in the sudden vortex of erupting water. Her hooves pawed frantically at the sand as she searched for it again. A plume of magenta water spread and dissipated across the pool. The air suddenly smelled of roses. A spout hit Phaedra square in the face. She closed her eyes, shaking her head to clear the water away.

"What have you done?" Jadwiga's ear-splitting shriek echoed off the cliffs. She lay half in the water, large fish tail flopping behind her. "You flooded my house. And—Augh! I'm a mermaid?!"

The sand settled. Phaedra quit panicking. The lamp was not far off, on its side in the clear water. The pink hue and the rose smell faded away.

Serves you right for babbling so much. Now we're matched. I'm a unicorn, a black unicorn in the desert heat, and you're now an aquatic creature in a land with very little water.

Jadwiga splashed water with furious fists. "I should have smelled the magic, but the stench of sweaty horse was too strong. I think this might be a shape-changing spring." She narrowed her eyes, still half-hidden under the filmy head scarf and bead fringe. "Wait just one moment. You've been here before. You were changed into a unicorn, weren't you?"

Phaedra shook her head, paused in confusion, then nodded.

Jadwiga backed away from the bobbing horn as rapidly as her fishy bottom half would allow. "Let me guess, you want me to use your first wish to turn you back."

Phaedra whinnied agreement.

"Sorry, sweetheart, horse noises don't count. You have to use words or I can't grant the wish. Rules are rules, you know." Jadwiga scooted backwards into a deeper puddle. "Besides, I'm a mermaid now, temporarily, not a djinn, so it's a moot point. The change spell doesn't feel very strong. Very temporary change. May as well get comfortable and enjoy it. Hey, I've got an idea. Take a nice long drink and we'll see what you change into. Might be something useful, might be something not. These things are completely random. But at least it would be entertaining. And while you're at it, you can fish out my lamp and set it on the shore to dry. Pour out the water first, otherwise the carpets might mildew." She flopped onto her belly and slid into the deeper stretches of the oasis pool. With a flip of her tail, she disappeared under the water.

This doesn't seem to be your first transformation, sweetheart. What were you before you became a djinn?

Phaedra eyed the water. She was beyond thirsty and it looked very cool and refreshing. She lowered her head, nostrils flared. It smelled like water, nothing more. With a mental shrug, she sucked in a long drink.

The cool water slid down her throat, easing the dust of the sandy trek. When she didn't change, she kept drinking until her thirst was satisfied.

She stood, fetlock deep, and waited while the water cleared. The lamp lay a few steps away, submerged on its side. A thin stream of fuchsia smoke leaked from the spout to dissipate in the pool. Maybe she'd caused the change spell when she'd dropped the lamp. If something of Jadwiga's had spilled and contaminated the oasis, it would explain a lot.

How do I know so much about magic? Was I a sorceress?

Phaedra closed her eyes and tried to imagine herself as a human. Two legs, two arms, hands, fingers, eyes facing forward. Her tail flicked a fly from her rump and broke her concentration. Try as she might, she couldn't forget four legs and the horn on her head, although the idea of hands seemed strangely familiar. She pawed the sand with her front hoof. Definitely not a hand, but still useful.

Blazes, but it's hot out here. Strange, I don't remember heat bothering me.

She trotted toward the stand of palm trees and the promise of shade. She splashed through the water up to her knees, then kicked up more. The cool droplets rained across her back alleviating some of the heat.

She passed from light to shade, then stopped dead. What was that smell? Strange, but familiar and not quite pleasant. She planted her legs and drew a deep breath through flared nostrils. Her ears twitched, alert for any sound. Something crouched under a bush, breath heaving though whatever it was tried to stifle it. She took one slow step toward the creature, teeth bared in threat.

It bolted along the edge of the oasis. Her teeth clamped shut on a ragged robe that tasted of rancid goat.

Delicious.

She planted her feet, staring in shock. She *wanted* to eat rancid goat?

The man she had caught shrieked, high and thin. He waved limbs so coated in dust he looked gray. He shimmied up and down in the robe trying to escape her hold.

She shook him until he stopped shrieking and wiggling. He hung limp, too heavy for her teeth. She dropped him into the water.

He screamed again, then stopped abruptly. He splashed as he sat in the shallow water, frowned, then splashed again. "No magic now? Where is the fish woman?" He glared at Phaedra.

She blew air through her lips, huffing loudly. It was as close as she could come to laughing. His hair framed his face in a most comical way, long and shaggy on one side, looking like he'd been sheared on the other side by a drunken shepherd. She stamped one hoof, then kicked toward the far end of the pool.

"Did I hear correctly that she is one of the all-powerful, mighty djinni of the desert?" His glare changed to an expectant look. "At least when she is not half-fish?"

Phaedra rolled her eyes.

The man rose to his feet. "If she is indeed a most magical djinn, then whoever holds her lamp is assured three wishes. Where is the lamp?"

It was Phaedra's turn to glare. She lowered her horn until it pointed at the man's throat.

He pushed it aside with an impatient brush of his hand. "You do not appreciate our opportunity, o most magnificent of stallions. I am Achmineedees, a scholar of no small renown. But alas, I have fallen on difficult times. The Sultan of Raisinetti did not approve of my sense of humor. And neither did his thirty-seven wives. He had me banished to the desert to perish of thirst. But fortunately, I carried a waterskin. I stumbled on this oasis not long ago but did not dare drink, especially not after seeing your companion transformed into a partial fish."

Phaedra tapped one foot in a most menacing manner. He thought she was a stallion and he still had the nerve to call himself a scholar? She lowered her horn again, letting the light gleam along its length, to sparkle off the end. It was a most pointed horn.

"Yes," Achmineedees continued after pushing the horn aside again, "as I was saying, we have an opportunity here. If you show me the lamp, once she turns back into a djinn, I shall be the one holding the lamp. I shall wish you to be human—"

Phaedra snorted. Something about being human didn't sit right.

"—for my first wish," Achmineedees continued as if she had not interrupted him. "Then I shall pass the lamp to you for your three wishes. But," he held one finger in the air, "you must return the lamp to me for my remaining two wishes or you will revert back to this form. I will make that a condition of my first wish. You make a magnificent unicorn, but I sense it is not your true form."

What if I'm getting to enjoy it? If I could speak, it would be quite a nice form to keep. She swished her tail, enjoying the slide of hair across her back. *Built in flyswatter, nice for traveling, a horn for menacing people. Really, what downside is there to being a unicorn? Aside from the penchant for virgins and the inability to speak. Why did unicorns want virgins anyway? They are rather tender and tend to be quite juicy with a nice crunch—*

"I said," Achmineedees said quite loudly, "do we have a deal?"

She hadn't been listening, she'd been remembering the taste of virgins sliding down her throat, their screams still lingering. Or was that sheep? Same difference. What had the silly man proposed? Ah, yes. He'd make her human so she could have three wishes. If she were human, she could speak and make wishes. Then she'd give the lamp to him for his wishes. She smiled inside where he couldn't see, not that unicorns could smile. They mostly stood in regal poses with the wind blowing their manes. Foolish beasts. That was the downside of being a unicorn, everyone else laughed at their boorish airs.

She whinnied and lifted one hoof.

"Close enough to a handshake," Achmineedees said as he touched her hoof. "Now, where is that lamp?"

Phaedra gave him her best "follow me" look, then turned to trot back across the oasis. The lamp lay on its side in the clear water, which had a decided pink tint again. The air smelled faintly of roses. Phaedra sneezed.

Achmineedees clapped his hands in delight then plunged them toward the lamp. He started shrieking as they dipped into the pinkish water. He kept shrieking while the spell wound up and around him, like a dancer teasing with her veils. The scent of roses waxed stronger until it became a cloying stench.

Phaedra turned her head, backing away and trying not to breathe. She didn't look back until the screaming subsided. It ended on a high and decidedly feminine note. Achmineedees was no longer a scrawny, unimpressive man. He was now a most buxom and shapely young woman. His, no *her,* hair was still a wild tangle sheared short on one side, long on the other. Even in the rancid goat rag of a tunic, she was quite becoming.

"What villainy is this?" Achmineedees clapped hands over her voluptuous lips. "Is that my voice?" She sang a trilling melody, then giggled. Then clapped her hands over her mouth again.

"Who is messing with my spells?" Jadwiga marched out of the deeper water, not quite back in her djinn form but much less of a fish and more of a human, albeit a male one now. She stopped short at the sight of Achmineedees. "You didn't! How did you?"

"I have no idea what you're babbling about." Achmineedees stamped her shapely foot, sending up a spray of pinkish rose-scented water.

Phaedra backed away quickly. She had no desire to be caught in whatever shape-shifting, gender-swapping magic Jadwiga kept in her home.

Achmineedees and Jadwiga dove for the lamp at the same time. Achmineedees held it triumphantly above her head. Her sleeves slid down to reveal slender arms. Jadwiga bellowed, deep and masculine, and reached for the lamp.

Achmineedees clutched it to her large bosom. "I wish for everything to be as it was!"

Phaedra ducked her head and charged forward, horn aimed for the loop of handle. She barreled between the two humans, knocking them both backwards into the water. The lamp clanged onto her horn just as everything slowed.

It was as if the world had suddenly been coated in honey. Jadwiga's bellow of rage dragged out as he tumbled in a spray of water. Achmineedees fell the other direction. Phaedra stumbled in the water on legs suddenly clumsy. The scent of roses thickened to an almost tangible level.

The sandy bed of the oasis pool rose to meet her. Slowly. Oh, so slowly. Her legs tingled, an itch that spread rapidly until every inch of hide shivered. She reached forward with one forefoot to catch herself from her fall. What landed in the water was not a horse's hoof. Not even close. Five very large clawed and scaled toes smashed into the sand.

The honey cleared. The rose smell shifted to sun, sand, water, and date palms with a thick overlay of wet rancid goat. Phaedra's second front foot smashed down. Five large claws dug into the bottom of the pool. Something metallic clanged against her forehead. She'd managed to catch the lamp on one of her horns.

Horns? Yes, horns. Five of them in a crown across my skull.

The weight of them was all too familiar. She whipped her massive tail and let loose a long bellow. She wasn't surprised to see flames shooting from her mouth.

"This is more like it." She turned to find Achmineedees sprawled on the bank of the pool, looking like a fish gasping for breath. She plucked him up with one front claw. He hung from his tunic, too shocked to move while she inspected him. He was as grubby and unkempt as when she first startled him from the bushes. She snorted a smoke ring into his face, then dropped him in a coughing heap on the shore.

"Your turn," she said, rounding on the djinn.

Jadwiga floated on her fuchsia smoke cloud at Phaedra's eye level. "You wouldn't dare hurt me. We have a treaty. Dragons don't interfere with djinnis and we leave your hoards alone." She folded her arms and tried to look defiant. Her nervous twitching destroyed the effect.

"Oh, I don't intend to interfere, but I'm still holding your lamp."

"Dragons don't get wishes." Jadwiga's voice squeaked and her lips trembled but she held eye contact.

"You offered me wishes when I was a unicorn. They are not allowed wishes, either, as part of the nonproliferation of magic treaty, unless my memory is false. Which it might be since someone turned me into a unicorn!" The last came out in a wreath of fire.

Jadwiga waved her hand, turning the flames to a shower of rose petals. "I was bored. Unicorns can't talk and so can't make wishes. Nothing would have come from it. And besides, I wasn't the one who turned you into a unicorn."

Phaedra narrowed one of her giant green eyes. "Are you sure about that? You seem to have plenty of transformation spells inside your lamp."

Jadwiga's face paled, color draining to leave even her smoke cloud white. "He made me do it!"

"Who?" The water around Phaedra began to steam.

"I have a theory," Achmineedees spoke.

"No one asked you." Phaedra kept her glare focused on the djinn as she reached behind to pluck the scholar from the sand. She dangled him from his tunic. "Shut up, silly little man."

Achmineedees snapped his mouth shut.

"He made me do it. I'm sorry I made you a unicorn. You were a very pretty one, too. I especially liked the black—"

"Stop babbling and tell me his name!"

"Wait," Achmineedees said as he waved a finger at Phaedra. "You're a mare, not a stallion?"

Phaedra spat out a stream of fire. The oasis boiled energetically.

Achmineedees let out a high-pitched scream as Jadwiga shouted a name.

Phaedra snapped her mouth shut then dunked Achmineedees toward the boiling water until he shut up. She stopped just shy of the surface. He tried to climb up her claw away from the steam. She shook him off onto the sandy beach.

"My own brother did that to me?" she said when it was finally quiet again.

"He said he'd arrange a fate worse than death for me if I didn't do it." Jadwiga cringed away from the angry dragon, but not very far. Phaedra still held her lamp. "He was going to make me marry him."

"The traitor who turned himself human and declared himself the Sultan of Raisinetti?"

Achmineedees gasped.

Jadwiga blushed. "He used all three wishes. I didn't have a choice!"

Phaedra chuckled. "Oh, this is rich. He was going to make you wife thirty-eight if you didn't turn me into a unicorn?"

"He was going to smash my lamp first. And the Lord of the Djinn was going to allow it." Jadwiga's voice trailed off into a mumble.

"What was that? I'm pretty good at smashing things, too." Phaedra reached for the lamp with two very large talons.

Jadwiga sagged into her pink cloud. "He said I'd overstepped my bounds and needed to be taught a lesson."

"You definitely need a lesson," Phaedra said. "Do you have a love potion in your lamp, by any chance?"

"What for?" Jadwiga lowered her eyebrows in a suspicious glare.

"Do you?"

"Yes." The djinn's shoulders slumped. "Your brother is horrid. I don't want to marry him. Not even a love potion will make me want him."

"It isn't for him. And I agree he's a toad. He's also about to be deposed." Phaedra smiled the frightening and toothy smile of a dragon. "For my first wish, Achmineedees here needs to be young, handsome, and a lot more muscular. And he needs to smell like something other than a rancid goat."

Jadwiga screwed up her face, fighting the wish. She finally sighed. "Since I promised you wishes, I have to grant them, despite the treaty. Done." She waved her hand.

"Hey!" Achmineedees cut his protest short when he caught sight of his new, much improved profile and haircut. He used a large scale on Phaedra's rump as a mirror, posing in front of it. She ignored him.

"Now it's time for that love potion." Phaedra pinched the lamp off her horn, then carefully turned it upside-down and shook it.

"Watch out for the china," Jadwiga shrieked. "It's Wedgwood. And probably smashed," she finished as Phaedra gave the lamp an extra hearty shake.

A small bottle of pink liquid tumbled to the sand.

"What's your third wish?" Jadwiga asked.

"Second," Phaedra corrected. "The love potion was not a wish. And don't try arguing semantics with me." She hissed a long streamer of smoke.

"Second," Jadwiga agreed.

"Achmineedees, pick up the potion and drink half. Then give it to Jadwiga." Phaedra smiled. "And when you have both drunk and looked deeply into each other's eyes until the spell takes full effect, I wish for us to appear at the palace of the Sultan of Raisinetti."

The dragon watched as the human and the djinn drank the potion, gazed at each other, and became totally smitten. She had to interrupt the kissing with a loud harrumph.

Jadwiga, enveloped in Achmineedees strong and muscular arms, waved her hand. "Done."

Air rushed past as they were whisked across the desert to the sumptuous palace of the Sultan of Raisinetti. They landed in the courtyard amid a screaming scatter of terrified guards.

Phaedra waved one clawed hand. "Citizens, behold your new Sultan and his Sultana."

"What about your brother?" Achmineedees whispered.

"Leave him to me," Phaedra answered. She blew a long stream of fire up the walls to set the blue and yellow flags ablaze. "For my third and final wish—"

"Yes?" Jadwiga tore herself away from the loving gaze of Achmineedees, but only for a moment.

"I wish you a long and happy life," Phaedra said, "as a human."

"Done. Wait!"

"Too late."

The lamp shattered. The fuchsia cloud of smoke disappeared with a loud pop. Jadwiga staggered on two legs. Achmineedees caught her in his arms. She blushed. They both smiled. The guards cheered hesitantly.

"Brother!" Phaedra stamped forward. "You are no longer Sultan here. Quit cowering in your palace and face your sister. You've got a lot of payback coming." She turned to look at the couple. "Rule well and wisely. And never meddle in the affairs of dragons."

She gave them one last toothy grin before snatching her brother from his balcony perch and flapping off into the sky. Her voice echoed behind her.

"A unicorn? Seriously? You are going to pay for years for that insult."

The Sultan's screams faded into the distance as the dragon disappeared into the maze of red rock and sand dunes.

The Wild Ride
Christopher Baxter

The dragon, a lumpy redspine, shot out of its enclosure into the canyon. It swerved, barreled, and bucked, trying to throw off the rider that clung to its back. The audience cheered as it belched gouts of flame and oily smoke. Its rider held himself too stiff, fighting against the dragon's movement instead of letting it lead, and was quickly flung free of his saddle. He crashed into the canyon wall just beneath the spectator galleries. From her spot at the edge of a stone platform on the lip of the canyon, Niketa winced and shook her head.

"How'd that fella even manage to qualify for the Dragon Ride?" Creyne muttered beside her, tugging his hat down over his eyes.

Niketa elbowed him, aiming for his ribs but only reaching his gut. "Be nice," she said. "You wasn't any better when you started."

"*I* heal quicker 'n most. Kid's gonna get hisself killed. Shoulda stuck to the Gryphon Ride for a few more years."

The rider, now unconscious, slid from the canyon wall and plummeted toward the enchanted white safety nets thousands of feet below. When he hit, an iron rod glowing with a faint blue light tumbled from his jacket to the red rocks and squat dry shrubs along the canyon floor. Niketa felt Creyna tense beside her.

"Oh, here we go," Creyne muttered. "Fella had a dragon prod on him." He crossed his arms with a glance down at Niketa.

She raised an eyebrow and watched the scene below. The two of them had been arguing about this for almost a month now—somehow, her fool husband had got it in his head that just *carrying* a dragon prod was enough to get someone disqualified from a rodeo. Niketa had told him time and again that it was only a disqualifying offence if you had to *use* the prod during a ride.

Down in the canyon, the rodeo imps darted around the Redspine, distracting it from turning on the unconscious rider below. One imp caught the dragon in the eyes with a soaked sponge, sending up a gout of steam. The dragon swerved, snarling, and snapped at the imp.

A glowing golden lasso arced out into the canyon and snapped around the Redspine's neck, reeling it toward the edge of the cliffs. The rodeo imps slipped away to fish the rider out of the safety net and onto a waiting flying carpet. One of them swooped down to the canyon floor, retrieved the iron rod, and returned it to the rider's jacket.

"See there?" Niketa said. "They don't care none. Only a flamin' *idjit* rides dragons without a prod. Just in case."

Creyne tugged his hat even lower over his eyes. His hair was dark and shaggy and his skin was deeply tanned, though still several shades lighter than hers. He worked his jaw like he was chewing on something unpleasant, which made his small tusks jut out over his upper lip—he had a spot of troll blood somewhere back in his family tree. Niketa usually thought it was cute when he was stubborn, but the man could draw things out too far.

"Just 'cause they didn't steal the man's property don't mean he ain't disqualified," he finally muttered. "You'll see—they won't post a time."

Niketa growled slightly and shook her head. *Stubborn mule.*

The sorcerers coaxed the Redspine into its enclosure, where it was given a haunch of beef to gnaw on while its caretakers removed its harness and checked it for injuries. The imps flew the unconscious rider up to the edge of the canyon, where healers rushed to revive him and tend to his wounds—it looked to Niketa like the kid's leg was twisted in a bad direction, and he almost certainly had a few broken ribs after hitting the canyon wall that hard. She knew just what the kid would feel like when he woke up.

A *clacking* sounded from the huge wooden scoreboards on the canyon walls; the gleaming numbers there spun over until they showed the kid's time. He'd stayed in the saddle for six-and-a-half seconds—one-and-a-half short of earning a score. Tough luck.

But it *was* a time, not a disqualification. "What did I tell you?" Niketa said, pointing at the scoreboard.

Creyne hunched his shoulders and shook his head. "He'd a gotten run off from a backcountry rodeo for that," he muttered, turning away.

Below the scoreboards were the galleries, carved into the walls of the canyon and shielded by ensorcelled netting. The crowd clapped politely for the rider, some with sympathetic *awws* and some with mocking whoops and jeers. Peddlers took advantage of the lull between rides to move through the galleries, offering spyglasses, fans, and a range of food from roasted bloodflower seeds to flaming salamander. Hucksters moved through the crowd as well, taking bets and hawking good luck charms of dubious quality. A few goblins climbed up onto the netting for a better view, only to be pelted with shouts and rocks by the portion of the audience whose line of sight they'd blocked.

The crowds cheered as the countdown began for the next rider. In the center gallery, the rodeo master stepped forward and blew a quick, high-pitched blast on his dragon-spine horn. A grey Deuschalin Cragger burst from an opening below the galleries, carrying another young buck as new as the last one.

Niketa didn't pay the show any more mind, though; her attention was focused on her husband. "Well?" she said. "I was right, wasn't I?"

Creyne turned and spat into the canyon. Then he shrugged. "Suppose you were. What of it?"

Niketa reached up under her coat and pulled her own dragon prod from the sheath on her back. "They're legal," she said, pointing the glowing rod at her husband, "and we're gettin' you one."

Creyne batted the rod away. "Put that away," he growled, glancing around the canyon at the other riders' platforms.

"What... you think *they* don't all have prods, too?" Niketa said, poking him with the rod. "We may not flaunt 'em, but you're the only one here fool enough not to carry one."

Creyne shook his head and squared his shoulders, looking out over the rodeo again. "Never needed one before, don't need one now."

Niketa clenched her teeth, glaring up at the man, but he didn't meet her eyes. She opened her mouth to say something that she already knew wasn't well thought out. But a deep, rumbling horn blast cut her off, shaking rocks and dust from the wall of the canyon. The audience's cheers doubled in volume.

The Northwestern Migration was nearly here. It was time to prepare for the Wild Ride.

Creyne watched the imps and sorcerers hurry to ensure that all of the rodeo's dragons were secure in their enclosures. On dozens of stone platforms along the lip of the canyon, the men and women who would compete in the Wild Ride hurried to make last-minute equipment checks and to hurl a few extra insults or bets back and forth.

He simply tipped his hat back and turned to face his wife. Their preparations were a little different from the other riders'.

"We're gettin' close," he said, smiling at her. "We do well enough this ride, and the next few . . . we could be buyin' our ranch by the time the season closes."

Niketa nodded, but she didn't smile. She didn't seem angry; just disappointed. She wasn't cursing and she hadn't even *tried* to hit him. That meant that this whole dragon prod thing was well and truly bothering her.

Creyne sighed and brushed a stray strand of his wife's black hair from her face. The rest was pulled back in a tight braid that was hidden by the hat hanging on her back. She wore riding leathers, just like his—protective jackets that laced up to cover the throat, heavy riding chaps, and tall boots with steel spurs. The clothing was deep brown, a shade darker than her skin. Her ears and eyebrows came to a slight point, a mark of her elfin ancestry—as was the vibrant violet shade of her eyes.

Creyne held up a small crystal sphere. Niketa glanced at the sphere with an eyebrow raised. As she studied it, the intense color of her irises faded to a pallid gray, and the crystal clouded over from clear to purple.

"I'm takin' the color of your eyes," Creyne said with a slight grin. "You can have it back after the ride."

"Where'd you get that?" Niketa asked, tapping the sphere.

"Won it in that card game with the sorcerers last week—the one you told me I couldn't win."

"Oh, you're just so proud of yourself, ain't ya?" Niketa poked him in the chest, and the corner of her mouth twitched, holding back a smile. Creyne grinned. That was more like it; there was no sense getting bothered over a disagreement just before a ride.

His wife reached up and ran a gloved hand along the stiff stubble on his chin; then, to his surprise, her finger slipped into his mouth and came to rest on one of his longer teeth that jutted out from his lower jaw. Her glove tasted odd. It had a faint metallic tang to it—a sign of magic. Before he could ask what was going on, she grabbed his tooth between her fingers and wrenched it out of his mouth.

"Flamin' shit!" Creyne shouted, grabbing his jaw and stumbling back.

Niketa grinned and held up his tooth. "I'm takin' your tusk hostage for this match, handsome."

"Ain't a tusk, woman," he mumbled, rubbing his jaw. "How the hell'd you do that?"

"Got me a special glove." She peeled the gray glove from her hand and dropped it and the tooth in a pouch at her waist.

"So you decided to take my flamin' tooth?" He spat the blood from his mouth. "I thought women were supposed to be romantic n' stuff."

"Damn straight," she said, poking him in the chest. "And I love your tusks—they're cute." Her expression went all disappointed again, and she needlessly adjusted his riding coat. "You be sure to make it back from this ride so we can find a way to put that back in."

"I'll be fine," Creyne grunted. "This ain't my first ride." His lip pulled over his teeth oddly now, but he'd manage; it was hardly the first time he'd lost a tooth. The pain was already starting to fade. He pulled her close, resting his chin on her head. "You just worry about gettin' *yourself* back in more-er-less one piece, hear? This crystal ain't near as pretty to look at as the real thing."

She nodded and squeezed him tight. He could just feel that blasted prod under her jacket. He shook his head, still flabbergasted. When had those become allowable? He couldn't believe he'd never heard it before. If his pa could have seen it, the old man would have raised hell against all these soft city slickers. If a rider was really talented, then they didn't need extra help. Most rodeo injuries happened too quickly for a dragon prod to do any good, anyway.

The horn sounded again—the Wild Ride was about to begin. He slipped the crystal into his jacket, and Niketa stood on tiptoe to kiss him. He smiled at her, and she smiled back. That was good; that was how a ride should start.

They turned and stepped to the edge of the platform. In unison, they pulled on their magic rigging gloves and their riding goggles. Niketa pulled her flat, wide-brimmed hat into place on her head, and Creyne pulled his hat down over his eyes.

A rust-red cloud of dust rose not far up the canyon from them, in the direction of the distant mountains. Down below, the crowds in the galleries began to murmur with anticipation. Creyne buckled the strap that would hold his hat in place, and Niketa cinched hers up under her chin.

They watched the distant cloud of dust as it drew near. When it reached the closest curve of the canyon, a swarm of wild dragons burst into view. They churned down the ravine like a flood, some skirting the sagebrush on the canyon floor while others darted up above the rim for a few moments and then back down.

The first of the dragons shot past the galleries below Creyne and Niketa's feet, and the audience began to cheer. The noise was quickly drowned out by the beating of wings, the rush of wind, and the snarls and roars of wild dragons.

Creyne pulled his bandana over his mouth and squinted through the dust to pick out the different breeds. Most common were lithe golden Sun Serpents, squat scarlet Redspines, and spindly brown Dirtnappers, but here and there he noticed more unusual colors. Spots of deep blue marked what had to be Northern Sea Skimmers come south for the migration; vibrant green Treetalons pressed through the mass, knocking smaller dragons aside with ease; and the occasional blotch of inky shadow even hinted at the presence of a few Blackflames darting along the edges of the canyon. Several packs of cloud-gray serpents were either Deuschalin Craggers or Stormchasers; those were impossible to tell apart from this distance.

Without looking away from the chaotic swarm, he reached out and took Niketa by the hand. She squeezed his hand in return. Out of the corner of his eye, he could see the other Wild Riders leaning over the edges of their platforms, ready. They waited.

The rumbling horn shook the canyon. Creyne released his wife's hand, and they jumped.

Creyne was lucky; he had a clear line to one of the lumbering Treetalons. The green brutes were vicious mounts, which would mean higher marks for him when he rode it out. He twisted to avoid getting clipped by a Dirtnapper's wing, and then he hit the Treetalon's flank with his arms outstretched.

He'd landed on its shoulder behind the wing, just to the right of the long needles that ran down its spine. Leather straps whipped out of his Rigging Gloves, snapping around the dragon's neck quick as spit. Then the real ride began.

The Treetalon immediately arched its back. Creyne was tossed up and then slammed back down against its flank. It knocked the wind from him, but he held tight to his rigging; if he relaxed his grip, the line would unravel. The dragon barrelled upward, spinning Creyne away from its body, and then twisted back to throw out a gout of sapphire flame that singed his boots. That was unusual; he'd seen Treetalons that breathed yellow or green fire, but never quite full-on blue. Fortunately, it couldn't quite twist far enough to burn him. He was in the one safe spot on its back, out of range of flame, teeth, talons, and tailblades.

His mount swerved back down into the canyon and slammed against the wall, prompting screams and cheers from the galleries above. Creyne got a faceful of dust and rocks; but once again, he was safe, protected by the dragon's spines and wing from the cliff proper. Under his bandana, he grinned; he'd landed this one perfect. Then a stray stone struck his still-tender jaw, and he cursed loud enough for a deaf mule to hear it.

The dragon spun away from the cliff. Creyne heard a scream as a rider fell past him, burning. He glanced back to see if he knew the man, and then blinked when his mount's tail thrashed into his view. This dragon didn't have any tailblades. All Treetalons had blades along their tails for hacking through overgrown forests.

Creyne suddenly became aware of an electric *crackle* in the air around him. Blue flames, no blades—this wasn't a Treetalon. It was an Emerald Shifter.

Everything seemed to slow for a moment; the air warped around him. Through the chaos of the swarm, he caught a glimpse of Niketa clinging to the side of a silvery Deuschalin Cragger. She looked in his direction with a frown.

He didn't have time to let go; he didn't even manage to curse. A flash of green light blinded him, and the rodeo was gone.

Empty silence rang in his ears, broken only by the thudding beat of the dragon's wings and the creak of his leather rigging. The Shifter bucked again, once, twice, trying unsuccessfully to dislodge him.

Creyne blinked, trying to encourage his eyes to adjust to the dim light. The air was cool and moist, and it smelled like a meadow in the rain. An endless expanse of teal clouds roiled beneath him; above, a slate-gray sky sparkled with golden stars that left blazing fire-trails as they swirled through the heavens. He was in the Aethereal Lands.

Mentally, he cursed his misfortune. Never in his entire life had he seen a Shifter flying with the Northwestern Migration—he'd never even heard of one living on this *continent.* How in the lost hells had he managed to land on such a rarity?

The dragon dove and jackknifed, still trying to dislodge him. But to his surprise, Creyne found himself smiling. This wasn't bad, not one bit. All he had to do was hold on until the dragon shifted back over to his world, and he would be fine. In fact, he'd probably get the highest marks in history for being the only man to ride an Emerald Shifter into the Aethereal Lands and back. He closed his eyes and pictured it, completely content. A perfect one hundred. The highest prize ever paid out. A dragon ranch in the high mountains. Just him, Niketa, and their hatchlings.

His mount swung around abruptly, and Creyne lost his grip on the rigging. He opened his eyes as the leather straps withdrew back into his gloves, confused. Part of him was shouting that this was bad thing, but he couldn't figure out why. He was falling toward the clouds, sure—but he was falling slowly, gently. He would be fine. It was just a shame that he didn't have Niketa here by his side.

Above him, the Emerald Shifter vanished with a flash.

Niketa clung to her Deuschalin Cragger as it bucked, trying to look around. Part of her wanted to believe that her eyes had deceived her— her husband hadn't actually disappeared, she'd just lost sight of him in the chaos. But she knew better. Somehow, impossibly, Creyne had landed on an Emerald Shifter. He was in the Aethereal Lands.

Her dragon spun. She clenched her teeth, fighting nausea, but refused to close her eyes. If the Shifter reappeared, she needed to see it. Creyne could ride it out. He could make it back. As long as he knew to hold his breath—the air in the Aethereal Lands was poison to mortals. Mentally, she cursed. She'd grown up there, among the elfin people; she knew the dangers of those lands. But she didn't speak of those times often. Did Creyne know what he faced?

The Deuschalin Cragger suddenly swerved, slamming her hard against its side. She cursed, gritting her teeth, and then reached for her dragon prod. Using it would disqualify her from a prize; but if Creyne didn't come back, no prize would matter anyway.

She jammed the prod against the Cragger's back and felt a *hum* as the magic began to flow. *Be calm,* she willed the beast. The dragon's flight immediately leveled out. With another thought, she sent the dragon climbing up out of the canyon for a better view.

The rest of the swarm barreled past them, with a few dragons thrashing about with riders still clinging to their backs. She could see a few flashes of green passing through, but none with a rider.

Then a brilliant green flash caught the corner of her eye. She swerved her mount around to find the Emerald Shifter had returned and rejoined the flow of dragons down the canyon—and it was riderless. She clenched her teeth, blinking back sudden tears.

No. No, she would not lose her husband. Not today. Not when they'd just been fighting.

She willed the Cragger to pursue the green dragon. When they were just above the Shifter, she took a deep breath and jumped.

She landed higher than she normally would, on the Shifter's neck just behind the head. The spines there caught her in the stomach, knocking the wind from her lungs. As the dragon began to rear, she thrust the prod against its scales, just at the joint of the neck and head.

The dragon calmed as she willed it. She took a moment to find better seating—she couldn't use the rigging gloves with the prod in her hand—and then closed her eyes, preparing herself.

Shift us over, she thought. *To the Aethereal Lands.*

The green light flashed through her eyelids, and the air was suddenly cool. The scent of it was achingly familiar; she hated it. She opened her eyes to find the rolling teal clouds of the Aether below her, and golden stars above her.

Find him, she willed, picturing Creyne in her mind's eye. *Take me to my husband.*

The dragon snorted and then swerved around. She held her breath as it dove toward the clouds; she'd been to these lands before, and the air wouldn't affect her like it would Creyne . . . but that didn't mean it wouldn't have any effect.

They pierced the clouds, sinking deeper and deeper. As her lungs began to burn, a shadow appeared ahead. She almost gasped in relief as it resolved into her husband, drifting gently with his eyes closed and a peaceful little smile on his face.

She stretched forward as the dragon approached, grabbing Creyne by the front of the coat. She pulled him across the Shifter's neck, just in front of her, and then willed the dragon to take them away from this wretched place.

With an emerald burst, they appeared beneath pale blue sky once again, the sun mercilessly bright. The bitingly cold wind hit them like a wall, sending Creyne tumbling away. She lunged to the side and caught him by the sleeve, barely managing to keep her legs wrapped around the dragon's neck.

She panted, gasping for air as she strained to keep hold of her husband and still keep the dragon prod in place. There didn't seem to be enough air. They were up too high, she realized. Thin ribbons of cloud whipped past them. The canyon was a narrow crack far, far below.

Creyne was blinking, beginning to wake. She willed the Shifter to pull around so that she could get her seat back. And then a sudden cross breeze pulled Niketa farther than her arms could stretch, and the dragon prod lifted off of the Shifter's neck.

The dragon immediately bucked, smashing Niketa's arm against her side. She felt her arm *crack*, and her vision flashed white. The prod went spinning from her suddenly numb fingers, and she and her husband went tumbling away into the open sky.

Creyne blinked, trying to wake up. His head throbbed with the worst hangover he'd ever felt. What had happened?

He'd been falling, he remembered. He was still falling. Someone was shouting. He looked down to find his wife clutching his sleeve, her teeth clenched and her other arm curled tight against her chest. She was pulling him . . . he looked down, over his shoulder, and realized that she was trying to angle them toward the canyon below, which was growing larger with every second.

Slowly, his mind began to grind into gear. He knew that even the enchantments of the safety nets wouldn't be enough to save them, falling from this height. How in the world had they gotten here?

A roar shattered through the wind, and Creyne looked up—past his feet—to find the Emerald Shifter bearing down on them with sapphire flames billowing from its maw. His mind finally snapped into full wakefulness. He grabbed his wife, twisting to shield her from the dragon's fire. Then he blinked. There, whistling through the air just a few feet away, was a dragon prod. He snatched it and turned to face the dragon.

Fire enveloped them. Creyne felt his bandana wither away in the heat. Through the shimmering flames, he glimpsed a forked, lashing tongue. Vicious teeth surrounded them. He slammed the rod up into the roof of the dragon's mouth and felt it touch flesh.

"Stop your flame!" he shouted. He'd never actually used a dragon prod before; it was supposed to communicate your commands to the dragon, though. Sure enough, the dragon's fire bled away in an instant. He and his wife were halfway into the dragon's mouth, but it didn't bite down on them.

"Slow us down!" Niketa screamed in his ear, clinging to his back. He looked over his shoulder and saw the canyon walls almost within spitting reach.

"Pull up!" he shouted at the dragon. "Level out!"

The Shifter immediately complied, spreading its wings and straining against the wind. Creyne and Niketa slammed against its lower jaw and held onto its teeth as it streaked into the canyon; he kept the prod firmly against its gums the whole way. Rodeo imps scattered out of their way, screaming in otherworldly languages. The dragon slowly began to curve upward again, and Creyne felt himself slipping down toward its throat.

Niketa grabbed his arm with her good one and braced her feet against the dragon's teeth. Then, with a heave, she threw them both free of its mouth. Creyne felt its teeth tug at his boot as he fell.

They slammed into the safety nets and each other. Once again, Creyne had the wind knocked out of him, this time by his wife's hip connecting with his stomach. Above them the imps darted and teased the Emerald Shifter. Snarling and hissing, it vanished with a flash.

They lay there panting. Creyne worked his arms free of the net and wrapped them around his wife. She rested her head against his chest.

"How's yer arm?" he mumbled.

"Prob'ly broken," she replied. "Just a little crack, though. You injured?"

He stretched slightly. His face stung and his side was throbbing. "I'm a mite singed. A little bit, but I've had worse. Maybe a broken rib or two."

"Nothin' else?"

He shook his head. "I'm all right."

"Good." Niketa whispered. Then she thumped him on the head with her fist. "You don't have to *speak* your commands with a dragon prod, idjit," she growled, yanking off her goggles. "You just *think* 'em—it's faster and easier."

Creyne stared at her. Her leathers were singed black and there was a sooty outline from her goggles around her gray eyes. Her cheeks were singed with a faint flush. He coughed up a brief laugh. "Give me my tusk back, woman."

Niketa blinked at him. Then she smiled. She wrapped her arms around him and pulled his head against her chest while she fished the tooth out of the pouch at her waist.

"There you go, idjit," she said, shoving it into his hand. "Now make my eyes pretty again."

Creyne pulled the crystal sphere from his jacket and held it up before her eyes. The color faded from it and drifted in wisps back to her eyes until the irises gleamed violet again. She blinked, smiled, and then pulled him into a kiss.

The imps helped them onto a magic carpet. As they raised into sight of the galleries, the crowds began to cheer. Niketa smiled; every spectator was standing, and many were jumping up and down. She'd never heard a rodeo crowd cheer so loudly or so wildly. Creyne squeezed her shoulder, and she hugged him back.

"Well that's nice, isn't it?" she said.

"Yeah." He looked down at the dragon prod in his hand. "Pretty sure they're still gonna disqualify us 'cause of this thing, though."

Niketa looked at the prod, then at him, and snorted. She wasn't getting into this again. "Don't expect an apology from me."

"Never crossed my mind." He shook his head and pulled his hat back onto his head. "Just a shame to miss that prize."

She rested her head on his arm. "Prizes at the Coasttown Rodeo next month are bigger, anyway." But even as she said it, she wondered if another rodeo was the best idea.

Creyne nodded absentmindedly, and she wondered if he was thinking the same thing. Then he hefted the dragon prod. "How much, uh . . . how much does one of these cost? We should prob'ly get another'n before we move on."

Niketa looked up at him. He didn't meet her eyes, and was instead intensely studying the glowing prod. She smirked and nodded, leaning her head against his chest. "Damn straight."

Rising Star
Michaelene Pendleton

I was plunging in a wind-shrieking dive, wings snicked in close to my back, riding the fine edge of control, claws spread, working my ribs like bellows to pump up my fire, anticipation dripping from both tips of my tongue, and dropping like fate on a frizzly-haired old mage robed in tatty blue velvet, when—BAM!—he slammed me with a bolt of magical dragonbane stronger than hammered lightning and twice as bright.

The blast fried all my senses, blinded and deafened me, flung me spinning down a long, dark tunnel, my wings flailing for lift and not finding any air to grab. Tumbling in a lightless void, sparked here and there with the tracks of stars. Freezing from a cold sharper than a Viking's nightmare of Hel, damping my fire to faint tendrils of smoke oozing out of my nostrils, icing over both sets of eyelids and turning my wing membranes as brittle as rime frost on a still pond.

The battle was a mistake from the beginning, a defamation of character leading to inevitable confrontation. I'd been accused of taking a young virgin girl. That was a long-bearded lie. I will admit that when I was not long out of the shell I appreciated the delicate savor of virgin flesh, boy's or girl's, but after laying my first egg clutch, my taste turned to full-grown males. Their meat was richer, stronger-flavored—in truth, gamier—than the pale flesh of young women. Anyway, the local maidens keep themselves starved down to skin and bone until they attract a mate. After that, well, while it is grudgingly permitted to take breeding females, my line has always had more care for our honor. There's not much sport in harvesting a woman too pregnant to run, or too concerned with protecting her young to have the sense to hide. And children aren't worth the bother unless you round up a gaggle of them.

I hadn't tormented and dined on anyone but full-grown males for two or three centuries, usually the ones who came proudly shouting what they thought was my true name, riding fat juicy horses and encased in metal shells which sizzled a nice crust on them.

Now there was true sport! Dodging their sharp, pointy little lances, huffing great gouts of dusky smoke, fending off swords with my claws, and finally broiling them medium-rare with one good blast of flame after enough tormenting to get their sap fully risen. Tasty, oh my, yes.

Unfair that I was banished from life and light for something I didn't even do.

Time had no meaning in the void, only emptiness and a great, aching loneliness that gnawed and rended my soul with fangs more terrible than any beast magical or mundane. Abandoned, my life ripped out of time, I floated through the beginnings and endings of worlds unknowing, alone and unmade, reined back from the black rage of berserker despair only by the raw, desperate need to survive. I am Draconis Verdigris. We do not give up.

With a concussion that rattled my brain inside the wedge of my skull, I dropped from the void into a night sky overwhelming with sound and color and scent. The sudden transition shocked my senses. I plummeted like a hunk of granite, falling, not flying, terrorized by the rush of warm and sudden life. By the time I got my wits about me, I was too close to the ground to do more than flare my wings and brace for impact.

I hit the ground hard enough to knock my wind out and snap two spines at the end of my tail. But I was alive.

The scents were alien to my nostrils, revealing a hot, dry, barren place instead of the forested fjords of home. A slice of moon showed me a land of blasted, jagged rock, sand still warm from the day's sun, strange twisted bushes and trees armored with thorns, powdered with dust. Unknown tracks patterned the sand and disappeared over rock, to reappear again in the next patch of sand. I recognized nothing.

I could hear the skritch of wind-shifted twigs against rock, the whisper of sand moving over itself, claw-scuttlings of tiny creatures, and once a wild wailing that could have issued from the stretched throat of a wolf. But no birdsong, no rill of water or the slow, cold conversations of salmon, no thrashing of brush as elks beat the velvet from their antlers.

My fire was almost out. I lay still, saving what energy remained to me. I can fast for a century or so if necessary but the lethargy in my long-sinewed muscles and the vast emptiness in my belly told me my time in the void had been much longer than two, three or even four hundred years.

I was too weak to hunt, too weak to even move. I lay with one wing crumpled under my body and couldn't shift enough to free it. I pumped my ribs and exhaled. No fire, just a whisper of smoke, not enough heat to warm a leftover snack.

Something moved across the sand in front of my nose. A blunt-tailed lizard, beaded black and orange across its back, moving slowly, its tail in counterpoint to its torso as it waddled cautiously closer, drawn by the fading heat of my body.

A lizard. A relative. An ancestor, if you believe the legends of the beginnings of our race. Which made eating it uncomfortably close to cannibalism.

Damn ethics, I was starving. I scooped it off the sand with my tongue. One crunch and it was gone. Barely a tidbit to my hunger, but its brief taste gave me hope. I cast out my senses, pushing back the creeping cold of death.

There were sparks of warm life all around me. I lay still and let mammalian curiosity bring the creatures within range of my glance. Once under my basilisk stare, they marched obligingly into my jaws. Rabbits, a porcine creature much smaller than the wild boars of home, a thin, slab-sided wolflike thing with dirty gray-yellow fur, each one renewed my strength, stoked the coals in my fire-chamber.

I didn't torment any of them. There is no honor in tormenting a creature too simple to fully realize what it has to fear. For tormenting to be honorable, as well as pleasurable, you need prey that can imagine its own demise, which leaves us with only humans, magpies, foxes, and two species of swine.

I couldn't yet fly, but I could stand and shake out my cramped wings, flex my talons, and stretch hindlegs and forelegs, surveying my length for serious hurt, and finding none. Able to move, I could hunt.

Cattle are the same the world over. Brainless and toothsome. I stalked a herd and killed four while they were still entranced, a quick slash of claw, eating two of them raw, choking down their uncooked flesh, feeling their meat and blood flood my muscles with life, fueling my fire. Three deep breaths. I raised my head, flexing my neck to clear the passage, and belched out a stream of fire that lit t he night sky and splashed liquid flame over rock and sand. I was alive! I shrieked my challenge to this world, a long ringing clarion that refuted death and said to all, "Beware. Hic est draconis!"

When the echoes of my cry died away, the night was utterly silent. Nothing moved, or hardly breathed. Life huddled close to the earth, frozen in terror, knowing with the memory of long-dead forebears that its only protection lay in invisibility.

I seared the other two dead cows and ate my first civilized meal by the graying light of dawn, relishing the hot, herbivore-scented meat, picking my teeth clean with splinters of leg bones.

As the sun tipped a horizon jagged with the backbones of mountains, I spread my wings, flexing the long vanes and stretching their prismed green-gold plates that lay flat along the reptilian curves of my body. The acid-washed bronze of spines, talons and the two spiraled horns that swept back from my wide triangular brow were gilded in the early light. From the egg, I knew that I was beautiful, but only now, after surviving the worst that magic could do, after eons in the void, rebirthed weak and helpless into a new world, only now did I know my own true strength. In this world or any other, I am fear. I am why men flinch and look up at the shadow of a crow.

With a strong downthrust of wing, I sprang into the air.

The ascending sun gave the air substance. I rose and soared, riding the warm currents with barely the flick of a wingtip for control, then diving, twisting, rollicking in the freedom of flight.

When I settled, I found myself looking down upon a very strange land. Not a forest in sight, no water, no villages or farmsteads, just sere, barren earth spiked with sharp upthrusts of gray and yellow rock as far as I could see.

In the cantilevered bone over my eyes, the pits that read the magnetic currents of the world swirled with nausea, telling me that, wherever I was, it was untold leagues away from my northern forests, a long way south and farther west than any seafarer had dared venture. In fact, if the men of my time who considered themselves learned were right, I should have been either in the middle of Oceanus Incognita or off the edge of the earth. Well, all Draconi know that the earth is not flat, but as round as a Saxon's skull, and I wasn't swimming. So much for learned men. The one thing I was sure of was that I had better come to like this place because it was going to be my new home.

After flying for most of the day, I was certain it was a home I would not have chosen. Too empty. Several times I saw flying things, never close enough to challenge, nor even to be sure that they were Draconi, especially since they flew with no beat of wing, incredibly fast and unbelievably high.

The ground below me was streaked here and there with straight paths of smooth gray stone. Along the lines moved what looked to be scarabs or possibly pill bugs, large beetles of ugly, flat colors. Bugs are not fit prey for an adult of my Line, but these were very large beetles. I cirdled down to have a closer look. Two of them stopped beneath me. One was a bilious brown and the other solid white with blue and red fires flashing on its back. They reeked of burning lamp oil, forge-hot metal, and some acrid effluvia that stung my nostrils. A man got out of the white one.

I went into a stall, forgetting to flap, in my amazement. What kind of world is this where men encase insects in armor and ride inside them?

The man walked up beside the brown beetle. I heard two loud pops and he sprawled on the ground. The brown beetle roared and ran away.

It's hard to resist running prey. I chased off after the beetle, overflying it, then flaring down in front of it. It shrieked and stopped. Two men leaped out, shouting in a tongue I had never heard but, with the inborn knowledge of all Draconi, could understand. They weren't being complimentary about my ancestry, nor were they offering me a proper challenge. In truth, they were downright insulting. They pointed their hands at me. I heard more popping sounds and something stung my breastbone.

Well, if they had no honor, I had no obligation. I charred them with one blast, setting the beetle aflame as well. As I reached to skewer dinner, the damned bug exploded! It blasted me muzzle over mead kettle, rolling me like a puffball along the ground. A piece of its armor whacked me between my horns and knocked me cross-eyed. It also burned my dinner to two lumps of cinder.

I settled for beef again that evening. Obviously I was going to have to learn more about this place before I could safely hunt humans here.

It took several days to find a cave. My new lair wasn't much of a cave, only a deep hollow in dirty gray sandstone rather than an arching granite cavern, mined smooth by dwarfs. Unwelcoming, too, with no seeping water for a bathing pool, and no heaps of shining gold to cozy it up a bit.

In truth, I was beginning to suspect that gold might be hard to come by in this country. There was no smell of it on the two men I hadn't eaten, and no lovely aroma in the air of new-mined gold freshly brought to light.

I had to keep reminding myself that I was fortunate to be alive. Despair became a new taste on my tongue. No honorable prey proclaiming challenge, no gold to be found. And in this world, I found I did not rule the skies.

One darkmoon night, I was frolicking in the air, playing with the winds rather than having a care for my safety.

The creature was on me before I was even aware of it. It came at me with a banshee shriek, riding the rumble of Ragnarok thunder, spewing a tail of fire, tossing me like a mayfly in its turbulent wake. It left behind a reek of oil and metal that told me it was akin to the ground beetles.

I lost a lot of sky before I got lift under my wings again. That may be what saved me. It had circled around at me, fire sparking from its rigid, back-swept wings. Something ripped through my right wing, shredding one membrane panel, flipping me over on my back. It was lunging down on me. Flailing at the air, all control gone, I was helpless. We were less than sixty rods above the broken ground, and I was looking Death in her cold eye, when it suddenly pulled up, screaming high into wider air.

I flared into a stall, and twitched down into a good-sized gully in the desert floor, making the best speed my wounded wing would allow. I could hear it above me, searching, but fearing to fly too low. When it was gone, I ascended and limped back to my lair.

My pride was badly dented that night. In the long hours before dawn, I wrestled with the demon of realization that I was no longer the most powerful being in the air. No griffin, no winged Sphinx, no Valkyrie of my time could have withstood me—any more than I could stand up to the unholy amalgam that had attacked me.

When it was coming straight for me, I had seen that men rode inside the armored flying insect. Could it be that in this place men had handfasted with the enemies of mammals and warm-blooded reptiles alike, and used them for steeds? What price had they paid, I wondered, for that evil alliance?

That was when I knew despair.

I took cattle for my hunger and stayed on the ground after dark, wrapped in self-pity, angry anew at my fate. Restless, wanting the world that was gone, trying to make sense of this new world.

I was lonely. No trembling wizards braving my hunger, outstretched hands offering jewels from Far Aegyptus in return for the knowledge they asked of me. No dwarfs bringing rough-hewn gold in worshipful tribute. No fields of harvesters to swoop down on just for the fun of watching them scatter. No long evenings of philosophical dispute with learned witches clothed in bone amulets and rivers of dark hair. No ritual challenge and combat.

No mate.

The hot nights stirred my blood. For the first time I understood the rampages of my southern kin among the men of the desert who wore curved swords and braided their beards for Allah. We Draconi of the northern mists and chilling rains are slower in our passions, but they are deep, deep as the black waters of the Ice Sea. Once aroused, we do not waver.

I kept a tight hold on my yearnings. Going berserker in my injured condition would be dog-stupid. But there is no challenge in preying on cattle, skinny deer, and the odd razorback or rabbit. Men are really the only fit prey, and I wasn't having much success hunting men. The rules had changed, and I didn't know the new ones.

One morning I woke to a low rumble and the insect reek. My first instinct was to burst from my cave, belching flame and ready to attack the creature that dared invade my domain. My recent experiences, however, counseled caution. I crept from the shadows into the lemon-yellow light of dawn. The rocky ground before my lair sloped down some way then leveled out into a smooth sand floor. Sitting on the sand, surrounded by its own stench, emanating waves of heat, was a bulky, blue-carapaced snout beetle almost as large as I am. Beside it, leaning on its long nose, stood a man.

Both my hearts hammered in my breast. He smelled of gold.

I couldn't take him while he was protected by the insect. With gold at stake, I didn't want the cursed thing exploding and destroying the beginnings of my hoard.

To lure him away, I stretched my jaws, tightened my throat, and began to sing. It was a song I had learned from the Rhine Loreleis, a wordless flow of music in a minor key, complete with two dark-hued harmonies that hinted of sensual twinings in the night, of love and lust and unearthly delight. The Loreleis always could weave a good tune.

It caught him. He turned his head, listening, not yet understanding. He drank from a glass bottle and I smelled the sharp bite of brandywine. One hand went to his mouth, a spark glowed, and smoke drifted from his nostrils.

Smoke? From a human?

He looked wholly human, and if he was a mage, he didn't dress the part. His trews were close-fitting dark-blue cloth, and his tunic was black leather, pigskin by its smell, open down the front. Under it he wore something white that came up close around his neck, but no sign of a weapon, not even a bodkin. I drew in a suppressed breath: gold glinted from his throat and one wrist. Saliva dripped from my tonguetips and I almost lost the thread of my song.

His boots scraped on the rock. When I saw the crown of his head, I reared up to my full height and fixed him with one baleful golden eye.

He stumbled to a stop, dropping the bottle, his mouth sagging agape, his limbs suddenly frozen. The insect didn't explode, no curses magical enveloped me. Finally something was going properly in this strange world.

I called him to me. He came, moving in the stiff-jointed way of the entranced. I studied him carefully while I held him in thrall—I'd had enough surprises. He seemed as human as men of my time. He wore his hair longer than the short helmet-cut of a cataphract, his jaw was beardless, and his eyes were covered by two round black pieces of glass. I was familiar with glass of magical properties, but this glass, whatever its purpose, gave off no arcane aroma. I touched him with the tips of my tongue, and he shuddered in a most human fashion.

I backed him against a slab of rock and curved both wings to fence him round before I released him from my stare.

For a really satisfactory tormenting, it's wise to wait them out in silence, let them speak first. Often those first words reveal their deepest fears, giving you a direction for the torment.

He was quiet for a goodly time, weaving a bit as if he were having trouble with his balance. He reached up and removed the glass things from his face, then ran a hand down his chin. His eyes, dark, bagged, and red-rimmed, touched me, slid away, then crept back. His voice was broken into bits like gravel in a streambed, hissing and rattling. "Oh man, I have got to lay off the booze, I'm losing it." He scuffed his hands at me. "Well, you just piss off. I don't need very large, lovely green dragons on top of everything else."

Obviously this man wasn't understanding his situation.

He put one hand against the rock to steady himself. "Go on, beat it. The rest of my life may be going down the toilet, but I refuse to have DTs, too. There are no dragons. I'm asleep. I'm dreaming you."

I chuckled and he cringed away from the sooty heat. I stretched out one foreclaw and delicately nicked the back of his hand. I licked a scarlet drop from the point of my claw. "Dreaming, are you?"

"Shit," he said.

He put the glasses back on his face. "All right, if you're going to kill me, do it. Get it over with."

He wasn't cooperating. Yes, he was scared, but by now he should have been down on his knees, babbling to various divine beings to intercede and save his paltry little life, which, in my experience, they never do. Circling deep in the currents under his surface fear was an urge to die almost draconian in its bleak intensity. A human with a Death wish? I'd thought that reserved for higher forms of life. This man piqued my interest. "Are you so eager to die?" I inquired.

His mouth twisted into a sour line. "That was my intent, yes. Why else come to the Mojave-godforsaken-Desert?"

"Why?"

"You tell me. The production company folded, I can't pay my bills, the producer's assistants' assistants won't return my phone calls, and my last decent client just went over to William Morris. Next thing you know, headwaiters won't seat me during rush hour. I'm not waiting around for the luncheon postmortems on poor old Terry Pierce's career, nice guy, just couldn't cut it, heard he slunk back into the Great Flyover somewhere, all that bullshit. A bottle of Halcyon, a quart of Stoli, and the whole problem fades away." He creaked out a laugh. "I sure as hell didn't expect to end up fried by a dragon, a mythical beast that doesn't even exist, which must mean that I'm crazy, too."

Although that didn't make a whole lot of sense, I was a little irked that he still didn't believe in me. "I am not mythical," I said. "I am an adult female Draconis of the Verdigris Line. I was thrown into your world by the magic of a second-rate wizard who got lucky."

"Magic? Not even a hack scriptwriter would believe that one. The only magic these days is in the movies." He went still, as if every muscle in his body were suddenly frozen. "Movies. Jesus, Mary and Joseph, if you are real—" He pulled off his glasses and took a step toward me.

I hissed and backed up. "You will find that I am very real. Pray to whatever gods you revere, man. I will give you that time."

He raised his hands. "Wait a minute. Stop. Can't we cut a deal here?"

Bargaining is an honorable reaction to tormenting. I raised my head and vented a little flame into the cool morning air. "What did you have in mind?"

Fire always shakes them. He managed to keep most of the fear out of his voice. "You don't kill me, and I make us both so filthy rich we'll puke."

Not exactly a revolutionary bargaining point, and rather indelicately stated, but he was trying. "You promise gold?"

"Gold? If that's how you want it, sure. Here," he tore the gold from his neck and wrist, "you want gold, take these. The Rolex alone is worth six thousand. Consider it a down payment."

I could feel a new wish for life born in him. That's what tormenting is all about, the rising and dashing of hope. The pleasure flowed through my body like sex or flight. "How will you get this gold you offer?"

"Just by signing papers, babe. You let me represent you, do an exclusive contract with me, and I'll have every major studio begging to use you. Shit, Spielberg and Lucas will go fucking nuts! You'll be the biggest thing to hit the movies since Godzilla!"

He continued in a language just as arcane as any first-water mage. His words didn't matter. I felt his excitement, the hot rush of his human desires, the need in his blood not only to live, but to succeed at this plan he was concocting. Humans are most interesting when they are fired with that singular drive to create. His life force burned more brightly the longer he talked.

"So," he finished, "have we got a deal?" He rubbed his palms together. His aura was vivid with life.

I looked down at him, holding my silence until both color and hope faded from his face. His shoulders sagged. "I think not," I said.

His eyes flinched but he stood his ground. "Nothing I can say will change your mind?"

I turned my head to fix him with the balefire of one hungry eye. In the act of inhaling a fire-breath, I hesitated. He was really quite brave, facing me with no weapons, almost as cast adrift from his referents as I had been in the void, yet controlling his fear. He had the desperate courage of a dragonet facing a phalanx of lancers. His visage was even faintly draconic, long and thin, bone-edged along its planes and hollows. His eyes and hair were black and shining like the scales of Draconis enbonii, the Line of my first chosen egg-mate.

And in truth, I was very lonely. My Line is more solitary than most, but here in this place of so many unknowns, I needed a touchstone to link me to sanity, even if it was only the limited conversation of a human. I had the suspicion I wasn't going to find another of my own kind.

I hadn't answered his question. When I released him from the entrancement of my gaze, he slumped against the rock at his back. "Okay," he rasped, "I get it." He dragged one hand over his face. "Can I smoke first?"

So I hadn't imagined it. It was against all reason, but I knew I had seen it. In the strange ages of change I'd missed, could humans and Draconi somehow have become kin? "Please do," I said.

He reached into his clothes and brought out a thin white stick. He put it between his lips, holding his other hand to its tip. I heard a small snick. And suddenly his fingers were aflame. It startled me, raising a wild hope, until I saw that he held in his palm a small metal device that actually produced the fire. He inhaled deeply, then let tendrils of blue smoke drift out of his nostrils.

Disappointment was as deep as the hope that had been vaulting. Not kin, then, not real fire. Still, it was something to note that down the ages, humans had retained enough memory of us to preserve our ways. To show that I accepted his reverence, I politely breathed some of my own smoke to join his.

He coughed. He looked up at me, a slash of smile pulling his mouth askew. "Go for it, babe. At least 'Death by Dragon' makes a better headline than 'Small-time Agent OD's.' Too bad no one will ever read it."

I sucked in a great draft of air, arching my neck, raising the points of my wings. White-hot the flame roared, incandescent heat, hissing and crackling, searing up my throat, out between my long jaws, to splash harmlessly over rock and sand, because at the last instant, I couldn't do it. I didn't want to kill him. I'd found food to sustain my body, uninteresting food, true, but enough to keep me alive. Now I needed sustenance for my mind. This man had the courage to pretend to laugh at Death. How could I kill a being capable of that?

"How much gold?" I said.

He opened his eyes. Dark hair stuck sweat-slicked to his cheeks. His voice was a whisper. "To tell the truth, I don't think I could figure your take of a ten-million-dollar contract and three percent of the gross, after my commission of course, right at this particular moment."

What amount of gold is honorable in this age? I suppose, like any other age, as much as you can get. In some ways, the world does not change. His two pieces of gold lay before me, throwing back the light with a soft gleam. Centuries of tradition named him prey, life to be tormented and taken. But the mind must rule the blood. I did not want to kill him. In this new world I could make my own rules.

I settled back on my haunches, tucking in my wings. As the sun rose to bake us in a welcome heat, between us we reasoned a bargain that would allow me to let him live. Against all sensible argument, I put my trust in him, agreeing to his plans, even telling him my True Name to seal the bargain, although he said we'd have to change it because Sigrigrantharisis was too long for something called billboards. There was much I did not fully understand in his words, but I could feel his eager interest in me.

By the time we parted, I was hungry enough that I had to stop looking at him. To hold me over until I could find acceptable prey, I asked for the insect.

"The what?"

I pointed with my snout. "The insect that carries you in its belly. The blue one down there, may I take it for prey?"

His teeth flashed white as he grinned. Strong, sharp canines, I noted. "It's not an insect, it's a machine."

"A mechanical device? Like a catapult or a wormscrew?" My voice held doubt.

"Sort of. Let me explain cars to you another time. Right now I've got the media event of the century to promote." He patted my slanting shoulder, a little hesitantly. "Babe, we are going to make so much money, it'll be indecent."

Just before climbing into his insect-car, he said, "Why didn't you waste me right off?"

If I correctly understood the idiom, some questions lie best unanswered. I hacked a blotch of smoke at him. He didn't ask again.

He had the courage to talk to me instead of immediately trying to skewer me with something sharp, and he was only the second human in my experience to recognize that, in truth, I am an exceedingly lovely green dragon.

In less than a quarter moon, Terry completed the arrangements for his "media event." On the agreed day, just as sunset turned to dark, he gathered a large assembly of humans known as flacks on a high butte of rock not far from my lair.

I followed Terry's instructions as if I were, in truth, born to what he called "show business." In the afternoon I ate several fat cows to curb my instinct to prey on humans, since even I could understand the consequences of such an action. I preened my scales and burnished my horns, spines, and claws until they shone like sea-gold. Then I lay hidden, waiting for Terry's signal.

In his parlance, we blew their socks off. Gliding silently, I swooped down on them from the rear, blasting a long stream of fire as I passed, then circling to hover, wings flared, spitting sparks and roaring in my most ferocious voice.

It was like stirring a nest of mice. Some froze in terror, some ran in wild panic. The running ones I turned back, showing off my acrobatic skill, diving and dancing in the air, huffing just enough flame to scare them without really hurting anyone. When they were all herded together again, I landed among their cowering forms, let off one last gout of flame into the black sky, then lowered my head so Terry could stand with his arm around my neck while he convinced the flacks that I was not, after all, going to eat them en brochette. When they found that I talk, they went wild, all yelling at once, popping flashing lights in my eyes. Terry controlled their questions, only allowing me to respond to the ones for which we had created answers that Terry thought would be acceptable to the media.

It was a stupendous success.

So here I am, the hottest star in Hollywood. I have my own dressing room, a converted semitrailer with my stage name in red uncial Gothic letters on the side. I get a hundred thousand per speaking appearance, my price for a cameo role is higher than Brando's, and the Koreans are negotiating for my endorsement on a theme park called DragonLand. Kitty Kelly is writing my unauthorized biography.

Terry makes all the deals. I can't fit inside the offices. Though if the negotiations aren't going well, we often arrange for me to stick my head in the window and huff a little smoke now and then. That usually simplifies the bargaining process.

My last feature was an FX film, with me playing two roles, good dragon versus bad dragon. I reluctantly allowed them to dye my scales, but only because Terry convinced me that I needed to be able to play against type for career longevity. He's now working on some deal where I get a "love interest." I've explained the draconian way of these things, but Terry insists that humans will like me better, and spend more at the box office, if they can anthropomorphize me. I'd rather be feared, but if it makes Terry happy and keeps the gold flowing in, I'll be lovable. For a couple of movies, anyway. Then I want Terry to buy an option on Beowulf so we can tell the truth of that story.

It's a fat, comfortable life. No knights trying to puncture me, no magicians hurling spells at me, no priests cursing my name for eternity. All the treasure any dragon could want, beautiful people sucking up to me and wanting their pictures with me in all the tabloids. I take my rest on a hard, lumpy pile of bright yellow gold. My own chef presents me with the tenderest pedigreed Japanese beef on the hoof and ready for broiling.

Still, I do miss the thrill of the hunt and the occasional torment. Terry is adamant that, no matter how toothsome, I'm not allowed to eat any more of my co-stars. I did charbroil that hairy little rat dog that supposedly saved the world from me in my first feature. Terry took care of the bad press and explained that it would be really hard to get parts if I kept that up, so I promised I wouldn't do it again.

But I don't suppose they'd miss an extra now and then, would they? Maybe a stuntman or a bit player? And, I promise, only after the production is wrapped.

The Diamond-Spitting Knight
S. E. Page

All of Millet's troubles began when she freed the fairy. Pixie Mab's wings were caught in the dewy cobwebs covering a mulberry bush until the orphan girl gave it a good shake.

"I am not your godmother, but I suppose I *might* spare you a small fairy's blessing," Pixie Mab said as she smoothed the torn gossamer ruffles of her gown. "How would you like to become a changeling and learn how to howl like an ogre and run wild with the unicorns?"

But Millet shook her head, very certain that she would prefer silver platters of tarts bathed in honey, satin dancing slippers, and chandeliers with more crystals than a starry sky. "Make me a princess, please, with a castle and a crown and *everything*—"

"Boring," Pixie Mab interrupted, rolling her eyes, "but as you wish." She waved a tiny rowan splinter of a wand before vanishing in a puff of periwinkle sparkles.

Millet patted the top of her head and was sorely disappointed to find only the usual tangle of red curls. Yet there was no time to search for her missing tiara as a royal hunting party charged into the meadow where she stood quite in the way. Millet opened her mouth to cry out a warning before their stallions trampled her under hoof, but found it impossible as something hard and cold rolled up her throat and clinked against her teeth. A torrent of sapphires slipped from her surprised lips and mixed with the clover.

"Halt!" King Wulfram shouted, and his hunters reeled their steeds to a sudden stop. A sharp glint filled the king's eyes as he glanced down at the dazzling mess of jewels and then back up at the orphan girl. "What a lovely little gem you are," he said. The new name stuck, and he promptly pronounced her his princess on the spot.

King Wulfram brought Little Gem back to his castle where she continued to spit out jewels faster than melon seeds: one bucket of rubies as large as a bear's eyes Monday through Thursday, a barrel of sapphires as bright as morning stars Friday through Saturday, and a ladle-full of pearls as blue as dove's eggs on Sunday. The daily jewels that Little Gem coughed up kept a very particular schedule, unless of course, she sneezed.

In such an emergency, Ole Maid Gertie unfurled a kerchief at the first hint of a scrunching nose, and Little Gem filled the cloth with emeralds and now and then, the odd peridot.

"Bless you, poppet," the old woman said after a particularly powerful sneeze. She dumped the glimmering stones caught in the kerchief into a scale and weighed them with a practiced hand.

"No thanks!" Little Gem said as she pinched her nose to keep from sneezing again. "One blessing is quite enough."

Little Gem supposed the fairy's blessing would be rather nice if only being a princess didn't come with so very many rules: never tell anyone of her gift, never give a single jewel away, but mostly, *stay* in the Iron Room.

"It's for your own good, my little gem," King Wulfram had assured her as he'd unlocked the black metal door and ushered her into the iron-walled room. "This is the safest place in the castle for a treasure as truly precious as yours."

Little Gem didn't mind spending her days in the Iron Room at first, for every corner of the treasury overflowed with peculiar splendors: a harp that played music even when no finger touched the golden strings, tapestries of snow white stags that galloped as if alive instead of silk thread beasts, and Faerie books that told new stories every night no matter how many times she turned the pages. How could she *dare* complain when she'd traded a dirty straw pallet and cold porridge for a downy pile of goose-feather pillows, and three hot meals brought to her by Ole Maid Gertie every day?

But as her time rolled by in a gilded haze, Little Gem felt a deepening pang of loss; she'd almost forgotten the springy feel of grass and how a clean slant of sunlight was so much brighter than the wink of gold.

King Wulfram came to visit Little Gem at noon, as he always did to tally and inspect the day's bounty of jewels.

"No diamonds today?" he asked, frowning at the silver pail brimming over with Tuesday's rubies as if it was a bucket of squirmy salamanders.

Little Gem bowed her head, for she'd never been able to spit out a single diamond, though she'd tried a thousand times. "No, Your Majesty."

King Wulfram kicked the pail over and rubies tinkled into every corner. "This humble pile of jewels is not nearly enough for my kingdom," he seethed. "I need diamonds, Little Gem, mountains of them! After all I have done for you, is it so *hard* to show me your gratitude?"

"No!" Little Gem said, her shoulders slumping under the weight of her own failure. "Perhaps I shall have better luck tomorrow. . . ."

"Tomorrow," the king agreed.

Alone once more, Little Gem picked up the empty pail and stared fiercely at the bottom. "Surely I can make just one tiny diamond," she whispered, but her tears were the only kind of jewel that plunked inside.

She fell asleep clutching the empty pail only to be startled awake by a loud growl at precisely midnight. The door to the Iron Room swung open as two guards entered and wheeled a large cage inside. Little Gem gawked in amazement at the young dragon the size of a pony snarling behind the bars. A tight silver collar pinched the emerald green scales on his neck.

"Beware you well, little lady!" one of the guards snickered. "That collar may keep the dragon from belching flames, but touch the vicious beast and he'll have your fingers for supper."

"Aye," the second guard cackled. "And clean his fangs with your bones."

The door to the Iron Room shut on Little Gem and her perilous new companion with a deafening slam. Tucking her hands deep into her robe's pockets—it didn't hurt to be too cautious as she was rather fond of her fingers, after all—Little Gem hid behind her pile of pillows and studied the monster. He stared back at her with equally curious amber eyes.

"*I* stole ten bushels of ripe summer pears," the dragon said, licking his dagger-length fangs with a satisfied smack. "That's how I got caught in the king's trap in the royal orchard. But what did a wee damsel like yourself do to get thrown into this fancy dungeon?" he asked.

Her pillows scattered as Little Gem stood up and glared at the dragon. "I am no prisoner, I *live* here. I am the princess of this castle, beast!" She grabbed a tiara hanging from the horns of a marble faun and crowned herself just to prove her point. Yet her hands clenched into fists as she wondered if the sly monarch hadn't tricked her, too, trapping her in the Iron Room with fine promises of being his fair princess.

The dragon snorted. "Well, you have very coarse manners for a princess; my name is 'Emeril,' not beast."

Little Gem's cheeks burned. "Forgive me, Emeril. I haven't always been a princess, only since I started spitting jewels." Coughing once, she spat up an oval Wednesday ruby in her palm. "Would you like one? I've heard that dragons are particularly fond of shiny things."

"That's very kind of you, but I fear my treasure hoarding days are over." Emeril curled his body in tight winding circles until he was one big scaly ball. "King Wulfram has decreed a glorious tournament tomorrow! Knights from all corners of the kingdom will joust in noble combat, and the champion will win the chance to slay a legendary monster at noon." The dragon gave a mournful sigh. "I suppose that's *me*."

"How dare King Wulfram make such cruel sport of you!" Little Gem said. She vowed never to give the king one measly gem ever again—or to let a knight harm a single scale on Emeril.

"No one may slay you if *I* free you first," Little Gem said. Seizing one of the many jewel-encrusted swords lining the walls, she hacked at the dragon's cage with all her strength, but her blows left only scratches in the strong black iron.

"You made a valiant effort," Emeril said after her seventh blade chipped and cracked, "but perhaps it's time to admit the truth: nobody ever rescues a dragon." A tiny flame slipped from his left eye and snuffed into cinders. "It simply isn't done."

A rebellious thought hardened inside Little Gem's heart, no bigger than the millet seed that once was her name: *Why not?*

When the guards came for Emeril in the morning, Little Gem stuck her nose in the air and pretended she was quite glad to be rid of her reptilian companion. But she hid a smile as their armor gave her an idea. The instant the lock on the Iron Room twisted tight, Little Gem ransacked every corner of the treasury for everything a knight might wear—a silver helmet, golden gauntlets, a lion-embossed breastplate and a wide-bladed broadsword. Her search took hours as only chain mail hammered by the hands of Faerie Folk had spells in the metal that would shrink it to fit her size. Donning her mismatched suit of armor, Little Gem stood by the door and waited for Ole Maid Gertie to bring her luncheon plate. She held her breath as the door unlocked barely ten minutes before noon.

"I brought toasted buns and cheese curds today!" the old woman said. She shuffled over the threshold and blinked in puzzlement. "Poppet?"

Little Gem slid swiftly behind her and slipped into the hallway. Dread pushed her feet faster as she wondered—was there still enough time to save Emeril from the despicable knights? Servants and nobles shot her odd glances as the short and strangely armored warrior clanked past them, but no guards stopped Little Gem as the helmet hid her face. She dragged her broadsword behind her as she followed the cheers of the tournament crowd to the courtyard.

Tapping the nearest man on the shoulder, Little Gem lowered her voice to a gruff pitch. "Where do I enter the tournament, Sir?"

"You're too late," the man said, pointing forward. "The champion kills the foul beast now!"

Chains fastened to rings in the ground kept Emeril trapped at the center of the courtyard. A knight with an ostrich-plumed helmet stood with his sword raised over the dragon's neck.

"*Stop!*" Little Gem commanded. Dropping the heavy sword, she pushed past the crowd and charged the knight. She tossed aside her helmet as the hard, stubborn shine inside her heart swelled and rose upwards to push against her teeth. She spat it out with all her strength and a radiant stone the size of an acorn smacked the knight's hand.

Relief filled her as he dropped his sword, but Little Gem froze as every gaze swung to the mismatched knight who had spat a flawless diamond with the force of a sling shot.

King Wulfram's eyes bulged with fury. "Get back to the Iron Room at once, Little Gem!" he bellowed.

"No." The girl spat another diamond lightning-quick that knocked the legs from the king's seat and sent him tumbling into the dirt. "That is not my name anymore. I am the Diamond-Spitting Knight!"

Turning to the dragon, she spat something bright and sharp as a star. Her diamond's aim was true and shattered his silver collar. Emeril shot a fire bolt that melted his shackles into a boiling puddle. Bursting free with a roar, he dove straight at the girl.

"Are you done playing princess?" he asked.

"Quite," she said.

Emeril dropped her between his wings. Together, the Diamond-Spitting Knight and dragon soared off on an adventure entirely of their own making.

Amélie's Guardian
Bryan Thomas Schmidt

Long ago in a land known as Glendon, there lived a young girl, whose name was Amélie. Her mother was a seamstress and her father was a soldier, a Captain in the Kingdom Guard, who'd been seven moons at war. They lived in a small village on the banks of the mighty River Rhi, surrounded by woods. They led a quiet life of farming and simple trades, far from the capitol.

Her mother's name was Mara, and her father's name was Ramon. Mara and Amélie had huddled together as Ramon and his men rode out one fateful day, straight down the main street, amidst the straw roofed cottages. Their horses whinnied with excitement as the villagers felt the vibration of their pounding hooves, and choking clouds of dust rose up, carried on the Autumn breeze.

Amélie buried her face in her mother's well-worn apron, her shoulder rising and falling to the rhythm of her sobs. Her mother kept a brave face, but Amélie knew she was worried, too. Late at night, as she lay restless, Amélie heard her mother's own sobs through the thin walls of their cottage.

The village itself, Tallerive, had not known conflict in many years and the surrounding woods were known to be safe and quiet. To keep her daughter occupied and avoid her sitting around worrying, Mara sent Amélie out each morning on a daily quest. One day might be to gather berries in the nearby woods, another to pick up freshly fallen apples. Amélie delivered eggs to the inn and gathered cloth from the weaver's. All the while Mara stayed home to feed the chickens, work on her sewing, and kept the cottage clean.

On one of these quests I met Amélie. I'd been watching her for a long while and found her intriguing. Her blonde curls bounced as she walked which was a kind of rhythmic loping with a spring in her steps. Her demeanor was one of curiosity and playfulness, yet I detected a sadness beneath it, echoed in her brown eyes. It touched me. She looked lonely, and that was something I understood well.

For years, I had occupied a mountaintop near the village, but because I never bothered the village, the humans never came to trouble me. I rarely approached humans because of their reaction. Adult humans would scream and hurl rocks or spears when I got too close.

But Amélie was a wee child, and except for worry about her father, she seemed quite fearless. My heart ached for her on the times I glimpsed her sobbing beneath the apple trees. Other times she talked or sang to herself as she gathered the fruit. Her lilting voice was a delight to my ears.

I chose to meet her one day atop a hill beside the apple trees. I went early, for Amélie always came mid-morning, and I wanted time to prepare so I could present myself well. I heard her singing first as she approached. The gentle wind seemed to amplify it somehow through the woods. I could make out every syllable long before I heard her feet rustling in the fallen leaves and brush.

In a few moments, she bounced into view. I saw her golden locks first, then her silky white skin and red cheeks. She began gathering the apples lying at the base of the trees. She seemed in better spirits than I'd seen her previously.

As she worked her way through the trees, I considered again how best to make my presence known. My kind are not known for their subtlety, of course, but at the same time, startling her didn't seem wise. So, as she continued singing and gathering, I decided to join her song. I'd heard her repeat the refrain several times already, so I waited until she finished the verse she was on, cleared my throat as softly as I could, and joined her on the refrain.

My voice, I'll admit, was rough from disuse. I lived alone atop a mountain, after all. Nonetheless, it wasn't the total disaster I'd feared. It took a few moments for her to realize she was no longer singing alone. As soon as she did, she stopped and whirled around, her eyes searching, until finally they found their way to the top of the hill.

Finishing the refrain's last line alone, I curved my lips into smile, taking care not show my sharp teeth lest I frighten her. I didn't speak, wanting to be sure I said the right thing. I feared she would run away, but her eyes never showed the fear which was most human's normal reaction. Instead, her head tilted slightly as her eyes took me in, and she set down her basket, She stepped closer to get a better view.

"You're a dragon, aren't you?"

I nodded, the smile frozen on my long narrow snout.

"Are you going to eat me?"

I shook my large head. "No."

"In my uncle's stories, dragons either eat you or burn you," Amélie said, her face twisting in a quizzical way as she thought. "You don't look so scary to me."

I laughed, relieved. I couldn't help myself, but the sheer volume made her step back toward the woods, looking as if she might run. "No, I won't eat you, I promise. I came here to meet you."

"Meet me?" She stepped forward again, clearly intrigued. "Why?"

"I've been watching you for some time now. You're quite fascinating."

She shook her head, an amused smile crossing her face. "I'm just a little girl."

"Yes, and I'm just an old dragon, but still, I find you interesting."

Amélie laughed, a charming high pitched sound which warmed my heart. The sound was filled with joy and a sense of freedom I longed to know, as if she had not a care in the world. Oh to know such freedom! I was rapt with fascination.

"What's your name?" Amélie started slowly climbing the grassy hillside toward me.

"My name is hard to translate into human," I told her, trying to come up with something she could understand. "You can call me whatever you'd like," I finally said.

She smiled as she stopped beside me, then moved slowly around, examining me without fear. "You're very green, you know. And very big, too." She crinkled her nose. "You smell funny, too."

"I smell like all dragons, I suppose." I tried not to be offended, reminding myself she meant no harm. Besides, she smelled odd to me, too.

"Perhaps I should name you something grand." She put a finger on her mouth thinking.

I smiled, liking the sound of it. I wasn't familiar with human names, but I hoped it was grand. "I like that."

Amélie giggled. Her face took on a serious look. "I think I shall name you Johannes. Okay? "

"Johannes?" I thought it over, trying it on for size. It did sound somewhat regal to me, very formal and proper it seemed. "Okay, Johannes it is."

She nodded with approval and smiled again. "My name is Amélie. I'm from Tallerive. Do you know it?"

I nodded and smiled back. "Indeed. I live atop the Mount to the East."

"Shadow Mount?"

So that's what the humans called it! As I considered the meaning I remembered it did cast shadows over their village in late morning, before the sun rose to its afternoon peak and started its descent. "Shadow Mount, yes." I nodded.

"Is it scary? Father and Mother told me stories of large creatures and people who disappeared there long ago." She shuddered at the memory of them.

My mind raced to find words I could tell her which wouldn't make her fear me. Dangerous creatures dwelled there—direwolves and bats and trolls—and the few human adventurers who'd tried to climb it usually died at the hands of one or the other. Only one had made it to the top and confronted me but that had been long in the past. I'd meant to spare him but he came at me with a sword, and I'd had to defend myself. The stench of burning flesh haunted my memory causing me to cringe. I'd always tried to live in peace with the world around me. It gave me no pleasure watching him die.

"It's been my home for many generations," I explained. "It's not scary to me, but there are creatures about who might do harm to someone like you."

Her lower lip curled up over its companion a moment, then she shook her head and spread her legs in a defiant stance. "I'm not afraid. My daddy would protect me." She paused, her eyes turning sad and looked at her feet. "If he were here."

My heart melted at seeing her pain. I wanted to reach out and comfort her, but one of my hands was twice her size and I feared crushing her by accident, so I sat where I was.

"He's gone to war," she told me, not knowing I already knew. Sadness darkened her face like a shadow. "But he's coming back to visit soon. My Mother got a letter today." At the mention of it, her smile returned and she did a little dance, sending her brown skirt fluttering around her long, skinny legs.

I laughed as I watched her. Such a delightful sight to behold. "You miss him a lot."

She nodded, glancing back at her apples. "I have to go back soon. My Mother will worry. She's waiting to make fresh apple pie." Her tongue slid quickly across her lips at the mention of it. From her face I could see it was something delicious. "But I enjoyed meeting you, Johannes."

"I enjoyed meeting you, too, Amélie."

"Will I see you again?"

"I hope so," I said as I watched her turn and bounce back down the hill the way she'd come. She went straight to her basket and picked it up, glancing back at me with a smile before returning to her gathering.

We visited daily from then on. I landed in a glen near the berry bushes or a brook near the path to the weaver's; somewhere close to wherever she was headed for the day. I made sure to avoid other villagers or their animals. Drawing too much attention would put an end to our visits, and Amélie appeared to enjoy them as much as I did. In fact, since we'd met, I hadn't seen her sob in the woods once. It was as if somehow my companionship made her feel less alone. I know my time with her had that effect on me. Both of us enjoyed each other's company, the only difficulty being the times she begged me to take her for a flight.

"What's it like to fly?"

"It's freeing." It was all I could think of.

"I wish I could fly." She looked up toward the puffy white clouds with a dreamy look. "It must be wonderful."

"It is until . . ." I stopped. Perhaps she was too young to know the dark truth of her people's relations with my kind.

"Until what?" Her eyes held the sense of wonder common to all younglings. Wide and brown, they looked at me as if I were the core of wisdom. It was impossible to resist them, as much as I tried.

"Sometimes people see me and they become afraid." I watched her for a reaction. "They try and attack me."

Her eyes watered and she ran toward me, wrapping her arms around my lower arm. It was so large her outstretched arms could only stretch part way around. "Why would anyone want to hurt you? You're so kind."

I closed my eyes at the warmth of her body pressed against mine. She softly stroked my scales.

"Your scales are soft," she said in wonder. "They look so hard."

I smiled. "They're my protection against enemies. They hold up very well when I need them, but they're like my skin, Amélie."

She smiled as she caressed them. "I like them." She stepped back so our eyes met. "Take me flying with you, Johannes!"

Fearing she might fall, I politely refused her. "I'm sorry. I can't."

"I'll be careful, I promise. Just a little flight. Not even very high. I want to know what it's like."

Each time I refused from then on, she had the same sad eyed expression she'd had whenever she spoke of her father. After several tries, she turned away and looked back down the hill toward her village. "Friends do things for each other," she half accused.

My heart ached to fulfill her wish, but how would she hold on? I couldn't risk it. I didn't know what to say, and, after a few heartbeats, she simply started her bouncing lope down the hill, not looking back at me, as she usually did when we parted.

The next day, she returned to her old self, running to hug me when she saw me in the glen near the berries. She chased me as I hopped and skipped just out of reach, using my wings for short bursts of flight, making her laugh and laugh as she kept trying to outsmart me. In the end, I let her catch me, and the joy on her face gave me a happiness I had never known. My life as a dragon had been so lonely. Amélie was the first true friend I'd had since I was a youngling, and had other dragons as my companions. I thought of her like family, although I tried to guard my heart.

As the day approached for her father's expected arrival, the energy radiating from Amélie grew more and more joyful. It felt as if all her cares had suddenly vanished. She spoke often of her father—how he used to tell her stories as he tucked her in at night, stories of knights and castles and princesses and battles. She knew her daddy was as brave as the men in those stories. She spoke of him as gentle and kind and wise and honorable. Hearing her describe him, I wished I could meet him, but then I remembered my previous encounters with human adults which hadn't turned out well.

It made me sad to only share a small part of her world. I'd grown quite fond of her and she of me. But Amélie herself seemed to enjoy our secret friendship. It was something of her own she didn't have to share with anyone, she said once. She called me her best friend, her guardian, making me promise I would look out for her until her father came home. I always promised when she said it, although I started worrying her father's arrival might bring an end to our encounters.

Finally, the week came for her father's homecoming. I watched from the woods as she and her mother waited anxiously outside their cottage. Smoke rose from the chimney and I smelled the scent of fresh baked bread, a smell I always associated with the village.

Her mother kept busy sweeping and doing laundry, but Amélie sat patiently on a wooden bench, watching the road, her eyes anxious and excited. I sniffed the wind, searching for a scent of human sweat and approaching horses. For several daylight hours I kept vigil with her. But no one came.

Her mother's face grew more and more concerned, her eyes darkening with worry as her face dropped into a frown. She went behind the house twice, wiping tears on her stained apron where Amélie couldn't see her. And finally, as the sun arced overhead, preparing to start its descent in the west, she called Amélie to her, handed her a basket and motioned toward the woods.

I found her near the apple trees, landing on the hill where we'd first met. She paid me no attention, sniffling as she gathered apples, her shoulders drooping, her eyes fixed on the ground near her feet. I ached with all my heart to reach out and comfort her, but the trees kept me from drawing near, and it seemed obvious she wanted to be left alone.

As she returned to the village, the basket half-full, I made a decision and launched myself with a running start. I soared high amongst the clouds, following the road leading from the village, the route she'd told me her father would come. The wind caressed me as I soared, a pleasant feeling I always enjoyed. I flew what seemed like a long time, but, from the sun's lack of movement, I could tell little had passed. I heard them before I saw them—the sharp clash of swords, the high screams of horses. I could smell their sweat and hear their shouting. I knew the sounds of battle and willed my wings to move more swiftly.

I found them at a crossroads, fighting face to face, dozens of companions dying all around. Her father looked tired and older than I remembered him. I knew then their fighting had been long and terrible. He and one of his soldiers stood outnumbered by the enemy, who had three archers on horseback firing at them from a rise, while five others surrounded them with swords.

One of the enemies, who appeared to the leader, raised his arm and his men stopped waiting. "If you surrender now, your lives will be spared," the leader shouted.

"If we surrender now, our lives are worthless," Amélie's father answered. "Honor and glory to the King!" He raised his sword and his companion did likewise.

The enemy soldiers laughed. "Your honor will be your end," the enemy leader responded. He lowered his arm and his men moved in.

Swords clanged and men grunted. I could see Amélie's father was exhausted and could barely lift his sword. His companion took a sword through the stomach and fell to his knees, his life's blood watering the parched dirt.

They needed me! Swooping down from behind, I blasted the archers with fire from my mouth. They shrieked as their clothes caught fire and uselessly tried to escape into the woods. I continued down toward the others. Spotting me, the enemy soldiers yelled and swung their swords over their heads in desperation, ducking as I flew past. I turned my head and blasted two of the enemies with flames. I then swung back up to circle around.

As I came in the second time, I saw some of the enemy mounting their horses. Apparently they'd done the damage they intended and had no desire to stick around and fight a dragon as well. Amélie's father collapsed in a heap, as if his legs could no longer hold him. I dropped down and landed nearby. He turned his head toward me, his face showing resignation to whatever fate might bring.

"I have no strength left to fight you dragon," he said. "I'm at your mercy."

I looked him over, trying to decide what to do. Then I took a running start, reaching down to grab him with my talons. I arched back up into the clouds, returning the way I'd come toward Tallerive where my sweet friend would be waiting. He relaxed in my grip, hanging there as if he'd fallen asleep, but I glanced down once and saw his eyes examining me.

As I flew, my mind raced, trying to decide how I could return him to Tallerive without raising alarms. If I left him in the woods, Amélie and her mother wouldn't know to find him there. But if I took him to the village, the men might attack me on sight. In the end, I knew I had no choice, so I flew over the village once, before I came in for landing on the main road near his family's cottage.

Two women removing clothes from a line screamed and ran as they saw me, calling for their husbands. I set Amélie's father gently on the dirt and prepared to take off again as Amélie and her mother appeared in their doorway. Her mother's face filled with fear as she saw me standing over her husband, but Amélie brightened, her face lighting up with a smile as she ran toward me. Her mother and father both called for her to stop, but she didn't listen. She embraced her fallen father.

His arms wrapped around her. I heard men shouting as they came up the road. I had only moments before they'd arrive to engage me, so I smiled at Amélie as she hugged her father.

She looked up at me, tears streaming down her face. "Thank you, Johannes. I love you."

I choked back my own tears as I nodded and ran up the road, launching myself into the air.

I heard her father ask: "Who's Johannes?" behind me as I disappeared over the trees into the woods, heading for my mountain home.

For the next week, I saw Amélie only from a distance. She did her usual chores, but I kept my distance for fear the adults might be nearby to protect her from me. It was always the same, in every town, with every race of humans. Dragons were feared and hated—the enemy. No matter how she explained it, they'd never understand. I had to prepare myself for the loss of her companionship. I hoped I was wrong, but I had to be ready.

"Johannes! Where are you?"

Her voice echoed through the trees and cut through my fears like a sword through flesh. I circled down in an arc toward the glen near the berries. It sounded like her voice had come from there and my nose detected the scent of humans. I peered through the trees trying to spot those golden locks, but with the first snowfall, the canopy was layered in white, covering the gaps in the trees.

Setting aside my worry, I swung down and landed in the glen near my usual spot. As I turned toward the now bare trees, Amélie came racing toward me, a thick shawl wrapped around her shoulders. Her curls bounced as bounded toward me and smiled with delight.

She swung her arms around my neck as she reached me, caressing my scales. "I missed you, Johannes!"

"I missed you, too." And then I saw them. Her parents stepped out from behind the thick trunks to watch us cautiously.

Sensing my concern, Amélie stepped back to look me in the eye. "It's all right. They came here to meet you. I told them all about us." She patted my neck. "Don't be afraid."

As she waved at them, her parents approached with trepidation. "You saved my life, dragon," her father said as he drew near.

I nodded. "Your family needs you."

"We're so grateful," Amélie's mother wiped moisture from her eyes.

"It is I who am grateful. For the friendship of your daughter."

Her father smiled. "Dragons and humans are not known to be friends."

"Johannes is a good dragon," Amélie said. "He's my guardian." She smiled at us, as if dragons and humans should always have been friends

The adults and I laughed.

"We know that, dear." Her mother tousled Amélie's hair as she placed an arm around her shoulders.

"But he never let me fly with him." Amélie frowned.

"It's quite amazing," her father teased.

"No fair!"

Her parents and I shared a laugh again.

"I don't want you to fall and my talons might crush you."

"I have an idea about that," her father said. "Meet us here tomorrow."

The next day, they returned with a leather horse harness her father had modified. It fit Amélie securely and had a handle where I could clasp on with my talons and carry her safely. Their confidence amazed me. "You would trust me with her life?"

"You proved trustworthy with mine." Her father nodded as he finished helping Amélie into the harness. Lovingly, he snapped the last fitting and made sure her shawl was secure around her. "Everything is fine," he reassured Mara, who stood nearby, looking slightly worried.

Amélie smiled, then hurried over beside me, waving. "Come on! I'm ready!"

"As you wish, little one."

And with that I lifted off, hovering just above the ground as her father rushed in, ducked underneath and held the harness handle up so I could grasp it. My talons closed tightly around it and I tugged gently. It moved with me.

With a nod from her father and wave from her mother, I took off, carrying Amélie into the clouds. She laughed with delight, pointing at the village as she saw it beneath us. She pointed at the mountain I called home, at the river, and the hill where we'd met. I told her stories about all of them, recollections from the hundreds of years I'd lived here. When she grew quiet, I guessed perhaps she was overwhelmed. I flew in silence, letting her ponder what she'd heard and seen.

I returned her safely after a daylight hour to where her parents waited in the glen. Our daily visits resumed after that, and although she occasionally brought her parents, mostly she came alone.

Long ago in a land known as Glendon, there lived a girl, whose name was Amélie. Her mother was a seamstress and her father was a soldier, and her best friend was a dragon.

She came to see him every day, introducing him to her husband before they married, and bringing her children to play with him. As she grew, their relationship transitioned from mere companionship to a sort of mentoring.

The loneliness which had once haunted the dragon was never known again. Even the villagers welcomed him with open arms, calling him "Amélie's Guardian." Their friendship became legendary. He became part of the family, and he protected the girl and her village for all of his days.

Aer'Vicus
Jodi L. Milner

Deep within the rich earth, under layers of rock and mineral, beyond the understanding of the men who dwelt above, slept Phaedra, the red dragon. The marbled walls of her immense cavern had been blasted smooth with the heat and the fire of the dragons who had come before. Veins of rose quartz threaded around and through the walls, pulsing with the beat of the dragon's heart. In the center of the cavern stood an immense shining pillar of rose quartz.

Century after century, Phaedra the Red had protected the settlement that turned to village, that turned to town, that turned to city, that turned to the gleaming prince among cities, the citadel of Chalsis. Century after century, she listened to the trembles of the earth, the vibrations of the air, and the whispers of the stones above her, ensuring that the harmonies of life blended properly, and all was well.

Until it wasn't. A dulling, a dimming of the earth's vibrations, shook her from her pleasant dreaming. Something had changed, something small, something large. The great red dragon breathed onto the wide fire-polished stone floor and summoned a spell. Magic wove into the veins of crystal and gathered before her into a hovering sphere. She peered into the sphere and saw her city, far above her. Bright white marbled cathedrals and tall proud libraries were flanked by pockets of green. Gardens filled with statues and walkways rested peacefully as they breathed in the warm spring air and soaked in the early morning light. Still, the errant vibration, the wrongness buzzed in Phaedra's ear like a gnat.

She studied the sphere, following the path of wrongness, the trail of misaligned noise, of disharmonious music, until she reached the wide circle marking the citadel's heart. The proud glowing crystal Aer'Vicus rose up from its centermost point. It was the very same crystal that stretched its roots reached deep into the ground and pierced the center of her cavern. Aer'Vicus had stood long before the druids had wandered in the deep forests, long before memory.

Aer'Vicus's song had changed. No longer did the great crystal vibrate in tune with the earth. The two melodies now fought against each other and the crystal grew weaker because of it. Should Phaedra allow it to continue, the great crystal would fracture and shatter. Phaedra's cavern would collapse. The gleaming citadel of Chalsis would crumble and fall.

Within her mind, a fragment of memory stirred from a thousand years before, dull and half forgotten. The crystal required a sacrifice and it was Phaedra's legacy to complete the task. Another memory floated to the surface, this one broken into pieces like a dry leaf crumpled inside a fist. She could not do this alone, her own rumbling vibration that sung with the earth had changed when Aer'Vicus had changed. The raw edges of her melody ached where a part had been torn away.

In the distance, the piece of broken melody called to her, wanting to return. The vision within the sphere led her deep within the library, behind the long dusty shelves of scrolls and leather-bound tomes, across the beautiful hand-tiled floors, to an alcove lit by a single candle. There she saw a girl bent over an ancient crumbling book. A smudge of ink stained her chin and cheek. A paper filled with line after line of tidy notes rested under her outstretched hand.

The girl lay fast asleep, still clutching a quill in her delicate hand. A dark drop of ink dripped from its sharp tip onto the table. Her unnaturally white hair spilled around her head in a halo. Embedded within the girl's heart, Phaedra's missing melody sang a mournful tune.

Awake, girl. Come to me.

Within the sleeping girl's dream, words echoed, entering her mind like a worm. Like a summons. A deep stirring, unlike one she had ever heard or felt before, vibrated within her, ringing her bones with their song. And with it, the stern face and long pointed nose of a great red dragon.

Ianthe bounded awake, gasping and reeling. The weight of the solid marble bench kept her from tipping backward to the floor. A sheen of drool had worked its way under her face. She rubbed the wet off with an ink-stained sleeve and blinked. Something had woken her. She blinked again, trying to grasp the wisps of the dream already slipping away, a red dragon, an urgent need, breaking, discordant music, and bitter melancholy. She struggled to make sense of it.

The open tome before her related the history of the city, of the origins of the ancient buildings and their eccentric architects. Her task was to find evidence of secret rooms and passages between the five massive structures that ringed the citadel's central plaza and shining rose-colored obelisk. There, in the detailed margins of the book, mostly filled with ivy and birds, hid a carefully detailed red dragon. She wiped the nib of her quill and set back to work. The library warden, Master Timon, demanded she finish before the end of the day. Lord Kyril of Stormhold had waited long enough for the answer to his query, and patrons like him kept her fed and kept her candles lit.

Come to me, Ianthe.

The sound in her head rang as clear as the iron bells hanging in the tower of the Cathedral on the opposite side of the great circular plaza, mixed with the rough grating of one heavy stone being dragged over another. It pulled at her, lifting her to her feet, guiding her through the long shelves of the library, across the cupolaed study hall filled with color from the ring of stained-glass windows high above, and past the head librarian's book-stacked desk. Master Timon hunched over a book no larger than his palm with his glasses perched on the tip of his abnormally long nose. His many layers of sweaters, cloaks, and scarves poked out at all angles like feathers, making him appear like a long-legged, long-billed water bird, all bones and beak. She prayed he wouldn't notice her passing.

Come to me.

Again, the voice drew her through the looming doors of the library and tugged her down the stairs and into the great circle. It guided her steps, leading her around to the garden space stretching between the library and the House of Justice. Within the garden, a white marble statue of a dragon, with its wings outstretched and its eyes shining, stood tall in the center of a trickling fountain.

She stopped in front of the statue, taking in its terrible majesty, its noble wisdom. "It is you who called me, great statue?"

The statue said nothing.

Come, child.

The pull came once more, guiding her past the fountain and the statue and down a narrow footpath that wound between arching beech and alder trees. It plunged deeper into the wilder, untamed garden, through choking bushes to a small clearing no wider than her outstretched arms. A wall covered in moss and ivy bordered the far end. Between strands of ivy, a marble dragon's head peeked out. A stream of water bubbled from its mouth and poured into a scalloped basin. Again, the pull guided her steps. She pushed past an overgrown cypress to the area behind the wall where she uncovered a narrow opening and a set of equally narrow stairs.

The pull led her down dark, twisting stairs deeper and deeper until she could no longer see. She pressed her hand against the rough dry wall beside her to keep from losing her balance on the stairs as she plunged ever deeper into the earth.

The base of the stairs opened into a small empty chamber where the air hung heavy with dust and a sharp smell Ianthe didn't recognize. She followed a small trail of light, shining from an unknown source ahead. The small chamber opened into a vast cavern, so big that Ianthe hugged her arms to her chest to not feel so small. A crystal shaft stood tall and domineering before her in the center of the space, larger than her imagination allowed. She hugged her arms tighter and stepped closer, again drawn by an invisible thread. Glowing crystal flowed away from the top and bottom of the crystal pillar like the branches and roots of a great tree and spread across the floor and up the walls in intricate rings and graceful knots.

The color of the crystal triggered a vision of the grand plaza somewhere high above her. It couldn't be, surely this wasn't the same crystal as the great Aer'Vicus that stretched from the center of the plaza to the sky.

A dry sliding rattle echoed from the shadows on the far side of the chamber, along with a sound that reminded her of the great heaving bellows in the iron works where Master Timon had once taken her. A great scaled head shifted, not ten paces from where she stood, and a great glowing amber eye opened and blinked.

"Hello, little one," the same granite scraping voice from her dream greeted her.

"Impossible." Ianthe tripped and fell to the smooth glassy floor as she retreated away from the dragon's massive head with its knife-like teeth and hungry tongue. The hard edges of the mournful song within her softened in the presence of the dragon and grew quiet and content.

The dragon regarded her carefully with its golden eye. "You feel it, don't you? There is a rightness when we are close. Don't be afraid. I'm called Phaedra."

Ianthe crossed her legs beneath the fabric of her loose-fitting dress. While the cavern wasn't cold, being in the presence of this great dragon sent shivers through her. "I am Ianthe." She bowed her head.

"You have been schooled by the masters themselves, spending your time in the histories, and had your nose embedded in books. Have you read of me? Of my ancestors?"

Ianthe thought carefully, fearful that an incorrect answer might anger the great beast. "There's not much in the histories about dragons." She swallowed. "I'm sorry."

"Pity." The immense head gave an imperceptible nod, seen only in the eyes and the slightest dip of the jaw. "This great city has stood for thousands of years, far longer than any city in existence. Have you ever wondered why?"

The presence of the great crystal pillar captured Ianthe's attention. She imagined it thrusting up through the earth to where its tip breached the center of the plaza. "The Citadel of Chalsis has never been defeated, never seen the ravages of war. Its citizens have protected it and preserved it."

"Oh, the arrogance." The dragon rolled her eyes and huffed. "This city is protected by more than the efforts of man. This obelisk contains the power to repel ill, war mongers, plagues, pestilence, and tremors. It strengthens the walls, firms the foundations, and keeps the fresh waters flowing." The mighty beast shook her head and exhaled through her nose. The warm blast tossed Ianthe's pale hair.

"Why have you summoned me? Why am I here?" Ianthe asked, feeling small and highly edible near the immense dragon.

"The Aer'Vicus is weakening." Phaedra lifted a taloned claw and gently wiped the side of the column. A smear of glittering fragments stuck to her scales. "I cannot strengthen it alone. Its song has changed. If something is not done, this fair city will fall to ruin."

Ianthe uncurled from where she was sitting and approached the glowing pillar. She placed her palm against it and for a moment thought she heard strained harsh tones. "That can't be true. Everyone knows Aer'Vicus is eternal, unchanging. Priests pray to it morning and night. At the feast of Mlinzi we leave offerings and raise our voices in song." She removed her hand from the pillar and studied it. Tiny flakes of crystal sparkled in the rosy light. Ianthe shook her head. If Aer'Vicus was not eternal, if it could fail, then everything she had built her life around could fail and fall as well. She felt as if she were falling, as if someone had shoved her from the highest peak of the looming spire of the cathedral. "I can see it, feel it even, but my mind does not want to accept it. It should be impossible."

"Sometimes the impossible happens. It's why I'm here. My task is to strengthen the crystal when the time comes." Her voice grew softer. "That time is here, but I don't know how." Phaedra lowered her head. "In this we are bound. I need you so together we can correct the imbalance and strengthen the crystal. I can't do it alone." Her burning golden eyes closed. "There is something in you, something special. I know you can feel it."

The dragon closed the gap between them and allowed the tip of her nose to brush Ianthe's arm. The song that felt broken inside Ianthe when she stood alone felt whole here next to the dragon. They were as two pieces of a puzzle, meant to be together.

"I'll go back to my master, tell him what's happening. Maybe he will know what must be done."

Phaedra bowed her head. "Go then, but be quick. Each passing hour the crystal's song grows more desperate."

She found Master Timon in his tiny cluttered office, perched on a tall stool to reach the top of the stack of books piled one on top on another. A thick layer of dust obscured the titles on the spines. Ianthe stifled a sneeze that threatened to erupt. She told him about the dragon and the crystal. He listened on, expressionless and unamused as he searched through the volumes. He selected a slender volume from the stack and slid it out with great care before returning to his upholstered desk chair and sinking down into it. "I have no time or patience to deal with this dragon fantasy you've concocted to get out of your work." He studied the cover of the book in his hands. "I just had an exhausting discussion with Lord Kyril. You haven't finished your report for him yet."

Ianthe rested her forehead against the worn wood of the doorframe. "Please. You must believe me. I've never tried to get out of my work before. Why would I do it now?" She studied the palm of her hand for any trace of the glittering flakes she'd seen down in the cavern. Nothing.

"You've become a young woman. Perhaps a gentleman has captured your attention and you wanted to spend an afternoon with him." Master Timon peered at her from over the piles of books stacked on his desk with a twinkle in his eye. "How should I know what youth get up to these days?" He snatched his quill from its stand along with a sheet of paper. "Get the report for Lord Kyril done before nightfall and I won't have you scrub out the library's collection of inkwells."

She wanted to snatch the quill from his hands. "I'm telling you the truth. You must help me. There must be a book that talks about where the Aer'Vicus comes from, about dragons. Are you even curious in the least bit?" She leaned on her knuckles on the edge of his desk, being cautious to not disrupt any of the stacks of books. "Why won't you believe me?"

He cleared his throat. "Because you are a no one. You have no titles, no influential parents, no riches, no standing." He set down the quill and wove his fingers together over his feathered layers of clothes. "It's as if you are a mouse standing on a corner of the road squeaking as loudly as it can about the surprising lack of cheese in its life. No one listens because no one cares about the well-being of mice." He sighed and looked out the grimy window. "It's the same for you. No one cares about what you have to say."

His words withered her like a fallen leaf under the hot sun. As an abandoned child, she knew she was no one important. If it wasn't for Master Timon taking her in, she would have lived and died on the streets. He had served as the only parent she had ever known and a poor one at that. She knew her place; he didn't need to remind her, but the melancholy song haunted her thoughts. Phaedra needed her. "It doesn't matter what you think about me. What matters is that you help me find the information I need. Please, at least tell me if there is mention of where Aer'Vicus came from. I'll do the rest."

Master Timon adjusted the narrow spectacles that had slid down his long nose. "As much as I would like to believe you, none of the histories support your claims." His tone softened. "There isn't mention of a dragon beneath the stones, let alone one who can sense the state of our fair city. Put the matter out of your mind. This fascination of yours was all a dream." He tapped a sheet of paper perched on top of one of the piles of books. "Finish your report tonight or you'll have to answer to Lord Kyril personally."

"Yes, Master. Right away," she answered through clenched teeth. The dragon wasn't a dream, this song inside her wasn't imagined. She would search the library herself, the second she finished her duties, until she found something.

She returned to her alcove and cleaned the nib of her quill and quickly set to work copying passages and drawing conclusions as Master Timon had taught. Darkness came and plunged the pages before her into shadow. She lit her candle and continued to write.

Return, Ianthe.

One page remained, only one more until she finished her task. Ianthe pushed away the dragon's call and pressed on, scratching the quill across the paper faster, all while trying to keep her script neat enough that it could still be read. Rushing meant errors, and errors meant she would be punished. Master Timon would make her scrub the floors for a week or dust the endless shelves of books from top to bottom if there were too many.

Phaedra's call grew stronger, making her quill slip and scratch on the page. She cursed and wiped the nib clean once more. The dragon had been silent for hours and could surely wait another few minutes for her to finish. With a final neatly dotted period, she dusted the page to set the ink and blew it clean.

Come to me, Ianthe.

The call pulled her from her chair. She dashed, papers in hand, through the long, winding shelves and toward Master Timon's desk. He wasn't there. She hurried to his cramped office and found it empty. He couldn't have gone far, the large front doors had not been locked for the night.

A noise from outside caught her attention. A crowd gathered around the great Aer'Vicus. She pushed her way through, stomach sinking. Should the mighty crystal have already broken or crumbled to pieces, no force on earth could repair it. Master Timon stood in the center of the crowd next to the crystal, his hand resting on its shining surface.

Ianthe forced her way through the dozens of people separating her from the obelisk and her master. He opened his eyes and stared at her with a grunt. "During the evening devotion a piece came free from the base here." He opened his hand to reveal the tiniest piece of crystal, no bigger than a fingernail. "Come with me."

Phaedra's summons filled her mind, making her head feel as if it were splitting in two. "No. The dragon is calling me. I must go."

"What is this nonsense?" Master Timon glowered down at her.

"I must return to her." Ianthe gripped her head. "Do not try to stop me."

He pulled a dingy handkerchief from his pocket and tucked the tiny crystal fragment into it. "I'm coming with you."

This sudden change stopped Ianthe short. While her words had done nothing, the fleck of crystal in his pocket must have scared him. "Follow me." She hurried back through the winding garden and down the dark spiral stair.

"What took you so long, little one? Our time is fast running out. Splinters of the Aer'Vicus are beginning to rain down. What have you found?" Phaedra stood tall, her movements agitated and sharp, almost snakelike, as her neck twisted back and forth.

Master Timon shuffled into view, eyes suddenly wide, hands reaching for something solid to hold onto. "In all my years. The legends are really true." He gripped Ianthe's arm to steady himself before bowing low. "You must forgive me, Great Dragon. I didn't believe the girl."

Phaedra shuffled back, her claws raking the glasslike stone at her feet with a screech. She did not respond to Master Timon but spoke to Ianthe instead. "He doesn't belong here. He's not part of the music. He must be destroyed." Her eyes flashed dark and she opened her mouth wide. Blue flame curled in the back of her throat.

Ianthe jumped in front of Master Timon and spread her arms wide, blocking him with her body. "Stop! He might have the answer we are looking for," she shouted over the flailing mass of dragon. "I forbid you to roast him alive. We cannot succeed without him."

Master Timon didn't shrink back from Phaedra's display. If anything, it awakened his curiosity. "I assure you, I want to help, nothing more. Please don't cook me." The gleam of discovery shone in his eyes as he traced the rose-colored threads extending from Aer'Vicus and wrapping around the great subterranean vault.

Phaedra's noise and stomping caused more glittering flakes to fall like gentle snow. Tiny cracking noises filled the air. She calmed and settled on her haunches still breathing hard. "Forgive me, my fear got the best of me."

Master Timon approached the wide crystal pillar reverently, as a supplicant would approach deity. "It is forgiven. I haven't made things easier. I'm sorry."

Ianthe didn't dare break the quiet. While near Phaedra, their twin songs hummed in harmony together and were complete. Another tiny flake of crystal floated down from the lofty ceiling. Waiting wasn't an option. "How long do we have?"

The red dragon closed her eyes and sound filled the air, vibrating the soles of their feet. "A day, maybe two. Please hurry."

Master Timon led Ianthe through the wide halls of the library, oil lamp held high above his head. With each turn the halls grew narrower, unfamiliar. In the many years Ianthe lived in the great building, she had never been down this way. Judging from the chipped plaster and dusty cornices, no one else had either.

From deep within the lower levels of the library a new song filled Ianthe's mind. It pulled her and guided her much like Phaedra had done the first time Ianthe had been summoned.

Master Timon faltered at a junction of two identical hallways. "I know it's down here. My blasted memory is not what it used to be."

Ianthe didn't listen. Her feet followed the trail of song turn after turn until she was stopped by a door. On the door, in a piece of cunning carved relief, was a curled dragon. She set her hand on the door, searching for a knob or latch, but found none.

She rested her head against the carving, trailing a fingertip along the dragon's spine. "How do we open it?"

Master Timon patted at the pockets draped around him until he was rewarded with a jingle of metal keys. "Here, it has to be one of these."

Ianthe took the heavy ring, but when she returned her attention to the door, she found it was missing a keyhole as well. "No, it's something different." She leaned against the door, pressing her ear to hear the sound, feel the vibration of its song. As soon as she did, the door creaked inward and opened a fraction. She pushed harder, the scales of the relief biting into her palms, until it had opened enough for her to pass through.

"What is this place?" Ianthe asked as she entered the tiny room. Like in Phaedra's cavern, the walls curved into a circle. At the centermost point a white marble pillar held a single rose-colored crystal the length of Ianthe's forearm and about as thick. One end was pointed, much like the obelisk in the center of the great plaza.

Master Timon stayed in the doorway, not moving to set even a single foot into the space. "No one remembers when this came, it has always been here. I think it might have been here since before the great library was built over it."

The crystal continued its song, urging her to touch it, to pick it up. She brushed her finger against the smooth hard edges, the sharp point. A gentle glow shone beneath her hand and the crystal warmed under her touch. With the greatest care, she picked it up.

The vision came without warning, catching her in its grasp with such force she had to grab the edge of the pillar to keep her knees from buckling out from underneath her. In an instant, understanding washed over her. This process had happened before, girls like her had existed throughout time. Even before the city had been built, a temple of the dragon had been built around the rose obelisk by the druids who first found it. All the memories were there, locked into the crystal in Ianthe's hands.

She felt a rush of power awaken within her, a raw energy, a dragon energy. The vision opened to show her the girl who came before, Ianthe's predecessor. She watched on as the girl used the crystal to bond with the dragon and together, they formed a bond that strengthened the Aer'Vicus for another 1000 years. The vision took her breath away. She knew what had to be done, and how to do it. With the lesser crystal in hand, Ianthe made her way back to her dragon.

Master Timon rushed after her. "What is it, girl? What must be done?"

Ianthe didn't stop to talk to him, didn't dare. The knowledge the lesser crystal gave her filled her with such energy and fear she was afraid to stop and risk letting her nerves get the better of her. If so, she wouldn't be able to start again.

"You must tell me." He had fallen behind, his old creaky joints slowing him down.

Again, Ianthe could not answer. The weight of the crystal pulled her back to the dragon, to her fate, to her death. This would be the end of her and in a way, she had been prepared for it since her birth. Holding the crystal made it real. Master Timon needed to stop shouting at her, to be silent.

"You may watch, but do not interfere. The fate of the entire city depends on it." The words sounded hollow and distant in her own head.

Back in the cavern, Phaedra lifted her head as if a great weight held her down. "You found it. I felt it. Heard it. The song was so beautiful." Her eye shimmered with a tear. "Aer'Vicus returned my memories to me, as well as the memories of those who came before. Those memories hold me down, I can't bear it. I know what must be done."

Master Timon hung back in the smaller chamber leading in from the spiral stairway. Ianthe couldn't take time to explain. The wrongness of the vibrations filled her with unrest, with an itching that couldn't be scratched. The disharmony needed to me made right.

"May I see it?" Phaedra asked, lowering her great head. "May I see the lesser crystal?"

Ianthe held the long crystal in front of her. Another cracking filled the air, louder, and more insistent. Small stones fell from the ceiling, clattering on the glassy smooth floor. Master Timon drew back further into the safety of the smaller chamber, his stork-like outline barely visible.

Phaedra touched the crystal in Ianthe's outstretched hand with the tip of her nose and took a deep breath with her eyes closed, as if contact with the stone filled her with a greater awareness, with a sense of peace and solidarity. "You know what to do, don't be afraid."

Ianthe climbed astride the great dragon's back and crawled forward to where the head met the neck. In front of her, at the base of Phaedra's neck was an indentation and a series of missing scales. The crystal in Ianthe's hands grew warm in anticipation, the warmth spread up her arms and blossomed at the hollow in the back of her own neck. The warmth soon turned to fire, piercing Ianthe, and burning at her bones.

"Why do you hesitate? This must be. Waiting will prolong the agony for both of us." Phaedra's voice was breaking. Tremors shook her body and her breath came in tight gasps.

Ianthe set the point of the crystal against the center of the indentation. Phaedra held her breath, her muscles locking rigid in anticipation. The burning intensified. The stone in Ianthe's hands began to glow white, its heat too much for her hands. Aer'Vicus glowed white in response.

"Make the bond Ianthe. All will be well, I promise," Phaedra ordered. The words pierced Ianthe's mind.

With one confident motion, Ianthe clenched the stone and plunged it through the dragon's skin. The world turned white and stood still. The flecks of crystal raining down froze in place, and the bright light of the twin crystals filled the space, filled Ianthe, filled the dragon beneath her.

Ianthe clung to the crystal embedded in Phaedra head, knowing if she were to let go everything would fail, all would die, the city and the thousands living there would not see another morning. All turned to brilliant light, the stone, the pillar, the dragon, and Ianthe. The mark of the dragon spread down from the back of Ianthe's neck, down her arms, down her chest, her legs. Scales appeared. She was falling, flying, changing.

Phaedra's memories flowed through the crystal and became a part of Ianthe. As Ianthe grew, Phaedra changed, the vibrant red of her scales faded, resembling blood tinged water, matching the rose crystal, matching the floors and ceiling of the great chamber. The pulse of her heart echoed along the stone, echoed in the obelisk, echoed in the swirling and branching threads of crystal lacing through the walls and floor of the cavern.

A bright white stream of flame burst from Phaedra, heating the brilliant obelisk. Immense power flowed from her into the stone. The room grew hotter and hotter until Ianthe thought she would burn and turn to nothing.

She kept her hold on the lesser crystal even as her hands began to change into claws. Her awareness was dimming, there was too much heat, too much magic, too much sheer power flowing through the room. Phaedra's pulse beat within her, keeping her heart moving when Ianthe was sure it would fail.

Another jet of white flame, and another, and then the flecks of stone stopped falling. The room grew white hot and surged with the power pulsing between them.

Phaedra's deep red scales turned entirely white, and then even the whiteness began to fade until the pulsing glow of the crystal threads in the floor were visible through her. Another jet of white flame, weaker this time, lit the room. They were coming further and further apart. The white-hot glow of the walls cooled back to the swirls of glittering marble.

Still, the tones and vibrations clashed. Ianthe's task was not yet complete. She opened her maw and released a jet of white flame toward the great Aer'Vicus, marking it as hers. The flames wrapped around the crystal and shot along the webbing network of threads along the ceiling and floor. The discordant tones of the crystal, so wrong in her ears, realigned and straightened to once again form the tones of beautiful music of an earth well-tended, and a city well-protected. In her golden scaled claws she gripped the lesser crystal.

An immense fatigue struck Ianthe. Phaedra was gone, having fulfilled her destiny in giving her magic to the great crystal, and transforming Ianthe into the new guardian of Aer'Vicus. And yet, Phaedra was not gone, as her experience, her memories, and her life were now one with Ianthe.

Soft footsteps approached. Master Timon crept forward, his hands gripping one end of a scarf that worked loose. Ianthe yawned and tucked her wings around her. Her eyes refused to stay open.

"Sleep now, sweet Ianthe." He slipped the lesser crystal from her claws. "I'll keep this safe for you."

Loyalties

Josh Brown

I.

Jinari stood at full attention, back straight, chin down. Her hands were at her sides—her right hand resting on her thigh armor, her left palm lightly brushing over her leather scabbard. The armor she wore was a mix of items that were mostly pulled from dead bodies in the wake of battle.

Leader of her clan, the Kur-hik, a human tribe known for being skilled warriors in battle, Jinari didn't look particularly threatening herself. In fact, strip away the armor and weapons, and she might be mistaken for a nursemaid, a far cry from warrior and clan leader. Not at all athletic-looking, she had soft features, smooth skin, brown shoulder-length hair, round cheeks, caring eyes, and a warm smile. The softness continued down her body, which was quite womanly, with gentle, round curves, enough to make any male, no matter his race, linger his stare. The only things about her that were not soft were her feet, which had known countless days of travel throughout her life, and her hands, which had gripped many a weapon in many a battle throughout her life.

Jinari stood in front of Gar-Dum, an Orc, and the leader of the Vulgar-kin. Gar-Dum was High Orc Chieftain of the Empire of the Black Moon banner, and had succeeded in bringing together the strongest clans of the trolls, goblins, giants, and "evil" men, Jinari's clan among them. He was old, but still very capable, and still able to defeat giants and trolls in one-on-one combat rather easily. He sat upon a stone throne on a rigid platform, brownish-green trolls on either side of him, his personal bodyguards.

Gar-Dum's head and face were completely hairless, and he wore no crown, helm, or any other type of headdress. Gar-Dum was missing his right ear, presumably lost in combat of some sort, and the remaining ear was so notched and ragged it looked to be only half there. He wore only a fur loincloth and boots, presumably made of the same fur. He slouched in his throne, as if this whole affair was of little interest to him. A human female, wearing nothing but a thin, white slip of fabric wrapped around her waist, glided up the stairs and handed him a dark chalice. It looked to be iron, but Gar-Dum held it as if it were a feather. He took a sip, and addressed Jinari.

"I need you to travel to the eastern caverns," he said, tilting the chalice in his hand, still seemingly disinterested.

"Yes, Lord Gar-Dum," Jinari bowed slightly. She waited for him to say more, but he did not. "May I inquire on the nature of the mission, my Lord?"

Gar-Dum looked up from his chalice and met Jinari's eyes. A chill shot down her back. She stood perfectly still, doing her best to resist the urge to shudder.

"There is a weapon in the caverns," Gar-Dum said. "If found by the Man-kin it could be used against us. I need you to find it, and destroy it."

"My Lord," Jinari said, "the eastern caverns have quite extensive tunnels, and having never traveled there myself, I am not familiar with its layout."

"Not to worry," Gar-Dum said, waving his hand dismissively. "I have arranged for a guide to travel with you."

As if on cue, a stunted, grotesque figure waddled the room. He had an oval-shaped head with a tuft of coarse black hair sitting in a mess on top. He wore a dark green cloak that was thrown back over his shoulders, revealing a thin layer of hair that swept across the majority of the blue-gray skin of his egg-shaped body.

The hair was thickest at his midsection, a large matted triangle completely covering the space between his thighs. In fact, Jinari questioned if it was indeed his own hair, or if it was perhaps fur or a garment of some sort. His bulbous eyes studied Jinari in a way that made her feel uncomfortable.

"A goblin?" Anger flared in Jinari's voice. Her statue-like stance was broken as she took a half-step forward, her arms coming up.

"Is that a problem?" Gar-Dum asked, raising an eyebrow, still slouched. He took another sip from his chalice, keeping his eyes fixed on Jinari.

Jinari let her arms fall back to her sides and retreated a step. She shrank back and looked to the stone floor. "No, my Lord." She said sheepishly.

"Good," Gar-Dum said over his chalice. "This is Uskor. He will be guiding you through the eastern caverns."

Jinari carefully regarded him and inclined her head slightly.

"He knows exactly where and how to find what we are looking for," Gar-Dum continued.

Jinari waited a long beat before speaking. "Which is what, my Lord?"

Gar-Dum glanced over at Uskor, wild grin still plastered across his face, then back at Jinari. "Uskor will allow you the details of the mission as they are needed."

Jinari did not like that one bit. But what was she to do? She could not defy Gar-Dum. "Very well, my Lord."

"Very well indeed." Gar-Dum tossed his chalice aside. The muscles in his chest quivered as he moved. "Choose three members from your clan. Make sure they are your best. You will set out with Uskor at daybreak."

Jinari bowed deeply, then backed away, exiting Gar-Dum's chambers, a rotten feeling swelling in the core of her stomach.

II.

Jinari waited for Uskor at the camp fire, three of her most trusted Kurhik clansmates, all female, silently accompanying her. Anessi was older than Jinari, her long mane of silver hair belaying that fact. She wore dark red robes. Around her waist was a fur belt fashioned from a wolf that Anessi had killed herself. On the belt hung adorned with several small leather pouches, each containing some sort of powder or herb used in her magic. She leaned on her staff, which was roughly half a head taller than her, and had runes carved deep all up and down it.

Anessi was a magic user. At one time, her magic was used only for healing, but after joining with the Vulgar-kin, Jinari had utilized her skill more and more for destructive things such as bringing fire down on the enemy in battle, calling a swarm of insects, firing lightning form her staff, conjuring force fields, and so on. Jinari had even asked Anessi to use a death curse on occasion. Jinari knew that the death curse was something that Anessi did not like doing, but she complied with Jinari's requests nonetheless. She always did.

Jinari sighed. It was simpler times before the war. Before she had made the decision for her clan to join the Vulgar-kin. She could see the fear and confusion in many of their eyes, but all Kur-hik followed her without question. Always. Before the war, there was peace. The Kur-hik clan spent most of their time farming the land, tending to their animals . . . tending to their families. Today, the lands were dry and barren, the animals have died of disease or famine, and most everyone in the clan have lost at least half their family, including Jinari.

Jinari's own family had included five children with her three male consorts, her eldest two daughters so close to partaking in the rituals of adulthood. Now they were dead. All her children were dead. Slaughtered like animals by a neighboring tribe of humans, the Darhatlor. But Jinari had staged a brutal retribution. She gathered the remains of her Kur-hik and struck down a retaliating blow the very next morning, crushing the surprised Darhatlor.

As she stood over Omarothu, the Darhatlor Chieftain, she asked him why they had attacked her. He coughed blood, and his reply was simply: "Man-kin." Since then, Jinari has turned the Kur-hik into a tribe of fearsome warriors, joining the Vulgar-kin in a shaky alliance to further her crusade in obliterating the Man-kin—the humans aligned with them, the elves, the dwarves, and whoever else got in the way of her mission of vengeance.

Next to Anessi were Tutia and Kelen, Jinari's most skilled warriors. Like Jinari, Tutia and Kelen were dressed in a mish-mash of armor and clothing mostly stripped from fallen soldiers in battle. They both looked quite interesting, with the mix of furs and skins, bronze, and rusted steel. Tutia carried a heavy two-handed broadsword, while Kelen had a bow and quiver strapped across her back, and several daggers sheathed around her belt.

The four of them stood silently around the fire, taking in the smell of the damp, burning wood and the crackling sounds. A coarse voice came from behind.

"All ready, I see?"

They all turned in unison to see Uskor, cloak wide open, hands perversely placed on his hips.

"Yes," Jinari said evenly. "This is Anessi, Tutia, and Kelen." The three women did not move.

Uskor was all nose and ears as he looked the three of them up and down, taking his time to study their every last feature head to toe. Jinari had no doubt they felt every much as violated by his eyes as she did when he first looked upon her.

"Very well, we shall go then." Uskor turned to leave, his long ears flapping ever so slightly, and Jinari and her three Kur-hik followed.

The first leg of their journey was made in silence. Uskor walked, Jinari and her Kur-hik followed. Sometimes Uskor used roads or trails, other times he cut directly through a forest or large clearing. It made no difference to Jinari, she and her Kur-hik were accustomed to traveling through all types of terrain, from mountains high to valleys low.

Uskor abruptly stopped at dusk, threw his pack down, and announced they were making camp for the night. He told Jinari to start a fire, then disappeared into the brush.

"Where's he going?" Tutia asked.

"Who cares, as long as I don't have to stare at his back any longer," Kelen said as she began looking around for sticks.

"Or smell him," Anessi added.

Jinari smiled to herself as she began to help look for wood for the fire. Tutia dug out a small fire pit while the rest managed to gather quite a bit of wood, enough for the night at least. Jinari piled some into the pit and looked at Anessi. Anessi stepped forward, lifted her right hand palm up, and whispered something so soft it was inaudible. She blew into her palm, and black dust swirled in front of her and floated to the fire pit. Fire erupted with a *whoosh*.

Anessi stepped back and looked at Jinari, who felt Anessi's eyes burn into her own. Anessi didn't care for using her magic on such trivial things, things that didn't really need magic. Jinari looked to the ground. looked away.

The four sat around the fire trading wine skins, bread, and light conversation. "When will we know what it is we are looking for?" Tutia asked.

"Soon enough," Uskor's raspy voice came from the shadows as he materialized in front of the fire. He threw three rabbits down at his feet. "I brought dinner."

The Kur-hik and the goblin sat in silence as they cooked the rabbits. Jinari wanted very much to prod him for information, but waited until he was finished eating.

"This weapon," Jinari began. "Is it enchanted?"

"In a way," Uskor replied, holding his gaze into the fire.

"Is it large?" Jinari asked.

Uskor let silence hang for a moment before he replied. "Yes."

"How are we to destroy it?" Kelen asked.

Uskor lifted his eyes from the fire and looked at Kelen, then to Jinari. He reached into his cloak and pulled out what appeared to be a flattened rock. He held it up for all to see. It was about the size of Jinari's hand, and was covered with small, raised bumps. It was deep crimson in color, and occasionally flashed a reflection of the fire, curiously, as it did not appear to be smooth or shiny in any way.

Uskor grunted, and tossed the rock into Jinari's lap. She picked it up, and immediately had a sinking feeling in her gut. Her head felt light, almost dizzy. Her face felt flush, her fingers and toes began to tingle. She thought she knew what it was, but refused to allow herself to believe. She looked to Anessi, whose eyes were as wide as she's ever seen them.

"Is this a . . ." Jinari's voice cracked, and she couldn't even finish her own sentence.

"A dragon scale," Uskor said, a proud grin plastered across his misshapen face. He looked around, waiting for the reactions.

"Are you saying we're looking for a dragon?" Tutia said, a twinge of disbelief in her voice.

Uskor did not answer, instead holding a stare in Jinari's direction.

"Impossible," Jinari said, meeting Uskor's stare. "Dragons haven't existed for hundreds of years. The last dragons died out with fall of the Migar, during the Age of Winds."

Jinari remembered when she was a young girl, listening to the elders' stories of dragons and Ages past. There were stories of heroes such as Yerik the Whitehood riding dragons into battle, defeating armies of giants or trolls in one fell swoop. *Giants and trolls*, Jinari thought solemnly, the very creatures she had now aligned her clan with.

"It exists," Uskor said, shooting a quick glance to each that sat around the fire. "I've seen it myself. We must destroy it before it is discovered by the Man-kin. They have a ways of controlling it, a way to use it against us in the war. If that were to ever happen, if they had just one dragon in their favor, we would surely be defeated."

"Control it?" Anessi arched an eyebrow. "How so? Through magic?"

"Not exactly," Uskor replied.

"Why do we have to kill it?" Kelen inquired. "If it can be controlled why can't the Vulgar-kin use it?"

Uskor gave her an even look. "Dragons would not trust the Vulgar-kin. Giants, orcs, trolls," he paused for a beat, "and *goblins*, among other things, are a dragon's enemy. Only humans who are pure of heart have been known to ride a dragon. I've heard stories of dragons aligning with elves, but as far as I'm concerned they are stories, nothing more. Could we try? Sure, but Gar-Dum would rather not take the risk, since, as it is, we seem to be winning the war at the moment."

Jinari let out a quiet sigh and studied the red-orange flames of the fire. She had given up so much when she made the decision to join her clan to the Vulgar-kin. It seems she could add her humanity and the respect of her Kur-hik to that list.

"This is wonderful," Tutia burst in, rising to her feet. "We get to kill a dragon? We'll be heroes! Legends! They'll write songs about us!" She threw a fist into the air.

"Uskor, tell us more about the dragon, and how you propose we kill it," Jinari said.

"Killing it is your job," Uskor said with an awkward snicker. "Did Gar-Dum not make that clear? But I will offer you more information as you need it. In truth, I am simply your humble guide. I get you in, and get you out, provided you remain in one piece after accomplishing your mission." He paused and looked around, smiling. "As for the dragon itself, what's to tell? It's big, it has wings, its scales are hard as rock, and it breathes fire."

Silence held. Jinari looked form the fire to Anessi, who was looking at the fire, glanced up at Jinari and held her gaze briefly, then shifted her attention back to the fire. Jinari looked back to Uskor, who was already rolling over and stretching out on the ground. "I'll take first watch," she said. "The rest of you get some sleep."

III.

The next morning Jinari opened her eyes to find everyone else packing up camp in silence. She looked at Uskor, who was standing about twenty paces apart from the rest of the group, looking impatient.

"Are we ready?" Jinari said to her Kur-hik.

"Yes, my lady," Tutia replied. And their journey continued.

Again, they traveled mostly in silence. Kelen passed around some more bread, and they ate as they walked. Uskor seemed to be walking in erratic patterns, making a sharp left or right turn, but they followed all the same. When the sun was directly overhead, Jinari noticed the ground was becoming moist.

"You're leading us into a marsh," she called up to Uskor.

Uskor made no reply. Jinari looked to Anessi, who returned a concerned glance. They continued to follow the goblin. Soon, the grass sloshed under their feet. Not long after that, their feet were immersed in water up to their ankles. Eventually, the cold, murky water nearly reached their knees.

"Uskor, enough of this," Jinari halted and her companions followed suit. Uskor also stopped, and turned to regard her. "Do you intend for us to swim to the eastern caverns?"

Uskor's mouth contorted into a crooked sneer. He opened his mouth, about to speak, but before he formed any words there was a shriek at Jinari's back. As she turned she heard splashing, and saw Kelen struggling to hold her balance. Tutia drew her sword, and Anessi balled her fist, drawing energy within.

"Kelen!" Jinari shouted over the splashes. "What's got you?" Jinari turned her head back to glance at Uskor, who was hastily climbing up the nearest tree.

"It's a hand!" Kelen shouted in return. "With claw—"

Before Kelen could finish she was pulled all the way down with a mighty splash. The chilly, dingy water of the marsh sprayed up into everyone's faces. Everyone except for Uskor, whom was busy getting as high as he could in that tree.

Tutia fished her left hand into the water, her broadsword tightly gripped in her right. She pulled up with a grunt, and Kelen burst out of the water gasping for breath. Jinari heard the muffled sound of Uskor shouting something in the distance. His shouts were muffled by high-pitched hissing and spitting sounds. Jinari's breath shortened. She whirled around to see four Lizardmen facing her. One was holding a crude wooden spear; the other two simply bore their large talons and swung their thick, spiky tails menacingly behind them.

Jinari looked to Kelen and Tutia, and saw two more Lizardmen stalking near them. That made five in all, and four of them, not including Uskor, who was now about fifteen lengths up in a tree shouting something Jinari could not fully hear.

Kelen pulled her bow and notched an arrow. Jinari slowly pulled out her axe. The Lizardmen drew nearer as they continued with their menacing hissing sounds. Jinari nodded in Anessi's general direction. Anessi shot her arms straight above her into the air and shouted, "Sangazae!"

In a course of a split second, everything became dark, then was illuminated in a brilliant flash of light. Jinari blinked spots away from her eyes, and saw the three Lizardmen nearest her staggering. The one had dropped his spear, and was bent over with his claws in the water, trying to fish it out. Jinari moved, a cry of defiance singing out as she lunged forward and cocked her axe behind her head. She came down with all her strength and momentum, taking the Lizardman's head off, and its left arm as well.

Jinari then dropped to one knee with a plunging splash. She brought her axe parallel with the ground and brought her torso around in a fierce twisting motion. Once she had nearly made a full rotation, she released the grip on her axe, allowing it to sail through the air with a mighty hum. Jinari's axe buried itself deep in the chest of a Lizardman, much to its surprise. The Lizardman staggered back, looked down at his chest, then dropped, dead before he hit the water.

Without even thinking, Jinari shouted again and charged the third Lizardman. The scaly foe staggered back, a little due to fear, but mostly in surprise. Just before Jinari reached him, however, and arrow pierced its neck. The Lizardman reached up to touch the arrow, attempted to make a hissing sound that sounded more like a choking gurgle, and fell to its death. Jinari stood and pivoted to look at Kelen and Tutia. Two Lizardmen lay in the waters near them, two arrows protruding from each their bodies. Kelen held her bow at her side, one hand near her quiver, ready to grab another arrow. Tutia's blade was clean. She resheathed it, looking disappointed.

"Well done! Well done, indeed!" Uskor was already bounding over from the tree he had taken refuge in. He was visibly excited. "You see," he said as he rejoined the group, struggling to catch his breath, "that dragon should be no problem at all."

IV.

After the group had emerged from the swamp, they built a fire to get warm and dry. There was not much time to spare, and Uskor kept pushing to move on, so their clothes really only got about half dry. But half dry was far better than soaking wet.

The sun had fallen, and Uskor led with torchlight. Jinari found herself surprised when Uskor announced they had reached the caverns. She expected them to be at the base of a mountain or along a hilltop at the least, but they were in the middle of a forest, not surrounded by mountains but rather the tallest trees she had ever seen.

Uskor beckoned for help as he began clearing foliage. Tutia and Kelen lent a hand, while Jinari and Anessi stood back and watched, both with folded arms. Before long, palms and vines were cleared, and a large, dark opening stood before them. Tutia and Kelen stepped back to fall in line with Jinari and Anessi. Uskor looked back, gave a small grunt, and entered the cavern mouth. Jinari followed, Anessi behind her, then Kelen, with Tutia last.

The light vanished almost immediately, though it did not seem to bother Uskor, who continued along as if everything was perfectly visible. Anessi whispered something to herself, and the top of her staff began to glow with a blue light. It gave off a tremendous amount of light, though there was not much to look at. The cavern walls were reddish brown and damp, streaks of water occasional seeping through a crack or small fissure. There was no sound, save the faint scrapes and shuffling of their feet. Jinari didn't speak for she did not know how far the sound might carry.

Uskor moved along at a brisk pace, not pausing or hesitating when the tunnel came to a fork. He knew exactly where he was going; or, at least, he certainly gave that impression. They continued along like this, moving in a single file line in total silence, for what seemed like hours. Jinari felt they were moving at a slight downward angle all the while. She began to worry about finding their way out.

"How much further," Jinari whispered to Uskor, her soft voice carrying faint echoes.

Uskor turned to face her. His bulging eyes looked almost luminous in the blue light of Anessi's staff. He nodded, and pointed ahead, and continued walking. Jinari took that to mean that they were close, and indeed, after a few more paces, she could see a faint light. She signaled for Anessi to dim the light on her staff. Uskor stopped and the mouth of some sort of opening, and Jinari came up alongside him.

What she saw made her heart skip two beats. The cavern opened into an enormous space, with other tunnels and openings surrounding the large cavern, some smaller than the one they were standing in, others over fifty times larger. A large fire burned at the far end. Jinari saw the glint of gold and silver, the sparkle of fine jewels, all piled in heaps and heaps throughout the cavern. Everything had a brilliant shine, nothing was dull. In the middle of it all she saw the dragon, curled up and sleeping as if he were an old dog curled up at his master's feet.

The dragon was enormous, Jinari estimated him to be at least on hundred lengths from head to tail. His body was covered in rigid-looking brown-red scales, his midsection beneath his folded leathery wings rising and falling slightly with his sleeping breaths. Jinari drew in a breath—his head was covered in boney spikes that protruded out the top and sides. Large pointed teeth and fangs were also visible, even though its mouth was fully closed.

"You and your two warrior girls will climb down here," Uskor said in a whispered tone. "The mage and I will remain here. We will create a distraction. When the dragon looks up, strike him high on the neck, where the jaw ends and the neck begins. This is a vulnerable spot."

"The only vulnerable spot?" Jinari asked, raising her brow, not taking her eyes of the massive creature.

"The most vulnerable spot, and easiest for us to access," Uskor replied. "You could poke it in the eye, but that's not going to kill it, only upset it greatly. Stab and cut high on the neck, and he not only loses its ability to breathe fire, he eventually dies as well."

Jinari blinked. "*Eventually?*"

"It will take some time, yes. How long, I do not know."

Jinari took a deep breath and summoned Anessi, Tutia, and Kelen to her. She gave instructions, and motioned Tutia and Kelen to follow her down the cliff into the dragon's main chamber.

Jinari took short, slow steps, being very careful to make as little noise as possible, No noise at all was ideal. Tutia and Kelen followed silently, and closely, behind. The closer they came to the dragon, the more her heart raced. She gripped her axe tight, and close to her body. Soon they were within twenty paces of the dragon's head. She could feel the warmth of its breath. One of its wings twitched a bit. Jinari froze, holding her breath, terrified. She looked back to Tutia and Kelen. Both were frozen like statues. She craned her neck a bit more to look further back and up at Anessi and Uskor. Uskor motioned with his hand as if he wanted Jinari to move a closer. The dragon's wing twitched again. Jinari swallowed, and slowly continued forward.

After six or seven steps, Jinari froze again when she heard what sounded like a muffled screech. It seemed to have come from the direction of the dragon, but it did not sound like something that would come from so large a creature. She looked around, then back to Tutia and Kelen. Tutia's expression was unreadable, Kelen simply shrugged. Jinari turned back and took another step forward, and that's when she saw it.

From underneath the dragon's wing emerged a small creature, no bigger than Jinari's own torso. Its skin was smooth and of a dark-purplish hue. It walked on all fours and had two protruding lumps on its back. Two more creatures, exactly the same features, also came out from beneath the dragon's wing. Jinari's heart sank at the sudden realization that the dragon was not a *he* at all; it was a *she*, and these were her offspring.

Jinari glanced back, giving Uskor and Anessi a frightened look. Uskor smiled and said something to Anessi, who raised her staff. They were about to create the diversion. Jinari was sure they had not seen the baby dragons. In a panic, she shouted, "Wait!"

Her voice echoed loudly, causing everyone's shoulders to tense. Anessi stood motionless, her staff high in the air. Jinari heard the baby dragons' screeching sounds again. She turned and saw the large, open eyes of the dragon staring directly at her, Tutia, and Kelen. The baby dragons were playfully wrestling with each other near the dragon's nose. The dragon lifted her head, her eyes still trained on Jinari. Jinari felt a puff of hot air as the dragon exhaled.

"NOW!"

It was Uskor's voice, and before his voice's echo could bounce there was a crackle and a brilliant flash of light. The dragon wailed, and brought her head back down in an apparent effort to protect her babies. Tutia called a battle cry and ran toward the dragon, broadsword held high. Kelen stood her ground, her bow notched and trained in the general direction of the dragon.

"Tutia, wait, no!" Jinari called after Tutia but it was too late. The dragon simply effortlessly brushed her head to the side, catching Tutia on one of its boney spikes, impaling her. Blood spurted in all directions. Tutia cried in agony as the dragon lifted her head and tossed Tutia aside in a motion akin to a nod. Tutia was dead before she came back down to the cavern floor.

Jinari did the only thing she could do at that moment—she turned and ran, grabbing Kelen's arm and pulling her along. Uskor and Anessi were not retreating, however. They were in fact running toward the dragon. Her feet still moving, Jinari turned to look back. The dragon was bringing her head down to her babies, not paying the intruders any mind at the moment. "We have to get out of here!" she shouted as they met Uskor and Anessi.

"No!" Uskor shouted back. "We have a task to complete! Kill the dragon, and its offspring!"

"I will not!" Jinari said firmly.

"You will kill the dragon and its offspring, or die trying! That is your mission." Uskor trembled, visibly upset.

Jinari took a breath. She looked to Kelen, then to Anessi. Uskor drew a long dagger, and moved past Jinari in the direction of the dragon.

"Uskor, no!" Jinari's head swirled. She wanted to grab Kelen and Anessi and run, but found her feet unmoving. The dragon saw Uskor coming, and her eyes narrowed in anticipation. Before she could think of what to do next, Jinari felt something hiss past her ear. Kelen had fired an arrow, and it struck the dragon in her eye.

The dragon roared in pain, and brought her head up, exposing the babies. Uskor raised his dagger, and made directly for them. Kelen notched and drew back another arrow, but Jinari used the handle of her axe to knock the bow out of her hands. Kelen grunted in frustration, fumbling to reach for it on the ground.

"Anessi, we have to stop him!" Jinari gave Anessi a pleading look, and Anessi nodded in understanding.

Jinari moved after Uskor, a good ten paces behind him, and heard Anessi's low voice chant something. Mere steps before he reached the baby dragons, magic wind blew Uskor backward off his feet, landing in front of Jinari. Without hesitation, she lifted her axe, then brought it down onto Uskor's neck. He was dead before he even knew what was happening.

"Jinari!" Anessi's voice came from behind, and when Jinari turned, she saw Kelen aiming an arrow directly at her. Jinari heard the dragon's roar once again. On the ledge, Anessi wrestled Kelen, each attempting to overpower the other. Jinari ran back to them, but before she could reach them, Kelen pulled her dagger and stuck it into Anessi's side. Anessi staggered back. Jinari raised her axe as she came closer, hesitated for a brief moment, then buried her weapon between Kelen's shoulder blades. Kelen stumbled forward and fell face first on the rocky cavern floor. Her axe still buried in Kelen's back, Jinari knelt to Anessi's side.

"I'm okay," Anessi grunted, trying to get up, dagger protruding from her hip.

"Stay down," Jinari gently pushed Anessi back down, simultaneously pulling the dagger out of her side. Anessi groaned, but fished a pouch from her belt, and sprinkled the contents onto her wound.

The hair on the back of Jinari's neck stood up, and she whirled around to see the dragon's head, complete with an arrow protruding from her eye, a mere five paces from them. The dragon was unmoving. Jinari moved toward it.

"Jinari!" Anessi's cry was pleading.

"Stay there," Jinari said calmly, slowly moving toward the dragon. "Don't move."

The dragon remained still as Jinari walked right up to her and gently put a hand on her snout. The dragon's hot breath caused beads of sweat to form on her neck and forehead. Jinari reached up and grabbed the arrow, pulling it out. The dragon winced and wailed in pain, letting out several short breaths with hints of smoke from her nostrils. The dragon turned her head and looked down to her babies, looked back to Jinari, then brought her head down right in front of the human's face. Jinari again gently put her hand on the dragon's snout.

"Yes," she said in a soothing tone, stroking the dragon's snout as if it were a kitten on her lap. "I am Man-kin, not Vulgar-kin. Thank you for reminding me of this."

The dragon puffed, then turned to retrieve her babies, who were still squealing and wrestling with each other, seemingly oblivious to the entire situation.

Jinari turned and walked back to Anessi, who was now standing. "What will you tell Lord Gar-Dum?" Anessi asked.

"Nothing," Jinari replied. "We're not reporting back to Gar-Dum. We will retrieve our clan, the Kur-hik, and seek out the rest of our people—the Man-kin."

"How will we get out of these caverns?" Anessi asked. "Without Uskor, I fear we will not be able to backtrack out steps. We could end up walking for days before we find out way out."

Jinari looked over to the dragon, whose babies were crawling back into the safety and comfort of her wing. "Why walk," she said, her lips curling into a grin, "when we can fly?"

Ash and Blood
Hannah Marie

Chapter One

Eva coughed up ash and dust as she fought her way out of the cellar. The heavy oak door crumbled between her fingers, singeing the rough skin of her palms. Even after three days, the embers burned hot against her hands. The house had collapsed on top of the cellar door and had it been any other disaster—a hurricane, tornado, flood—she would have been buried alive.

She was fortunate it had been fire.

She pushed her way through the crumbling wood and stepped into the sunlight.

Gray. Gray and red and orange. Everywhere. Ash coated everything that wasn't still burning. What once had been a thriving village full of tailors, farmers, weavers, and bakers now drifted away on the wind.

The Queen's judgement was swift and terrible, riding the sky on wings and breathing fire. This village, Eva's village, would be a warning to the others who wished to disobey.

Eva turned around and looked at the wreckage of her house. In the cellar, she had heard the screams of her mother and sisters, had felt the blazing heat of the flame, and done nothing. What could she have done?

She bent and pulled at a board. It came away in pieces.

They were still under there. Buried by fire and wood and ash.

Tears ached in her throat, but she shoved them back down, bundling her emotions into a tight ball in the middle of her chest. There would be time enough for tears after.

She slipped back into the cellar and collected a few items in a bag.

Things she would need for a journey. Things she would need for revenge.

"Hello?" The voice trembled on the air.

Eva flinched, her hand tightening around the pack.

"Is anyone alive?" It was a man's voice, laced with shock and fear. "Is anyone alive?"

No. They were all gone. Every last villager burned alive in their homes, in the streets, and in the market. Everyone was ash and bone.

Eva scrambled out of the cellar. The voice came from what was once the town square. She padded down the cobblestones, stepping around wood and bones.

A man stood by the small fountain full of gray water, thick with sludge, his arms hanging limply at his sides. He stared at what was once the marketplace. His patched brown coat and purple felt hat didn't belong in this world of soot and smoldering flames.

Eva approached, her shoes noiseless. "Who are you?" The words were born from a throat ravaged by screams and smoke.

With a shout of surprise, the man jumped backwards, almost falling into the fountain. Eva watched dispassionately as he regained his balance and braced himself against the stone ledge. He stared open-mouthed at the apparition. Eva knew she looked a sight. With pale gray hair, clothes, and skin, she looked more dead than alive.

"I'm Timas the tinker." He pointed at the pack on the ground. Tin pots, pans, and cups spilled out of it. "I come to Rose Haven every year for the Reina Day Celebration."

Eva blinked ash out of her eyes and then turned her head, taking in the devastated village. "We won't be celebrating the Queen's birthday this year."

"But the festival next week . . . I mean . . ." The man tugged at his beard. "What . . . what happened?"

Eva shouldered her pack, already dismissing the tinker. "Some of our men joined Huru's army. The Queen found out."

His face paled. "Traitors?"

Eva turned her head sharply and stared at him. "Traitors or no, judgment has been rendered." She waited until he lowered his eyes before she looked away. "Don't stay here. It may come back." She moved through the square.

"Wait!" he called.

Eva paused and looked over her shoulder. Memories of laughter and kisses and love assaulted her, choking her in a way that the ash never could. They were dead. All of them. And maybe she was, too.

"Where are you going?" the tinker asked.

Eva took a good long look at the square, committing it to memory. She would need this later. When she could feel again.

"To kill a dragon."

Chapter Two

The Queen preferred solitude after a raid.

Morley balanced the tray on one hand and knocked gently on the ornately carved door. Leaves and flowers and small woodland creatures grazed his knuckles, frozen in the grain of the wood. As always, he searched the carvings until he found the mouse. He swore it was alive, darting between vines and hiding behind the larger animals. But no one believed him. It was just a wooden mouse, carved into the Queen's door.

He knocked once more for good measure, just loud enough to make his presence known, then bent to place the tray on the ground. The china and silver rattled gently, rippling the soup and shifting the plate of grape tomatoes, before settling against the flagstones. The Queen preferred solitude, but she also expected supper to be served promptly at ten o'clock.

He straightened and his eyes darted once more to the door. There! Just behind the griffin's talon. He leaned forward to confirm. Yes, he could just make out the small rump and the long, skinny tail.

The door slammed open.

Morley snapped into a bow, the Queen a blur of red, black, and white. "Your Majesty!" he exclaimed.

"Is it finished?" Her voice was tired, wispy, and her words fluttered in the air like moths around a flame. "Has it spread?"

Morley raised his head slightly and stared fixedly at the black embroidery adorning her red skirt. *Has it spread?* Like wildfire. Rose Haven was no more, burned to ash and dust, and haunted by the ghosts. The city hissed the fate of the traitors beneath dark eaves and in seedy taverns. The courtiers murmured behind painted faces and gilded fans. And when whispers of the fiery dragon wreaking death and destruction, leaving no survivors, finally reached Morley's ears, he knew it to be finished. The dragon did its job well.

He made sure to keep his voice level as he answered. "The entire country now understands what happens to those who oppose Your Majesty. The tale was carried by the witness of a tinker, or so I understand."

"And Huru?" She bit the name and it snapped in her mouth.

Morley straightened just a bit more. "No word."

"Our men remain under his command?"

Morley's throat dried and he nodded.

"I see." The skirt moved out of his line of sight, leaving the door wide open.

Understanding the unspoken order, Morley retrieved the tray and slipped into the Queen's room.

When she was younger, and happier, she had resided in the royal apartments on the third floor. Morley remembered games and laughter. He remembered chasing the young princess down the hall, catching her in his arms, and lifting her onto his shoulders. He remembered the Queen standing at the window with one hand on her belly and the other caressing her King's cheek. He remembered how fond she was of her people. And most of all, he remembered the kindness of those days.

That was then, in the Before.

He placed the tray on the blackened surface of the table and stepped back, surveying the small, cramped quarters of the tower room. It was meticulously neat and clean, but a far cry from the majestic rooms downstairs. The circular space held a small, canopied bed, a table and two chairs, a wardrobe, and a locked trunk. The one and only window opened onto a balcony barely big enough to fit two people.

It was closer, the Queen had insisted when she moved in. And she needed to be closer.

No one had asked closer to what.

"Morley?"

His heart ached at the sound of her voice. "Yes, my Queen?"

She stood at the window, gazing out over the city. She used to wear her hair loose and soft, piled on top of her head or cascading down her back. The honeyed waves were a magnificent compliment to the golden crown balanced on her brow. She still wore the crown, but the hair was scraped away from her face and held captive in a bun at the nape of her neck. A black snood ensured that the strands stayed in place. It was too severe for Morley's Queen. It made her older, harsher, more . . . hateful.

Her eyes slid to him, as though she could hear his thoughts. "Are you mine, Morley?"

He placed a hand on his heart. "Always, my Queen."

She nodded, her eyes softening. And just for a moment, she was herself again. She opened her mouth to say something and paused, her attention captured by movement outside. Morley stiffened.

"Leave us."

The command came cold and harsh, accompanied by the blossoming scent of scorched earth and metallic blood. Morley's skin tightened around his eyes and he bowed, backing slowly out of the room. As he shut the door, he saw the Queen on the balcony, one hand stretched into the night sky. A huge golden talon curved around the eaves as the dragon nestled onto the roof.

"Are you mine?" the Queen whispered to the beast.

One golden eye peered into the room, lighting on the Queen and burning with an inner fire. Tendrils of smoke spiraled from nostrils as the dragon peeled back its lips to answer.

Morley shut the door.

Chapter Three

One of Huru's soldiers found her on the fourth day. She didn't mean to kill him, but he rushed at her with a sword. She ducked under his swing and jammed her mother's second-best kitchen knife under his arm. He made a gurgling noise, his eyes widening, and backed up a step. Eva's hand still gripped the knife and she stumbled with him. His arms came down around her like a hug, his sword point scraping the dirt behind her. Warm blood pulsed over her hand. She tightened her hold and tugged at the knife.

The soldier opened his mouth to say something and coughed. Blood splattered across Eva's face. He fell to his knees, taking her with him, and they knelt face to face. It could have been a kind face, with wide, child-like eyes, and full cheeks. But right now, his face was smeared with tears, blood, and fear.

"I'm . . . I'm sorry," she said, but it was too late.

His head tilted back and his sightless eyes focused on the sky.

She knelt with him, supporting his weight, frozen in this moment.

She killed this man.

She wondered if she should have felt anything. But she just felt . . . tired.

She shrugged out of his bloody embrace and crouched by his body, her hand still attached to the knife buried in his side. It wouldn't come out. It went in so easily, parting the skin and muscle just below his armpit, and now it wouldn't release its hold.

She used both hands, braced her feet against the dead man's side and pulled. The knife scraped free with a fresh river of blood. It poured over her hands, warm and wet.

Eva's heart raced and her lungs gasped for air. Her stomach clenched.

Funny how the terror hit after the danger had passed.

She stumbled away, dropping the knife, and vomited. She emptied her stomach of her meager breakfast and then continued spitting up yellow, foamy bile. She wiped her mouth, shuddering as the blood transferred from her hands to her lips.

A rustle in the brush drew her attention from the dead man at her feet.

A soldier, his sword aimed high, stepped forward. And another, this one holding a halberd. And one more with two knives.

Eva held out her bloodied hands, defenseless.

The man with the sword approached cautiously. "Gavin?"

Eva closed her eyes.

Gavin.

The name burned across her skin. His name was Gavin.

The swordsman growled and Eva opened her eyes to see the sword swing down. She stared at the blade glimmering in the sunlight and waited for it to bite into her neck.

"Hold!"

The command had an immediate effect. The swordsman pulled back and turned, stiffening his posture.

A man approached and Eva had heard enough stories to know him. The lightning blazing across his chest and the heavy double blades in his hands identified him as General Huru himself.

His eyes glittered darkly in the shadows of his helmet.

"Gavin?" he demanded.

"Dead." The swordsman jerked his head at Eva. "Her doing."

Huru considered Eva for a long moment. In one motion, he sheathed the double swords at his sides. "Bring the Blood-Wraith."

Chapter Four

They tied her to a tent pole in full view of the camp. Both Huru's soldiers and Rose Haven's traitors gave her a wide berth, their expressions ranging from angry to fearful and everything in between. Someone spat at her and it landed in her hair. Eva didn't care. She leaned forward, her shoulders and wrists pulling against her bonds. She embraced the sensation. But even the pain was dull.

"Blood-Wraith." The voice was soft and familiar.

Eva blinked. She tilted her head back and peered through the curtain of her hair at Brodie Hammond. He stood in front of her, a cord of wood in his arms.

Two months ago, he had let his forge grow cold as he packed a bag and said goodbye to his wife and three sons. Two months ago he had followed Huru's red flag and the promise of gold and mercy. Two months ago, he had left, believing that by joining Huru's army, his family and village would be protected from the coming battle. And for two months, they were.

Eva stared at his wide, honest face. He knew. Somehow, he knew that Rose Haven was gone.

"Blood-Wraith," he said again, "were there any--" He paused and swallowed. "Were there any survivors?"

How much had she changed to become so unrecognizable? She had played with his boys all her life. He had mended more than one of her scrapes as a child. And last year at the Harvest Festival, she had shared her first kiss with his youngest, Uther.

The urge to shout his name and throw herself into his familiar arms became unbearable. She opened her mouth to identify herself as the only survivor, but bit her tongue before she could speak.

Brodie's family had burned to ash in an instant.

How could she be the only survivor? How could she tell this man that his entire family was destroyed, that his entire village was destroyed, leaving only one empty girl alive?

Eva met his eyes. The bleak shadows lurking behind his gaze told her that Brodie already knew that they were gone. But he needed to hear someone say it aloud. He needed *her* to say it aloud.

Her chest ached with guilt and sorrow. She gripped the emotions tightly to herself, but they burned their way up her throat, forming words.

"No," Eva croaked. "No survivors."

Brodie held her gaze for a long moment, then nodded. Without another word, he turned and moved to the pyre in the middle of camp. He placed his cord of wood carefully in place and then stepped back, staring at the unlit pyre. By the slope of his shoulders and the shaky breaths, she knew he was thinking of his wife and children and their painful death.

Dragon's fire was, at least, quick. Eva doubted anyone had suffered very long.

Her eyes slid to the pyre.

Unlike whoever was going to burn on that.

The tent flap behind her flicked open and General Huru stepped forward. Out of the corner of her eyes, Eva could see the edges of his hauberk and his black boots. She tensed.

"It's time," he said, and strode to the pyre.

A woman followed close behind. The feathers braided in her white hair and cloak of multi-colored fur declared her to be the General's Sibyl. She moved through the gathering soldiers and stopped at the head of the pyre.

"Bring the fallen," General Huru commanded.

Eva let out a breath as four men carried a shroud-wrapped body to the pyre.

She had heard of the barbaric practice of burning the dead, but had never witnessed it herself. She watched as they carefully laid the body on the pyre and lit it. Her skin crawled with a burning sensation as flames licked at the body. She felt as though she were on the pyre, slowly burning. Eva doubled over, her shoulders and wrists straining at the ropes, and gasped with pain.

There, in that moment, she heard the Sibyl's voice begin a familiar prayer. She lifted her head and met the Sibyl's eyes across the distance. She heaved a breath as the holy woman spoke the final phrase.

"From ash we were born and to ash we return."

Chapter Five

They left her tied to the tent until the pyre burned to dusty white embers.

Eva thought she would have been accustomed to the smell of burning flesh. She leaned against the pole and stared into the night sky. The scent clung to her hair and coated her skin. She would never be rid of it. Death had found her four days ago and she feared it would never let her go.

A movement at her periphery drew her attention as General Huru stepped into view. He had removed his helmet and his hair was pulled back in a knot of braids. The black paint smeared across his eyes and temples did nothing to disguise his glittering gaze.

"Blood-Wraith," he said, dipping his head slightly, "are you satisfied? Or do you require more sacrifice?" He gestured to the glowing pyre behind him.

Eva's eyes slipped past him to the dying fire. "Why do you call me that?"

He grinned, feral in the moonlight. "I'll show you."

His knife nicked her wrist as he cut through the rope. She didn't react and he didn't apologize. With his hands on her shoulders, he drew her into the tent and deposited her on a roughly-cut chair.

"Look." He held a small mirror in front of her face. "A Blood-Wraith."

The creature in the mirror drew back in dismay. Wild hair surrounded a gaunt, wide-eyed face, both caked in ash. Dried blood painted the mouth, chin, and cheeks. Angry red burns glowed through the ash on collar bones and forearms.

This wasn't Eva. It was a monster born of flames and fury. Eva fisted her hands in her lap. And if that's all she was, then she would do what she must.

Huru nodded in satisfaction, as though he understood her grim acceptance. "A Blood-Wraith," he said again. He settled in an equally-uncomfortable chair and stared at her. "Why are you following my army? Why did you kill one of my men?"

Eva's gaze snapped to him. He didn't appear angry, merely curious. For a brief moment, she wondered what her punishment would be for killing one of his soldiers.

Not that it mattered. How could he punish her if she were already dead?

When she didn't answer, he leaned forward. "What do you want, Blood-Wraith?"

He held intelligence in his gaze, and a fierceness that would have frightened her had she not already survived a dragon.

"I . . ." She trailed off as the tent opened, admitting the Sibyl.

"The questions can wait," the wise woman said. "First, let's see what we are dealing with."

General Huru sat back as the Sibyl retrieved a wash basin and rag and proceeded to clean every inch of Eva's exposed skin. The Sibyl worked in silence with Huru looking on. Eva cringed in pain as the rag found the burns on her forearms and the back of her neck. The feathers in the Sibyl's hair brushed against Eva's clothing and came away gray. After several painful minutes, the Sibyl straightened, glanced at her ash-dusted clothes, and sighed.

"Well?" Huru asked.

The Sibyl moved to the side, revealing Eva to his curious gaze. "Not a Blood-Wraith. At least, not yet."

Huru nodded. "Just a girl. For now."

Eva found her voice. "What do you want with me?"

The general and the Sibyl exchanged glances. Huru nodded and the Sibyl turned back to Eva.

"What do you know about the Queen's dragon?"

Eva paused, the screams of her family echoing in her ears. Her hands trembled. Days ago she was consumed with household chores and the best way to get Uther to ask her to the Reina Day festival. And then, as she sat in the cellar peeling potatoes for the feast, the Queen's dragon struck. One moment the house above her echoed with footsteps and chatter and the next it was filled with the roar of fire and the dying shrieks of her family. And the dragon waited. For three days it waited in the square, flaming anything that moved. And Eva waited, frozen in the cellar, listening to the dying cries of the townspeople, listening to the terrified screams of the few survivors as they broke free to encounter a dragon face to face, and listening to a dragon breathing in and out, patient and calm.

What did she know about the Queen's dragon?

"Everything," she whispered.

The Sibyl nodded and untied a small scroll from her belt. "The stars speak to us, did you know?" She unrolled the scroll, pressing it flat against the table. "They told Huru to take command and they told us when to march on the capital. The scourge of the Queen's dragon cannot stand. Our people have suffered long under this beast. Too many sons and daughters have been lost to its appetite. Too many mothers have cried for vengeance. And now we march on your land, to defeat your Queen and her dragon."

Eva watched as she traced the patterns on the scroll. It was full of swirls and lines, like writing, but much more complicated than anything Eva had learned from her mother. Instead of forming distinct words and sentences, the marks flowed into each other, like one never-ending word.

"The stars spoke to us of a Blood-Wraith, paving our path to victory, the only one to defeat a dragon." The Sibyl pushed some long, gray hair behind her ear, her eyes intently fixed on Eva. "The stars spoke of you."

Eva shook her head. "I'm not a Blood-Wraith."

Huru stood up, his dark gaze locked on the gray girl. "Not yet. But you could be." He squatted in front of her. "And so I ask, Blood-Wraith, what do you want?"

Eva stared at the general and his Sibyl and licked her lips. She still tasted ash.

"I want to kill the dragon."

Huru didn't scoff. Instead, he leaned forward. "Is that so?"

Eva's fingers clenched at her skirt. It had once been a pale yellow, made of the softest wool, crafted by her mother's own hands. Eva's mother had made matching skirts for all three of her daughters, because yellow was her favorite color.

Eva thought of the other two skirts, with delicate pink roses embroidered on the hem, now burned to ash, and took a deep breath.

The knot in her chest pulsed with anger and guilt, but she forced it back down. "It is."

He stood and held out his hand. "Then you'll need something better than a knife."

Chapter Six

Morley had proven himself a coward years ago in the Before and he did so again now as he stood just outside the entrance to the throne room, waiting for the screams and crying to stop. Once they did, he straightened his doublet, nodded curtly at the soldier standing guard, and slipped through the doorway.

The room held remnants of past opulence—the giant chandelier hanging from three stories above, the hand-cut marble floor, and the heavy iron-wood throne—but they were mostly obscured by the damage to the room. The throne sat at the far end, in front of what used to be large windows overlooking the valley. The windows and part of the walls to either side had been removed some time ago to allow a larger entrance for the Queen's dragon. The flying buttresses and two thirds of the balcony seating had also been removed to allow the dragon room to stretch wings and turn around. The remaining walls and ceiling were braced with hastily-constructed columns of wood and rocky remnants of the stone wall.

In the Before, courtiers had crowded the throne like cloying flowers reaching for the sun. But now . . . Morley deliberately kept his eyes on the Queen, ignoring the courtiers huddled at the back of the room, clinging to the walls like dying vines.

The Queen watched him approach and beckoned him to her side. Morley climbed the three steps of the dais, doing his best to ignore the sounds of rending flesh and breaking bones coming from behind the throne. He placed a hand on his heart and bowed, his eyes desperately searching for a single stone not stained with blood.

"Morley." His name exited her lips as a sigh. "Rise."

He straightened and focused on the fresh droplet of blood staining the dove-gray silk of her collar. "My Queen. I have news."

Her eyes brightened despite the massacre taking place behind her. "Of General Huru?"

Morley tilted his head to one side. "Related, yes."

She leaned forward. "Don't leave me in suspense."

He glanced unnecessarily over his shoulder. With the sound of a masticating dragon and weeping courtiers on the other side of the room, there was little chance of being overheard.

Yet he still whispered the news.

"There have been reports of a Blood-Wraith."

The Queen's eyes widened and she slowly rose to her feet. "A what?"

Morley didn't repeat himself. He knew his Queen too well to make that mistake. "It joined Huru's company last night."

The Queen's mouth opened and when she spoke, it was a scream. "Get out!"

Morley bowed again, letting her anger wash over him and splash against the courtiers at the other end.

Morley remained in place while the courtiers scrambled to exit the room. Once the doors slammed shut, he lifted his head. His Queen stared at him with tears in her eyes. His breath caught in his chest. She was still so young. He longed to wrap her in an embrace, as he did many times in the Before, and press his lips to her hair. He wanted to tell her that despite the sorrow and the pain, she was strong enough to bear it.

"Where is it?" she demanded.

Morley returned his eyes to the floor. It would never be the way it was in the Before. His Queen wasn't his anymore.

"In Huru's camp. In Einsburg."

She whirled, robes flapping wetly against the flagstones. "Find it!" She commanded. "Fly!"

Morley kept his eyes averted as the dragon swallowed its final morsel and spread its wings.

"Wait!" The Queen rushed around the throne, heedless of the fresh offal soaking her slippers.

Morley moved back, unwilling to eavesdrop on her whispered words. As he stepped off the dais, his foot kicked something down the steps. He bent to pick it up and froze.

It was a small, pink slipper with pearl beading sewn into the shape of a flower.

Less than an hour ago, he had met the owner of that slipper. The child had been so excited to meet the Queen and had lifted the hem of her dress to display her new slippers. She had informed him that she brushed her fiery red hair and chose her pale blue dress all by herself. She had wanted to know if the Queen was nice, if she was pretty, if she would like her new shoes. Morley had ignored the anxious mother and chatted with the girl as he escorted her, her mother, and her two older brothers to the throne room.

And now . . .

His eyes darted around the dais, taking in the scraps of fabric soaking in pools of blood, the chunks of bone and flesh littering the floor, and the strands of fiery red hair caught in the arm of the throne, where a child had tried to hide.

With trembling hands, he lifted the slipper from the floor and cradled it.

He didn't realize he was shaking until the Queen placed a hand on his shoulder.

"They were traitors, Morley," she said, her voice pitched to affect stern sorrow. "Their father and husband attempted to flee to Huru's army. They had to be punished."

Morley kept his head bowed. "Even the children?"

The Queen's breath shuddered, but when she spoke, the words flowed like water. "They were traitors all, and had to be an example for the court. I can't make allowances for anyone, no matter their age. You understand, don't you, Morley? I can't allow traitors to go unpunished, children or no. You understand, don't you? Tell me you understand."

Morley took a deep breath and looked his Queen in the eyes. "I understand, my Queen."

She nodded. "Now go, bring me word of the Blood-Wraith's death."

Morley bowed and turned to go.

"And, Morley?"

He paused and turned. "Yes, my Queen?"

"Are you mine, Morley?"

He clutched the slipper behind his back as he bowed. The pearls, smooth and wet against his palm, felt like tears. "Always, my Queen."

Chapter Seven

Alone in his room, Morley put his head in his hands and cried. It was a relief to find out that he still could. He cried for the children he had led to slaughter, for the bloody future that lay ahead, and for his Queen, for the child she once was and for the monster that she became.

After his tears were spent, Morley dried his eyes with a monogrammed handkerchief and, despite the summer heat, started a small fire in the brazier. When the coals were hot and red, he gently lowered the pink, blood-stained slipper into the brazier. As the scent of burning silk filled the air, he knelt before the brazier and watched the flames consume the small shoe. His throat burned with the urge to pray, but he resisted. There would be no forgiveness for his part in this child's death. There would be no forgiveness for any of them.

When the slipper was nothing more than ashy flakes on the coals, he stood and crossed to the shelf at the head of his bed. He paused, listening for footsteps, and, after hearing none, carefully retrieved the book from its hiding place.

It was bound in green leather, barely bigger than his hand, and slim enough to be concealed within the pages of another book. The word "Draxoni" blazed across the cover in slightly raised letters.

Dismissed by historians and scholars alike, Gurye's Draxoni was filed next to myths and legends. The ancient language in which it was written was full of misspellings and punctuation errors. Most libraries had removed the book altogether, finding no value in a poorly-written dragon tale.

Morley moved to the desk at the window where he had better light, and a view of the Queen's room across the courtyard. The dragon had built an aerie on the roof of her tower, lined with torn silks and shiny gold coins that winked in the sun.

Nothing but the best for the Queen's dragon, everyone said. Probably better than its meager horde in the mountains or across the desert.

Most of the courtiers suspected what Morley knew for a fact; the nest was also filled with bones, most of them human. The constant diet of traitors and cattle seemed to fill the dragon's belly, but never satiate its appetite. No one knew what would satisfy the dragon, not even the Queen.

Morley squinted at the aerie.

And that was the problem, wasn't it? No one really knew anything about the dragon. It had just appeared one day, unexplainably bound to the Queen and her will. Morley recalled the day the Queen had exited the chapel, a horse-sized dragon at her side. She had been dazed, confused, and couldn't tell Morley where she had found it. And, since that day, it had grown in size and power. Some days, Morley wasn't entirely certain who was in control, the Queen, or her dragon.

With his attention split between the southern sky and the book, Morley did his best to concentrate on the words scrawled across the page. Behind each slash of ink was another, lighter mark, dismissed and unrecorded by history. Morley had first noticed the pale marks years ago as he read the tales to a young princess. He began studying them in earnest when she found her dragon. They told a very different story, one unfit for children's ears. Instead of the bumbling adventures of Yulrick the squire, it was a desperate tale of war, bloodshed, and pain.

Morley had forced himself to learn the archaic language in which it was written. The process of translation mired now and again by his lack of knowledge and was constantly interrupted by trips to the library and careful—oh, so careful—discussions with the clergy.

He found his place toward the end of the book and followed the words with his fingertip. It took him almost an hour, but he managed to translate the next paragraph, recording it on rough, hand-made paper.

When the paragraph was complete, he stared at the words struggling to understand what he had written.

He bowed in his grief. And his tears hardened to anger. And his anger turned to fury. And when he lifted his head, behold, a dragon stood before him. He put forth his hand and the dragon did again likewise. For the dragon was him and he was the dragon and together in their guilt and hatred, they raged.

Morley looked out the window to the Queen's tower.

Tears, anger, guilt . . .

His eyes slid from the tower to the grand chapel at the other end of the bailey. In the middle of the chapel, carved in pure white marble, lay the reason for all of it. For a week after their death, the Queen remained in the chapel, caressing the stone face of her husband and kissing the marble cheek of her toddler son.

Fury and hatred . . .

The dragon had appeared one week after they were buried.

He looked down at his translation.

For the dragon was him and he was the dragon and together in their guilt and hatred, they raged.

Standing alone in his room, staring at the Queen's tower and her dragon's aerie, Morley whispered, "Together they raged."

Chapter Eight

The Sibyl smeared ash from the funeral pyre across Eva's face. She was a Blood-Wraith, and as such, would wear a dead man's bones.

"It is fitting," the Sibyl said as she ground the dust into Eva's hair, "that you wear your first kill into battle. His ghost will frighten your enemies."

Eva trembled in the early morning air. The Sibyl had bathed her, fed her, and let her sleep in a warm cocoon of furs and wool blankets before waking her early this morning with whispered instructions to follow. She exchanged Eva's worn dress for loose trousers, a gauzy shirt, and a fitted leather jerkin with bone plates, all dusted with the same ashy gray from the pyre. The ashes coated her skin, her hair, her clothes, working its way into every crack and crevice in her skin. But this time she was coated with a stranger instead of her family and friends.

Pieces of Gavin's bones still burned with residual heat from the pyre. Ordinary fire was not as hot as dragon fire, Eva found, and so the bones took longer to break down. A long arm bone and half of his jawbone glowed with heat, but the rest had dissolved into ash.

"And if his ghost does not frighten your enemies, he will, at the very least, hide your scent." The Sibyl lifted a bowl of blood, collected from a recently slaughtered goat, and plunged her fingers into the viscous liquid.

Eva shuddered as she smeared the blood across her eyes, and down her chin. To be a Blood-Wraith, she had to look the part. And Blood-Wraiths were, by their very nature, bloody.

The Sibyl stood back to observe her handiwork. "There. Now you are a true Blood-Wraith." The Sibyl placed her hands on Eva's shoulders. "Do you understand what you must do?"

Eva stepped out of her hold and rubbed at her eyes. "Yes." She whispered the word. If she said it any louder, she thought she might scream.

For a moment, the Sibyl's eyes softened. "You will be with them soon."

Eva nodded. There was nothing more certain. "I know."

The Sibyl bent her head and whispered a prayer. Eva let the words slip off her skin where they pooled at her feet, forgotten. She stared through the camp at the horizon. The sun was rising, but she was just as dead as before. Nothing had changed.

Huru was suddenly at her elbow, one hand holding a shortsword, and the other holding the reins to a horse. The horse, too, was covered with ash. It stood placidly, tilting its head this way and that, and ash drifted to the ground with each movement.

"Is the Blood-Wraith ready?" Huru's eyes kept sliding past her, as though she was gone already.

Eva placed a hand over the small pouch tied to her waist. After three years of study, the Sibyl said that this was the only way to kill a dragon. Poison of the foulest kind lay on her hip, all she had to do was administer it. It would work. Or it wouldn't. Either way, her problems were solved.

"I'm ready." Her voice was reed-thin, like the wail of the wind through trees.

He boosted her onto the horse without another word, handing her the shortsword to buckle at her hip. He stepped back and turned his face to the sun. Eva took this moment to study him. Without his warpaint, he appeared younger, more vulnerable, despite his size. She wondered if his entire campaign rested on her shoulders. She wondered if she failed, if he would die.

A part of her was slightly dismayed to discover that she didn't care either way.

"We will be right behind you." The Sibyl handed Eva the reins. "You will succeed."

There was a lie in those words, carefully layered over with good intentions. But Eva just nodded and tugged at the reins, directing the horse north. The Sibyl may have waved farewell, but Eva didn't look back to see.

A few scattered soldiers stood as she rode by to watch her pass. Sometime in the night, the main body had broken camp and moved on, but they would not be accompanying her to the Queen's castle. Blood-Wraiths traveled alone.

She kept her eyes straight ahead, ignoring the blessings and curses tossed her way. Revenge would not be had by exchanging words with these men. Revenge would be had by killing the dragon.

And the only way to kill a dragon was not by meeting it head-on. It was through subterfuge and cunning.

And this was why, when the dragon descended on the camp, spewing fire and shrieking in rage, Eva hardened herself against the screams, stiffened her shoulders, and rode hard with flames chasing her back.

Chapter Nine

After two days of hard riding, her horse finally collapsed. She slit his throat and left him in some poor farmer's field, the blood watering a fresh crop of wheat. She continued the rest of the way on foot. The Sibyl's directions skirted around the town to the north side of the curtain wall where the forest slowly encroached on the castle. Beneath a bramble of thorns, she found the crumbling hole in the stone and crawled inside. There, the muted sounds of soldiers training lulled her into a dreamless slumber.

The lack of sound woke her. She crept into the open bailey, finding it deserted. The sun had gone down while she slept and the stars twinkled brightly in their dark bed. With a hand on the pouch at her hip, and the other clutching the short sword, she darted into the deeply shadowed crevice between a chicken coop and a pig pen. The animals were missing, nothing more than a few drifted feathers to indicate that they were here at all.

Eva waited one hour, then two, as the clouds chased each other across the moon. When she was certain the castle was asleep, she emerged from her hiding space and hurried across the open yard.

The southern tower was her goal. The dragon slept there each night. If Eva could make it to the roof, her task would be accomplished.

Locked.

Eva leaned her head against the door and tried the handle again. It still wouldn't budge.

The ache in her chest threatened to unravel.

Of course it was locked. She was a fool to think that the Queen wouldn't safeguard her dragon.

The knot of emotions began to loosen and she stepped back, pressing her hands to her chest, her head bowed.

There would be a way. There had to be a way.

The sound of a door opening behind her forced her into the shadows. She held her breath and watched as a man made his way across the yard, illuminated by a single candle on a tray held with both hands. The dishes on the tray and the key ring on his belt clicked and chimed with every step on the cobblestones. Eva's eyes narrowed. His halting walk and thinning white hair indicated an advanced age. But his shoulders were broad and his limbs strong. It was unlikely that she could subdue him and take the keys.

He approached the door to the southern tower and paused, his eyes lifted toward the sky. He mumbled what sounded like a prayer, and balanced the tray with one hand, unlocking the door with the other. As he hooked the keys back to his belt, he paused, noticing a smudge mark on the door.

Eva clutched her sword.

It was the ash from her forehead.

She had killed a soldier with nothing more than a butcher knife. She could certainly kill an old man with a sword.

He muttered something and rubbed at the mark with his sleeve, buffing it from the wood. When it was cleaned to his satisfaction, he opened the door and stepped inside, the tray rattling with each step.

Eva waited a moment, then followed.

The winding stairs were tall and narrow, but Eva managed them easily, taking long strides as she climbed. The flickering candlelight above her wavered in the darkness, and then paused. A moment later, the man knocked on a door.

Eva froze as the door opened and a woman's voice echoed down the stairs.

"Morley."

The tone, the sigh, the emotion, felt familiar. Eva crept upwards, keeping to the shadows, and peered at the landing.

The old man bowed at the waist, the tray carefully shifting in his grip. "My Queen."

She was beautiful. Standing in the soft glow of candlelight and framed by an intricately carved doorway, she was everything Eva imagined the Queen to be. Her eyebrows arched above wide, purple eyes. Full, pink lips lent a softness to a face with sharp cheekbones and a pointed chin. The crown on her head was heavy and golden, inset with bold red jewels. Her heavy brocade gown brushed the floor in perfect pleats.

But there was . . . something else. A darkness clouded her eyes and pulled her lips into a frown. And there, like a shadow, it stood behind the Queen, wrapping tendrils around her heart.

"Are they routed? Do we have them?" She demanded answers and the man delivered.

"Yes, my Queen. What is left of Huru's army is being led here as we speak." Morley straightened and the tray rattled again. "With Huru himself in chains."

The Queen smiled and withdrew into the room. After a moment's hesitation, the man followed and the light dimmed.

Eva fingered the pouch hanging from her waist. The poison was like a pulsing heartbeat, urging her upwards. She quickly crossed the landing, and hurried up the next flight of stairs. These led to a small hatch in the roof that opened easily at her touch. The hinges were well-oiled and well-used. She clambered onto the roof and stood with her arms outstretched, facing the aerie.

"Dragon," she called, her voice strong against the night wind.

Nothing.

The pouch burned at her side and the fury in her chest boiled, aching for release.

She crept towards the nest, her breath hitching with every step.

It was empty.

Sticks, silks, and gold formed the nest, with bones scattered across the floor.

She looked up. If the dragon wasn't here, where was it? The starry sky was empty of all but the stars, moon, and a few wispy clouds. She frowned and turned back to the nest.

A scrap of yellow caught her eye.

With halting steps, she walked around the pile of sticks, silks, gold, and bones, and touched the scrap of yellow wool. It was a torn strip of a skirt, with delicate pink roses embroidered on the hem.

With controlled horror, she lifted it from the nest.

It belonged to one of her sisters.

"Cara," she whispered, her gaze taking in the broken bones scattered around her. "Hamar."

There was no answer. Of course there was no answer. She stood on nothing but bones.

She turned her face to the sky, rage boiling in her chest.

A large hand covered her mouth, muffling her scream, and pulled her down to the roof. She stiffened and attempted to reach the short sword, but his arm pinned hers to her side.

"Quiet, Blood-Wraith," the old man said, holding her tight against his chest. "The dragon comes." He released his hold and tilted his head to the sky. "Quiet, or we're both dead."

Eva followed his gaze and saw on the horizon a pale shape gliding silently through the stars.

The old man placed a finger on his lips. "Stay silent, and follow me." He turned to go.

"Why?" Eva's whisper came out harsh and raw. "What do you want?"

"What do I want?" His eyes closed for a moment, and when he opened them, they glared fiercely. "To kill a dragon."

Chapter Ten

Morley stared at the girl sitting on the bed across from him, her legs drawn up to her chest, a scrap of embroidered wool clutched in her hands. She was gray. Everywhere gray. From the top of her head to the soles of her boots. The only break in color was the rusty brown stripe running across her eyes from temple to temple and the stain covering her chin and dripping down her neck.

She was a Blood-Wraith. But was she *the* Blood-Wraith? The one Huru's people prophesied would defeat the Queen's dragon? Looking at this girl, Morley didn't believe it.

"Did that . . ." He gestured to the yellow cloth in her grip. "Someone you know?"

She lifted her eyes and nodded.

Morley closed his eyes. Another added to his sins.

"Sometimes it—the dragon—brings someone home to . . ." He bit his lip and sighed. Explanations wouldn't help. "I'm sorry for your loss," he said finally.

She wrapped the fabric around her wrist, knotting it tightly. "You serve her. The Queen."

Morley nodded. "I do."

"*Why?*" The question snapped against the wall. "Why do you serve her and her dragon? They have murdered women, children, innocent people. Everyone I care about is dead because of them. So, why? Why do you serve them?"

It would take far too long to explain. The years and years he spent watching over and guiding a young princess engendered a love and loyalty that even when tested at its breaking point, held firm. How could he explain that watching that princess become a just and benevolent Queen brought him more joy than he could possibly contain? And that watching her descend into madness with a dragon on a leash brought immeasurable sorrow? How could he explain? He didn't try.

Instead, he stood and opened his cabinet, retrieving some wine. He poured it into two tin cups and handed one to the girl. He sat down at the desk and took a small sip. The girl watched warily, so he took a bigger draught, raising an eyebrow meaningfully. She glared, but still did not drink.

Morley leaned forward and laced his hands together, elbows propped on his knees. "I am looking for redemption, for me and my Queen."

The girl slid her legs off the edge of the bed and mimicked his pose. "And I am looking for revenge."

Morley nodded. "Then perhaps we can help each other."

He held his breath as the girl stared at him, examining his face and deciding whether or not to trust him.

Finally, she nodded and, with eyes fixed on him, took a sip of wine.

And Morley's heart sank.

Chapter Eleven

The Blood-Wraith walked to the throne room in chains.

The shackles on her wrists chafed and, as Morley pulled her along, finally broke through her skin. Blood appeared and oozed down her wrists, staining her hands. Morley pretended he didn't see it and the girl made no sounds of distress.

Morley glanced back at her to see her eyelids heavy and her limbs weighed down. She had yet to fully wake up from her drug-induced slumber. He had stripped the girl of her sword and, more importantly, of the pouch of poison on her belt. But he left the ash and blood. The Queen would want a good show.

For a moment, he thought about turning back. He could go back to his room, let the girl recover, and set her free. There was no need to go through with this.

And then he thought of his Queen, carelessly striding through puddles of blood and around piles of bones to stroke her dragon's cheek.

The story in the Draxoni book had ended badly. He had finished translating it last night while the girl slept. He couldn't leave his Queen to that fate.

He tightened his grip on the chains. He told himself that it was better this way. He told himself that she wouldn't feel anything.

He'd tell himself anything to make this seem like less of a betrayal.

The two guards outside the door stepped in front of Morley, blocking his way.

"What have you here, Morley?" Connor asked, his voice pitched low.

Morley tugged the Blood-Wraith forward, ignoring her stumble and slurred curse. "A gift for the Queen and her Dragon."

Connor stared at the girl, his face paling. He never could handle the sight of blood very well, and with the stains on the girl's face and the new blood dripping from her wrists, the guard looked positively ill. Morley always thought it odd that he became a palace guard instead of a blacksmith like his father. He jerked his head at Nicko, the other guard, and stepped back to his post.

Morley, his heart pounding in his chest, tugged the girl forward.

The throne room was full. Courtiers lined the walls, their expensive, finely-wrought garments muted and plain. The Queen's soldiers and guards stood in a ring just in front of the courtiers, their uniforms dusty and stained from battle.

The Queen stood on the dais in front her throne, addressing the room. Behind her stood her dragon, wings folded across its serpentine body and arched neck stretched high. Its golden eyes scanned the room, passing quickly over Morley and his prisoner, and its tail twitched and curled around the dais steps.

And lined in rows and rows in the middle of the room stood the dirty, bloody, beaten soldiers of Huru's army.

Skirting the edge of the room, Morley led the Blood-Wraith through the courtiers, earning a few wide eyes, but no exclamations. No one dared make a sound while the Queen spoke. As they approached the throne, he could better hear the Queen's words.

She always did have the talent for diction.

"--who have thought to murder me, you who have longed to destroy my kingdom, you *traitors*, look where your general has led!" She flung back her long sleeves and walked to the edge of the dais. "Do you believe in mercy?" Her harsh whisper echoed through the room.

Morley halted at the edge of the dais. Huru himself was in front of his army. He knelt, clutching a bleeding wound in his side, but his head was held high. This man had pride and it would take more than a dragon to take it from him. His Sibyl knelt at his side, her left side badly burned. Most of the hair on her head was missing and she wheezed when she drew breath.

"Mercy?" the Sibyl croaked. "Mercy will never be had from one such as you."

The Queen paused and her Dragon lowered its head, drawing even with its Queen. She reached out a hand and placed it on the Dragon's cheek, eyes pinned to the Sibyl. "You are right." She addressed the entire room. "Anyone who opposes me will not receive mercy!"

The dragon's lips peeled away from its teeth and Morley stepped forward, dragging the Blood-Wraith with him. He bowed, placing a hand over his heart.

"My Queen."

She paused and the dragon turned to stare down at them.

"Morley, what do you have?"

Morley raised his head, tugged the chain, and flung the girl to the floor. "I have your Blood-Wraith."

Chapter Twelve

Eva's knees hit hard, drawing blood. She caught herself on her hands and struggled to lift her head. The man, Morley, had drugged her, and she couldn't shake the dense fog clouding her mind. She heard the Queen and Morley exchanging words, something about the dragon and a Blood-Wraith and a celebratory drink.

She blinked at her gray hands, wrists shackled and bloodied. Everywhere she looked was gray and red. She stretched out her fingers on the stone and the shackles shifted. A scrap of yellow caught her eye. She focused on it, noticing the embroidered roses soaking the blood from her wrist.

The fog cleared.

Cara and Hamar. One of her sisters was eaten by the dragon and her skirt used to line its bed. Her village was burned to the ground, taking her family, her friends, and her life with it. And she was here, a prisoner in chains on the cold floor.

The Queen and Morley laughed above her and she heard the clink of silver on glass. The dragon's hot breath blew down, flattening her hair and clothes. If she looked up, she would see the maw of the dragon. She wondered if her sister was frightened when she faced those teeth. Did she shriek and cry? Or did she submit to her fate?

Eva bowed her head to the floor and felt the knot in her chest burst. Emotions poured out of her. Guilt, grief and anger swirled together and became rage. She hated the Queen and her dragon. They would both suffer.

She was here as a prisoner, but she was also here for revenge.

With her head bowed and her eyes squeezed shut, she screamed in fury and grief.

An answering wail echoed above her, combined with the cries from the crowd and the shriek of the Queen's Dragon.

Eva lifted her head.

There, between her and the Queen's dragon, stood another dragon, ashy gray, with red eyes and snout, snarling in rage.

Chapter Thirteen

Morley dropped the pitcher of wine and it shattered against the stones. At the sound, the smaller dragon leapt.

The entire room held its breath as the gray dragon latched onto the larger dragon's neck. The golden dragon roared and flung itself into the air, crashing against the ceiling.

One dragon was frightening, but two were terrifying. The crowd descended into madness, clawing at each other to exit the room.

Morley dragged the Queen off the dais and hurried to the wall, positioning his body in front of hers. She stared upwards, her wine-stained lips parted, goblet in her hand.

"Morley, what . . . what . . ." She was again a bewildered child.

This was the second time Morley had observed her like this. The first was in the Before, when she lay curled against her husband and child's tomb, wondering what happened. Then, Morley had the painful task of explaining to the young Queen that her King and husband had been loyal all along and that the real traitor was the snake of a chamberlain whispering in her ear. Morley told this wide-eyed child that the traitor had confessed hours after the King had succumbed to the poison his wife had carefully slipped into his wine, unknowing that he sometimes gave sips to their child.

And now, he had another unenviable task. His chest caved as he slipped the now empty pouch out of his pocket.

"My Queen." He shouted to be heard over the screaming crowd.

She ignored him, staring at the dragons raging in the rafters above her. "My dragon is injured. Look!" She pointed a finger at the golden dragon.

Morley spared a glance at the battle above them. The gray dragon had positioned itself on the bigger dragon's back, claws digging into scales and its teeth latched on the back of the golden dragon's neck. Droplets of blood rained down on the crowd, sizzling where they landed. He dropped his gaze to the Blood-Wraith. She stood still, her hands outstretched, eyes closed, ignoring the dragon blood dripping down her face and hair, burning away the ash rubbed into her skin.

The Queen dropped the goblet of wine and grabbed his arm. Morley closed his eyes at the feel of the red wine soaking his trousers. One more task. One more explanation.

"Stop them, Morley! Stop them!" The Queen shrieked as loud as her dragon.

Morley grabbed her shoulders and shook her. "My Queen! Listen to me! You don't have much time!"

She froze, her eyes widening on his. "What . . . do you mean, Morley?"

"You've been—" He swallowed once, twice, then managed to get the words out. "You've been poisoned, my Queen."

She stared at the pouch in his hands, then touched her tongue to her lip. "The wine."

He nodded, blinking away tears.

The Queen sagged and Morley stretched out a hand.

"Why?" she whispered.

"I had to, my Queen. I had to." He gathered her into his arms and sank to the ground. He cradled her as he had for many years, tight against his chest, with her ear pressed to his heart. "Do you believe in mercy, my Queen?"

She coughed, wet and bloody against his chest. "For you?"

Morley bent his head to hers and let the tears fall, flowing down his cheeks and washing her face. "For all of us."

The Queen convulsed in his arms, her hands clawing at his shoulders. When she spoke, her voice was broken and small. "I thought you were mine, Morley. I thought you were mine."

He tightened his hold on the child he had loved for so many years and ignored the dragons raging above them.

"Always, my Queen. Always."

But she was already gone.

Chapter Fourteen

They buried the Queen next to her husband and child in the chapel, an effigy carved out of pure white marble atop her tomb. The remaining lords and ladies attended, each one wearing somber grays and blacks, with white roses in their grip. The funeral didn't last long and even the Bishop exited the chapel when it was done.

Eva watched the funeral procession from atop the southern tower, her dragon at her side. The aerie had been cleared of the gold, scraps of fabric, and bones, but remained a perfect perch for the ashy gray dragon with the blood-red eyes.

Eva stretched out a hand and her dragon bowed its head, leaning into her touch.

She was afraid to learn her name. She was afraid it would be her own. They were connected in ways that she didn't understand. Every time she touched the smooth gray scales she felt boiling emotions just under the surface, but Eva herself felt calm and detached.

It didn't make any sense.

But nothing about this made sense.

The door in the roof clicked open and the dragon turned its head. General Huru held out a placating palm.

"Easy, dragon."

Eva placed a hand on her dragon's neck and she settled. "She won't eat you."

Huru winced as he climbed onto the roof. "I was talking to you."

Eva scowled, then paused. Irritation was the first real emotion she had felt since the dragon appeared.

Huru carefully picked his way across the roof and then stepped into the nest, sitting down next to Eva. He watched the chapel for a moment, then turned and stared at the pyre in the bailey. They had gathered wood and cut down trees for three days to make one big enough, piling the wood high on top of the dragon where it had fallen. Eva's gray dragon would light the pyre later this evening, when the people had gathered to watch. It wasn't every day that the soldiers and courtiers and village-folk received vengeance for the death of their loved ones.

"My people will finally have peace." Huru said, his face hard.

Eva thought of Rose Haven, burned to ashes. "So will mine."

"Your Queen became a monster, Blood-Wraith." Huru turned, eyeing her and the dragon at her side. "My Sibyl may have passed through the veil of death, but I learned a great many things from her. Namely, how to kill a dragon."

Eva nodded, but her fingers curled against her dragon. The beast hissed at the General, then returned its gaze to the chapel.

"I know," Eva said.

Huru ran his hands down his face, smearing the blackened stripe around his eyes. "And I will know where to find you."

"That you do," Eva agreed.

He nodded and clapped her on the shoulder. "Good luck, Blood-Wraith. I hope we never meet again."

Later, as the pyre burned, Eva leaned against the wall in the bailey. Her dragon lay curled at her feet, tail twitching as it watched the fire. Morley approached from the shadows, giving the dragon a wide berth, and stood next to her.

"They want you crowned." He watched the blaze for a moment, then said, "The title of Queen comes with many responsibilities." He turned toward her. "Your people come first. No matter what."

Eva nodded in agreement. "I will remember."

She examined him, taking in his somber clothing and the white rose pinned to his jacket. She thought of the Sibyl throwing herself in front of a dragon to save the life of General Huru. And she thought of Morley taking the Queen's life to save her soul. And a phrase rolled around in her head. She tasted the words in her mouth, disliking the flavor. But she said them anyway.

"Are you mine, Morley?"

The old man froze, his eyes drifting to the chapel doors. In the flames reflected in his eyes, Eva thought she saw a deepening sorrow.

"No," Morley finally answered. "No, I'm not." He met her eyes and took a deep breath. "But I will help you. To the best of my abilities, I will help you become a good Queen."

Eva nodded and his honesty warmed something in her chest. She squatted beside her dragon and ran a hand down its crest. Emotions boiled beneath the scales, but the rage was fading. She stood, squaring her shoulders and the dragon lifted her head.

"Then let's begin."

Therapy for a Dragon
Sam Knight

"THE DRAGON WOULD CREEP INTO MY ROOM EVERY NIGHT AND whisper to me," Majorie said distantly. It was strange to be able to look back on such terrible times fondly. She had never dreamed those nights, filled with such fear and danger, would be the ones she treasured most, the only ones when she had been allowed to be a little girl.

"And what would it say?"

The bespectacled man impatiently tapped his pencil against the side of his clipboard. The rapid ticking sound echoed in the small green-tiled room, making it feel even more closed in than it had before. They had been over this many times before. He didn't even ask her about the dragon anymore, only the words.

"That words were magic," she finally answered. "That they had power."

"What kind of power?" he asked. It was one of his standard questions. They had been over this a dozen times at least.

"Every kind of power that matters." One of her standard answers.

The man sighed heavily, blowing the air out through pursed lips. His frustration was showing through. Today, for the first time, he had sat where Majorie could actually get a good look at him.

But she didn't bother.

She had been in this room too long to care. When he had first come to ask questions, weeks or maybe months ago, she had strained to see him at the edge of her sight, fighting against the restraints to turn her head far enough to see his form in her peripheral vision. But now she didn't care what he looked like. It wasn't worth irritating the bedsores to turn her head and see.

"Your words didn't have the power to save your family."

Majorie blinked, becoming aware again of the crack in the ceiling that looked like a wilted lily. Though she had stared at it for what seemed like an eternity, she hadn't actually seen it for a long time now.

He had mentioned her family before, but never so directly. So . . . accusingly.

Something had changed.

She turned her head and met his steel gray eyes.

He was losing his temper.

"Words killed my family." It was impossible for her not to see the images of the soldiers dressed in black, claiming to be peacekeepers.

"Bullets killed your family." His voice was cold. Not merely distant as his tone had been in the past, but cold and heartless. Hateful.

"Bullets fired by men because of words said to them," she countered.

"So yours are not the only words of power?" The man raised his eyebrow, seemingly genuinely interested in what she had to say for the first time in a long time.

"All words are power."

"Are my words power?"

In his eyes, Majorie thought she finally saw what this man was looking for.

"Are they?"

"I was asking you the question."

Majorie resisted the temptation to respond with another question. There was something in his eyes, in the desperate way he suddenly needed to know the answer to this question when all the rest of the questions had been asked with such a clinical affect for so long now.

How long had she been here? She looked back to the crack in the ceiling. It seemed to her that once it had not been a wilted flower, but a blooming one. Nonsense, she knew, but how long had she been here?

"Why do you not answer me? Do you have no respect for your elders? Is that why your family died? Because you went against their wishes and spoke your traitorous words to anyone who would listen?"

Majorie almost felt the cold emotions stir to life within her. Almost. It wasn't time for them yet. For now, she still needed to remain numb.

"My family died, as did so many others, not because they listened to my words, but because the monster who controls this country is afraid of my words," she said.

"The words of a little girl. Why should anyone be afraid of the words of a little girl?"

"I don't know. Why should they?" Majorie gave in and returned questions. "Who should be afraid of someone who is too young, the wrong gender, the wrong religion, the wrong race? What words could someone so worthless possibly speak that could impact anyone or anything?"

"You are still so insolent. Even after all that has happened to you. To your family. Do you really think these words that you speak are so powerful? Who is here to hear them? What can they do?"

"You are here. And you are hearing them. They will eventually free me. They will eventually free everyone." Majorie tried to shift on the bed, but against her restraints she was only able to move millimeters. "Can you not feel them affecting you?"

The man chuckled humorlessly. "I became immune to the tears of little girls many years ago."

"I am not crying. Nor am I begging. But your claim that I am does not surprise me. I would expect no less from the lapdog of a lying, murderous, petty dictator."

The room seemed to hold its breath as the echoes of those words faded.

"I am no lapdog. And your great leader is no petty dictator."

"But you admit he is a liar and murderous?"

The man stood. "I think perhaps you need more time alone with your words so that you can learn to choose them more wisely."

"That might not be wise on your part. I may finally come up with the words to free myself."

Walking to the edge of the bed, he looked down at her with cold eyes. "You really don't understand your predicament, do you?

"I guess I expected too much from a little girl. I should have realized that it was all coincidental. A confluence of events. There is no way anyone could have planned such an uprising against me, let alone a silly little girl and her family." He dropped the clipboard and pencil upon her bound legs. "I have no further use for you."

Majorie looked away from the crack to meet his eyes.

"Ah. So now you see who I am. Your deceitful words could never have turned me against myself. They are not so magic after all."

Majorie smiled and a giggle escaped her cracked lips.

"You have gone insane? Good."

"No." Majorie shook her head. "I finally figured out the magic words to free this country. The magic words to be rid of you."

The man snorted. "Words are just words. They are not magic."

"But they are. And so are dragons. And the right magic word, said to the right dragon, is all I need."

"Then say your magic word, stupid child. Say it now, for tomorrow I will have you publically executed for treason."

Majorie nodded. "Please," she said quietly.

"Please?" he snapped angrily. "Do you think you can beg of me now?"

"Oh, I wasn't talking to you. I was talking to the dragon. And that is the magic word. Please."

"Bah!" The man spun on his heel and into the jaws of the waiting beast, which snapped down violently, with an echoing chomp.

Majorie smiled at the shimmering outline of the dragon as it chewed. "Thank you," she said.

Taking Wing
Julia H. West

Sofria sat on one corner of the widest street in Tarnisi, on the plaza right outside the Guild Hall. Papa Matteo carried her there every morning, sat her down on a piece of old sacking, and arranged her twisted, stick-thin legs in front of her. Then he set her cup near her, growled, "You'd best make more today than you did yesterday, or no supper for you," and left.

A fine drizzle dampened the plaza. It always rained in Tarnisi, it seemed to Sofria. She pulled a rag over her head to try to keep dry, or maybe get slightly warmer, but the cloth was already soaked through. She leaned back against the building, to take advantage of the overhang of the Guild Hall's roof, but that didn't help much. The Guild Hall was very tall—taller than the Cathedral across the plaza. There was too much rain, and not enough shelter.

People hurried past her, women holding shawls over their heads, men with capes and broad-brimmed hats to keep them dry. Some even spattered water onto Sofria as they splashed through puddles, but acted as if they didn't see her sitting there. She was used to that. The fine ladies holding their gowns out of puddles paid her no heed. Only people like the stout woman with three small children trailing behind her, all holding hands, noticed her.

The stout woman stopped in front of Sofria. "You're soaked through, child," she said.

Sofria just nodded. Of course she was—it was raining.

"Don't you have a shawl? Nothing but that old rag?"

"It's all I got," Sofria said. "Papa can't spare nothing for a shawl."

"You poor thing." The woman reached into her skirt and pulled something from the pocket hidden underneath. "Here, at least you don't have to starve while you're wet."

It was a whole bread bun. Sofria looked up at her and smiled. "Thank you so much, my lady!" she said. Sofria had discovered that everyone liked to be called "my lord" or "my lady." It made them feel important, even if they had red chapped hands from doing laundry, like the stout woman did.

The woman blushed. "Eat it quickly now, child. Don't let it get all soggy." She tugged at the children, who had stared at Sofria's twisted legs in their much-mended stockings the whole time, and bustled off across the plaza.

Sofria ate most of the bun, and hid the rest under her skirt where she hoped it wouldn't get too wet. She liked it when people gave her food. If she ate it before Papa Matteo came back, he'd never know about it, and couldn't take it away or say she had already eaten, so he didn't need to give her supper.

It started raining harder. The water that fell on the roof of the Guild Hall dripped from the mouths of monsters, one on each corner of the building. They decorated the Guild Hall, but also kept water from cascading off the roof and soaking people beneath. Or so Osanna the storyteller said. Channels on the roof gathered rain water and sent it to the monsters, who spewed it into gutters like the one not far from where Sofria sat. Sofria didn't like that gutter—it stank of rotting vegetables and old fish, and chamberpots people emptied into it. Papa Matteo said the smell was a blessing to her. No one else wanted a corner that stank. So she sat in a place where many of Tarnisi's people passed every day, and some might feel pity for her and drop coins in her cup.

The monster nearest Sofria was fat and round, with clawed feet and a very wide mouth. Its wings were folded along its back, and its back legs gripped the edge of the roof far above her. She couldn't see many details of the monster—it was too far up—but she had sat beneath it for eight years, looking up at it until it seemed like a friend. She sometimes imagined that wide mouth, when water wasn't pouring from it, saying things like, "I'm watching you, Sofria. Someday I'll take you away from Tarnisi."

But now the water dripping from the monster's mouth became a heavier stream, splashing into the gutter near Sofria. She couldn't imagine it talking when so much water poured from its mouth, so she sat sadly, shivering a little, as people dashed past and paid her no heed.

Near midday the rain slackened. Sofria sat up from her miserable wet huddle in time to see a man in brightly embroidered clothing, with a sword at his hip, hurry past. Even though he seemed not to see her, he dropped a coin in her cup. Sofria smiled. She would have at least one coin for Papa Matteo. Maybe he wouldn't beat her tonight.

The sun broke through the clouds, and Sofria raised her face to its warmth. Above her, the stream of water falling from the fat monster's mouth dwindled, and Sofria imagined it licking its lips and saying, "That was a fine meal." She imagined it shifting its wings a little, getting more comfortable on its perch atop the Guild Hall. *Does the monster have a name?* Sofria thought. *What can it see from up there? The golden statues in the Cathedral? The Duke's Palace? Heaven?* Sofria didn't know much about heaven. Sometimes men in black gowns stood in the middle of the plaza. She remembered everything they said, though it never made much sense. They shouted about how good people went to heaven when they died, and wicked people went to hell. It seemed heaven was above her, higher than the top of the Guild Hall. Hell sounded like where she lived with Papa Matteo—hot, crowded, and stinking. She didn't want to go there.

With the sun out, and the streets drying, people slowed their steps as they crossed the plaza. The storyteller, Osanna, took up a place on the rim of the fountain. Soon children—and some older people—gathered around her, sitting cross-legged on the cobbles. Today the story was about a hero who had gone through many trials to find and kill a dragon. Osanna's words came clearly to Sofria as she described the dragon. Tall as a cottage, with scaly back and wings. It had claws on its four legs, and a mouth full of sharp teeth. It opened its mouth wide to breathe fire.

Sofria considered the monster far above her on the roof of the Guild Hall. It had wings, and four clawed legs, and a mouth that opened wide to . . . spout water. Was the monster above her a dragon, then? A dragon that breathed water instead of fire? She imagined asking it that. "Are you a dragon?"

It laughed, a great bellow of a laugh. "I can be a dragon if you want me to, Sofria," it said.

But the dragon in Osanna's story was wicked, and killed people and ate their sheep and cattle. "You're not wicked, are you?" she imagined asking the monster above her.

"Not all dragons are wicked. Do you want me to be wicked?"

"Oh, no!" Sofria had seen enough of wickedness in her life, and didn't like it. She liked good people, such as the stout woman who gave her the bun, and the man with the sword who dropped a coin in her cup.

"Then I will not be wicked. I will be a good dragon for you, Sofria." Sofria smiled, and realized she had missed the rest of Osanna's story while talking with her dragon.

"Do you have a name?" she imagined asking her dragon.

It made a gruff noise, as if clearing its throat. "I have been called many things."

"What do you mean?"

"When I drip water on people's heads, they look up at me and yell things like," the dragon paused, then said a few words that Sofria knew were not very nice. Papa Matteo yelled them at her and the other children when he was angry.

"Those are *not* good names," said Sofria solemnly. "My name is Sofria. You need a good name, like that."

"When I was being carved, my maker called me—"

A woman with a wrinkled face and a threadbare green shawl came up to Sofria, smiling. "I have something for you, little girl," she said. "My own little girl grew up and doesn't need it anymore." She took a red ribbon, rather frayed but quite long, from her pocket and put it into Sofria's hand. "Such a cheerful color, red," the woman said. "I hope it makes you happy."

Sofria stared up at the woman, lips trembling. "It is beautiful," she whispered. "I've never had anything beautiful. Thank you, my lady."

"Shall I tie it in your hair?" the woman asked.

Sofria was about to say no, that if Papa Matteo saw it he would take it away to sell, and then decided she could wear it for *part* of the day. "Yes, please," she said.

The woman smoothed Sofria's hair, put the ribbon around the back and over the top, wrapped it twice, then tied it atop Sofria's head. "There. May it bring you joy." She patted Sofria's shoulder and hurried away before Sofria could thank her again.

That was the last pleasant thing that happened to Sofria for most of the rest of the day. Two boys splashed water from the stinking gutter onto her, laughed, and ran away. A man with puffy sleeves and very tight trousers told her beggars shouldn't sit in front of the Guild Hall, that it cheapened the building in people's minds. A puppet show set up in the plaza, but since the stage faced toward the Cathedral, all she could see was the curtain covering the people who made the puppets move.

As evening drew near, Sofria took the ribbon from her hair and stuffed it up her sleeve so Papa Matteo wouldn't see it. She was certain the bread the stout woman had given her would be her only food for the day. She had one coin in her cup—the one the man with the sword had given her. Papa Matteo would curse at her and give her no supper.

She bit her lips, hoping that Papa Matteo wouldn't beat her, and looked up at her dragon. It had been telling her something when the kind woman came up. They had been talking of . . . names.

"Dragon," she imagined saying to it. "I'm sorry. I've ignored you."

"Most of the city ignores me," it answered. "I am far above their heads. But you, so small below me, you have watched me for a long time."

"You have wings! You could fly away from here. I . . . I can't walk. I have to be carried."

"But I am bound to this building. My wings are for nothing but show."

Sofria sighed. "Then we are both bound here. I'm glad I can talk to you. Now . . . what were you saying, that your maker called you?"

"Pietra," said the dragon. "But he laughed when he called me that."

That was not one of the bad words that Papa Matteo shouted. It sounded nice. Pi-e-tra. Pi-e-tra. "I like that name," said Sofria. "May I call you Pietra?"

"Of course you may." Was it the sun in her eyes, or did the dragon—Pietra—shift its wings? She knew it could not, for it was stone. But she could imagine. And she imagined that it stretched its smooth—not feathery like a bird's—wings a bit, then settled them against its back again.

A man in brown brocade with huge sleeves, slashed so gold showed through, dropped a coin into Sofria's cup, never meeting her eyes. He walked up to the great doors of the Guild Hall, pulled them open, and entered. Moments later, a woman with very wide skirts and sleeves dropped another coin into Sofria's cup. "Thank you kindly, my lady," Sofria called after her. Three coins. Perhaps she would get supper tonight after all.

The next day was sunny, and Sofria gained far more coins than she had on the wet day before. People stopped and talked to her, and the stout woman came by again and shared sugar candy with Sofria.

"What's your name, child?" the woman asked. When Sofria told her, the woman introduced herself. "I'm Betani, and these are Ercoli, Luania, and Vinela." She pointed to her three children, who stood staring at Sofria's legs.

Ercoli, the boy, took a deep breath and then asked, "What-happened-to-your-legs?" all in a quick breath, as if he was afraid she might bite him for asking.

"I was born this way," Sofria said. "I've never been able to walk."

"Oh, you poor thing," said Betani, the stout woman. "How do you get here?"

"Papa Matteo carries me."

"And just leaves you? A little girl like you? My boy Ercoli is eleven, and you look much younger."

"I don't know how old I am, but I might be eleven too," said Sofria. "I remember eight years here in the plaza, after my mama died, and before that when I was little I begged with her."

"Eight years here! Well, I'll watch out for you if I can. I collect and deliver laundry all over this part of the city. Be well." She took her children by the hands and they threaded between people, crossing the crowded plaza.

Sofria made the sugar candy last most of the day, sucking on it little by little. As the day waned, a man sitting on the rim of the fountain throwing bread to the pigeons gave her the last piece. He must have seen her watching him, wishing she were a pigeon. The bread wasn't even stale.

After she thanked the man and he left, smiling, she leaned back and looked up at her dragon, Pietra. "Today was a better day, Pietra," she imagined saying.

"I like the sunshine, too, although I fulfill my function when it rains."

"What does that mean, 'fulfill my function'?" Sofria asked.

"I was made to drain water off the roof. It makes me feel good when it rains and I can do what I was made to do."

"Do you think I was made to be a beggar, because of my twisted legs?" The idea did not make Sofria feel good. In fact, it made her sad.

"No, because you are more than your legs. You have a mind, and you are good at imagining things. See how you have learned to talk to me."

Sofria turned that idea over in her mind. If she imagined she talked to Pietra, and Pietra told her nice things, was it just herself telling herself nice things? Those thoughts just confused her, so she stopped thinking about it. She would just enjoy talking to Pietra.

"Do you ever wish you could do something besides what you were made to do?" Sofria asked. "You have wings, and they were made to be a part of you. Do you wish you could fly?"

Pietra was quiet for a long time. Sofria thought about how marvelous it would be to fly above the city, looking down at the people walking through the plaza. She had never been outside the city. If she could fly she could see forests, farms, and other cities besides Tarnisi—things she heard of in Osanna's stories.

Finally Pietra said in a husky voice, "I would *love* to fly. To feel wind beneath my wings, to soar over the city, to see something besides the people below me and the Cathedral across the plaza—that is my dream. I was not made to fly, but I *wish* to fly."

A huge idea bubbled up in Sofria. "If you fly, I can ride you and fly, too! It would be wonderful. Far above the stinking gutter, and the boys that splash me or steal my coins."

"If *you* imagine us flying, we can fly."

Of course that was true. But before Sofria could try to imagine flying, a crowd of boys ran past and she had to sweep her cup under her skirts to keep them from kicking it over. Then two women in bright-colored gowns bustled past, dropping coins into the cup she had just replaced near her feet, without even looking at her.

The sun disappeared behind the Guild Hall and Papa Matteo was coming across the plaza toward her, so Sofria shoved the last of the bread the pigeon man had given her into her mouth. It was gone by the time Papa Matteo strode over, looked down at Sofria's cup, and grunted.

"You did well today, girl," Papa Matteo said. He emptied Sofria's cup into his pocket, handed it to her, then bent to pick her up.

That night, supper was stale bread and a few vegetables floating in broth that might once have had meat in it, before it was served to the children. After supper, Papa Matteo sent the children to bed. Sofria lay on her straw pallet listening to the other three girls breathing. She tried to imagine how Pietra would fly. The dragon had a round, wide body, and the smooth, ribbed wings grew from its shoulders. Yesterday she had imagined it lifting those wings, spreading them a little bit. If Pietra spread its wings all the way, they would each be as long as its body. Sofria had watched pigeons hopping about on the plaza, spreading and flapping their wings. Pietra's wings had no feathers. How would that change how it flew?

Pigeons fluttered about a lot. Sofria couldn't imagine Pietra fluttering. Those sleek wings would rise and fall smoothly, quietly, without all the bother that pigeons made. She imagined Pietra flexing its clawed toes, the ones clutching the roof so tightly. Little by little the tight hold it had on the roof loosened. It spread its wings wide in the night. Sofria imagined the stars shining down, and maybe moonlight—though she couldn't see moonlight, for she slept in a cellar room with no windows. With a push of its strong legs, Pietra released its hold on the roof of the Guild Hall.

Pietra's wings spread even wider as they caught the air. Although its body was round, and made of stone, it wasn't fat or heavy. Somehow Sofria knew that. Its wings held it up easily. Could it hold her, too, if she sat on its back? She didn't weigh much.

Strong wings flapped slowly, and Pietra circled over the plaza. Lights shone from Cathedral windows below. Pietra turned, then flew in a straight line toward where more lights blazed, farther away in the city. Was that the Duke's Palace? The dragon flew without making a sound, the long wings only flapping enough to keep Pietra aloft. When it reached the lights, it circled, watching people in fabulous costumes dancing in a courtyard below.

Since Pietra had never used its wings before, it was getting tired. It swooped back toward the Guild Hall and dropped quietly to the roof. Its strong back claws gripped the edge, it folded its wings, and once more became a motionless monster looming over the plaza in the center of Tarnisi.

A drizzle met Sofria when Papa Matteo carried her out of the lodgings the next morning. The cobbles were already wet when he set her down next to the gutter outside the Guild Hall. There wasn't enough rain yet for water to pour from Pietra's mouth, but occasional drips into the gutter splashed stinking water onto the cobbles. Sofria pulled the rag over her head and sighed. Today would not be as good as yesterday.

She huddled close to the Guild Hall's stone wall to keep from getting splashed by people hurrying past, and looked up at Pietra far above her. "Did you enjoy flying last night, Pietra?" she imagined herself saying to the dragon.

"Yes, yes!" came Pietra's joyful reply. "It is better than I ever imagined! To see more of the city than just the Cathedral, to move on my own, to be free of the Guild Hall's roof. Thank you, Sofria."

"I'm glad you are happy," Sofria said. She paused a moment, biting her lower lip, then said, "Do you think I might fly with you some time?"

"I'm sure you could," said Pietra. "You are small and I am large, and my wings are very strong."

"But what if someone saw us?"

"Do you want them to see us?"

"No! This should be a secret. Everyone would point and stare. 'See the stone monster from the roof flying about the city!' they would call, and the city guard would no doubt shoot arrows at us." The idea of all those people staring at her frightened Sofria. She didn't mind people stopping and talking to her, in her place against the Guild Hall's wall. But having them all stare at her as she did something they had never seen before—no, that would be too scary.

"If you don't want them to see us, they won't see us," said Pietra, and Sofria knew it was true. This was *her* imagining, things she didn't want to happen would not.

"When can we fly?" she asked Pietra. "I don't think I can get out at night. Papa Matteo locks the cellar door."

"Right now would be good. No one is paying attention to you, so they won't notice if you're gone. Who would look up at the roof in the rain to see that I'm not there?"

"Right now?" Sofria took a deep breath, and her heart started pounding with excitement.

"Right now." Pietra slowly spread its smooth, ribbed wings, then pulled first one, then the other clawed back foot from the roof. It swooped downward, circling the plaza, and came to rest on the cobbles in front of Sofria.

Sofria could hardly breathe, her heart was beating so fast. She reached out to touch one of Pietra's feet. This close up she saw webbing between the claws. The dragon spread one of its wings over her head to shield her from the rain.

"How do I get onto your back? I can't stand on my own." Had she been able to stand, she might be able to reach over Pietra's back and pull herself up.

"Crawl onto my foot," Pietra said. The dragon flattened itself to the ground, and when Sofria dragged herself onto its foot, she found herself lifted toward its back.

"Grab the base of my wing and pull yourself up on my neck."

"Will it hurt you?" Sofria asked breathlessly.

"I'm made of stone. You cannot hurt me."

With arms strengthened from dragging herself everywhere she wasn't carried, Sofria grabbed Pietra's wing and pulled herself onto the dragon's neck. It took her some time to arrange her legs astride the dragon, as she could only move them with her hands. But finally she sat atop Pietra, just in front of its wings.

"Lean forward and grasp my neck. I don't want you to fall."

Sofria leaned forward and put her chin on the top of Pietra's head, between its eyes, and wrapped her arms around its neck. It didn't feel like stone, but smooth, warm skin. She was shaking with excitement, but trying to take in every detail of the moment.

"Ready?"

"Yes!"

Pietra pushed upward with strong legs, and began to beat its wings. With every beat, Sofria and the dragon rose above the plaza. Soon they were higher than the top of the fountain, then higher than the statues atop the Cathedral's great doors. When Sofria realized she could see the roof of the Cathedral itself she wanted to shout, 'We're flying!' but it came out in a shaky whisper. "We're flying."

Rain misted around them, and Pietra said, "I don't want to fly much higher, or we'll end up in the middle of a cloud."

"A cloud! You can fly into a cloud?" She had never imagined such a thing before.

"I can, but we don't want to. It's cold and wet, and I can't see anything."

"Have you been in a cloud before?"

"When clouds settle low over the plaza, I've sometimes been inside one for hours. I don't find it exciting."

Pietra circled over the plaza one more time, so Sofria, peeking over its shoulder, could see how tiny the people below looked. Then it flew in the direction it had gone last night.

"Is that the Duke's Palace?" Sofria asked, as they flew over a building much larger than most in the city, with towers and porticos and many windows. Last night its courtyard had been lit up and glittering with people in colorful clothing. This morning it was empty and wet.

"Yes. It is one of the most beautiful buildings in the city—besides the Cathedral, of course."

It seemed to Sofria that the dragon's wings were beating slower. "Are you getting tired?"

"I haven't used my wings in all the years since I was made. Until I strengthen them, short flights like this are all we can make." Pietra lifted a wingtip to turn and Sofria watched people, carriages, and horses, like tiny dolls, in the streets below them.

There was bustle and activity at the edge of the city, though she couldn't see much besides movement. "What's over there?" she asked Pietra.

"I don't know. We'll have to explore that another day."

Back at the plaza Pietra waited, flapping its great wings, for people to move away from where Sofria usually sat. Then it settled to the ground with hardly a bump, but the wind from its wings blew hats off men halfway across the plaza.

Sofria slid from Pietra's back, then crawled back to where her now thoroughly soaked piece of sacking still lay on the cobbles against the side of the Guild Hall. "Thank you, Pietra," she said. "That was the best thing I've ever done."

Pietra turned its head, smiled at her in a wide-mouthed grin that—rather to Sofria's surprise—revealed no sharp fangs, and said softly, "I am always ready to help you, Sofria." Then it hopped into the air and flew back to its place on the edge of the Guild Hall's roof.

For the rest of the day, Sofria hardly noticed if it rained or the sun shone. She re-lived the pictures of Tarnisi from the sky over and over, reveling in soaring above the city she had seen so little of in her life. When Papa Matteo came to pick her up, she was so quiet that he said sharply, "Are you getting sick? I can't support a useless beggar in my household."

"No," Sofria said dreamily. "Just tired. It was cold today, and I shivered a lot." She was used to telling lies like this to Papa Matteo.

He rattled the coins as he poured them from her cup. "You got enough coins. Good. You can warm up at the lodgings."

A few days later it was sunny in the morning, but then clouds blew in and rain started misting down. "Can we fly again?" Sofria asked Pietra, looking up at it on the edge of the roof. "What happens if you are not here to 'fulfill your function' and gather water from the roof?"

She imagined she saw Pietra's shoulders rise and fall in a shrug. "My fellows on the other corners will have to drain more water. I'll be back before anyone notices I'm not there, unless it rains very hard, and I don't think you will want to be flying through that much rain."

"You're right."

Pietra dropped to the cobbles near Sofria and she pushed her battered cup, which already held two coins, into the pocket tied around her waist under her skirt—and felt the red ribbon the kind woman had given her. She crawled across the ground to Pietra and onto its foot. It was difficult to pull herself up onto the dragon's back. "Would it hurt you if I tied something around your neck to help me climb up?" she asked once she had settled in front of its wings.

"As I told you before, I am made of stone. You can't hurt me."

Sofria took the ribbon from her pocket and looped it around the dragon's wide neck. It was barely long enough. She tied a good tight knot. That should do. She held on as Pietra hopped into the air, wings spread. This way she didn't have to sprawl over Pietra's head, holding onto its neck. She could see more when she sat up straighter.

Pietra flew toward the edge of Tarnisi, where they had seen so much bustle two days before. It was even busier today. She thought of how an ant hill between two cobblestones had looked when a boy kicked it and the ants swarmed everywhere. People ran about, setting up booths rather like the one for the puppet show. There were horses and wagons, people carrying great bundles and boxes, and so many other things Sofria nearly fell off Pietra's back trying to see it all. "What is this?" she asked.

"It's the fair," Pietra said. "People come to Tarnisi from all around to buy and sell. It lasts for two weeks, and is one of the most exciting times of the year for the city."

Sofria had heard of the fair before. Papa Matteo sent all the other children there to pick pockets, but he never took her. The others brought in so much during fair time that Papa Matteo never seemed to mind much when her cup was nearly empty.

"There are acrobats!" she cried. "And jugglers! How I would like to go to the fair."

"You had best not," Pietra said with sadness in its voice. "There are so many people that we would certainly be seen."

"Oh." Sofria was disappointed, but she was used to not getting what she wanted. "Maybe when I'm older."

Pietra soared on past the fair, to where the muddy pasture land ended and something dense, green, and mysterious began. "What's that?" asked Sofria.

"The forest," the dragon said, swooping lower so she could see it more clearly. "Many, many trees. Animals live there, and birds. Tarnisi gets much of its wood from this forest."

Sofria had heard of forests before, in Osanna's stories. There were magical creatures who could grant wishes or steal everything you owned. There were dangerous people and talking animals. The forest sounded as interesting as the fair.

"Can we land so I can see what it's like from the ground?" asked Sofria. "All I see now are leaves, waving in the wind and covered in raindrops."

"That sounds safer than the fair," said Pietra, and angled lower in the sky. It found a clearing in the trees and set down neatly, not catching its wings on any of the trees' branches.

Immediately Sofria found wildflowers growing in the clearing, and looked up to see a bird—not a pigeon!—watching her from a branch. "This is better than the fair," she told Pietra. "There everyone would stare and think of me as the crippled beggar. Here . . . I can be whatever I think of!"

Pietra chuckled, a gruff sound from its stone throat. It hopped toward the trees, where Sofria heard a sound like the fountain in the plaza's center. But this was no fountain. Water ran along the ground, then gathered into the biggest puddle she had ever seen. There were little animals beside the puddle.

"What are those?" she asked Pietra.

The dragon put its head down slightly to look at them, and Sofria leaned past its eyes to see better. The animals were small greenish creatures with big mouths and eyes. When Pietra's shadow fell over them, they hopped into the water.

"Sofria, those are . . . those are my kin." Its voice sounded strange.

"*Dragons?*" Sofria asked, astonished. "I always thought they were much bigger, like you."

Pietra shook its head from side to side, nearly dumping Sofria on the ground. "No, these are frogs."

There were frogs in some of Osanna's stories. Something magical always seemed to happen to frogs. "Did a witch make you into a dragon?"

"No, I was made to look like a frog. A frog with wings, like no natural frog has."

Sofria thought about that. "Do other dragons look different from you?"

"I suppose so."

"The monsters on the Guild Hall and the Cathedral all look different, so if they are all dragons, that makes sense." She paused, then added, "But you are the best dragon of all, Pietra."

It rumbled something shyly at her, then said in a sharp whisper, "Someone's coming. Stay perfectly still, and don't make any noise." Pietra crouched, staring at two trees on the other side of the clearing.

Three men leading a donkey appeared from between the trees. The donkey was piled high with bundles, all tied together so they wouldn't fall off the donkey's back. Sofria wondered if they were making their way to the fair and became lost. They crossed the clearing, stepped over a fallen log near where Pietra crouched, and then disappeared into the forest again.

Pietra didn't move, so Sofria remained quiet, though her mind was full of questions. Why was Pietra so concerned? Who were the men? After what seemed a very long wait, Pietra finally said, "Those are thieves. All those bundles on the donkey were stolen from merchants on their way to the fair."

"How do you know?" Sofria whispered.

"I have watched thieves from my perch on the roof for many years. I . . . know how they act, how they move."

"What should we do?"

"Follow them," said Pietra. "Find out what they're doing with their takings."

"An adventure!" breathed Sofria. Osanna told stories about adventures. Sofria had never thought *she* might have one.

Sofria didn't ask Pietra how it knew where the thieves were going. She just sat on its back, holding onto the ribbon around its neck so she wouldn't fall off when it hopped. When they came to a tumbledown little house in another clearing, Pietra stopped in the shelter of the trees. The donkey was tethered outside the house, but the men were not with it. "The thieves are in that hut," Pietra whispered. "Stay perfectly quiet, and don't move."

Sofria slumped down between Pietra's eyes, staring at the hut. She could hear voices and movement. She wanted to ask Pietra what it thought the thieves were doing, but it had said 'stay perfectly quiet,' so she said nothing.

A thumping sound, more talking, then the splintered door swung open and the three men she had seen before came out. They were arguing. "And I tell you again that we *can't* sell it now, with the fair here. Everyone would know where we got it," said a stocky gray-haired man.

"Just a few things, so I've got coin to spend at the fair," wheedled the youngest man, with tangled dark hair and a face smudged with dirt.

"Leono says no, we don't do it," said the third man, medium sized and wearing a stained smock. "Move on out now, let's get home so no one knows we been here."

The youngest man, his mouth pursed obstinately, led the donkey off and the oldest pushed the door shut behind them.

After waiting quietly for the thieves to get some distance away, Pietra hopped over to the door. It shot out its tongue, grabbed the door, and pulled it open.

"That's a good trick," Sofria told the dragon.

One of the hut's walls had collapsed inward, and there were gaping holes in its roof. The floor was dirt, now quite muddy and churned up.

"They didn't do a very good job of hiding their takings," said Pietra.

Sofria looked around, but couldn't see the bundles from the donkey anywhere in the tumbledown hut. She was about to ask Pietra what it meant when it hopped over to where the wall had collapsed into the hut. With its tongue, it lifted the piece of wall, made of sticks with straw and dried mud flaking out from between them, enough to show Sofria a pit hidden beneath it.

"There's more here than they brought in just now," said Pietra. It carefully pushed the crumbling wall up until it stood propped against one of the remaining walls. "Look there."

The hole was lined with coarse cloth so the bags of goods wouldn't get dirty. There were bundles of clothing, rolls of cloth, pots, and wooden plates. Sofria saw a green shawl and thought of the woman who had given her the ribbon. Wouldn't it be lovely to exchange that tattered old shawl with this bright new one? And that roll of cloth. There should be enough there for clothing for all Betani's children.

"Can we take some of it?" Sofria asked. "I want to give it to people who have helped me."

"Don't you want anything?"

"Papa Matteo would notice and take it away to sell."

With Sofria directing, Pietra hooked the cloth, the shawl, and a man's cap from the pit with its tongue. It flipped the goods back up over its head to Sofria, who arranged them carefully along the dragon's neck so nothing would fall when they flew. Then it carefully replaced the fallen wall the way the men had left it, and went back outside.

The rain had stopped, and Sofria worried that she wouldn't get back to her place in the plaza in time to collect more coins. She didn't want her day of adventure to end with a beating from Papa Matteo. They were over the city before she wondered how she would get her gifts to the women—and the cap to the man who had been feeding the pigeons.

"I can't keep these things with me," she told Pietra, gazing down at the people in all their colorful clothing crowding the streets now that the sun had come out. "Papa Matteo will take them."

"I'll get them to the proper people." Pietra circled over the Duke's Palace, then followed the street to the Cathedral plaza.

"How do you know where to take them?"

"I see and hear much, up there on the Guild Hall's roof."

When Sofria slid from Pietra's back to the cobbles in front of the Guild Hall, she left the shawl, the bolt of cloth, and the cap behind. Once Pietra had returned to its place, she could see the cloth, one edge flapping gently in the breeze, still draped across Pietra's neck.

That night, lying on her mat with the other girls, Sofria imagined Pietra flying across the city. The dragon found the lodgings where Betani and her children lived, eased their door open with its tongue, and set the bolt of fabric inside. The old woman who had given the ribbon to Sofria lived in an upper room, and she slept so close to her open window that Pietra could spread the shawl across her. The man who fed the pigeons was a baker, and Pietra left the new cap on the counter in his shop.

When the fair opened, the city became a different place. The plaza was quieter; most people, including the storyteller and the puppet show, were at the fair. The old woman with her new green shawl brought Sofria a bit of cheese, and Betani stopped by every evening after she delivered the laundry she had washed, to tell Sofria of what she had seen at the fair in the few moments she had been able to attend.

Sofria and Pietra flew over the city every day, but for very short flights. They circled the fair to watch acrobats and jugglers, see the strangely-dressed merchants from all across the land, and listen to the music wafting up from far below.

"There are farms, towns, and cities beyond Tarnisi that we can visit when we have more time." Pietra circled the fair once again and veered off to go back to the plaza.

"I'll need a warm shawl if we do that," said Sofria. "It gets cold high in the sky, especially when it's raining."

"We could go back to the thieves' hoard. There should be something warm there."

The next day when rain started misting down Sofria and Pietra flew to the tumbledown hut in the forest. They landed in the clearing just as the young man with the tangled dark hair came out of the forest whistling, with an axe over his shoulder. He nearly fell over backward when he saw Pietra. "A demon from hell!" he screamed, and swung his axe at the dragon.

Pietra hopped backward, raising its wings to keep them out of the way of the axe. Sofria held on tight to the ribbon around the dragon's neck, thinking, *Why can that man see us?* But when she was imagining people not seeing them, it had been crowds of people, the people in the city. Whatever it was that made people not see Pietra once it left the roof of the Guild Hall, it must not work here. Or she had been careless. The other children at Papa Matteo's lodgings teased Sofria about being careless.

The young man ran at them again, swinging the axe. Its wicked sharp edge caught Pietra's wing tip, and a piece shattered off.

Pietra tried to hop into the air, but it had backed too far into the forest, and its wings caught in the branches above them. The dragon shook itself, and Sofria lost hold of the ribbon about its neck. She slid to the ground near a tree's trunk and her hair tangled in bushes growing at its base.

Just as the axe came down again, Pietra hopped forward, so the side of the axe's head bounced off its rounded shoulder. Sofria yanked her hair free from the branches and began crawling, making sure she was not in Pietra's path as it hopped out of the way of the axe.

A branch she grasped to pull herself along came free of the leaves and twigs littering the forest floor. It was twice as long as her forearm and rather stout, so she held onto it as she awkwardly pulled herself forward.

She could not fight the young man—he moved fast, and she couldn't even stand up. But the heroes in Osanna's stories often used trickery. The next time the man lunged toward Pietra, Sofria shoved the branch in between his feet, tripping him. The axe flew from the man's hands as he flung his arms out to catch himself, and the blade came down right between Pietra's bulging eyes.

While the man was down, Sofria dragged herself quickly to him, and rolled to one side so she could prop herself up on an elbow. With the branch in the other hand, she smashed its knobby end down on his head. He moaned and twitched, then lay still. Had she killed him? She did not want to kill him, but he was attacking Pietra.

Sofria used the branch to push herself to a sitting position and turned to look at Pietra. The axe had hit the dragon in the middle of its head and shattered it. Pietra's wide mouth and eyes were in pieces on the ground, with the axe lying atop them.

"Pietra!" Sofria screamed. She crawled forward, pulling herself up on one of its webbed feet, and touched the side of its neck. It no longer felt like soft, warm skin—it was stone, cold stone, a headless body of a monster crouched in the forest. Sofria sobbed, leaning against a stone knee, all her hopes of adventure shattered along with her only friend.

The sun breaking through the clouds reminded her that she had no way to get back to the city. She could die out here in the forest. There was no way for her to get food, and it would take days to crawl as far as the edge of the fair. There were blankets and clothing—maybe even food—in the hoard of stolen goods in the hut behind her, but without Pietra to lift the fallen piece of wall, she could not get to them. If the thief she had hit woke up to find her here, he would probably kill her. She should leave quickly, as he was starting to groan.

The red ribbon was still tied around Pietra's neck. It was rather grubby by now, and even more frayed than when Sofria had received it, but it might be her only link with Pietra now. She untied it, and was about to put it into her pocket, when she decided that she wanted Pietra to have it after all. She started searching through the grass, picking up pieces of Pietra's head and finding where they fit, with the thought that maybe she could hold them together with the ribbon. All the while her memories of the many times she had talked to Pietra, and flown on its back, played through her head.

She got Pietra's head re-assembled, though there were still small pieces of stone missing, powdered into the grass beneath the dragon. She wound the ribbon around its jaw, trying to hold the wide mouth together, keep the bulging eyes from slipping downward. She ran her fingers along the cracks, smoothing them.

The young man groaned louder and struggled to push himself to a sitting position. Sofria crouched low behind Pietra's body so the man couldn't see her. He put a hand up to run through his hair, where he probably had a knot the size of a goose's egg, and opened his eyes. He looked straight into Pietra's shattered face.

With a terrified scream, the man wavered to his feet and stumbled off into the forest, leaving his axe behind. Would he bring his companions back? She did not want to stay here long enough to find out.

Sofria turned to say goodbye to Pietra. She reached out to touch its shattered face and saw that the break lines were closing up, almost as if they healed.

"Pietra," she whispered. She ran her fingers along the breaks, feeling them smooth out and fill in. Moments later Pietra's wings began to twitch, and then the dragon shuddered and blinked its eyes. Sofria had never noticed before that the eyelids moved *up* when its eyes closed.

"Pietra!" She flung her arms around the dragon's neck and began sobbing again, in relief and joy this time. One of its wings came down to shelter her until she sat up and wiped her face on her sleeve.

"Hmmmphg." Tears turned to giggles as Sofria realized she had bound Pietra's mouth shut. She untied the ribbon and the dragon opened and closed its mouth, blinked a few times, and then cautiously shook its head. "Sofria, what happened? I *felt* myself shatter."

"That man hit you with his axe. Then I hit him with a stick, and when he woke up he ran away."

"But how did I . . . ?" Pietra tilted its head sideways, lifted its front legs and looked at its feet. Then it peered up toward its wings, spreading them to their fullest span. "I am whole. I am not shattered."

"You were, but . . . I think this ribbon is magical, Pietra! When I tied it around your head, it put all the pieces back together."

Pietra laughed—a shaky laugh, but with a note of the booming amusement it had shared with her when she asked if it was a dragon. "That would be the way it worked in one of Osanna's stories."

Hearing Osanna's name reminded Sofria that she must get back to the city. The sun moved westward, and she had no coins for Papa Matteo today. "We should go back," she said.

"We came to get you a shawl, and that we shall do." Pietra hopped to the hut's door and pulled it open. It took but a moment to prop the broken wall up, and then Pietra did something Sofria had not expected. With tongue and front legs it gathered up the heavy cloth lining the pit into a great bag, which it pulled out of the hole. "See if there is rope in here," it directed Sofria. She pawed through the bundles and packages until she found one tied with rope. She untied it, dumping the contents of the bundle in with everything else without even looking at it.

"Now find yourself a shawl." She had seen one—a pretty blue one, with beads at the hem—and quickly found it and draped it over her shoulders. Pietra bunched the top of the cloth together again. "Take this rope and tie up the top good and tight, so I can carry this big bundle with my feet."

She did that, weaving the rope through holes she found in the cloth and knotting it tightly. Then she tied the ribbon around Pietra's neck again. It dragged the big bag of goods from the hut, leaving the wall propped up and the door open.

"Let's fly!" said Pietra. Sofria pulled herself onto its back and held onto the ribbon as it pushed upward with its strong hind legs. Between its front feet it held the bundle.

Sofria leaned over Pietra's head, between its eyes, and looked down at the forest below them. She stroked the soft skin that did *not* feel like stone. All there were to show for the dragon being shattered were some thin lines, like scars, across its face.

At the edge of the forest Pietra found a great tree, taller than its neighbors, and hung the bundle from a high branch, close to the trunk so it couldn't easily be seen. Then the dragon glided across the city toward the plaza.

Remembering how the young man had seen them, Sofria thought very hard about *not* being seen as they flew over shops and houses, the Duke's Palace, and a church not nearly as fancy as the Cathedral. Sofria slipped from Pietra's back at her usual place on the plaza as the sun sank behind the Guild Hall.

She had just pulled her cup from the pocket under her skirt when she saw Papa Matteo across the plaza near the Cathedral steps, talking to a man. When she lifted her arm to run her fingers through her hair, tangled from branches and flying, she remembered the pretty blue shawl over her shoulders. There was no time to hide it. Papa Matteo turned, saw her, and strode across the plaza toward her.

"Where have you *been*, girl?" he bellowed.

All thought fled from Sofria's mind. He had come to the plaza before she got back with Pietra. He knew she had not been in her place. What could she tell him? "I had to pee," she blurted.

"I would have seen you if you were at the gutter." Papa Matteo stood over Sofria, tapping a stick he held in his right hand against his left fist. His gaze moved up and down her body, then he reached out with the stick to lift the shawl from her shoulders. "And where did you get *this*?"

"It was a gift."

"Why would anyone give *you* a gift? You're a broken, worthless piece of trash."

"I am *not* worthless." The caution that usually kept her silent had left her today. "I bring in coins for you every day. What do I get for that? Many times you don't even feed me, and you beat me for things that aren't even my fault."

"Don't sass me." Papa Matteo raised the stick.

Sofria lunged for the stick. Caught off guard, Papa Matteo wasn't holding it tightly, and she wrenched it from his hand. Remembering the man in the forest, how she had hit his head, she brought the stick down with all her strength on Papa Matteo's right arm. He howled and cursed when it hit, and seized the stick with his left hand and pulled it away from her. Though not regretting what she had done, Sofria cowered, hoping he wouldn't hit as hard using the left hand.

"You worthless beast!" he screamed. "I don't need you. No one needs you." He lifted the stick again . . . and it was seized from behind and pulled away from him a second time.

"Leave that child alone!" Betani stood there, holding the stick out of Papa Matteo's reach. Behind her crowded many more people, all of them glaring at Papa Matteo.

A huge argument began, with people shouting, and Papa Matteo cursing. Sofria sat up straighter, listening as Betani told Papa Matteo that he had no claim on Sofria, and she wouldn't allow the child to live another day with such a bully. With the crowd booing him, Papa Matteo strode off across the plaza, holding his right arm close against his chest.

"Thank you for watching out for me," Sofria said to Betani, her voice shaking more than she had thought it would.

"I never liked the looks of that man," the stout woman said. "I was sure he beat you."

"Yes." Sofria found she was shaking all over. Papa Matteo was gone, but now what would she do? Could she live in the forest, and have Pietra bring her food?

Most of the crowd had left now, laughing at how they had got the better of Papa Matteo. Betani turned toward the fountain, and Sofria saw that the woman's three children sat there, probably to keep them safe if there was fighting. Betani waved at them to come, and they did.

Ercoli, the boy, pulled a little wagon behind him. The youngest girl was riding in it, but when they reached Sofria, the child hopped out. "I washed every scrap of clothing and linen in my neighbor's house," said Betani, "and he built this for me. Do you like it, Sofria?"

There was a cushion in the bottom, made of some of the cloth Sofria and Pietra had left at Betani's house. "May I?" Betani asked. Sofria wasn't sure what she meant, until she reached toward Sofria, and the girl realized Betani wanted to lift her into the wagon.

"Of course," said Sofria, breathing quickly, excited and scared both at once.

When she was settled in the wagon to Betani's satisfaction, the woman said, "Would you like to live with us? We don't have a lot, but it sounds like it's more than you are used to."

"Live . . . with you? I think I would like that. I can pay my way. You can bring me out here every day, same as Papa Matteo did."

"No more begging," said Betani. "I'm sure there are other things you can do. Can you sew?"

"No, I never learned how. I don't know anything except begging."

"Well, no time like now to learn." Betani tugged on the wagon's rope, and it began bumping over the cobblestones of the plaza.

Sofria turned to look at Pietra, clinging to the roof of the Guild Hall. It lifted a wing, as if to wave to her, and tears filled her eyes. Would she be able to have adventures with Pietra again? "When I'm old enough, I'll come back for you, Pietra, and we will travel the world."

"I am made of stone. I will be here for you."

Osanna the storyteller sat on the rim of the fountain, her back to the Cathedral, waiting as children gathered at her feet. Something caught her attention—something fluttering in the breeze, high above her head, She looked to the top of the Guild Hall to see something bright, perhaps a ribbon, about the neck of the nearest gargoyle. How—and why—had anyone climbed that high to tie a ribbon on one of the great stone statues? That was a story she would someday like to tell.

Lullaby

John D. Payne

As plaintive cries from the nursery chamber intruded on the unconscious bliss of slumber, I curled up in a ball, wrapped my wings more tightly around myself, and squeezed my eyes shut. "Go back to sleep," I whispered to myself. And to the children.

No good. Their voices kept rising, both in pitch and in volume, until the shrieks stabbed their way into my skull and banished sleep completely. Maybe permanently. With a heavy sigh, I gathered the strength to heave myself up and out of bed.

"Sweetheart," Sam asked, "why do you do this to yourself?" He had the uncanny ability to jump in an instant from deep sleep to coherent conversation. It was perhaps the second worst thing about him.

"Unngggh," I replied. Well put, I told myself. You truly are a gifted communicator. A real wordsmith.

"Just let them cry," Sam said. In the darkness, I could hear him shifting his weight to prop himself up, accompanied by the ringing, watery tinkle of precious metals and jewels being displaced by his movements. At this sound, the cries from the children grew louder. More heart-wrenching. More insistent.

"I'm coming, I'm coming," I grumbled. I regretted the words as soon as they were out of my mouth. Poor things. They didn't mean to wake me. They didn't know, couldn't know. They were so small, so helpless.

"It won't kill them to wait," Sam said. I couldn't really see him, but I could sense him lying close to me in the darkness. His recumbent form was the one source of warmth in the otherwise frigid sleeping chamber.

"It might kill me." It ought to get easier to ignore their crying when I was more tired myself. But if anything, exhaustion made it worse. At this point, as sleep deprived as I was, it was a special kind of torture. It must have been, or I never would have considered getting out of my warm bed and onto the cold floor.

Our chambers should have been warm, since they were built into the side of a fire mount that still had a few active lava tubes. But we had given the warmest room to the children. It was the right decision, but it meant that my floors were always cold. That annoyed me.

I stoked this spark of annoyance until the flames in my belly grew bright and hot. Then I opened my mouth and uncorked a spray of fire on the floor until the stones gave off a dull, red glow. There. Much better. I got out of bed and put my feet down, and enjoyed the warmth.

Sam shook his head. "We've talked about this. Every time we get up—"

"Every time *I* get up."

"Hey, now. You know that's not fair."

My head whipped around and in an instant I was facing him on all fours, wings spread and tail lashing from side to side. In the faint but growing glower, the light tinged an angry red by its journey outward through my flesh and my scales, I could see him lift his forelimbs in surrender.

"Fine." He rolled his eyes. "Every time *you* get up—"

"Thank you," I murmured, my belly fires slowly cooling.

"—it reinforces the pattern. Behavior rewarded is behavior repeated." He took a deep breath. "I'm sorry, sweetheart. But there's only one way out of this cycle, and at some point we're going to have to grit our teeth and do it."

I considered that for a moment, but renewed cries from the next chamber interrupted my train of thought.

"At some point, fine. But not now."

"If that's your decision," he said, "then I'll go. It's my turn." He heaved himself upright, which set off a new cascade of gems and precious metals.

I reached over and gave him a pat. "No, I will."

He hesitated.

"Stay," I said. "I mean it. Go back to sleep."

"Well, that's hardly fair to you."

"If you go, I'll lay awake anyway. One of us might as well get some rest."

He chewed on this for a moment, and then said, "Okay. But I take the next shift." Then he rolled over and was instantly asleep. Which is the very, very worst thing about him.

I checked the larder and found nothing that would soothe the brood. So instead of going straight to the nursery, I popped outside briefly to scoop up a few morsels. All the while, I cursed the past version of myself from the last time they woke up.

"You could have set something aside for next time," I muttered, feeling more than a little hungry myself. "But no, you wanted to go back to bed. Lazy cow. Think of someone else for a change." My future self nodded in approval, taking my side. But my past self didn't even bother to respond. She just slept.

Flying through the nearby valleys as quickly as possible, I tried to focus on the task at hand and not get distracted looking at the scenery. The children were still hungry and crying, after all. But I couldn't help noticing that our pest problem was back.

Humans, it looked like. Or maybe Elves. Either way, it was quite a big colony from the look of things. And it seemed like Sam had just cleared out the dratted things, but of course you never really got rid of them permanently. Like a persistent rash or a chronic cough, the infestation just kept recurring.

I made a mental note to mention it to Sam when I went back to bed. He would handle it; he always did. And come back covered with scratches and bites all over, every time. Poor dear. He was so cute when he complained about his little wounds. Thinking of it brought an involuntary smile to my face and a warmth to my belly.

He really was very sweet, I thought, turning a dreamy and languorous spiral in the air. A good provider, a doting father, a fierce protector. A fine mate. And nearly my size. Well, at least three-quarters my size. Very respectable, for a male.

The warm summer breeze felt good in my wings, and I felt lighter and lither than I had in ages. Part of me yearned to climb and soar and ride the winds until I became one with them, floating like a cinder in the smoke.

But the children needed feeding. So I swooped back home, limbs and jaws laden with delectable nibblets. Sam was absent from our sleeping chamber, but I found him in the nursery. From the look of things, he had tried in vain to appease the children with the meager scraps he had been able to scrounge and now was attempting to pull rank on them, silly thing.

"I am Shamel-Shesha, the Enduring One," he cried, sounding more desperate than commanding, "I rule all things from the molten core beneath to the empty void above. Please stop biting me!"

Suppressing a smile, I rushed in to Sam's aid. Murmuring to them in my most soothing tone, I pulled each of the little dears off of their father, which in most cases elicited a shriek from both parties.

The babies were, by and large, easy to mollify. They didn't have long memories. You popped something sweet in their mouths and they would latch right on and forget why they had been crying in the first place.

Sam was somewhat more difficult to appease. Instead of going back to bed, he just stood there rubbing his wounds and heaving pained sighs. The faint light coming up from the lava tubes left much of his face in shadow, but it wasn't hard to see that he was upset.

I wanted to go to him, to take him in my arms, or at least to run my claws along his dorsal spines, the way he liked. But I was lying on the floor of the nursery, encircling the brood with my body and tail and cuddling them close with one wing. They had stopped crying, but if I put them down, we'd be right back where we started in a heartbeat.

So I gave Sam what I hoped was a sympathetic smile. "I'm sorry, dear. They really got you good this time, didn't they?"

"Yeah." He sucked in his breath as he craned his neck to examine a particularly nasty-looking bite under his left forelimb. "Those little teeth. So very sharp."

"Well, they're at a curious age," I said. "Maybe they just want to know what Daddy tastes like."

With my attention on Sam, one of the little ones decided to make a break for it, and attempted to wriggle free. I quickly swept her back with my free wing, which she bit.

"Mommy, too, apparently," he said.

"Apparently." I pried the scamp loose and plugged her little mouth with a half a cow's head that one of the others had dropped. Soon, she was happily (and noisily) enjoying her treat and seemed to have no more interest in escaping. "It's a phase. They're less than a century old. They'll grow out of it."

"Yeah."

For a while the only sound was the slurping and smacking and crunching of the children feeding. Very messy, of course, but also very cute.

I looked up to see Sam still standing there, watching me.

"I . . ." He hesitated, then threw his forelimbs up in the air. "I thought you were going to feed them."

With my free wing, I gestured expansively at myself and the children, a mute answer to his accusation.

"Yeah, now you are. But I thought you were going right then to feed them. And instead, you went I don't even know where, while they just got hungrier and madder and louder. So, there I am, lying there listening to this and wondering what in the name of Alala is going on because you told me to go back to sleep because you were going to handle it. If you wanted me to take a turn, you could have just said so. I offered, if you remember."

He shot me an accusing glare.

I glared back. "We didn't have anything to feed them. I stepped out for literally less than two weeks to grab them something to eat."

"Two weeks is a really long time for them. And they don't like waiting."

"What should I have done instead?"

"You could have said something. Let me know. I would have been happy to go in and entertain them while you were out."

"Evidently not, since that's what you did and you aren't happy."

He flexed his claws in frustration and exhaled a stream of bright orange flame.

I shook my head, searching for the words that would help Sam see how ridiculous he was being. But before I could unleash the stinging rebuke I was carefully constructing, I noticed that the children had grown noisy again.

Looking down, I realized that in my irritation I had unconsciously let my belly fires grow hot, and it was making the brood restless. Some of them were trying to climb out of the protective ring I had made with my body, others cried plaintively, and one seemed intent on chewing my wing to shreds. The whole point of coming in here was to soothe them, and instead we were stirring them up with our argument.

"Sweetheart," he began, sounding very, very tired.

"One moment, please," I said.

With some effort, I tried to calm myself and cool my temper down from a boil to a simmer. As the scales on my abdomen grew less scalding, the children once again let me draw them in close. Feeling them wriggling happily in my limbs, snuggling up tight, it was easy to let go of the anger.

Sam stepped closer, his neck and head hanging low and his wings dragging on the rough stone floor of the chamber in mute apology. Looking abashed, he leaned down and placed a kiss on my forehead.

"Forget I said anything," he said. "Stupid of me to pick a fight."

I lifted my head to rub the dorsal spines slowly against the sensitive skin under his chin, eliciting an involuntary shudder of pleasure and a low rumble of satisfaction. "Don't give it another thought," I said. "We're both exhausted. That always has us at each other's throats."

"True." After a pause he nipped at my neck playfully.

I smiled. "Go back to bed, dear. I'll get the children to sleep."

He hesitated, looking for a moment as if he were about to say something, then nodded and left.

"All right," I said to the children. "Who's still hungry?"

They all were, of course. I did my best to distribute the livestock equally, so that everyone got a nice, full tummy, but some of the brood were more aggressive and so got more than their share.

In scarcely more than a few days, all the food was gone. Most of the brood were stuffed up nice and plump, their eyes heavy and their limbs limp and languid. They hardly stirred as I lowered them back down into an inactive lava tube to sleep. There they curled up in a heap, one on top of one another, sharing their warmth as their unconscious bodies struggled to digest the massive feast.

Soon, there was just one left, the littlest. Having fed poorly, she fussed and cried and would not be contented.

"Now, now," I said, stroking her as she writhed in my limbs. "You're just fine. No need to cry. Everything will be just fine."

A pang of guilt struck me as I uttered the words, because in truth I was worried about her. We both were. Sam had said that she wouldn't last long enough to get her wings. I hadn't said as much out loud, but couldn't help but share his opinion.

That's why I had already given her a name. Belinda. Bright One. She was less than half the size of her brothers and sisters, but her eyes were sharp and attentive. More than any of the others, she made me wonder how much she understood.

"I know you want more," I said, lifting her up to my face, "but there is nothing left for you."

She stopped crying for a moment and leveled a gaze at me that was nothing short of a unspoken accusation.

"I'm sorry. Next time I'll bring more. And I'll make sure you get your share."

Screwing up her little face, Belinda wailed in a voice that was louder than I could have believed from such a tiny creature. I held her close and jiggled her up and down lest her cries wake Sam, or the rest of the brood.

"Hush now, hush."

After what seemed like years, but was certainly no more than a week, Belinda finally quieted down. But she wasn't sleeping peacefully in my arms, her face wore a look of such terrible betrayal that it absolutely broke my heart.

"All right, all right. We'll go grab something."

Holding tiny Belinda close to my heart, I went outside to see about something to eat. I couldn't see anything right away, which was irritating because all I really wanted to do was get this little one fed so I could go back to sleep. Nursing my irritation into a flame, I burned back the vegetation creeping up the sides of our mountain and immediately spotted a crispy herd of blackened deer.

"Mmm!" I murmured to the bundle of wiggles in my forelimbs. "Roasty-toasty treats. Let's give them a try, shall we?"

Belinda tried the deer, and loved them. But despite her evident pleasure and my own impatient coaxing, she seemed determined to take her sweet time eating them. Not wanting to waste the time, I looked around to see if there was anything else that needed doing while I was outside.

My gaze was drawn once again to one of the pest colonies, just outside the circle of burned-back vegetation and apparently completely unscathed. Annoying, but easy to fix.

I blew an experimental jet of flame at the nest, but it was made of stone and didn't combust well. So all I really did was stir things up. A whole host of the nasty critters came boiling out of every crack and crevice, many of them headed straight for me.

"Oh, no, you don't." I put my foot down and squashed several of the ugly things flat. "No itchy bites or scratches for me, thank you."

This made little impression on them, so after a few more desultory stomps, I decided to let Sam handle this once he was up. Suppressing a yawn, I scooped up Belinda along with the rest of the charred herd of deer, and headed back inside.

Cradled in my forelimbs, she was asleep before we got back to the nursery chamber. Asleep, and adorable. A delicate little baby snore whispered out of her slightly-parted mouth. Her long tail drooped, the tip occasionally twitching. And somehow the most adorable thing of all was her grotesquely swollen belly— her skin stretched, her scales straining to contain a meal that probably doubled her mass.

"Aw. You finally got a good meal, didn't you?" I stroked her little nose, and the ghost of a smile flitted across her face. "That's all you needed. Just a tummy full of yummy food, and now we can all have a good rest."

I stooped to lay her down amid her siblings, and she instantly awoke, crying lustily.

Of course.

I sank down to the floor of the nursery chamber. And maybe it was the sleep deprivation, but I felt like having a bit of a cry myself. I'd been up for weeks now— maybe months. It had been nearly a century since I got a decent sleep. Why had I sent Sam back to bed?

"All right," I told Belinda, jiggling her up and down. "You're as tired as I am. So why are you still awake? What's wrong? You're not sick. Do you want something? It can't be food. We already took care of that."

She slapped petulantly at me and hissed.

"What are you mad at me for? I'm trying to help, here. If I knew what you wanted, I'd give it to you. Believe me. There's nothing I'd like more. If I only knew what was going on in that little head of yours."

She whined and struggled, shaking her head rapidly back and forth like she had a sheep in her mouth and was trying to break its neck.

I laughed. "Or is there nothing going on at all? I mean, you're not even a century old yet. There are humans that live that long. I think. And they're certainly not intelligent." I sighed. "Maybe you're so young you can't even really comprehend your own self. You don't know if you're hungry, or thirsty, or sleepy, or hurt. You're just unhappy, so you cry. That's all there is to it."

As if on cue, she started crying again. I got up and walked around with her, which seemed to help.

"Here am I, one who has ascended beyond the realm of the clouds, to touch the Boundless and hear the music of the stars. And what defeats me? An unhappy child."

Wait.

The music of the stars?

"Do you want to hear a song?"

Instantly she quieted, her bright eyes wide and looking right at me.

"I guess you do."

And so I sang.

At first it was wordless. But at some point, I'm not even sure when, words came. I sang about a little baby named Belinda, and her mother and father who loved her. I sang about brothers and sisters, sleeping cozy and warm all together. I sang about the safety and strength of the mountain all around us.

And then I sang about the humans. I don't know why. It was stupid. They were pests. I probably still had some stuck to the bottom of my feet. But holding this little one, this youngling, I couldn't help but think about other tiny creatures, whose lives were measured by the spastic flickering of day and night instead of the graceful, steady cycles of sunspots.

I sang about a baby human, and the mother who held her and rocked her in their own little home of stone. I sang about the baby being tucked in with all the other children, resting warm and safe and quiet.

For whatever reason, it did the trick. She stopped fussing, closed her eyes, and slept. She never stirred, even when I put her down in the lava tube with her siblings and one of them rolled right on top of her. Thank goodness for small miracles.

I made my way back to bed. It felt indescribably wonderful to be off my feet and lying down. There was a pleasant clinking as the piles of precious stones and metals shifted to accommodate me. Sam stirred.

"How'd it go?"

"They're down, all of them. Hopefully that's the last disturbance."

He grunted. "Well, whether they sleep a long time or not, I've got next."

"All yours."

He leaned over and kissed me.

"Is there something for them to eat?"

"Yes." I yawned. "Near a whole herd of deer."

"Good. Anything else I should know about?"

"No, nothing." I turned over, wrapping my wings around myself. "Oh, except for . . . Have you seen the human colonies out there?"

"Humans? Looked like elves to me."

"Whichever."

"Already on my list. I'll get rid of them first thing."

"Actually, I was thinking that maybe we could leave them there. Just for a while."

"You want me to—?" He cut himself off and blew out a long breath. Then he shrugged. "Whatever you say, dear. Sweet dreams."

"Sweet dreams."

He, of course, was snoring almost instantly. It really was unfair. Especially since I was wide awake, despite the peace and quiet that reigned in our chambers once more.

For some reason, my mind kept going back to our pest infestation. What would it really be like to live a life so brief? To feel yourself dying from the very moment you were born? Even if they were intelligent, how could they possibly care about each other, about their young, the way we did? Such a creature simply didn't have the time to invest in the raising of a child, especially given how fragile they all were.

Yet I couldn't help but think of that human mother from my song, rocking her own little babe to sleep. The image haunted me, no matter how I told myself that this was only a lullaby made up on the spot to calm a restless child.

Now it was my turn to be restless, my poor, exhausted mind seizing upon disturbing impossibilities. I rolled over and thought about waking Sam for a moment, but then told myself not to be silly.

"Settle down. Go to sleep."

I closed my eyes and listened to Sam's slow and steady breathing. After an increasingly fuzzy eternity, I at last felt myself drifting off. As sweet slumber came to claim me, two last thoughts crept in to trouble my dreams.

If humans really could sing songs to their young, what would they sound like? And if they could tell tales, what would they say—about us?

Rain Like Diamonds

Wendy Nikel

The queen hoarded the barrels of seed, keeping them locked within her coffers among the diamonds and gold and strings of perfect pearls, remnants of the former days of prosperity and excess. The seeds would receive neither sun nor water nor nutrients from the soil until unlocked by the shining key strung around her neck. Day after day, she sat upon her throne, and the villagers lined up before her, pleading. It was only her loyal guards, with their sharp swords glimmering, who kept the villagers from severing her neck to get at that key.

"Have mercy!" They cried as though their tears might change her mind.

"Our children need nourishment!" They shouted as if she, too, hadn't been watching her own son grow thin and wan and dull.

"Just one barrel! One barrel will keep us alive for a few days longer!"

She held her chin high, her eyes downcast and sorrowful. "I cannot."

Though it broke her heart, she spoke the truth. It was true, the meager meal would sustain them for a day or two. But that would be one less barrel to plant when the famine ended, when those that remained stood a chance.

Nothing had grown for many seasons, till all the people's cupboards, barns, storehouses, and cellars were empty. All that remained within them were empty jars, dust-lined shelves, and—if one breathed in deeply—the haunting memory of the scent of food.

Yet even if the queen had thrown the seeds to those standing beneath her balcony, had given the seeds to the kingdom's best farmers, it was futile. Nothing would grow, and their hunger would not be satiated. Nothing would grow until the dragon-scorched earth was healed.

A messenger burst into the throne room. His gait, once like a thoroughbred's, was now the spindly stumble of one whose legs were too thin, whose ankles too prone to turn.

"My queen! The sorceress has spoken!"

The queen rose from her throne, for this news was long-awaited. Since first the crops refused to grow, the sorceress had been locked in her tower, spending countless hours staring into her scrying pools and crystal balls, searching for an answer.

"Well? What is it?" the queen demanded.

"You must see her, in her tower."

The queen climbed the spiraling stairs to the castle's dreary north tower. Though winded, she pressed on, for the task of climbing a staircase was so small compared with what her people had already suffered.

"Sorceress!" she called as she entered the chamber. "Sorceress! What am I to do?"

The sorceress's voice echoed through the chamber, coming from nowhere and everywhere at once. *"One shall weep at the foot of the tree, and the rain shall fall like diamonds on the earth."*

Throughout the kingdom, the queen sent the order, and on the following morning, every man, woman, and child arrived at the palace gates. The captain of the guard barked out directions, and the queen led the procession. The feeble and sick were carried or slung into carts. Their loved ones pulled them along, for throughout the entire kingdom not a single horse or donkey remained that hadn't been made into soup. The queen led the mourners from tree to tree, pausing at each one to tearfully recall those who had succumbed to the famine, until they'd traversed the entire kingdom and their eyes were as dried-out as the parched earth. Yet still, the rain refused to fall. Defeated, the queen turned away and locked herself up in the palace.

That night, the men, restless with no fields to tend, gathered at the tavern, though they'd long ago brewed the last of the hops. They muttered and grumbled against the weather, the fields, and even the queen herself.

"The dragon," Thummander said, raking his hand through his beard. "The dragon was the beginning of this trouble; nothing has grown since it scorched our fields."

"Let's do away with it," Leverett said. He slammed his fist on the table. Their voices, hoarse with thirst, rose in agreement and they conspired together all night. The dragon, they agreed. There was nothing else for them to do, nothing else they could do, except to kill the dragon.

Though the hour was late, the men requested an audience with the queen. They told her of their plan, and she reluctantly consented.

"It will do no good," she warned, but allowed them to proceed through the once-lush forest that now stood like an oversized bramble-bush, full of thorns and prickers. At least, she considered, this quest would make them feel useful.

In the inky blackness of night, with their torches burning brightly, they crept to the dragon's lair. The beast exhaled smoke with each sleeping breath, and if the villagers could only overlook its enormous size, they might have seen how the creature was really quite peaceful, like the cats that had once dozed at their hearths, before the rats had all been killed and the cats became more valuable for their meat than for their ability to hunt.

The men had disguised their scent by carrying pine branches, native to the hill near the dragon's cave. Carefully, they dropped the branches and the strongest of the men clamped an iron band snugly around the dragon's snout. The dragon woke with a start, its pupils like coals in its fiery eyes, but the men held tight to the chains and together dragged the creature down to the castle.

The villagers' triumphant cries rose with the morning sun, and golden light trickled through the brittle branches of the rosewood. The queen looked out from the balcony at the crowd below her.

"We've captured the dragon!"

"Come, watch it die!"

The queen felt the heat of their anger and shivered at the coldness in their voices. The enormous eye of the ensnared dragon stared at her, knowing. Yet what was she to do? She raised her scepter to give the command, but at the last moment, a small boy rushed forward and fell upon the beast. The queen gasped. It was the prince.

"Please, mother," he begged. "Please, don't kill it. Will there ever be a more wonderful creature? Please, spare its life. Send it away from this place, if you must, but don't kill it. I beg you! Please, show it mercy."

Glistening tears crept down his face and landed at the base of the tree. They darkened the soil as the roots soaked them in. The crowd stared as green life burst forth from the tree. First, tiny specks of color, then long, lush leaves spread across the tree's outstretched branches. They were so startled by the transformation that they loosened their grasp on the dragon.

Seeing its only opportunity, the beast lunged forward, flapped its wings, and launched itself skyward with the prince still clinging to its back.

"My son!" the queen called, but the dragon rose into a dark, heavy cloud. Just as they disappeared, the sky burst open and rain poured down. The crowd cheered and danced about, splashing in the puddles and laughing, seeing only the rain. They rushed to the castle and broke into the queen's coffers, but she made no move to stop them, for she saw only the final glimpse of her son, her son who had saved the kingdom. The son she'd never see again.

And her tears fell like diamonds on the earth.

Here by Choice
Gerri Leen

Tien Shen watched as Kuan Yin lounged by the waterfall, trailing her hand back and forth through the water as she stared up at the clouds overhead. A subtle odor of lotus surrounded her, reaching him where he sat. She gleamed like an emperor's pearl, if a distressed one. She cocked her head, listening for some sound and frowning deeply.

"What do you hear?" he asked. He heard nothing, not even with his dragon-keen ears.

She didn't answer him, so he tried to assess her mood. Her eyes glinted and for a moment, he thought he saw tears, but then she seemed to force a smile as she laid her head back onto the hard ground. But he could tell she was still listening, that not even the waterfall could drown out whatever it was that called to her.

"What is it you hear?" he asked again.

She finally looked over.

"Everyone."

This was how she was. This was how she answered. As if she could not spare the breath she no longer needed. She had achieved enlightenment; Nirvana waited. Why was she wasting time lying by this river not answering him?

"You don't have to stay, dragon." She sounded as if she wished he'd go.

"It is my honor to guard those who will enter Nirvana." Although in this case, it was rather a pain as well.

She lifted her head and gave him a look that could only be considered amused—at his expense. Then she lay back again and closed her eyes.

He made sure no one would threaten her before settling down some distance away, and she glanced at him, as if checking that he hadn't gotten too close. He seemed to make her unhappy, had since he'd told her he was her guide to paradise's door, but he didn't know why that distressed her. So many were striving for Nirvana; she'd achieved it, but no joy lit her face.

Letting his head come to rest on the softer scales of his side, Tien Shen listened to the water. The roaring sound of the river crashing over the rocks lulled him into sleep.

He woke slowly, blinking to clear his eyes. Then he blinked again, not believing what he saw—or didn't see: the woman he was supposed to protect was gone.

He closed his eyes, trying to find a trace of her with his inside-eyes. Nothing.

He listened, heard only the cry of the hawk, the grunt of the tiger, and the swish-snap of a squirrel in the underbrush.

He sniffed, breathing in the scent of evergreen; of hard, sandy soil; the blue smell of water; the hot, red odor of the pepper flowers he loved to eat. But no scent of pearls and lotus, no trace of the woman who had ridden the wheel of life until she'd earned paradise.

Taking to the air through force of will, he soared, annoyed by an eagle that flew near and peered at him, as if unsure how an un-winged thing like Tien Shen could live in its world. He roared at the bird, and the eagle flew away, but not without a defiant cry.

"Kuan Yin?" He formed the words slowly, sending them out into the world. They fell to the earth as rain, the drops merging to form the symbol for her name.

She didn't appear. She didn't call out. He still couldn't smell her. And the earth didn't give her up, didn't whisper to him that she'd been there. So he flew on.

He called for her over and over. Frogs echoed her name, but they were just playing. A deer bolted from a thicket as Tien Shen's calls grew more frantic.

One woman, ready for paradise, and he had lost her.

"Dragon," he heard in his inside-ears, and then he saw her with his inside-eyes. She was with a group of women who were studying a writing of a kind he'd never seen before. Curious, he settled on the ground just beyond them.

One of the women let out a little squeak, but the rest went on writing, not even looking over. The first woman stared at him, as if she could not believe what she was seeing.

"Chao Ma, pay attention to the lesson," Kuan Yin said softly, and the woman bowed and went back to creating the simple letters, so long and angular compared to traditional writing.

Tien Shen inched toward Kuan Yin, until he was right next to her, and she turned to look at him. He found he couldn't meet her eyes. But what did he have to feel guilty for? He was only trying to do what he'd been told. To see her safely to her rightful reward.

"I worried you, dragon?" The lotus smell changed, grew spicy, and he imagined it was regret that caused it.

"You did." He sighed and wished he could tell what she was thinking.

"I'm sorry. I don't wish to cause pain, even to you."

He accepted her apology—weak as it was—with a nod of his head. "It's time to go, my lady."

"Do you know why they're here?" She glanced down at the feet of one woman. They were bound, and Tien Shen knew the woman would hobble a little as she walked.

"They're bored?"

"Hardly." Kuan Yin laughed, and her laughter was cold and hard and full of pain he didn't expect. She glanced again at the feet of the woman. "I think it's less cruel to simply cut them off."

To his shock, he felt her hand on his back. "The language is called Nushu." She rubbed his neck softly, her fingers hitting spots he hadn't even realized were itching. "It's a language only for women."

He knew women were denied education. "You taught them this?"

"As I was taught."

"Who first handed you the brush?"

"I don't remember. So many lives. So many first lessons."

But he suspected she remembered every one of those lessons. His look must have told her he didn't believe her, because she laughed, and this time her laughter was like a brook as it bubbled over smooth stones or like the sound the sun made as the clouds tickled it.

The sounds of paradise—why was she waiting? She leaned against him, her fingers still working their magic on his scales.

"Why are we here?" he asked her.

"I'm here because I want to be. Why are you here, dragon?"

"To serve you."

She looked displeased. "That's the wrong answer." And like that, she was gone.

He sighed, and Chao Ma left her writing and walked over to him. She reached out, then jerked her hand back.

"It's all right."

"You don't bite?"

"Well, I won't. This time." He let out a little rumble of pleasure as she traced the pattern of his scales. Her touch moved him almost as much as Kuan Yin's. He was used to spirit creatures, insubstantial and fey, with touches just as light, not this more substantial rubbing.

"Why do you study the language?" he asked her.

She swallowed hard. "Because it gives us some measure of freedom. It allows us to have secrets. No man can read it."

"Why do you need secrets?" Secrets were never a good thing among dragons. They usually meant something bad was going to happen.

"My husband is cruel to me. Tan Lao's husband cheats on her. Mei Ling's brother sold her to an old man she doesn't love."

"How is your husband cruel?" Tien Shen did not care about the others. But this woman who was scratching his back deserved better.

"He yells. Hits, sometimes. Not all the time. Just . . . when he's angry."

Tien Shen sensed Kuan Yin reaching for him, the sound of her voice loud in his inside-ears. He heard the creak of the door between the worlds being opened, the rustle of a beaded curtain being pulled back. "I have to go."

"All right." But Chao Ma held on to him.

He rested his snout on her arm for a moment, was surprised to see tears in her eyes. She pulled away, but one of her tears fell onto his leg, and it burned as it sank into his scales.

Kuan Yin called again, and he forced himself away from Chao Ma and appeared where he felt his charge calling from.

Kuan Yin stood in front of the brightest light imaginable. It was so beautiful—Tien Shen never tired of seeing the sight, but then it wasn't one he saw very often. Those who attained Nirvana were few.

Soft breezes blew out of the light. A subtle smell of flowers and spices wafted over to him. Kuan Yin's scent seemed to grow in reaction, sweet and strong and still distinct even among such glory.

"Dragon?" Her voice was so small.

"You must go." But then he heard it: a small sob. And another. And another. His leg where Chao Ma's tear had fallen began to burn again.

Kuan Yin turned and stared out at the world, her back to Nirvana. Her eyes welled up, then she blinked, and the tears ran freely down her cheeks. He moved closer, lifted his leg and let her see that the scales where the woman's tear had fallen were turning silver.

"I hear them all, Tien Shen," she whispered. "The cries of the whole world."

He nodded. "I hear them now, too." He looked past her, at the beauty that was Nirvana. At the peace it promised. It was everything this remarkable woman had worked for.

It was what Tien Shen wanted for her.

And yet . . .

"I can't go just now." She took a deep breath. "I'm needed here."

The beaded curtain fell back, dimming the light. The breeze died, and the smell of Nirvana's flowers became fainter and fainter, as the scent of Kuan Yin grew.

Compassion. This was what compassion smelled like.

She turned to look at the door. "I'm needed here."

It slammed shut.

But the light remained. Growing brighter and brighter, and Tien Shen realized it was coming from her.

"My Goddess," he murmured, bowing his head. As he looked down, he realized the silver patch on his leg was reflecting her glow.

"There's much to do," she said, pulling the light around her like a cloak. It finally dimmed, drawn inside her. But he knew she could call it back if she wanted to.

He studied his leg; it still shone just a little. Even with no light to reflect.

She began to walk back into the world.

He hurried to get in front of her, and her eyes flashed with annoyance. Then he knelt, and said, "You should ride. I can be of help to you."

She touched his head before hugging him hard, her face pressed against his. Then, without a word, she jumped on his back and waited.

He listened and heard the loudest cries to the east. Without asking her, he flew for the rising sun.

Her hand tightened on his neck, and she sang a song he didn't know, her voice beautiful in its rawness.

"You gave up paradise," he said softly.

"How could I go there when even one person suffers?"

He had no answer to that. Only, he'd seen others do it. Perhaps Nirvana wasn't for the perfect. Maybe it was for the almost perfect. And someday they'd be back again to find perfection by helping those who still strove—and hurt.

"But it was beautiful, wasn't it?" she murmured. "And it smelled good."

He knew it was the last she'd ever say about it.

Dragon's Hand

David VonAllmen

THE CHAINED KING. FLAMING GOAT. MOON OF DAY.
Jane pinched the squares of heavy paper hard enough to turn her fingertips white. She'd finally drawn the hand of cards that would end her years of searching.

Or she'd drawn the hand of cards that would damn her to a lifetime of sorrow. She couldn't say which it'd be just yet.

"Make your play, Indian woman," the graying soldier across the table grumbled, just loud enough to be heard above the string quartet playing in one corner of the saloon.

Jane studied the illustrations' hard black lines and whirling brushstrokes of color. Her eye could almost make out all manner of stars and charms that promised fortune but never delivered. That was nothing new to Jane. Fate had dragged her along one dusty horse trail after the next for near on two years, always whispering that what remained of her tribe was just one more town away, always promising that her daughter was almost within reach.

She placed Moon of Day face down on the table but didn't take her fingers off it just yet. The card was powerful, but mighty unpredictable.

Jane looked up, hoping to read something in the expressions of her opponents. The soldier wore a tattered cavalry jacket and a six-shooter on his hip. His dark eyes darted endlessly around the room and every time the batwing doors thumped open his hand jumped to his gun. To Jane's left was an emaciated man whose slim suit hung loose, as if God forgot to add meat and fat before stretching skin over his bones. He sat still as a corpse. The woman to her right wore a schoolmarm's buttoned-up navy blue dress, her hair in a tight bun. She dabbed tears from her eyes with a lace handkerchief, but smiled relentlessly, like a showgirl on stage. The players' faces gave away nothing.

Jane started to pull back the Moon of Day card, but stopped herself. If she didn't play it, she'd never get a chance this good again. The game was the last hope she had to find her six year-old . . . No. Her daughter would be seven by now, wouldn't she?

Jane and her three opponents flipped their cards face up. The others eyed Jane with the flat look of practiced gamblers, surely surprised the quiet Indian woman in britches and shirtsleeves was crazy enough to lead with Moon of Day. What did they expect? None sat down for a hand of cards in Gideon's Saloon unless desperation had driven them at least halfway down the road to madness.

The game was seven-card Sorte. The stakes were luck itself.

"You look like you've been on the trails for a long time, dearie," the schoolmarm said, her tone so polite and friendly it was impossible to believe it was sincere. Jane reckoned the woman intended it that way. "What tribe are you?"

"Guachichil," Jane lied with practiced ease. It was an instinct every member of her tribe grew up with. Fortune hunters were always on their tail, looking to cash in on the riches to be had from selling their blood to those who knew the ways of spells and conjuring.

The dealer flicked another card to each player. Their table sat in the middle of a crowded saloon furnished as if it was a betting parlor for European royalty. A score of oil lights shone from each of the chandeliers floating a dozen feet above their heads and plush green velvet cushioned their seats. The décor matched nothing else in the border town of El Perdido, its humble buildings painted burnt red by dust that hung so thick you could taste iron in the air.

Jane picked up her card. Black Flower. Her jaws tightened.

"Guachichil . . ." The emaciated man's voice was never more than a whisper. "From dead in the center of Mexico, isn't that right?"

Jane nodded. She tilted the brim of her gaucho hat to keep the light off her pupils. If you looked real close, they weren't quite round, weren't quite human. They pointed, every so slightly, at the top and the bottom, as if she'd had a reptile for a grandmother. And that wasn't too far from the truth.

"Well it is such an unexpected delight to have you join us," the schoolmarm said. "Many saloons don't allow your kind inside." She plucked a card from her hand and placed it face down in front of her.

Jane pulled The Chained King from her hand and laid it face down. The four players flipped over their cards. As the last round was dealt, Jane struggled to sort out the ranks and realms and trumps her opponents might be working toward. Her head swam. There were too many possibilities.

She reached for her final card, praying the fates might smile on her just this once.

A voice like a cannon blast rang out across the saloon.

"You dumb sumbitch!"

Gideon himself, owner of the saloon and just about everything else in El Perdido, held some confused-looking sap by the lapels. A cigarillo bit between his teeth, he stood atop a dais three steps above the rest of the saloon and smashed a handful of cards over the fellow's head. He wore a red silk shirt, busy with embroidery, over a hairy body thick with muscle and fat. He put Jane to mind of a costumed circus bear she'd seen once. No amount of dressing up would ever rid the beast of the killing instinct coursing through its veins.

Gideon pitched the man backwards, right off the edge of the dais. By all rights, the fellow should have tumbled feet-over-rear and cracked the back of his skull open on the hardwood below. Instead, the fellow's heels caught each step, then his feet wheeled and danced him across the room, body titled too far to catch his balance. His clumsy jig took him to the far end of the saloon and out the batwing doors.

The dealer and the soldier chuckled in an easy sort of way that told Jane they'd seen this kind of thing before.

"Doesn't much care for losing, does he?" the emaciated man said.

"Losing ain't been a problem for him for, oh, going on six years now," the soldier said. "It's all the winning that's made him so ornery."

"He'd be the first I've ever met who grew tired of winning," Jane said.

"He lived for the thrill of the wager," the soldier said. "And then he trumped a Thirteenth rank Endeavor set. He won't never lose another hand of cards so long as he lives. No thrill to be had in that."

The luck of the Thirteenth rank was powerful and unending. The Endeavor realm ruled over any kind of effort or undertaking. If Jane had that kind of luck, whatever direction she picked to go searching for her daughter would turn out to be the right one, and before she knew it her little girl would all but fall out of the sky into her arms.

She picked up her final card. Dreamer in Mourning. The schoolmarm had played Three-Tailed Fox followed by Half Coin, and looked to be building a mid-rank set in the Opportunity realm. Jane would have to play her Dreamer in Mourning card to win.

In Sorte, the cards were both the game and the wager. If Jane's set outranked the schoolmarm's, she'd win that Opportunity luck, and the schoolmarm would lose it in equal measure. It was exactly the kind of luck Jane needed to provide a clue where her tribe had disappeared to. But she'd be laying down high-rank Coincidence set. If the schoolmarm's third card trumped her, Jane would likely spend years narrowly missing her tribe at every turn.

Jane squeezed her right hand into a fist, trying to fight off the tremble that had overtaken it. She pulled Black Flower from her hand. It stood little chance of winning, but if she lost her bad luck wouldn't be so terrible.

"You know, I heard a number of those poor reds down in Mexico were slaughtered two years back when blood hunters came through those parts," the schoolmarm said, her smile beaming as she played her final card face down. "They were chasing rumors one of the tribes down there were dragons."

Jane froze with Black Flower between her fingers. The woman had seen the shape of her pupils. She knew what Jane was.

The dealer, the soldier, and the emaciated man all studied Jane. Surely, they could hear her heart pounding like the gallop of unbroken horses. Surely, they realized what she was. She had to run, while she still could. The saloon was full of desperate men, and it wouldn't be long until one of them tried to collect her blood.

But wasn't the whole world full of desperate men? If she didn't take this last chance to find her daughter, how long until one of them caught up to her child?

Are you okay, my precious girl? Are you still alive?

I'm okay, momma. Grandpa's taking care of me. I miss you.

Her daughter's voice in her head was just imagination, nothing more than that. But hearing her daughter say she was alive and unhurt was the only thing that'd kept Jane from losing her mind to madness, even if it was only make believe.

Jane replaced Black Flower in her hand. She drew out Dreamer in Mourning and laid it face down on the table. The schoolmarm watched the change of cards and her tear-strained eye took on a gleam of satisfaction.

The four players flipped their final cards. The schoolmarm had played Cracked Lantern. Jane had her outranked. The schoolmarm's smile twisted into something savage.

"Well . . ." the schoolmarm said, her voice hollow.

The ink burned off her cards, illustrations disappearing as wisps of colored smoke rose from them and faded into the air. The Opportunity luck Jane took was Fourth rank, which meant her luck would only last until sunrise, but that luck would be powerfully strong.

The schoolmarm stood abruptly, backing into a man walking past. The whiskey he'd been carrying splashed across the front of her dress, his glass clanked across the varnished floor.

"And there I had you figured for a lady who scares easy," the schoolmarm said. She wiped at the whiskey stain with her handkerchief as she strode away. The schoolmarm hadn't figured out what Jane was. She'd just been poking, trying to unnerve her.

"You really Guachichil?" the soldier asked.

"Yeah," Jane said. "Hadn't heard of that trouble the lady was talking about. Was she trying to play me?"

"Probably," the soldier said. "Had other Guachichil come through here some months back."

Every muscle in Jane's body locked up. Her people had come through this very town. It had to have been them. Her newly-won Opportunity luck had struck already. She dug fingernails into her palms to keep tears from pooling in her eyes.

"Haven't seen another Guachichil since I left home," Jane said, fighting to keep her voice steady. "Happen to know which way they went?"

"Heh." The man's eyes landed on her for just a second, then bounded away again. "You just won the strongest set I've seen in a while, and you're looking for a favor from me?"

"Alright," Jane said, in a way she hoped sounded friendly. "We'll help each other out. What is it I can do for you?"

"Gimme some time to think it over while I try to win some luck of my own," the man said.

Another gambler slid into the chair the schoolmarm had occupied. The dealer looked at the deck and frowned.

"Only fifteen cards," he said. "Someone dropping out?"

"I'm done for the night," Jane said, standing. She looked to the soldier. "I'll be waiting out front when you're ready to ask your favor."

The man met her eyes just long enough to nod. Jane made for the door. She could only hope that whatever the soldier knew, it would finally put an end to her years of searching. She'd grown weary of lying, of stealing, of doing terrible things just to survive.

Pomogi mne.

The voice in Jane's head wasn't her daughter this time. It was the voice of a man she'd known two years back. A withered man, his limbs as thin and pale as the branches of a birch sapling in winter. A man she shared no language with, but had been forced to share a cage with. A man whose eyes had begged her for help. A man she had left to die.

She hadn't had a choice. She had to keep moving until she found her daughter. She'd only done what she had to.

I will find you, my precious girl. I've won strong luck to help me. Just stay hid until I get there. Promise me you will.

Okay, momma. I promise. I'll hide where the hunters won't ever find me.

Jane waited outside the saloon for hours, watching stars inch across the sky, too rigid with excitement and fear to sit. The night air returned the heat it had soaked up all day. Sweat and grit lined the cracks of her skin. It seemed nearly every patron stumbled down the saloon's porch steps before the soldier in the battered cavalry jacket hurried past.

"I know a place we can talk," he said, with barely a glance in her direction.

She rushed to catch him. "Hold up, now. Where are we going? Do you even know where those Guachichil went?"

The man turned down the alley between Gideon's saloon and the next building over. As soon as she rounded the corner, Jane knew she was in trouble. The worst kind of trouble.

The soldier stood between two thugs, one holding a pistol, the other a length of iron. Jane faded back. A blow like the kick of a mule stuck her full in the back. She collapsed face down in the dirt, blood rising in the back of her throat. Head dizzy with pain and lungs refusing to draw breath, Jane's only thought was for regaining her feet. She got no further than hands and knees before the toe of a boot cracked her ribs and she flopped belly down again.

"Stay down," the soldier commanded. "Ain't no point in fighting. Told Gideon what you was and he sent us to corral you, and you know Gideon's endeavors can't never fail."

Eyes blurry from tears, Jane could see one thing plainly enough: the thugs coming for her with a rope, like she was runaway cattle. Her only chance was to shift shape.

She never truly felt her body grow, never felt the wings sprout from her shoulder blades or talons rip through the leather of her boots. Instead, it was as if the fangs and red-brown scales and all the rest were always there, only she'd forgotten about them, and now her senses were waking up to them once again. Feeling her weight was like standing up after a long sleep, feeling the power of her muscles was like suddenly waking from a dream.

If the thugs had been able to hold onto their bravado, they would've laid into her the second her first scale appeared. But Jane had yet to meet the man who didn't cower back upon seeing a woman transform into a dragon. A moment later, she'd gained her full height – triple that of the largest quarter horse – and her wingtips scraped the alley walls.

The thug with the pistol fired a shot. It struck her neck, cracking a scale. She howled in pain and lunged forward, swiping at the man with her front claws. The fellow had been smart enough to stay out of reach, but couldn't help jumping back. Just as he did, the man with the iron bar darted forward. But he didn't have an iron bar anymore.

The man flung a handful of white powder, fine as flour, up into Jane's face. She reared back, but not fast enough. Fine-ground salt bit into her eyes. To a human, it would have been irritating, painful even. To a dragon, it was like being splashed with acid. The salt stung her scales and worked its way between them, stabbing her skin. Each draw of breath sucked more of the salt into her lungs, where it tore at her insides like the bites of a thousand tiny spiders.

The salt wouldn't kill her, but that wasn't the point. All they were trying to do was get her to shift back to human form. No matter how much she fought the urge, she wouldn't last but a few seconds until she did just that.

Blinded and panicking, Jane roared and flung her tail about, smashing the man who had snuck up behind her against the saloon wall. She tromped forward, hoping to feel one of the men crushed beneath her claws. Like the inhale of a man who'd been underwater too long, Jane could do nothing to stop her body from shifting and shrinking. With only a second or two left, she drew a lungful of air and exhaled an orange blaze of fire.

Flames crackled up the saloon wall as Jane lay face-down, naked in the dirt, her human body trying to cry the salt out of her eyes. When she managed to look up, all three thugs were closing on her. By the scowls on their faces, she figured they were going to give her some extra bruises before tying her up.

A rapid thumping of boots raced up behind her. Painful as it was, she managed to swing her head around to see a pale man running her way, hauling a bucketful of water. He was aiming to save Gideon's saloon from going up in flame.

No. His eyes were fixed right on her. The water was meant for her.

Just as he skidded to a stop and reared back to heave that water, the bottom fell out of the bucket and every last drop splashed to the ground.

"Asher, you miserable ol' loser . . ." the soldier growled. "What the hell do you think you're doing?"

The man named Asher stood blinking, a look of shock on his face, as if he'd been sleepwalking and suddenly woke to find he'd stumbled into a wolf's den. His distraction gave Jane the only chance she was likely to get. Biting her teeth against a cry of pain, she leapt to her feet and ran like the devil himself was just a step behind her.

A gunshot hammered her ears. One stride later, Jane reached the end of the alley and dodged behind the corner of the saloon.

Whatever Asher's source of water, the trail of spills he'd left were big enough to be seen in the moonlight, she could follow along and find it herself. The thugs wouldn't be but a few steps behind. As soon as they rounded the corner, they'd have a clear shot at her.

Just as another shot exploded, she saw it, and it was better than she could've hoped for. A watering trough. Jane didn't slow one tick before diving in head-first. The warm water stank of horse hair. She snorted it up her nose, hoping to take in just enough to clear her nostrils. Jane gagged and choked, but the burn left her skin as the salt washed clear.

Bullets thunked into the side of the trough, one after another. It was too late. The trough shattered with a crack like thunder. Jane exploded up into dragon form, waves of water and shards of wood scattering a score of paces in every direction.

If the thugs had any salt left, they'd lost the nerve to give it another try. They turned tail and ran. Jane spit a burst of fire after them to make sure they knew what they'd get if they somehow found that nerve again.

Jane let her dragon body unform. The sensation of her tail whipping behind her faded into a ghost of itself, then disappeared completely. Bit by bit she lost any sense of touch in her wings and claws, until she dropped into a human body and her mind almost couldn't imagine the feel of any other.

Dripping wet, she sagged with exhaustion. Only rage kept her on her feet.

Damn those bastards. That was supposed to have been her Opportunity. She'd won the luck, and Sorte cards never failed to deliver luck to the winner.

Pain stabbing her ribs with every movement, Jane pulled the duster off the thug she'd smashed against the wall and tugged it on. She had neither the time nor inclination to check if he was still breathing.

"Who are you?" she demanded, glaring at Asher. "Why'd you try to save me?"

Asher curled in on himself, shoulders hunched and head down, like a dog with a cruel master who expected another blow to come at any second.

"I'm nobody," he said. He turned to walk away.

Jane caught his arm and spun him around.

"How come roping me didn't work out for Gideon?" she asked.

"It weren't him doing the deed," Asher said. "His luck falls off sharply when it ain't him actually doing the endeavoring."

An alarm bell clanged and folks rushed from their homes to see the bright blaze crawling up the side of Gideon's saloon. Jane slapped her gaucho hat back on her head. She stared at Asher, a deep frown pulling down her mouth.

"This weren't no business of yours," she said. "Why'd you go risking your life to help a stranger?"

Dancing firelight lit up one side of Asher's trembling face. "What's it matter?" he sputtered in a burst that was a bark of laughter and a cry of anguish both at the same time. "My life ain't worth living. Only hope I got left is that Gideon'll get angry enough to shoot me dead."

Jane stared at him a moment longer while the gears in her mind clicked into place.

"You were on the losing side, weren't you?" she said. "When Gideon won that Endeavor luck, he won it from you. Now anything you try to do fails. Even when all you're trying to do is end your own life."

Asher said nothing, just stood there fighting to hold back tears. And like everything else the man aspired to do, he failed.

For a flash, his eyes were those of another man. A man Jane had left to die in a cage.

Pomogi mne.

They'd been the only words he'd uttered, almost too weak to hear. Though she didn't speak a word of Russian, there was no mistaking when a man was begging for his life.

Jane turned from Asher and set out walking with purpose. The voice of the Russian followed her.

Pomogi mne.

They'd shipped him across the Atlantic in an iron cage, to sell to the highest bidder. It had been darn near impossible to believe he could turn himself into one of those fearsome dragons they say terrorized the Ural Mountains so many years ago. Frail as a water reed and halfway starved to death, dragging him along would have slowed her down too much. She'd had to leave him behind. Her daughter needed her.

Why'd you leave him to die, momma?

I only did what I had to, sweet girl. It won't matter once we're together again. You'll never know the horrible things I had to do to get to you.

The townspeople all stood lined up on either side of the road, gawking like Jane was lead horse in a circus caravan parading itself through town. She met the stare of a tall fellow still dressed in his nightclothes.

"Gideon," she growled.

The man pointed down the road to a castle of a house, so tall and wide it seemed to be pushing the neighboring buildings aside. Jane marched for it. She'd pull her Opportunity right out of Gideon's hide if that's what it took.

"Gideon!" she bellowed up at the balcony jutting out from the second floor of Gideon's mansion. "Come face me yourself, you coward!"

A moment later, Gideon stormed out onto the balcony. He stared into the distance, where men ran in circles around his saloon, shouting and throwing water on the dwindling flames. Gideon's eyes shifted, glaring down at her as if he couldn't believe she had the nerve to still be alive.

"You want a real game of cards?" she called out. "I got some Opportunity luck I need to use up before sunrise. Come face me in a game of thirteen-card Sorte." Jane turned, then shouted back over her shoulder. "That is, if your place ain't burnt up, yet."

It must have been the whole town that packed in Gideon's saloon, crowded around the playing table, come to see the woman crazy enough to play Gideon in a hand of thirteen-card Sorte. The stakes were higher than seven-card by a mile. And then some. That was the point. Jane was going to use her Opportunity to win enough luck that she couldn't help but find what remained of her tribe. She could only pray her daughter was still alive and with them.

Lingering smoke filled the room, the scent of charred wood thick enough to give Jane a headache. She sat wearing nothing save her hat and the oversized duster, dirt rubbing in the cracks between her bare toes. Gideon stared at her as he lit a cigarillo and blew a cloud of sweet tobacco smoke across the table. He didn't smile, but his eyes shone, wild and alive. The soldier and the other thugs who attacked her stood behind Gideon like he was their shield. Asher hid among the crowd, where Jane wouldn't have noticed if she hadn't been looking for him.

The dealer fanned out twenty-six cards into two rows representing the thirteen realms of luck and the thirteen ranks of luck. They were simple, single-color icons, but once the dealer flipped them face down and started shuffling, they mixed like shades of paint. Hidden from every eye in the room, each became a unique combination of realm and rank, 169 different possibilities. Somewhere during the shuffling, it was impossible to watch close enough to say exactly when, the number of cards changed, so the deck wound up with exactly enough cards for everyone at the table.

The dealer flicked three cards to each of them and Jane scooped hers up. The Dancing Madman. Skeleton Knife. Candle of Memory. They didn't add up to much. Skeleton Knife was easily the highest rank, so she played it face-down on the table in front of her. Gideon looked up at her and frowned. Annoyed by how fast she made her decision, she had to guess. What did he expect? She wasn't going to beat him with strategic thinking. Her Opportunity luck was either strong enough to give his Endeavor luck a run for his money or it wasn't.

Gideon laid down his card. They both turned over. He'd played Golden Fish. He had her outranked. But it was only the first card.

The dealer tossed another card to each of them, adding Liar's River to the two cards she still held. What matched up strong with the Skeleton Knife she'd already laid down? It didn't take but a second before the answer hit her.

Gideon had led with Golden Fish. That almost always built a set in the Endeavor realm. She already had a high trump for that realm in her hand. She just had to play Liar's River next, then Candle of Memory the last round.

Was it possible Gideon might draw a combination to come back over the top? Hell, the man was playing with all the luck in the world in his pocket, the long odds against that didn't make a whit of difference. But morning would break soon, and the luck she'd won promised to deliver by sunrise. This had to be her Opportunity. It had to be. Fate was laying it out clear as day right in front of her: he had the beginnings of a high-rank Endeavor set and she had the three best cards in the deck to win it from him.

Gideon laid down his card. Jane played Liar's River face-down behind her Skeleton Knife card. They flipped.

Empty Mirror. He'd played Empty Mirror. It was exactly what she'd hoped for. He was building an Endeavor set and she had him trumped. There was only one card in the whole 169 that could save him now.

Jane's hands shook. Gideon looked up at her with a smirk. He thought she was nervous about the cards. Years of perfect fortune had robbed him of his instincts. He couldn't see she'd already all but won. She wasn't shaking from nerves. She was . . .

Why exactly was she shaking?

When you come back to me, who will you be, momma?

Who will I be?

You stole from them that had nothing to spare. You let a man die in his cage.

I only did what I had to. To find you. So I can protect you. When we're together again I won't have to do such things anymore. You'll never have to know what I've done these past couple years.

Life ain't gonna get any easier, momma, not for us. A time'll come that you'll hurt someone and I'll see it. I'll know what you've become.

No. I . . .

You can't return to me, momma. Not like this.

But I have to. This luck will be gone by sunrise. This right here's gotta be my Opportunity. It's gotta be. 'Cause if this ain't it . . . what is?

The trembling in Jane's hands threatened to shake her cards free. She slapped them face-down on the table and intertwined her fingers, squeezed as hard as she could. The shaking wouldn't stop. She stood, knocking her chair over. The crowd whispered and snickered.

"This ain't poker," Gideon said. He lifted a snifter of whiskey to smiling lips. "Can't fold and walk."

She would play away from the trump. That's what she'd do. Whatever card she drew next, she'd make the lowest set she could, take whatever bad luck was her punishment. She didn't have another choice. She couldn't face her daughter now. Not like she was.

Jane fought to smooth out her lungs' jagged gasps. They stared at her, every last soul in the crowd. Some with amusement, the more kindly folks with sympathy or even horror, guessing from her expression she was about to get loaded down with a terrible affliction of bad luck.

Her eyes stopped when they met Asher's. Though she would have sworn it was impossible, those eyes carried even more sorrow than when she first saw them. This time, the sorrow was not for his own plight. It was for hers.

Pomogi mne.

Fate was offering her an Opportunity all right. But it wasn't the chance to win luck off Gideon.

Jane's hands stopped shaking. The dealer tossed her last card to her, but she didn't pick it up. Still standing, she lifted the Candle of Memory card off the table and held it out, back side facing Gideon.

"I've got the Candle of Memory," she taunted, forcing her smile wide. "And you're working on an Endeavor set. I have you trumped."

Fury wasn't the only emotion that duked it out for control of Gideon's face, but it was the clear winner.

"You're lying, red woman," he said, voice tightly reined in. "Trying to fool me into playing away from the Endeavor realm 'cause you ain't got the cards to beat it."

"Then lay it down if you got the guts. But I know you don't."

Gideon bared teeth bit together in anger.

"Even with more luck than any other man alive, you're too cowardly to play at me. That's why you sent thugs to ambush me, 'cause you were too cowardly to try and rope me yourself."

Gideon's face burned red and his cheeks trembled. Whatever he was itching to say, his temper had boiled the words right out of his mouth.

Jane placed the Candle of Memory card face down on top of her other unplayed cards. She couldn't play it, yet. Not if she wanted her trick to work.

Then she did something she'd never done before, something she'd have no faith in trying if luck weren't on her side. She started a shape shift she had no intention of finishing. Just enough to get scales growing across her chest. Just enough so that her eyes burned bright orange and her pupils melted to black slits and bone fangs snapped inches from Gideon's face when she leaned forward with a wicked smile and whispered, "Your move."

Gideon threw himself back from the table, jumped to his feet, and fired a shot from his six-gun before anyone else in the room had a chance to so much as blink.

The bullet shattered a scale on Jane's chest, a sharp point of pain exploding across her torso. Goading Gideon into firing on her had been Jane's aim, but still the shock swept her legs out from under her. Forehead pressed against the hard varnish of the floor, she fell back into fully-human shape and coughed blood into her hand. Likely as not, she had a fractured rib.

After the screams and gasps faded away, the crowd closed in to see whether Jane was dead. The dealer knelt to speak to her.

"Are you alive?" he asked. "Can you continue?"

Jane groaned and gave a slow, slight shake of her head, made like she was trying to speak but couldn't quite manage. "Asher . . ." she said.

"Asher?" the dealer asked. With that, every head in the crowd spun about until they locked on Asher. Startled as he was, the man's usual hunched-shoulder posture momentarily disappeared.

"What the hell?" Gideon bellowed.

"A game of Sorte can't be stopped before the final cards are played," the dealer said. "If she can't continue, she's allowed to pick her replacement."

Gideon's face fought with itself again. This time, he wrestled a confident smile into place.

"What's the point in letting him finish her hand?" Gideon laughed. "I can't lose and he can't win."

Asher looked at Jane, unsure. Jane herself wasn't so sure of her plan. She had to trust that this was the moment her Opportunity luck had brought her to.

Asher shambled forward, lowered himself into the seat, and picked up the cards. Jane had to stifle a whimper as a pair of men hooked their arms under hers and hefted her into a chair.

Asher didn't hesitate. He plucked the Candle of Memory card and laid it face down behind the two Jane had already played. Gideon paused just long enough to scowl, caught himself, and smacked his final play card down with a tight-lipped smile. The two players flipped their cards face-up.

Gideon had played Orphan of Night. The overconfident fool had actually completed the Thirteenth rank Endeavor set. The color burned off his cards, turning them white. But not nearly so white as Gideon's face.

The stunned crowd didn't make a sound as Asher stood, plucked a cigarillo from Gideon's shirt pocket, and bounced a match off the table. The match lit when it struck the wood surface and popped right up into Asher's hand. The new king of El Perdido puffed his cigarillo to life.

Gideon yanked his six-gun from its holster and aimed the barrel at his temple. Asher slammed his fist on the table, bouncing the opposite side up and knocking the gun from Gideon's hand.

"Fate ain't gonna let you off that easy," Asher said. "All you woulda done is hurt yourself bad enough to spend the rest of your life regretting the attempt. But thank your lucky cards I'm gonna be a damn sight kinder to you than you ever was to me."

Jane stood, painfully, one hand over her ribs. She limped toward the door.

"Why'd you do that?" Asher called after her.

"Got my reasons," she said without looking back.

Jane stepped out into the night. The first dim hints of dawn lightened the horizon. Asher followed, as did most of the crowd. He hustled to get in front of her.

"I owe you a debt, now," Asher said. "A mighty big one. What is it you're doing here? What is it you want?"

Jane struggled to hold back tears as she met his eyes.

"My people came through here a few months back, with my little girl. All I want is to find them." She nodded toward the soldier. "I think that fella may know something about where they went."

Asher turned his gaze to the soldier, who startled back.

"We gonna do this the hard way, or you gonna tell this lady everything you know?" Asher asked.

"They asked the way to Las Cruces, that's all I know," the soldier said in a rush. From the fear pulling his eyes wide, there was little doubt he was telling the truth.

Jane dropped her gaucho hat in the dirt and let the borrowed duster fall to the ground. She stood naked in the middle of the road, staring over the hilltops to the west, where bright stars sparkled against the indigo sky.

I'm so sorry, my beautiful girl.

It's okay, momma.

Can you hang on just a little longer?

Yes, momma, I think I can.

Scales sprouted from Jane's skin. Toenails grew into talons. The ground receded in her view, the crowd gasping and backing away as she gained her full height.

Jane leapt into the air and beat her wings, picking up speed until the ground below became a blur.

I will find you soon. I promise.

Take out the Trash
Melva L. Gifford

Here I am, the ideal student, sitting at my easel, treating the scroll before me like the priests' holy wine. I'm in my second year of magic school. I'm studying a levitation spell, nibbling away on a mecca root when ol' Stop-and-Go Pordal struts in.

"Shantell, your turn to take out the trash."

Then he strides off before I can say anything. He's been giving me the dirtiest jobs ever since I caught him spying in the girls' quarters. I had just learned how to stun and froze him in position by the window for all to see.

Some of the sorceresses started calling him Peekee after that. I still call him Stop-and-Go. It fits better.

The masters assigned him kitchen duty for a full moon for his punishment.

He hasn't forgiven me since.

He thinks I'm nothing but a chambermaid because I'm only a second-level sorceress. Until I claim my wizard sense, I'm treated like the former. So what could I do? I wish I could find some kind of personal project to keep me busy.

Emptying the trash wouldn't be so bad if it was just the scrap spells from the more experienced trainees. But no, they also have to dump the first yearlings' rejects in as well. Have you ever smelled a half-conjured demon fermented for over a week?

No wonder so many of the masters' beards are white. The Psi nets are never strong enough. They're always leaking or losing something along the way to the vac pit.

I walk into the room, and just as I expected, the bag's filled to overflowing. The area is a mess. There are demons, zaps, fireballs, whammies, giants, dragons, potions, and Hades knows what else. Most are spells that never came into full realization. There's a monstrous tentacle weaving itself lazily above the rim of the net. Its acting like it's already high from the demons' fumes. After taking one whiff myself, I'm sure of it.

Why me?

Nothing to do but throw the lot of them in the vacuum pit. The tricky part is getting the thing to the pit, especially with weak Psi nets.

Because of Stop-and-Go's harassment, I'm now an old pro. Too many incidents from other apprentices' trips to the vac have taught me to take precautions. I step up to the net, keeping my skirt hem clear of possible entanglements. It's taller than me and almost reaches the high ceiling. A good reduction spell should cut the thing down to size. So, I cast the spell and watch as the occupants shrink to the size of a chair.

The thing keeps moving since some of the spells within it haven't fully deactivated.

I bend over the bag and quickly lean back to let one particularly powerful wisp of odor pass. Hades, it's strong. Whammies and zaps almost spill out of the bag, some barely hanging over the edge. When I begin to close the top, several fall out. They immediately activate, stinging and singeing my feet. My resulting list of obscenities would impress a warlock. They're all centered on Pordal. Thankfully most of the zaps fall back into the bag when I shake the net.

Zaps and whammies, in their solid state, look much like frozen lightning bolts. They always seem to find a way to poke you in the ribs. I seal the bag with an echo patch—the most powerful sealing spell I know.

Seeing how the potions and powders seem to always settle at the bottom, I try to put as much echo underneath the bag as over the top. Feeling reasonably protected, I touch the net's surface, probing with my fingers. Every kind of spell seems to be in there. Yep, they must have gone through a full session of Wizardry 101 to get all these rejects. It takes me only a minute to find what I'm searching for.

He's a big one, and only partially deflated.

A Giant.

Why can't everyone deflate their Giants fully before throwing them away? A Giant is eighty percent air. If you have a deflated Giant in the trash, it can help you with the lifting. All you have to do is give it a gentle tap on the head—just enough to aggravate it so it'll puff up. When the

Giant rises, then, the entire bag will rise, too. Makes it easier to carry the thing outside.

Of course, you have to watch that you don't hit them too hard. Heard a story once where a first yearling was taking out the trash. Made the mistake of giving the Giants a royal whack and it got 'em mad. Puffed 'em up all the way—all of them. Got the rest of the spells activated too. The yearling soon found himself floating up in the air, hanging onto that bag for dear life. He was yelling at the top of his lungs.

What a sight!

The Giants were having a grand old fight up there.

Thankfully, a couple of apprentices were also archers. Got their bows out and started shooting. Said it was great to have a moving target like that. 'Course the bag came down, and the yearling came after and got tangled in the tree.

It took a week for the school to clean up and catch all the mess. Made a school project of it.

So anyway, I lift the bag. Can't levitate it. You can only levitate stationary objects. The dragons inside keep shifting from side to side as if they're sitting on a hot pile of gold. It's hard getting a firm hold on the net. The Psi shield is already wearing thin in some areas, especially at the bottom. I would try to add another echo patch, but I have to see what I'm doing and the bag's in my way. Hades, I remember what happened the last time a bag broke open.

There was a student once who took out the trash without trying to patch up any leaks. There was an unusual amount of love potion at the bottom. He went almost the entire length of the path before he got a whiff. Then it was too late. He went under. It was love at first sight. A guy looks kind of silly kissing the ground like that. Took the Masters a while to get him under control. They repaved the path. Got rid of the soil by putting it under the mattress of a man who complained of insomnia. He loves to sleep now.

Keeping the bag in my arms isn't a problem yet, even though Giants and monsters can complicate things if they are too close together. If they start fighting they'll wake the dragons, and you'll end up weaving all over the place trying to get to the vac pit.

Oh, no! A cool dampness presses from inside the bag, kinda soggy and mushy. It's beginning to seep through onto my arm. My heartbeat quickens. If it's a fireball, I'm in trouble. Improperly deactivated fireballs turn into a cold liquid which acts as a powerful adhesive. It took the masters several days to separate a student's leg from the Psi net when some fire juice leaked onto her.

Not knowing the most dignified way to panic, I slowly move my hand away from the wet spot.

"Ribbit."

Oh, Hades!

I contemplate fainting from relief, but the trash is in the way. I'll faint later. I probe the bag's surface, recognizing the outline of a frog—several frogs. There must be a mini-course on witchcraft going on at the school.

Maybe there's something to my classmates' increasing complaints about warts. Though they shouldn't leap to conclusions.

I start up the path in a reasonably straight line (dragons permitting) when I hear something.

A voice?

What now?

It comes from the trash bag. Clutching the container against me, I place my ear next to the bag. It's a voice and he is quoting—

Philosophy?

Well, this little frog is still trying to turn into a prince. It would seem that the mind was willing but the body—it wouldn't make it. Guess it's trying to find a good role model.

I press on, ignoring the frog as he proclaims, "There were two peasants walking down a street . . ."

A dragon hiccups and shifts and I lunge to the right, trying to keep my balance. I'm getting annoyed.

Not too much farther to go. I try to hurry but then, just as I'm on the verge of reaching the vac pit—

The Giant lets out a burp and down goes the bag.

That thing's heavy when you have to rely on your own strength. With the Giant's levitating air gone, mass returns, and I almost gag when the Psi net tears as it hits the ground. I hear protests from the dragons and another Giant wakes up, along with two more monsters. I don't take time to see what kind. The contents of the bag begin attacking one another.

The rip in the net widens. If anything gets even partially outside the net, it'll return to normal size. Then the real trouble will begin.

The bag moves of its own accord. I hear the outcries of several monsters and Giants as they wallow at the bottom. A dragon bellows. The escalating battle shakes the entire bag. It starts to lean.

Hades!

I pray for a miracle.

Nothing happens. Panic appears to be the only alternative. If I try to touch the bag, I'm certain the netting will totally dissolve.

If I can convince the monsters and Giants that they're being challenged by something fiercer then them—

I levitate; a wind is tugging at my hair. I'm glad I braided it. Floating to the center of the pit, I bellow at the bag, imitating the occupants' various calls. But my verbal challenge can hardly be heard over the din.

I strain my voice to its full capacity, lowering it to sound more fierce.

The bag turns, moving toward me, closer and closer until—

Down it goes, into the vac.

What a relief.

I float carefully back to the edge, glad to stand on firm earth again. There is a silvery liquid shining on the edge of the hole. I'll avoid that. Then realization dawns. I've finally found something to do with my spare time until I acquire my wizard sense. I can work on something that could make me rich and famous!

I'll create a double-ply Psi net with an echo in between trash bags. That could hold nearly anything, guaranteed never to leak. The apprentices would certainly be Glad—so would my money pouch.

With a new purpose, I start back to the study room.

I now have some spell casting to do.

Burying Treasure
Alex Shvartsman

The wizard rode a cart full of gold into the village. The wooden cartwheels creaked, protesting the enormous weight of coins and miscellaneous trinkets that filled the cart to the point of almost overflowing. The coins shifted and jingled as the horse pulled the cart forward on an uneven road, their sweet sound summoning gawkers much faster than any magic could have.

"Now that's something you don't see every day," Hurlee said to her twin sister as the two of them watched the cart make its way down the road.

Burlee grunted assent, the straw she was chewing on teetering at the edge of her lip, then got up and headed over for a closer look.

"Careful," said Hurlee. "Anyone flaunting such riches is either very dangerous or dangerously stupid. Or both."

Burlee turned back for a moment, straightened the iron-studded jacket of her old military uniform, and nodded at Hurlee, who was wearing the same outfit. "When did that ever stop us?"

Hurlee reached toward her sister, wanting to hold her back, but thought better of it. She lowered her hand, and reluctantly followed Burlee instead.

The cart came to a stop. The entire village gathered to see what the wizard would do next. A pile of coins, jewelry, and small trinkets glimmered in the sun, awing the onlookers. A small gargoyle rested atop the treasure. It glared at the villagers, making sure no one got any ideas.

Hurlee hung back, close enough to observe, but far enough to quietly retreat in case there was trouble.

"I need a pair of guides," declared the wizard. "Young people who know the nearby woods. A gold coin is offered in payment."

There was no shortage of volunteers. Villagers jostled each other for a chance at earning the princely sum.

Burlee pushed and shoved her way to the front of the crowd. And although Hurlee was still conflicted, she followed right along.

"What do you seek in the woods, Sir Wizard?" asked one of the village elders.

"A place to bury this treasure," said the wizard. His gargoyle purred loudly and shifted to find a more comfortable spot. It cuddled up to a jewel-encrusted chalice.

"Why would you do such a thing?" asked Burlee, devouring the gold with her eyes.

"The Emperor decrees it," said the wizard, "to help the economy."

The villagers murmured.

"I thought them dragonses liked to hoard treasure," said Olaf. A tall, lanky youth, he made up for what could be generously described as below-average wit with excess enthusiasm.

"Quiet, fool." An elder glared at Olaf. "Don't disrespect the Emperor in front of our esteemed guest."

"Indeed," said the wizard. "His Majesty is long-lived, and his complexion is, perhaps, a little scaly, but vicious rumors of dragon blood in his lineage are falsehoods told by anarchists and malcontents. You would do well to discourage such talk."

"Won't happen again," said the elder.

"The Emperor plans ahead," said the placated wizard. "Word of the treasure will spread. Knights and adventurers from other lands will come to seek it. They'll spend coin in taverns and inns, patronize blacksmiths and apothecaries. They'll pay a special tax levied on all seekers. This is called tourism."

Hurlee was well-familiar with the Emperor's eccentricities. The new ruler signed a peace treaty with the orcs, inconveniently interrupting the conflict that had been successfully ongoing for over a hundred years.

Hurlee and Burlee had enlisted and were just finishing their training when the Emperor had cut down the size of the army. They were sent back home with nothing to show for their effort but a pair of hand-me-down oxhide uniforms. Thousands of young men and women who counted on the war for their employment were now back in their villages, struggling to adjust to this new peace, and to find work. Still, dumping gold into the ground like some storybook pirate was highly unusual, even for the Dragon Emperor.

"You," the wizard turned to Olaf. "Do you know these woods well?"

Olaf nodded enthusiastically.

"You're hired." The wizard scanned the crowd for another recruit.

Hurlee thought that the wizard wasn't particularly discriminating. Drawing his attention might be enough to be picked. She wasn't thrilled about getting involved in this crazy scheme, but there was no other work to be had in the village that didn't involve tending the fields, and she and her sister needed the money.

"Won't the adventurers stop coming once the treasure is found?" Hurlee asked.

"That's why I need guides. The treasure must be hidden so well, it'll take decades to find."

"My sister and I know the best hiding spots," said Hurlee. "Our father was a famed hunter. He showed us places so remote even the wild beasts would have a difficult time finding them."

Hurlee stood still, praying that none of the other villagers would speak up and tell the wizard that their father was actually a cabbage farmer. But others knew better than to incur the ire of the sisters.

The wizard sized them up. "Twins, eh?"

"Idontical," said Olaf.

"Don't you mean *identical*?" asked the wizard.

Olaf scratched his head. "I mean, I don't know how to tell them apart."

The wizard chuckled. "I'll hire the two of you for the price of one. Do we have a deal?"

The wizard and his three guides wandered in the forest all day, looking for a perfect spot.

Despite their exaggerated claims, Hurlee and Burlee did know the land very well. They'd spent their entire childhood exploring the nearby groves, picking mushrooms and berries, and snaring an occasional hare.

The three young villagers shared the secrets of their forest with the wizard. They followed deer paths to small clearings, far away from where any people might tread. They pointed out holes created by generations of woodpeckers, deep enough to conceal a purse of coins. They showed him uprooted trees with tangled roots that formed perfect hiding places for a larger cache. The wizard rejected them all, and urged his poor horse ever deeper into the woods.

It was slow going. The wizard's cart did not navigate easily through the wild growth of the forest. The gold pile jingled precariously each time a wheel hit a protruding tree root. On several occasions the wizard was forced to unharness the horse and levitate the cart over a particularly rough patch of terrain. Hurlee watched in awe. This was real magic, far more impressive than the healing salves and love potions brewed by the local hags.

As they walked, Burlee passed the time planning on how to spend the gold they'd been promised.

"We should buy new clothes," she said. "I'm sick of wearing this ratty uniform. I want to wear green again."

"Green does not flatter your skin tone," said Hurlee. "And besides, we should invest the money into something more practical. We could buy a horse. That way we could try for jobs guarding nobles' carriages and merchant caravans."

"I'm going to buy a goat," said Olaf. "It's cheaper than a horse, and I'll get all the milk and wool for free."

Having not found a satisfactory location by nightfall, they were forced to set up a makeshift camp under the open sky. Burlee started a fire and the four of them shared an evening meal.

"I still don't understand," Hurlee said, exploiting the chance to chat up the wizard. "Can't the Emperor make better use of his gold than to leave it lying around in some ditch? You know, hire more soldiers, pave the roads, that sort of thing?"

"His Imperial Majesty has thought of everything." The wizard poured himself some wine from a large flagon he produced from the back of the cart. He did not offer any to his companions. "Since the gold will be hidden, rather than spent or lost, the exchequer will issue paper money backed by its value."

"Coins made out of paper?" Burlee snorted. "That's a wild thought. They'd be ruined by the first rain. Besides, paper isn't worth very much."

"The value of the paper money is guaranteed by the Emperor," explained the wizard. "So each note will be worth exactly as much as a gold coin.

It's a novel concept and it may take some time for people in the countryside to get used to, but we're already having some success introducing the new currency in the capital."

"City folks might be too stupid to tell paper from gold, but we ain't," said Olaf. "You best plan on paying us with the real deal."

The wizard promised that they'd be paid with actual coins, and didn't seem interested in any further conversation.

That night, Olaf tried to steal some of the treasure.

Hurlee had known this would happen. She could tell from the way Olaf kept glancing at the cart, his face alight with greed. So, when the fire went out and everyone settled in for the night, Hurlee willed herself to remain awake.

Both Burlee and the wizard were fast asleep, exhausted by the day's journey. Even the wizard's horse was snoring lightly. Hurlee pretended to be asleep, but instead watched out of the corner of her eye as Olaf got up, checked to make sure his companions weren't alert, and crept toward the cart.

The gargoyle was curled up atop a gilded plate, covering its face with a winged paw. Asleep it looked like a big, gray cat. Very quietly, Olaf reached into the cart and palmed a large nugget. The gargoyle was up immediately, hissing and screaming and clawing at Olaf with its sharp talons. Olaf dropped the nugget and staggered back, clutching at the shallow, bleeding cuts along the length of his right arm. The gargoyle perched at the edge of the cart and hissed at Olaf until the wizard, roused by the noise, waved it off.

"You're lucky Maynard didn't rip off your face," the wizard told Olaf. "Go clean yourself up. Next time you try to steal, or interrupt my sleep, I'll turn you into something unpleasant."

Olaf skulked off toward the nearby stream. Hurlee finally allowed sleep to claim her.

By the late following afternoon Hurlee feared they'd be spending yet another night in the forest. But to her great relief, the wizard found what he decreed to be a perfect hiding place, far from where any hunters or gatherers might roam.

The wizard produced a pair of shovels from the bottom of the cart and instructed his guides to dig a hole. He rested in the shade while Olaf, Hurlee, and Burlee worked, sweated, and cursed.

"Look at us," said Burlee, "reduced to digging around in the dirt. If we wanted to do this sort of filthy work, we could have remained on Father's farm."

"It's paid work," said Hurlee. "It's not perfect, but we need the money to see us through until we can find something better."

"There is nothing better," Burlee said bitterly as she drove her shovel deep into the moist earth. "We might as well get used to handling a shovel, because there's no room for our skill set in this weird new age of peace treaties and paper money."

"You can't give up hope," said Hurlee. "We're young, and we're smart. We'll adjust."

"Your problem is, you're too picky," said Olaf. "Shovelin' is good work, when you can get it." He put his back into it to underscore the point.

"Shut up, Olaf," said Burlee. She turned to her sister. "Take the shovel. It's your turn to dig."

When the hole was deep enough, the wizard placed a few handfuls of gold into a sack and lowered it to the bottom. He then motioned for the others to begin refilling the hole.

"That's it?" asked Burlee, eyeing the lion's share of the treasure that remained on the cart.

"Our empire is vast," said the wizard. "Hiding smaller amounts of treasure across the land will serve the Emperor's plans better than a single large trove."

Covering the hole with freshly dug earth was easier work than digging. Afterward, the wizard made Olaf collect some leaves and twigs to cover up the recently disturbed patch of ground.

Halfway back to the village, the wizard stopped the cart. "Now that the treasure is hidden, I must remove your memories of its location with a spell. Then you'll be paid."

Hurlee had expected something like this to happen. After all, burying treasure would be pointless if one left behind three greedy and highly motivated locals who knew exactly where to look. If anything, Hurlee was relieved that the wizard hadn't planned on a more severe and permanent solution to this problem.

"This won't hurt very much," the wizard promised. He beckoned Olaf to him.

The wizard touched Olaf's forehead and recited a spell that he said would drain away the memories of the past few days. Olaf lumbered off like a drunk, looking like he just got hit in the head with a rake. He appeared to be stupefied by the experience, but with Olaf it was rather difficult to tell.

Burlee was up next. Hurlee watched her sister step forward, and an inkling of a plan began to formulate in her mind. Burlee was right; they couldn't just wait around and hope for their circumstances to improve. She saw an opportunity, and she was going to act on it.

While the wizard was reciting his spell for the second time, Hurlee touched Olaf's shoulder and pointed at the cart.

"Look. Gold," Hurlee whispered.

Olaf's eyes grew wide as he discovered the treasure. Without the memory of Maynard to restrain him, Olaf stumbled toward the cart. The gargoyle hissed in warning, baring its teeth at the hapless villager. And while the wizard, who had just finished enchanting Burlee, was distracted by the commotion, Hurlee traded places with her twin sister.

Hurlee counted on the wizard not being able to tell the two of them apart. Their army uniforms hadn't helped the sisters land the cushy bodyguard or sentry jobs they had hoped for in the past, but in this one instance, the matching garments might help them secure their future.

Having made certain that the treasure was safe from Olaf, and Olaf was safe from the gargoyle, the wizard turned his attention back to the sisters. He gently nudged Hurlee, who was standing in front of him with as blank an expression on her face as she could muster, out of the way, and grabbed Burlee.

Hurlee watched as the wizard zapped her poor sister with another forgetting spell. She wondered if Burlee would lose a few extra days' worth of memory, or just forget their forest adventures that much more thoroughly. Either way, she reckoned it was well worth keeping the memory of where the treasure was. Even the small portion of the cart's riches that the wizard had left behind was enough to set them up for life.

The wizard let his guides rest for a few minutes, until they regained their senses. Their old memories of the forest were unaffected and so they had no trouble finding the way back to the village. There, the wizard paid them, just like he promised. He was even kind enough to let the other villagers know that the guides' memories had been erased. That way no one would think of trying to force the treasure's location out of them.

Hurlee waited for over a day, to make sure the wizard was gone and not coming back, before she shared the secret with her sister. Burlee was so excited by the news that she didn't even grumble too much about being made into the lightning rod for the wizard's forgetting spell. The twins immediately decided that such information was best kept away from Olaf. So it was just the two of them sneaking out of the village to claim the treasure.

They traveled back to the site, dug up the still-fresh earth, and retrieved the sack. But when they opened it, there was no gold at all. The sack was filled with rocks.

Burlee examined one of the rocks and tossed it aside. "That treacherous wizard must've enchanted these rocks to look like treasure, and kept the real gold for himself," she said.

"For his purposes, the rumor of hidden treasure is as good as the real thing," reasoned out Hurlee. "This way, the Emperor can keep his riches and still get adventurers to come searching for them."

Frustrated, Burlee kicked some dirt back into the hole. "But then, why bury the rocks in the first place?"

Hurlee mulled it over. "The old warlock must've suspected that some of our memories might eventually return. If so, he couldn't risk not going through with the charade."

"What a cheat!" Burlee continued to rile herself up. "We should go back home and let everybody know the truth. Screw up his convoluted plan. That'll show him!"

"No," said Hurlee, after thinking hard for a while. "No, we shouldn't. I have a better idea."

Hurlee picked up a shovel and began to fill the hole again. "Let people think that the treasure is buried somewhere in these woods," she said as she worked. "We aren't supposed to remember exactly where, but we're the local guides, and we're the ones who showed the wizard all the likely hiding spots. This information will be worth something, once the adventurers come."

Burlee was beginning to understand, annoyance and disappointment draining from her face as she listened to Hurlee's plan. "The Emperor wants these treasure hunts to help spur the local economy? Well, we're part of the local economy, too. There's no reason why we can't cash in."

"It won't be long until the adventurers show up," said Hurlee. "There will be no shortage of demand for guides, then."

"There must also be other ways to profit from this," said Burlee. "Let's get some parchment and start drawing maps. Two . . . No, three silver coins for a genuine treasure map sounds about right."

"That's the spirit, sister," Hurlee clapped Burlee on her leather-clad shoulder. "Who needs the dangers of the orc wars, or the tedium of sentry duty? We're getting into the tourism trade."

Dragon in Distress
Mercedes Lackey and Elisabeth Waters

"Ah, my heart, and a-a-a-ah my heart,
My heart it is so sore,
Since I must needs from my love depart,
And know no cause wherefore..."

THE LIGHT TENOR VOICE WAFTED INTO THE CAVE WITH THE spring breeze from the ledge outside where the prince had been spending his days for the past two weeks. Unfortunately, since both of the cave's occupants were tone deaf, the melody was wasted on them. The words, however, were another matter.

Princess Rowena, who was sitting cross-legged on the floor going out of her mind with boredom, looked up at her companion. "Do you suppose that means he's going away now?" she asked hopefully. "He's been out there for quite a while."

The dragon smiled, an expression that did not look as forbidding as one might suppose. Her life had become much more amusing since Rowena had moved in with her, following the receipt of a birthday gift from her Aunt Frideswide which had been chosen with more poetic license than common sense. Boredom was the bane of a near-immortal's existence, which was probably why the dragon had agreed to foster Rowena when the princess had decided she did not wish to return home. So far the arrangement was working out quite well for both of them, although there were occasional drawbacks—such as the prince outside.

"I'm afraid not," the dragon replied calmly, using two foreclaws to pick up a particularly fine emerald from the pile of gems in the girl's lap and twist it so that it sparkled in the light from the fire in the back of the cave. "He's been here only two weeks, and he strikes me as the persistent type.

He could be here all summer—perhaps even until the snow falls." Her voice was wise with centuries of experience. "Princes as a whole talk a lot, sing romantic ballad after romantic ballad—"

"—after romantic ballad. Maybe he'd like to perish gallantly for love," Rowena suggested brightly, then sobered under the dragon's glare. "All right, it's not all that funny, but I'm getting very tired of being cooped up in here."

She sighed, which added an opal to the pile of gold coins and jewels in her lap. "Unrequited love is hell. And if he finds out about this—" she gestured at the gems which fell from her lips with each word she spoke, "he'll never leave."

"Just don't ask me to kill him," the dragon said tartly. "Those stupid princes taste dreadful, and they're difficult to digest."

Rowena giggled. "Especially if you eat their armor." Then she sobered. "You don't think he knows about the spell, do you?"

The spell in question was the birthday gift which had resulted in Rowena's sudden desire to leave home. Originally it had been the standard fairy tale version, where every word spoken produced a flower or a jewel. After Rowena left home and moved in with the dragon (that afternoon), the dragon, who had given Frideswide the original spell, had modified it somewhat, substituting gold coins for the flowers. Unlike roses, gold coins had no thorns, so Rowena was relieved by the change and more than happy to give the dragon the coins for her bed.

The young prince outside sang on. He could scarcely have found a less appreciative audience.

"It's not that I want him dead," Rowena sighed. "And I know that knights don't cook evenly and they're hard to digest. But still, it's a pain to be stuck here inside for weeks on end, especially when the weather is so beautiful outside. And if he doesn't go away soon, all the berries will be gone, and I wanted to pick a lot of them before the season ends. It's not fair!"

"True," the dragon agreed. "It's not as if he is a real guest. We're not obliged to entertain him or arrange our schedules to suit him."

"And it's all so pointless. Why did he come here to 'rescue' me?" Rowena frowned fiercely. "I don't need to be rescued! I'm much happier here than I ever was at home."

"You might wish to marry someday," the dragon offered, sounding amused, "and you don't get many opportunities to meet young men living alone here with me."

"If I were ever to marry, which I don't plan on," Rowena said firmly, "I'm sure I would want a husband who had some sense of self-preservation. Camping out on a ledge just outside a dragon's lair does not betoken any great degree of intelligence."

That actually provoked a snicker from the dragon. "You might try explaining that to him."

"Sure I could," Rowena said sarcastically. "I tried that four—or was it five—princes ago. That particular idiot insisted that I was bewitched and begged me to come away with him so that I could be freed from the nonexistent spell you have me under."

She grinned up at the dragon, in a lightning change of mood. "Besides," she pointed out, "It's very difficult to talk to anyone face to face without having him find out about Aunt Frideswide's birthday present."

It had been quite a shock for Rowena to wake up in this condition on her fourteenth birthday. The gems were all right, but the rose-thorns hurt. And she had known immediately what her fate would be if anyone discovered that she was producing something more rewarding than flowers; she'd have been locked in the palace treasury and forced to talk herself into exhaustion. Ordinarily, Rowena was something of a chatterbox, but there were limits!

Fortunately the dragon had carried her off that afternoon, before anyone at the castle realized why Rowena had locked herself in her room and was refusing to talk.

"There's a full moon tonight," Rowena said, still trying to find a way out of her current trap. "And I think he goes somewhere else at night to sleep, because I never hear him on the ledge after dark." She looked up at the dragon again with a touch of defiance. "I'm going to sneak out tonight and pick some berries; there's enough light for that at full moon. And if I don't get out of here for a little while, I am going to lose what's left of my mind!"

"Very well," the dragon agreed. "Just be sure that you're back before dawn."

"I shall," Rowena said grimly, "I've no desire to be carried off by anyone or anything, let alone some stupid prince."

Rowena left that night, and the dragon, listening carefully, heard no sounds of pursuit. But the girl was not back the next morning. This was enough to worry any foster-mother, of whatever species. The dragon left the cave two hours after dawn and flew a search pattern until midday. She couldn't see Rowena anywhere, and she knew that her search had covered more area than a human on foot could have gone in the time since Rowena left. There was also no sign of the prince or his horse. This could only mean one thing.

It was time to panic.

Rowena sat in the corner of a small, damp, uncomfortable cave and glared at her captor. Her wrists and ankles were firmly tied, although he had at least had the consideration to tie her wrists in front of her. And even with her ankles tied together she could still kick well enough to make him keep his distance from her. In fact, his shins were bruising nicely, and Rowena felt a certain amount of satisfaction in that.

"I am sorry for the lack of comfort in our accommodations, your highness," he said, "but if we leave this cave the dragon is certain to find us."

Rowena bit her lips. She would have loved to tell this idiot what she thought of him, his ancestry, his morals, and his singing, but she didn't dare open her mouth. He didn't know about the spell, and she needed to keep it that way. It had been dark when he grabbed her, so he hadn't seen the pearl that appeared when she screamed, and she'd kept quiet ever since. Of course, she had struggled and tried to run, which was why he had tied her up. So now she was wedged into this cave with him and his horse, until either the dragon found them or he felt safe enough to try to leave it.

"But you are safe with me," he continued, "and as soon as possible I shall take you home and ask your father for your hand in honorable marriage. I am Prince Florian of Astrefiore, at thy service, Princess." The prince stepped forward to make his bow, keeping a wary eye on Rowena's bound feet. "My eldest brother was among the guests at your birthday party when you were carried off, and he came home and told us of your abduction—and of how your own father forbade all of the princes gathered there to attempt your rescue!" He looked thoroughly indignant. "As it is the clear duty of a prince to rescue such an innocent victim, and as King Mark's unnatural command was not binding on me, I set out for the mountain where the dragon laired." He smiled sheepishly. "I'm a better minstrel than a fighter, so I'm just as glad that you were able to creep away without my having to fight the dragon. Of course," he added hastily, "I would fight the beast if it were necessary to insure your safety."

Chivalry is dead, Rowena thought morosely. *It's been replaced by total idiocy.*

Two women, one dark and one amber-haired, guided their horses on a barely-perceptible deer-track that threaded its way between decidedly unnatural trees. Fortunately, this set of trees whimpered and shrank away from the riders. They could, all too easily, have been reaching towards the women and their mares with avid hunger.

The last lot had, after all.

"I thought you knew your way around the Pelagirs," the dark-haired one said, rather crossly. Her companion didn't answer, but then, the remark had not been aimed at her.

:*I did,*: came a purely mental reply, in a tone of affronted dignity. :*It is not my fault that the forest has changed. That is the nature of Pelagir territory that has no Hawkbrother Vale nearby. You never asked me if I thought I could still find my way around this area.*:

The head of the speaker emerged from the underbrush, and the bushes there squeaked with alarm and pulled away. He was tall, dark, would have told you himself that he was a handsome fellow, and he was not human.

Nor was he a male in the strictest accounting. Warrl was a kyree neuter, a magically-made species with the coat and heads of wolves, the bodies of the great hunting-cats of the plains, the size of a young calf, and all of the intelligence of a human.

Of course, Warrl would have insisted that he was far more intelligent than any human.

Right now, his spirit-bonded friend, the Shin'a'in warrior Tarma shena Tale'sedrin, would have argued for the superior intelligence of the calf.

"Let it be, she'enedra," her companion, the sorceress Kethry, advised. "We're not in any danger."

"Now," Tarma replied darkly, though she did not elaborate. She didn't have to; Kethry already knew what the Pelagirs were like. This was not the first time that they had penetrated the wild lands where magic wars of long ago had warped and twisted the plants, the animals, and even the land itself into something strange, unrecognizable, and often deadly.

It wouldn't have been so bad if they had actually been in the forest on purpose—but they weren't. They were supposed to be on the way to Kata'shin'a'in, but the familiar road had inexplicably dwindled to a track, then a path, and now had become nothing more than a game-trail. Trying to turn around hadn't worked either; the trail vanished altogether when they tried that. Clearly, something wanted them to go in this direction, something magical. Tarma was hardly pleased. It was bad enough that much of their time was spent satisfying the demands of Kethry's mage-sword, Need—but to have some unknown magician trying to herd them to a completely unknown destination was intolerable! She was beginning to feel like some poor character in a play, bullied towards a confrontation known to the audience, but not to her.

She did not particularly like the feeling.

Suddenly the track opened up into a clearing. She urged her battlemare into it, disliking the whimpering trees and eager to put some distance between herself and them—and then reined the mare in abruptly when she saw what stood in the center of the clearing.

It was a doorway without a building, a beautifully formed arch of white stone taller than three tall men, and wide enough for a cart to pass through with space on either side. There was only one problem.

It shouldn't be here. There wasn't a single sign of the hand of man for leagues and leagues around.

Warrl stood directly in front of the portal, staring at it as if caught in a spell of fascination. All around the clearing, the whimpering trees with their thick, palm-sized leaves pulled their branches towards their trunks and shivered.

Kethry brought her mare up beside her partner's, surveyed the clearing, and wrinkled her brow in consternation. "The path ends here, doesn't it," she stated.

Tarma nodded gloomily. "And I'll bet you that if we try to retrace our steps, there won't be a path. We've been herded here like a couple of sheep—"

She would have said more, except that the space inside the doorway suddenly changed. Instead of the other side of the clearing, there was nothing there but darkness, a black void that Tarma shrank from without knowing why she did so. Whatever that thing was, she wanted no further part of it!

She started to turn her horse's head, determined to ride through and even over whatever animate plants wanted to get in her way—

But suddenly Kethry gave an all-too-familiar cry of pain, and spurred her mare straight at the archway. Warrl was right on her horse's heels, and in a heartbeat, the two of them were swallowed up in the blackness between the white stone pillars.

With a heartfelt curse, Tarma spurred her horse after, and followed.

"Warrl, I don't think we're in the Pelagirs anymore—" Tarma said weakly, looking around at the rocky and mountainous slope ahead of her. Sunlight blazed down from a sun near the zenith on the graveled path where their horses stood—it had been near sunset in the clearing.

Warrl did not dignify the observation with even a snort of derision.

It was possible to deduce some of what had just happened; Tarma had heard about magical doors into other places, often called Gates or Portals—obviously that doorway back in the clearing had been one such device. Something had made it active—and once active, whatever was on the other side had called to Kethry through the medium of the sword she wore, a blade called Need.

The sword responded to women in crisis, as the runes on her blade explained: *Woman's Need calls me/As woman's Need made me./Her Need must I answer/As my maker bade me.* Kethry had accepted a kind of soul-bonding with the sword as the price of the aid the blade gave her—Kethry, though completely untrained as a swordswoman, became an expert when the blade took over, and if she was wounded, the blade could and would heal just about anything. As a result, the greater the urgency of the woman in trouble, the worse the sympathetic pain Kethry would experience, unless and until she rode to that woman's aid.

Very nice for the women they helped, but not too damned convenient for Tarma and her partner.

No point in trying to throw the sword away, either; the farther Kethry got from it, the more it would call to her, and much too strongly to be denied. Relief would only come when Kethry found a successor to pass the blade on to—and even then, the sword would have to accept the new candidate.

"Where?" Tarma asked her partner curtly. Kethry shook her head as if to clear it, closed her eyes for a moment, and pointed up the slope.

"There," she said, her soft voice giving no hint to the firm will behind her pretty face and emerald eyes. "Whoever's in trouble, she's up there, and she is—must be—practically out of her mind with it. She's also a mage, but not of a kind that I recognize; that must be how she brought us here."

"Lovely," Tarma muttered. She stood up in her stirrups, and surveyed the countryside again. It was singularly unprepossessing. The rocky slopes boasted nothing much in the way of vegetation except for thick patches of blackberry bushes. At least, Tarma assumed they were blackberry bushes. There were berries in various stages of ripeness, from yellow-green to darkest plum, showing clearly against the foliage. If they were like the blackberry bushes of home, they'd be as thick with thorns as with berries. Tarma's long-dead love had called them "wait-a-moment bushes," because that was what anyone who tried to force his way through them was reduced to calling out, over and over again.

There appeared to be a path of sorts ahead of them, leading up to a cave with a generous ledge outside it. That was the direction Kethry was pointing.

There were no armies camped outside that cave, no signs of horses or other beasts of burden, no fires; whoever was in that cave was probably alone, or if captive, guarded by one or two people at the most. There was nothing to be lost in riding straight up to the cave-mouth and taking a look. Very few people outside the Shin'a'in Clans knew just what it was that Tarma and her partner rode—battlesteeds were easily the equivalent of two ordinary human fighters apiece, and when you added in Warrl, you had a force of the equal of any seven fighters. So if there was anyone nasty up there, he was going to get a major shock if he tried a direct confrontation. And just at the moment, Tarma rather hoped he would. She was truly in a mood to kill something.

"Let's go," she said, "I want to get this over with." And as her partner blinked in surprise at her apparent impulsiveness, she sent her mare trotting up the path to the cave.

She had been supposing all this time that her adversaries would, of course, be human, so when the monster snaked its head and neck out of the cave-mouth, all she could do for a moment was to freeze in place.

The monster seemed just as surprised as she was; it stared at her with its mouth—a mouth well-appointed with dagger-like teeth—dropping wide open in shock. Unfortunately, that only gave Tarma a much better look at all those teeth.

Whatever it was, it wasn't a creature like anything she had ever heard of before—except, perhaps, a cold-drake. This thing was the wrong color, but the size was right, and the long neck, and of course, all the teeth.

There was, presumably, a female being held captive somewhere in that cave. Maybe the monster was saving her for dinner, later; maybe it was just there to guard her. Whatever, the woman's distress held Kethry here until she was freed—and that held Tarma and Warrl. Tarma did the only thing a Swordsworn warrior could, under the circumstances.

She drew her sword, and with a Shin'a'in battle-cry, spurred her horse into a charge while the monster was still caught off-guard. That is, she started to charge. Kethry's shriek made her rein her mare in so quickly that the poor beast's hooves skidded and she slid to a most undignified stop.

"Tarma! Stop!" Kethry cried in real pain. "Don't! Need wants us to help the dragon!"

"Dragons," Tarma muttered, staring at their hostess in disbelief over a nice hot cup of tea. "Tea-drinking dragons. I must be out of my mind."

The dragon ignored her, as she had ignored Tarma every other time she had muttered something similar. It—she—was a very polite dragon, although a deeply distressed dragon.

She had every right to be distressed, though how that distress and the spell she had cast to bring her some help had interacted to open a portal between her world—which was obviously not the one that held Shin'a'in, since there were no such things as dragons in Tarma's world—and their world was a mystery White Winds Adepts would probably be debating for the next century or more. That didn't matter. What did was what she and Kethry were going to do about the situation that brought them here, since obviously the magic that had done so would not release them until they had.

"I'm dreadfully sorry now that I built the spell that way," the dragon was saying, apologetically, "But I thought I would probably be dragging in some reluctant knight or other, and well—historically my kind and theirs do not exactly get along. I built in coercions, and now I can't get rid of them."

Kethry nodded wisely, as Tarma sighed. "At least the track isn't even cold by Warrl's standards," Tarma put in. "I have to admit that you couldn't have deliberately selected anyone more fit to get Rowena back to you in a reasonable amount of time if you'd tried."

Warrl nodded. :*I really should get on the scent now,*: he said, his tone as sympathetic as Tarma had ever heard. :*Rowena is probably terribly frightened—*:

"Rowena is probably furious," the dragon corrected. "And if she starts telling him what she thinks of him—"

The dragon's voice broke on a sob, and her talons tightened on her own oversized mug until it broke, period. Tarma did not finish the sentence, for the dragon had revealed Rowena's "little talent" to explain why they were going to have to find the girl quickly. *Princes are always hard up for cash, especially younger princes. Once he finds out he has the equivalent of a mint and a mine in his hands, he'll lock her up so tight they'll have to send daylight to her by messenger.*

:*I'm on my way,*: Warrl said hastily, not wanting to be subjected to another bout of draconic tears and hysteria. The last bout had been quite enough for him.

I would never have guessed that dragons could cry.

Warrl vanished with alacrity, and Tarma decided to change the subject before the dragon broke down again. "Look, this idiot can't have gotten far with her. She isn't going to cooperate, and he is going to be far too gallant and polite to knock her over the head and bundle her off unconscious."

"That—that's true," the dragon sniffled. "Rowena didn't think much of him before, and by now, her estimate of his character has probably placed him somewhere below spotted newts. If he's lucky, she hasn't done anything to him that's permanent."

"Well, given that, how do you want us to get her loose?" Tarma asked. "I don't think you ought to appear; he might try something desperate."

The dragon winced, but nodded.

"We need to be smart about this," Kethry mused. "I—"

Then she flushed, and grinned. "You did say that her father forbade anyone to go after her?"

The dragon nodded again.

"Well," Kethry said slyly. "I have an idea that would provide the perfect explanation for why he did that, and possibly even prevent anything like this from happening in the future. Provided, of course, that your fosterling doesn't mind her reputation being totally destroyed."

Tarma looked closely at her partner, and as often happened, realized precisely what the sorceress meant; after all, it was an assumption—incorrect as it happened—that was often applied to her and Kethry. *Oh my ears! If she's thinking what I think she's thinking—*

The dragon lifted her head high, and cocked it to one side. "I don't think she would mind if it kept princes off the ledge, but what—"

:*I've found her,*: Warrl trumpeted in their minds. :*They aren't far away at all. Hurry up, though, I think His Highness is getting impatient.*:

"Let's go," Tarma said, jumping to her feet. "I want to get this over with. We'll explain on the way."

This prince, if not a complete idiot, was certainly the most incompetent person Tarma had ever seen. He hadn't left any kind of a guard on the trail outside the cave he'd hidden in, he'd picked a hiding place barely an hour away from the dragon's own cave, and he wasn't paying any attention to anything going on outside. *I guess this just proves that the gods watch out for fools and the mad*, she thought in disgust, as Warrl drove his horse off. *I can't think of any other reason why he's still alive.*

The sound of his horse galloping off—the fool hadn't even hobbled it!—finally brought him out of the entrance of the cave. He stared in shock at the sight of two grim-faced, armed women—with swords drawn—waiting for him.

Tarma was going to be the one challenging him, because Need had a tendency to over-react and they didn't want to kill or even hurt him. And right now, caught between the distress of the female dragon hidden out of sight behind them and Rowena's emotional state in the cave in front of them, Kethry would not be able to restrain the sword if she had to fight the boy.

Of course, there was the chance that he was a much, much better fighter than they thought. He could even be better than Tarma. In that case, they were not going to play fair. Kethry would move in and deal with him. Hopefully, she would be able to keep Need from inflicting anything too permanent.

"Stand forth, kidnapper!" Tarma growled menacingly. "I, Tarma shena Tale'sedrin, do challenge you as a cad and a miscreant. I challenge you for the welfare of the lady you have stolen. I challenge you to single combat for the hand of my lady and my love, the Princess Rowena!"

The look on the boy's face when she got to those final few words was almost enough to make her break out laughing. His eyes bulged, and his mouth dropped open, giving him an uncanny resemblance to a startled frog. The green surcoat he wore only heightened the resemblance.

"I—ah—" His mouth moved, but nothing more came out of it.

Tarma took advantage of his mental state to advance on him. He barely got his blade up in time to deflect her first move; he never saw the second. Her blow to the side of his head laid him out flat.

"Now what?" Kethry asked.

Tarma shrugged. "Go free the girl and explain the situation to her. She's the injured party. Let her decide what she wants to do with him. Personally, all I want is out of here."

:*He is a very good musician,*: Warrl put in wistfully. :*Truly a marvelous minstrel. I don't suppose—*:

"NO!" snapped Tarma, Kethry, and the dragon, all together.

From her position in the cave, Rowena had been able to hear clearly everything that was going on, but it didn't make much sense to her. First that incredibly odd looking animal had crept in and scared off the horse. She had seen it quite clearly, although she hadn't recognized it. It was like nothing she had ever seen before.

Warning the prince about what was happening to his horse was not something *she* was going to do; she didn't owe *him* any favors. She was prepared to watch the horse gnawed to bare bones before she opened her mouth, but she was just as happy when it was merely chased away—after all, none of this was the horse's fault.

But her mouth dropped open in astonishment when she heard the challenge. *Who is Tarma shena Tale'sedrin?* she wondered. *And what does she mean "my lady and my love"—I've never even met her!*

Then a very pretty young woman with amber hair came into the cave, cut her loose, helped her to her feet and held her up until the numbness wore off and Rowena could walk again. "It's all right, Rowena," she said soothingly. "My name is Kethry, my partner is Tarma, and I think you may have seen Warrl earlier. Your foster-mother hired us to rescue you."

Rowena had several questions about this 'rescue party' but she didn't know if it was safe to talk yet. So she remained silent as she followed Kethry out of the cave into the sunlight. The prince lay on the ground, but Rowena didn't spare enough attention to determine whether he was dead or merely unconscious. Kethry had obviously been telling the truth about who hired them; the dragon was perched on the trail just beyond the cave. Rowena ran to her and flung both arms around as much dragon as she could reach, which was most of one foreleg.

A scaly chin dropped down to pat the top of her head and then pulled back. "My poor child," the dragon said. "Have you managed to keep your mouth shut all this time?" Rowena nodded, her head still pressed firmly against the dragon's leg. "I'm impressed," the dragon chuckled. "I know it wasn't easy for you. But you can talk now. He's unconscious—"

"Not dead?" Rowena asked in mock disappointment, carefully palming two jewels.

"Rowena!" the dragon reproved her. "And Tarma and Kethry and Warrl know about your peculiar talent."

Rowena turned to look at them. Kethry smiled sympathetically. "It must be awkward sometimes," she said.

Rowena nodded. "But it's not so bad since the Lady Dragon modified the spell to get rid of the flowers," she said, carefully catching the jewels and coins in her cupped hands. "The rose thorns in the original spell really hurt!" She looked at Tarma. "Why did you call me your lady and your love? I don't understand that part—we've never met before, have we?"

Tarma chuckled. "That was to discourage further royal attempts at 'rescuing' you," she explained. "If you are thought to be a lover of women, most princes won't want you."

"What's a lover of woman?" Rowena asked, still puzzled.

Tarma sighed, and Kethry giggled. "Oh," Rowena said, realizing the class of information involved. "That's one of those 'you'll understand when you're older' things, isn't it?"

"Something like that," Kethry replied. "The idea is that when the prince tells this story, people won't bother you anymore."

"There's just one problem with that," Rowena said. "He's a minstrel—he's not going to tell *anything* accurately—or even close to it!"

"Damn," Tarma said. "She's right. We know how strange a story can become when a minstrel gets hold of it."

The prince stirred and groaned. "What happened?" He looked around, saw the dragon, and promptly fainted.

Rowena sighed. "He's a frog," she said firmly.

Pop! Everyone blinked at the sound, then looked at the figure on the ground. The prince was gone, replaced by a frog.

"How did you do that?" the dragon asked in surprise.

Rowena shrugged. "I don't know," she said. "He just seemed like a frog to me."

The dragon sighed. "I guess I'll have to start giving you lessons in magic. Wild talents are dangerous."

"So are some tame ones," Rowena retorted. "Look at my Aunt Frideswide."

"Can you change him back?" Kethry asked.

Rowena shrugged again. "I don't know," she said. "I don't particularly want to change him back, either—not after the way he treated me!"

"Well, you have to do something with him," Tarma said, "or he'll be outside your cave every time you look."

Rowena looked up at the dragon. "Can you do something with him?"

The dragon thought for a minute. "I'll set up a transport circle, and send him to wherever he's wanted or needed."

Rowena nodded. "Let's hope there's somebody who wants him then." She turned to Kethry. "You said that you were hired to rescue me. Did you," she looked from them to the dragon, "agree on a price?"

"We're actually getting paid?" Tarma said incredulously.

Rowena handed Tarma the jewels that had fallen into her hands with every word she had spoken since they had rescued her. "Would you prefer coins for the rest?" Tarma nodded, apparently unable to speak. Rowena cupped her hands in front of her face and chanted softly. When she lowered her hands, they were full of gold coins. She handed them to Kethry, who put them into her belt pouch. Tarma, still staring at the jewels, followed her example.

"Are you sure this is going to work?" Kethry asked the dragon anxiously, as she, Tarma, Warrl and their horses took their places in the carefully scribed magic circle.

The dragon could only shrug. "I can only hope. I am not entirely certain how I brought you here in the first place."

"Just get on with it," Tarma said, addressing a private and fervent prayer to the Star-eyed. The dragon closed her eyes, and inscribed a complicated figure in the air with one talon.

Then the world went black.

But instead of reappearing in the clearing in the Pelagirs, Tarma found herself standing alone, in a place of softly glowing mist, on a path of light. *The Moonpaths!* she thought, startled, *But why—*

"So," said a familiar voice, a hollow tenor, pleasant enough, but echoing as if the speaker stood in the bottom of a well. "Finally, we find you. Your spirits have been wandering, Younger Sister—wandering quite out of our world."

"What?" she asked, startled.

"You have traveled in spirit to a very distant place," her *leshy'a Kalendral* teacher told her. "Oh, do not mistake me, your venture was quite real, and as you know, you affected the world in which you walked quite decisively—but your true body was lying in your camp, where you were overcome by the dust of gade'shata. You, and your she'enedra both, your horses and your kyree." He tilted his head to one side. "We bent a rule for you, we, your teachers, and guarded you while you walked."

Tarma blanched. Gade'shata mushrooms produced a cloud of spores which were incredibly potent. Shamans sometimes used them to walk through other worlds and times, though at their peril. If she and Kethry had survived an encounter with those potent fungi, they were fortunate indeed!

"I shall not ask where you walked," the spirit-Kal'enedral continued. "You could only have been drawn to one who needed you profoundly. I will only say that you have been fortunate to have escaped this with a whole soul, and if I were you, I should be very careful to watch where I stepped in the future."

And before she could reply, the world vanished again. Only this time, she found herself lying cramped and cold on wet grass, soaked from head to toe by a sudden rainfall. She dragged herself to her feet with the help of a nearby sapling, scraping her wet hair out of her eyes as she looked around.

The mares were tethered nearby, shaking their heads as if dazed, the imprint of their bodies still marking the grass beside them. Kethry was blinking and sitting up; Warrl scrubbing at his eyes with his paws. It looked as if they had just made camp, for the remains of a fire smoldered in the light rain—and just beyond the fire, Tarma spotted the flattened shapes of decomposing fungi, their spores depleted. *The mushrooms*, she thought dazedly. *We camped next to the mushrooms, and the heat of the fire set their spores loose. Oh, the gods watch over fools and the mad*!

"What—was it a dream?" Kethry asked, dazedly.

"Yes—and no," Tarma croaked. "Let's get out of here while we can. I'll explain it to you on the road."

Kethry sighed. "It figures. Any job involving Need where we get paid would *have* to be a dream."

Contributor Biographies

Christopher Baxter got in trouble for reading books in class from kindergarten through high school. To stop his teachers from getting upset, he began writing stories instead (it looked like he was taking notes).

He works as an editor and writer. His short stories have appeared in the October 2016 and Spring 2018 volumes of *Deep Magic* e-zine, the *Best of Deep Magic* and *Put Your Shoulder to the Wheel* anthologies, and Immortal Works' *Flash Fiction Friday* podcast. You can hear his opinions about the *Star Wars* franchise on *A More Civilized Podcast*. He is blessed with the best wife and two adorable little boys. Find out more at writerinthehat.com.

Josh Brown has dedicated his life to sporadic rants and ramblings about comic book continuity, superhero superiority, and Han shooting first. He also writes poetry, science fiction, fantasy, and horror fiction. Find out more at his website, ninjamindcontrol.wordpress.com.

Jaleta Clegg was born some time ago and has filled the years since with plenty of make-believe. She writes science fiction adventure, fantasy of all flavors, and silly horror. When not writing, she enjoys playing with yarn, cooking weird vegetables, designing costumes and quilts, and generally messing around. You can find more about her at jaletac.com

Max Florschutz was born in the distant islands of Wrangell, Alaska, a fertile ground for adventure and imagination in equal parts. In 2013, he published his first book, and since then he has continued to delight audiences with works of science fiction and fantasy such as *Colony* and *Shadow of an Empire*. He is also known for the weekly series *Being a Better Writer*, aimed at examining all aspects of writing and how to best put them into practice.

You can find a full list of his books at his website, maxonwriting.com, as well as a titanic archive of writing articles on hundreds of topics, and even some free sampler stories. If you're looking for futuristic space battles, soccer-mom werewolves, or horseback chases through fantastical, magical, and foreboding deserts, there's a book for you on there!

Max currently lives in Utah, hard at work on more books to come.

Melva L. Gifford has been writing since her youth. She has fiction and non-fiction shorts published in various publications and websites. She won first place for her middle-grade book, *Operation: Middle School Madness*, at the 2016 Utah Arts Council. She's won two semi-finalist awards from the international Writers of the Future contest. Her fiction touches upon many realms, including childrens' mainstream, science fiction, and fantasy, as well as science fiction, fantasy, romance, non-fiction, and mainstream fiction for adults. Learn more on her website: melvagifford.com.

M. K. Hutchins regularly draws on her background in archaeology when writing fiction. Her YA fantasy novel, *Drift,* was both a Junior Library Guild Selection and a VOYA Top Shelf Honoree. Her short fiction appears in *Podcastle, Strange Horizons, Orson Scott Card's Intergalactic Medicine Show,* and elsewhere. A long-time Idahoan, she now lives in Utah with her husband and four children. Find her online at mkhutchins.com.

A Colorado native, **Sam Knight** spent ten years in California's wine country before returning to the Rockies. When asked if he misses California, he gets a wistful look in his eyes and replies he misses the green mountains in the winter, but he is glad to be back home.

As well as having been Distribution Manager for WordFire Press and Senior Editor for Villainous Press, Knight is the author of six children's books, four short story collections, three novels, and nearly three dozen short stories, including two media tie-ins co-authored with Kevin J. Anderson.

A stay-at-home father, he attempts to be a full-time writer, but there are only so many hours left in a day after kids. Once upon a time, Knight was known to quote books the way some people quote movies, but now he claims having a family has made him forgetful, as a survival adaptation. His website is found at samknight.com.

Mercedes Lackey entered this world in 1950 in Chicago, had a normal childhood and graduated from Purdue University in 1972. During the late '70s, she worked as an artist's model and then went into computer programming, ending up with American Airlines in Tulsa, Oklahoma. In addition to her fantasy writing, she has written lyrics for and recorded nearly fifty songs for Firebird Arts & Music, a small recording company specializing in science fiction folk music.

She has written over 70 novels, sometimes with one or more co-authors, and has created many different beloved fantasy and science fiction worlds. She has also written at least 50 short works, set in her existing worlds, and in others. Her husband (and sometimes co-author), Larry Dixon, is an accomplished artist and writer, as well. Find out more online at mercedeslackey.com.

Gerri Leen lives in Northern Virginia and originally hails from Seattle. In addition to being an avid reader, she's passionate about horse racing, tea, and whiskey, and her latest obsession is ASMR vids. She has work appearing in *Nature, Orson Scott Card's Intergalactic Medicine Show, Daily Science Fiction, Grimdark,* and others. She's edited several anthologies for independent presses, is finishing some longer projects, and is a member of SFWA and HWA. Visit her online at gerrileen.com.

Hannah Marie's first written story spilled onto the page at the age of 5 after watching too much *Sesame Street.* After graduating with a degree in theatre and collecting experiences and freckles in South Korea, she has since expanded her repertoire with more personal, unique work. Her first published work can be found in the anthology *Threads: A Neoverse Anthology Vol 1,* and her second can be found in *A Dragon and Her Girl.* She can be found on Twitter @ReadHannahMarie.

Jodi L. Milner is the author of the YA noble dark fantasy *Stonebearer's Betrayal* and has been published in several anthologies. When not writing, she can be found folding children and feeding the laundry, occasionally in that order. Visit her website at jodilmilner.com.

Joe Monson has worked as a paperboy, hot dog vendor, soda jerk, ice cream maker, volunteer missionary, teller, notary public, web monkey and designer, content writer and developer, collections manager, convention chair, guest liaison, art show director, newsletter editor, technical support analyst, customer service supervisor, network technician, satellite installer, and credit analyst. He currently translates and edits Engineer into English by day and expands the accessible knowledge of the world by night.

He edits the *LTUE Benefit Anthologies* series with Jaleta Clegg. The first, *Trace the Stars,* contained seventeen space opera and hard science fiction tales. This volume, *A Dragon and Her Girl*, contains twenty adventure fantasy stories featuring just what the title states. The next volume, *Twilight Tales,* will feature light horror stories. He has a number of other anthologies in various stages of completion.

Joe's one published short story, "Napoleon's Tallest Teamster," is found in *All Made of Hinges* from Immortal Works. He has three novels in a space opera adventure series in the works. He collects science fiction and fantasy art, but not as much as Paul (as if that was even possible). He lives in the top of the mountains with his wife, three children, and their pet library. Learn more about him at joemonson.com.

Wendy Nikel is a speculative fiction author with a degree in elementary education, a fondness for road trips, and a terrible habit of forgetting where she's left her cup of tea. Her short fiction has been published by *Analog, Nature: Futures, Podcastle,* and elsewhere. Her time travel novella series, beginning with *The Continuum,* is available from World Weaver Press. For more info, visit wendynikel.com.

S.E. Page writes stories about fairies, unicorns, dragons, and strange humans. She has an M.S. and certification in Secondary English and is co-editor of *Young Ravens Literary Review.* A Pushcart Prize nominee, her poems have been published in journals including *Connecticut River Review, Fresh Ink, Star*Line, Noctua Review, Bacopa Literary Review, Oakwood,* and included in the anthologies *Fire in the Pasture* and *Dove Song.*

As a child she dearly wished her first initial stood for something adventurous and dashing like Seraphina or Sapphira, but she has grown comfortable with being a Sarah. Two of her three favorite words rhyme: splendiferous and stelliferous; the third word is a secret. She writes about her novels at iffymagic.com.

Scott R. Parkin is an award-winning author, editor, publisher, and pop critic with more than fifty short story sales to a wide variety of venues, from romance to science fiction to absurdist slice-of-life to fantasy.

John D. Payne grew up in the American Midwest, watching the lightning flash outside his window and imagining himself as everything from a leaf in the wind to the god of thunder. Today, he lives with his wife and family in the shadow of the Organ Mountains in New Mexico, where he imagines that with enough concentration he might be able to rustle up a little cloud cover for some shade.

His debut novel, *The Crown and the Dragon*, is also a major motion picture produced by Arrowstorm Entertainment. His stories can be found in magazines (*Leading Edge*), podcasts (*The Overcast*), and anthologies (*All Made of Hinges: A Mormon Steampunk Anthology*). Find him online at johndpayne.com.

Michaelene Pendleton regularly attended *Life, the Universe, & Everything* in the early days. Her works have been published in *Omni, Asmiov's, Amazing Stories, Fantasy & Science Fiction, Century,* and *Dragon Magazine*, as well as in the *Washed by a Wave of Wind* and *A Dragon and Her Girl* anthologies. She had a passion for ancient Native American culture and archaeology from the Four Corners region of the American West, and co-wrote *Canyon Country Prehistoric Indians: Their Cultures, Ruins, Artifacts and Rock Art* (1979) with F.A. Barnes. She passed away on January 21, 2019.

Bryan Thomas Schmidt is an author and Hugo-nominated editor of adult and children's speculative fiction. His debut novel, *The Worker Prince,* received Honorable Mention on Barnes & Noble Book Club's Year's Best Science Fiction Releases, and his latest novel, *Shortcut* (forthcoming), is being developed as a motion picture by Roserock Films.

His short stories have appeared in magazines, anthologies and online and include entries in *The X-Files, Predator,* and Decipher's *WARS,* amongst others. As book editor for Kevin J. Anderson and Rebecca Moesta's WordFire Press, he edited books by Alan Dean Foster, Angie Fox, Tracy Hickman, Frank Herbert, Mike Resnick, Jean Rabe, and more. He was also the first editor on Andy Weir's bestseller, *The Martian*.

His anthologies as editor include *Infinite Stars, Infinite Stars: Dark Frontiers, Predator: If It Bleeds, Monster Hunter Files* (co-edited by Larry Correia and based upon his *New York Times* bestselling *Monster Hunter International* novel series), *Joe Ledger: Unstoppable* (co-edited by Jonathan Maberry, based upon his New York Times bestselling novels), *Decision Points, Shattered Shields* with co-editor Jennifer Brozek, *Mission: Tomorrow*, and *Galactic Games*. He has several original screenplays making the rounds in Hollywood. Visit him online at bryanthomasschmidt.net.

Alex Shvartsman is a writer, anthologist, translator, and game designer. His adventures so far have included traveling to over 30 countries, playing a card game for a living, and building a successful business. Since 2010, he has sold over 100 short stories to a variety of magazines and anthologies, including *Nature, Analog, Strange Horizons, Orson Scott Card's InterGalactic Medicine Show, Galaxy's Edge*, and many others.

He won the WSFA Small Press Award for Short Fiction in 2014 and was a finalist for the Canopus Award for Excellence in Interstellar Fiction in 2015 and 2017. Alex edits *Unidentified Funny Objects*, an annual anthology series of humorous science fiction and fantasy short stories. He's also the editor of *The Cackle of Cthulhu, Humanity 2.0, Coffee, Dark Expanse*, and *Funny Science Fiction* anthologies. His translations from Russian have appeared or are forthcoming in *The Magazine of Fantasy & Science Fiction, Apex Magazine, Samovar, Amazing Stories*, and other venues.

Alex resides in Brooklyn, New York with his wife and son. Find him online at alexshvartsman.com.

It wasn't until **David VonAllmen**'s high school professor thought one of his short stories was suspiciously high in literary merit and threatened to have him expelled for plagiarism that he realized he just might have the talent to be a real writer. David's writing has appeared in *Galaxy's Edge, Factor, Four*, the *Writers of the Future* anthology, and other professional publications.

David is the Grand Prize winner for the 2018 Baen Fantasy Adventure Award. He lives in his hometown of St. Louis with his wife, Ann, and children, Lucas and Eva, who write some pretty darn good stories of their own. Links to his works can be found at davidvonallmen.com.

Elisabeth Waters sold her first story in 1980 to *The Keeper's Price*, the first of the *Darkover* anthologies. She went on to sell stories to a variety of anthologies. Her first novel, a fantasy called *Changing Fate*, was awarded the 1989 Gryphon Award. Its sequel, *Mending Fate*, was published in 2016. She also writes short stories and edits anthologies.

She worked as a supernumerary with the San Francisco Opera, where she appeared in *La Gioconda, Manon Lescaut, Madama Butterfly, Khovanshchina, Das Rheingold, Werther,* and *Idomeneo*. Find out more on her official site at elisabethwaters.com.

As writers seem to do, **Julia H. West** has held many arcane jobs. When she was a quality control technician for ultrasound heart machines, video recordings of cross sections of her heart were shipped all over the world with the machines. She's also been a genealogical researcher, an office manager, a secretary, a desktop publisher, a digger at an archaeological dig, a quality assurance tech, a webmaster, an aircraft electrician (and aircraft battle damage repair instructor) for the Air Force Reserves, and a keyer for the United States Post Office.

Julia loves music, and sings with the Utah Filk Organization (that's not a typo: filk is music of the science fiction and fantasy community). She was a founding member of the Salt Lake City, Utah chapter of the Society for Creative Anachronism and still enjoys researching medieval culture. She was active in the Science Fiction and Fantasy Writers of America for over ten years, and was awarded the Service to SFWA Award for work on the Nebula Award reports.

Julia graduated Magna Cum Laude from the University of Utah with a BA in Anthropology. When people asked her what she would do with the degree, she'd tell them, "Write science fiction." Many of her stories incorporate fascinating bits of culture she discovered while studying. She has had fantasy and science fiction stories published in a number of magazines—including *Realms of Fantasy, Oceans of the Mind, Spider,* and *The Friend*—and anthologies, including *Sword and Sorceress* and *Lace and Blade*. She also sold a fantasy poem to *Enchanted*

Conversation. Many of her stories are now available as ebooks from various distributors.

West Jordan, Utah has been Julia's home for over 30 years. She lives with her husband, two daughters, and far too many Cat Overlords. Her website is at juliahwest.com.

Kaitlund Zupanic is a traditional and digital artist best known for her dragons. Through her artwork, she shares the universal story of life, facing adversity, surviving, and starting over. Her work has graced the interiors of *Spectrum 25, Infected by Art* (volumes 6–7), *The Art of Erica Lyn Schmit* (Bird Whisperers special edition), *The Elders Path* by J. D. Caldwell, *Mostly Anecdotal: Stories* by Norman Jenson, and *Unfettered III* (edited by Shawn Speakman). Her artwork depicting the Honey Island Swamp Monster appeared on the Travel Channel in the "Bigfoot of the Bayou" episode of *America Unearthed.*

The Fulton Library at Utah Valley University has some of her work displayed as a part of the *Roots of Knowledge* stained glass window installation created by Holdman Studios. She is currently focusing on oil painting and traditional illustration using the techniques of the old painting masters. You can peruse her art online at kaitlundzupanic.com.

Acknowledgments

As with *Trace the Stars,* a lot of people helped bring *A Dragon and Her Girl* to completion. Of course, there's Linda Hunter Adams, to whom this anthology is dedicated. You can read more about her in the foreword.

Kaitlund Zupanic, our wonderful cover artist, went far, far above and beyond with this cover. When I mentioned the idea to her, she was immediately interested. She offered to create a brand new piece of artwork for the cover, and donate it for use here. Kaitlund's work should be gracing works from the Big Five publishers, and I hope this anthology gives her a little more exposure for that. She is one of the most talented artists I know. Check out her work on her website (the link is in the contributor bios).

While volunteering at a booth at FanX in Salt Lake City, I met the ever gracious Mercedes Lackey. During our conversation, this anthology came up, and she offered to contribute a story for it. It's a wonderful story, too (co-authored by Elisabeth Waters). It was several months before I got to announce that to the world, and I was very excited to do so. Thank you for your generosity, Mercedes and Elisabeth.

One author whose work these pages contain is Michaelene Pendleton. Michaelene was a good friend whom I hadn't seen for many years, and we'd been in touch regarding the first LTUE benefit anthology, *Trace the Stars*. While she didn't have a story that fit that one, she said to keep in touch regarding future anthologies. When I contacted her about this one, she had just the story to submit. We had a verbal agreement to include the story, but then she passed away in January 2019 before sending me the contract. Thankfully, her close friend and (now) estate executor, Lola McElhaney, was kind enough to take care of things so we could include the story for you to enjoy. Thank you, Lola.

Once again, Dave Butler, Jeffrey Creer, and Douglas Cootey were great sounding boards for all my crazy ideas. Dave Doering, Marny Parkin, and JJ Safley were also very helpful. I appreciate Alexi Vandenberg and Kelly Taylor Olsen for providing a place to sell the anthologies to the masses at FanX. I also appreciate Erika Kuta Marler and James A. Owen for rooting for me. You guys are gracious and kind.

Jaleta Clegg, despite everything, was crazy enough (again) to agree to co-edit this volume with me. Her experience, thoughts, and hard work are very clearly evident in the quality of the works picked for this anthology. Without her, this process would have been far more difficult.

Thank you to everyone who submitted stories for consideration. The response was heartwarming and invigorating, and it was hard to narrow it down due to all the great submissions. Thank you for being willing to donate your story to this amazing cause, and I wish I could have included more of your stories here.

A really big thank you to all those whose stories were selected for inclusion. This anthology was a joy to put together. Thank you for your patience, your feedback, and your trust. I hope I have earned it in all our interactions. Thank you, Max, Megan, Scott, Jaleta, Christopher, Sarah, Bryan, Jodi, Josh, Hannah, Sam, Julia, John, Wendy, Gerri, David, Melva, and Alex. You are a credit to writers everywhere.

My lovely, patient Heather has been with me through thick and thin, and I appreciate her more every day. She is an inspiration to me and very supportive in this LTUE Benefit Anthologies project. My three angelic children have also helped me in many ways. Thank you for your patience, thanks for putting up with me, and thank you for your love and support.

I'm sure there are others I should have thanked, but whose names fell out of my brain as I was working on this. I apologize I didn't thank you by name. You are all wonderful.

—Joe Monson

Joe told me to write some words of wisdom, so here goes:
 Don't mess with dragons.
 Don't mess with women.
 Especially, don't mess with dragon women.

Linda Hunter Adams was one of the most encouraging, warmest souls I've ever met. It's an honor to be able to help bring this anthology together to honor her memory. I know she would have loved the stories in all their diverse styles and themes. But most of all, I think she would have loved the feeling of hope that runs through this collection.

Keep writing. Keep submitting. Keep loving life.

And keep believing in dragons.

—Jaleta Clegg

Story and Essay Copyrights

Stories published here for the first time unless otherwise noted. Listed alphabetically by author last name.

"The Wild Ride" © 2020 by Christopher Baxter.

"Loyalties" © 2013 by Josh Brown. Originally published in *Empire of Stone*, edited by Dara Syrkin.

"High Noon at the Oasis" © 2018 by Jaleta Clegg. Originally published in *Llama Tell You a Story*, by Jaleta Clegg.

"A Game of Stakes" © 2020 by Max Florschutz.

"Take Out the Trash" © 1986 by Melva Gifford. Originally published in *The Leading Edge* #12, edited by Karl F. Batdorff and Chris Halladay.

"Dragon Soap" © 2016 by M.K. Hutchins. Originally published in *Fireside Magazine* #38, edited by Brian White.

"Therapy for a Dragon" © 2020 by Sam Knight.

"Dragon in Distress" © 1995 by Mercedes Lackey and Elisabeth Waters. Originally published in *Sword and Sorceress XII*, edited by Marion Zimmer Bradley.

"Here by Choice" © 2010 by Gerri Leen. Originally published in *Life Without Crows and Other Stories*, by Gerri Leen.

"Ash and Blood" © 2020 by Hannah Marie.

"Aer'Vicus" © 2020 by Jodi L. Milner.

"Foreword: The Dragon Lady of Crandall House West" (essay) © 2020 by Joe Monson, except for the "Linda Hunter Adams" filk song. The author of the filk song is unknown, even after extensive research. Proper attribution will be made should the author be determined.

"Rain Like Diamonds" © 2015 by Wendy Nikel. Originally published on 4 September 2015 in *Daily Science Fiction*, edited by Michele Barasso and Jonathan Laden.

"The Diamond-Spitting Knight" © 2020 by S.E. Page.

"Li Na and the Dragon" © 2016 by Scott R. Parkin. Originally published in *Dragon Writers*, edited by Lisa Mangum.

"Lullaby" © 2016 by John D. Payne. Originally published in *Dragon Writers*, edited by Lisa Mangum.

"**Rising Star**" © 1993 by Michaelene Pendleton. Originally published in *Fantasy & Science Fiction*, June 1993, edited by Kristine Kathryn Rusch. Published by permission of the author's estate.

"**Amélie's Guardian**" © 2011 by Bryan Thomas Schmidt. Originally published in *Of Fur and Fire: Tales of Cats & Dragons*, edited by Dana Bell, Zeno Panagakos, and Diann Wacks.

"**Burying Treasure**" © 2015 by Alex Shvartsman. Originally published in *Chicks and Balances*, edited by Esther Friesner and John Helfers.

"**Dragon's Hand**" © 2018 by David VonAllmen. Originally published on Baen.com in 2018.

"**Taking Wing**" © 2020 by Julia H. West.

Do you love space opera and hard science fiction?

Read the first LTUE Benefit Anthology today!

hemelein.com/go/trace-the-stars/

Lightning Source UK Ltd.
Milton Keynes UK
UKHW010901110220
358532UK00001B/82